Steve Davis was born in Kidderminster and still lives in Worcestershire with his wife and two daughters. He is 62 years old, he loves dancing to club music, enjoys a game of squash and drinking beer. After leaving school, he trained as a carpenter and joiner but then moved into sales. He excelled in sales, selling pharmaceuticals, cameras and even shoes to customers all over the world.

He has travelled extensively throughout the world, for business and pleasure. His hunger for adventure and new horizons has propelled him through life with a driving passion. His life was almost brought to an abrupt end in 2014 when he suffered a terrible accident, leaving him with multiple injuries, including a broken back. Thanks to the air ambulance, four years later, he has made a full recovery.

He would be the last person to have ever thought he would write a book, let alone get it published.

Thank you to my wife, Jill, for her support while writing this book.

Steve Davis

THE DOOR

AUSTIN MACAULEY PUBLISHERS™

LONDON · CAMBRIDGE · NEW YORK · SHARJAH

A CIP catalogue record for this title is available from the British Library.

ISBN 9781528938204 (Paperback)
ISBN 9781528969468 (ePub e-book)

www.austinmacauley.com

First Published (2019)
Austin Macauley Publishers Ltd
25 Canada Square
Canary Wharf
London
E14 5LQ

I would like to thank Lynne and Bob Hill for their critique, also Tim Pawson for his totally honest thoughts on the book, he said it was Moorish. Also, AJ, who gave me so much IT support in producing the book.

Synopsis

Poppy Day is a young dynamic, very attractive young lady with a lust for life. Her blue eyes and radiant smile lights up the room, and people flock around her, like bees around a honey pot. With a body to die for and a thirst for living a fulfilled life, she is one in a million; always ready to help anyone, even strangers. She is a talented artist, painting wildlife, country scenes and wait for it, erotic fantasy art. A lot of her fantasy stuff comes from her outrageous sexual desires, and many of her paintings are of actual erotic encounters born from experiences in her short but exciting life. Sadly, she lost both of her parents in her early 20s, which made her more determined and self-sufficient than most young women at her age. In saying that, she has the most supportive friends, in Chloe and Kim, you could ever ask for. They call each other the three musketeers, because if any one of them get into trouble, the other two are there in a flash. Chloe is the boisterous one; no one pushes her around, you mess with her at your peril. Kim is the quieter one, but she is also very loyal to her friends.

Poppy's partner Simon Bridges who she has been with for ten years, turns out to be quite a cad, but also essential in her future life. Her desire to live in a large house in the country has been a dream for most of her adult life. Although neither of them realise it at the time, the purchase of the country house is paramount in dramatic, life-changing events to come. Poppy discovers that in the attic of the house lies a door, and it turns out to be no ordinary door. The 'Door' is an opening into her past, a chance to live her life again, taking a different path, allowing her to fall in love with someone she met ten years earlier. This is where Samuel Devere comes into the story. He is nothing like Poppy's partner Simon; and once Poppy sets out on the path of love, lust and romance, there is no going back. She becomes so smitten that a life without Samuel is unimaginable, so by talking with her friends in the future and Samuel in the past, she concocts a plan. Unfortunately, for Poppy, the path of true love is more complicated; and time travel turns out to be more troublesome and heart-breaking than she first thought.

They say that the path of true love is never straightforward. Poppy's path is no exception, and when you mix in, the intrigue of time travel and the complex nature of the time continuum itself, it turns out to be quite a ride. So although Poppy and Samuel set out on this exciting, heart-pumping ride of lust, love and friendship, towards the future, do they arrive at the end together? The only way to find out is to read on; just remember, in this life, not everything you see is as you might think. However, if deep down you believe, what you believe may well become true.

Chapter 1
Introduction

My name is Poppy, Poppy Day. I can hear you now, saying 'what a strange name', fancy calling your daughter Poppy when your surname is Day. Well, my parents must have had a sense of humour; I say had, because both my mum and dad have both passed away. First my mother, bless her, then some years later my father; they must have thought let's give her a name that sticks in your mind— well, it certainly does that. Also I'm sure, as I've gone through life, that having a memorable name has certainly given me an advantage, people remember me either from my name or I hope through my personality.

I'm a Gemini, born on the 18th of June 1966. Yes, you've worked it out. I'm 29 years young. I'm fit, I'm 5'7" tall, I would describe my figure as curvy. My bottom far too big for my liking; my breasts a firm 34"DD. I have brown hair and blue eyes. I play table tennis when I get a chance, and I hate losing. I love walking my dog; he's a terrier called Roscoe; he's my best friend ever; he never lets me down, and he's always pleased to see me. I also love being with friends, drinking copious amounts of Pino Grigio and having sex. Yes, I said 'having sex'. I love sex, especially out of doors or at least in different places, in the car, in the woods; it doesn't matter. It adds excitement and spice to something that's so important to most of us. Let's face it; it can be a little boring if you have sex in the same bed with the light off, every time! I say I love sex, I'm in a relationship, and my partner finds it a challenge to keep me satisfied; so over the past few years, my sex life has diminished dramatically. Yet my over-excited imagination is working overtime all of the time. Whenever I get the chance to frigg myself off with my fingers or my pocket-sized vibrator, I will. I do love my partner, but I also have needs.

When we first got together, we were at it like rabbits; but over the last few years, he has become less and less interested in me and more interested in his work and watching football on TV. May be he doesn't fancy me anymore, and he's shagging some piece of skirt where he works, but I don't think so; he's a little older than me, so perhaps he's lost the urge. Oh! Sorry, I'm talking about my partner, but I didn't tell you his name. His name is Simon, and he works in sales, always travelling somewhere, at home or abroad. He gets so excited about hi-tech stuff; I think it's something to do with security cameras, but I'm not exactly sure. The thing is he earns good money, which enables us to have the life we lead. If we had to rely on the money my business made, it might be a struggle. That brings me to my business; it's not much of a business as yet. I'm a struggling artist; and if I sell one or two paintings a month, I'm happy. I like to paint wildlife, country scenes, erotic art and animals, but getting known is a real uphill battle. I look at some paintings on the market, and quite frankly, they are technically terrible—heads too big, eyes out of proportion, colours wrong—just awful. But because the artist is known, or is in the right 'Art Society', the paintings sell for far more than I get for my work. Anyway, that's enough bleating from me. I will continue to promote my work and hope that one day someone with clout will discover me and my work and make me famous. I would just like to point out at this juncture that I'm not a slut. When I said I love sex, I didn't mean that I would sleep with any old Tom, Dick or Harry. 'May be Dick!' Only joking! I love sex, and the pleasure it gives me and my partner; of course, it's just that my sexual imagination is off the scale. I can be in any situation, and my mind will start drifting from normal thoughts to disgusting ones. For instance, the other day, I had to call an electrician out. I had a fault with some wiring. He turned up at the door, he was young, he had lovely blue eyes, a smile to die for, and all I could think of was, *I bet he has a massive cock.* I'm not sure all other women would have thought the same thing, or would they. The thing is I didn't try and seduce him. I let him get on with the job. I paid him in cash, and he was on his way; so no, I am not a slut, just a naughty, excited young lady. I've heard people say that sex is 40% friction and 60% imagination. I think it's more—90% imagination and 10% friction. I can have a fantasy in my head that's so vivid. I only have to rub my clitoris gently, and I'm all of a quiver, and I'm having an orgasm.

So I, for certain, have a vivid naughty sexual imagination, where I see things like they are really happening, which is why I get so turned on. Sex must be the best fun you can have, and it costs nothing. All you have to do is find someone who enjoys it as much as you do! So if you're thinking sex isn't that important in your life, put the book down—this book is not for you; go and buy something that interests you more, and you won't be wasting your time. On the other hand, if what you have read so far rings true in your mind, read on. Be prepared to be shocked; sometimes my descriptions of sexual scenes or actions can be raw and certainly vivid, and I prefer to use slang terms to describe sexual acts rather than words from the Oxford English Dictionary. In other words, this book is not for the light-hearted; more for the polite person in real life, but when it comes to sex, turns out to be really naughty and downright insatiable. I don't get turned on by people making love; it's all very polite, but it doesn't do much for me. I prefer a damn good shagging with a guy with a massive erect cock!

So there you have it, the introduction; you know who I am, what I do for a living, who I'm living with, and my inner sexual desires. I hope that you can relate to some of the experiences that unfold in the following chapters. I'm sure there must be thousands of people with similar mindsets to me, and I hope you like, rather than dislike, the person on this sexual roller coaster ride of sexual desires, kinky sex and intrigue. I wonder how many of us would jump at the chance to relive our lives again if that opportunity presented itself. To go back and not make the same mistakes again, to have a better, more-fulfilling life and to share it with a person who you truly love. The thing is this, do you believe in fate, or is your life mapped out for you at birth? I believe that your life is dictated by the actions you take in your everyday life, and you only have yourself to blame for the car crash or happy life that you may lead. Please enjoy the sexploits of Poppy Day.

Chapter 2
Country Abode

Simon and I had lived in several places together. We started out in a small flat, but having no garden to have barbecues in made us look for something a little bigger with a garden. We then moved to a three-bedroom-link detached house; it felt like a mansion after the flat. It was really exciting making it ours—buying new furniture, decorating it the way we wanted it. Unfortunately, Simon was terrible at DIY, so it usually meant me doing all the work. I'm pretty good at paper hanging, painting etc., and I will turn my hand to almost anything. Besides, it's a lot cheaper to do it yourself rather than pay a dodgy guy out of the paper, who you don't know from Adam. After buying this house and doing it up just the way we liked it, just 12 months later, we decided to move up the ladder once again; but this time, it would be the final move.

The house we were looking at was right at the top of our budget, and I was just about to knock on the door for our first viewing. When the door opened, a plump, rosie-faced lady bobbed her head out and said, "Hello, my dears, I assume you are the couple wanting to look around our house."

We entered and introduced ourselves, and the old man who was stood in the kitchen looked at me and said,

"I think we have met before young lady."

I was surprised. I had never seen the man before. I certainly couldn't recall it anyway.

"I'm sorry, I don't remember ever seeing you before."

I replied, in an apologetic voice. They then beckoned us to feel free and walk around the house on our own, which I thought a little odd, but we got on with it. I couldn't wait to see what it had to offer. It needed money spending on it, but it was to die for, set in two acres of land, a large duck pond, looking out over fields. Built in 1897, it had loads of character features; an inglenook fireplace, a stone cellar; in parts, the walls were two feet thick, made of sandstone. It had four bedrooms upstairs; the bathroom was downstairs which we would have to change. The most endearing feature being the attic room; to gain access, you had to climb a narrow, dogleg rickety staircase. At the entrance stood a ledge and braced boarded door, which creaked when I pushed it open. My heart was pounding, not from the ascent of the stairs, more from anticipation what we might find in the room. The first thing to hit you was the musty smell. I don't think the current owners used this room; the dust was thick on all the ledges. At the back of the room, set in the red brickwork wall, was a steel door painted black; it was quite formidable. It seemed out of place. I pressed down on the handle, hoping to gaze into the room beyond, but the handle didn't budge. Simon said,

"Let me have a go, you weakling."

He tried but to no avail. Strange, because the door had no lock. "It must have seized up."

Simon said, in a grumpy voice. I thought it was a little strange, but we moved on, gagging to look out of the window to see what delights the view had to offer. My word—such a pretty view over the garden and the duck pond. Ducks were quacking away; the male ducks chasing the female ducks, no doubt after a shag— typical males. The window was unusual because it had an arched top and reached almost to the floor, offering you the chance to sit in a chair and look out over the garden and pond. I thought this might make an excellent studio for me, where I could lose myself painting to my heart's content. Simon just saw the problems; loose plaster, damp on the ceiling etc.

"I really can't see what you're getting excited about."

He kept muttering. After looking at all the rooms, we descended the staircase and alighted into the kitchen, where the couple who owned the house were sat at the kitchen table, with a pot of tea and cake.

"I'm sure you will take a cuppa and a piece of cake before you leave," said the plump lady. Simon blurted out,

"Sorry, we don't have time today."

"Oh yes, we do."

I exclaimed. I was desperate to find out about the steel door in the attic. The plump lady, whose name was Susan, poured the tea.

"Help yourself to cake, homemade of course," she said, with a proud smile on her wrinkled face. Simon was losing his patience. I could hear him tutting away. He was so rude sometimes.

"What did you think of the house?"

The old man asked.

"It's very run down and needs a ton of work," Simon quickly retorted. The couple looked hurt and started to explain how they found it difficult to keep the house maintained with their ill health. I gave Simon the evils; he knew I was angry with him.

"It's a beautiful house, and we love it."

I said, in a sympathetic voice. Susan's face lit up; *she must have been desperate to sell the place,* I thought to myself. She looked right into my eyes, with such intensity and said,

"It's a special house. It will bring you such joy and happiness, you won't regret buying it."

Then the old boy chipped in, "I don't want to sell the house; it's just that my old body can't cope with the upkeep, so we are going to move to a bungalow."

This was my chance to ask about the steel door in the attic, it was intriguing me, "When we were in the attic, we noticed a door in the end wall; we couldn't open it. Where does it lead to?"

They both laughed, "Arrggh, the steel door."

They looked at each other; then the old boy started to explain, "When we moved in 25 years ago, we thought the same thing. We looked around the attic, tried to open the door, but it wasn't budging. After we moved in, I put WD40 on the handle, but it never opened."

He paused as another memory came into his thoughts, "One strange thing did happen a few months ago though."

Susan piped up quickly, "George, I don't think they need to hear your ghost stories."

"Oh please, please go on," I said, anxious to find out more.

"Okay! Well, one night, me and Susan were in bed. It was late when we heard a bumping sound come from the attic room above our bedroom."

Simon looked at me, raising his eyebrows, indicating for me to rush the old boy on. "Carry on, George," I said excitedly.

"It was strange because we never used the room. Anyway, I crept up the stairs, shouting 'Who's there' just before I entered the room. I switched the light on; the light switch is outside the door. I pushed the door inwards, then I heard this bang. It sounded just like metal hitting metal, just as if the steel door had been slammed, but when I tried the door, it was solid, as it always is. The strange thing was, it was really cold in the room, a bit like a cold fog."

"That's enough, George, you will be putting them off, buying the house, with all these silly stories," Susan exclaimed, "Anyway, in answer to your question, I think the guy who owned the house built it in for a joke, it doesn't lead anywhere; sorry to disappoint you." I have to admit I was a little disappointed. I thought it would have made a nice storeroom for my art materials; never mind, I still loved the house. We then finished our tea and cake and made our excuses to leave. As we left through the back door, the old man said,

"Young lady, I do recognise your face; are you sure you've never been here before?"

"I'm sorry! This is the first time, I've ever been here." It seemed to trouble the old man, but I definitely had never been here before. We set off home; both of us quietly thinking about the house and all the work it involved. Simon wasn't too keen; there was so much work to do, but I knew it was the house for us; there was something about the house that was calling me. When I first stood at the end of the drive on that first viewing, I looked up at the house, and I was drawn to it, like a magnet attracting metallic objects. I just knew I had to live there; why, I didn't know. All Simon could see was the money pit the house represented; he would have preferred a modern, all-done-up box with no hassle.

Over the next few days, I spent all of my time trying to convince Simon that this was the house for us; after all, he would be away working, while I spent most of my time grafting, trying to bring the property into the 21st century. Also Roscoe the dog would love having all that space to run around in; we might even get a few more pets to liven up the place; maybe some chickens or geese even, they would love the large pond in the garden. Eventually, I persuaded Simon to agree that this house offered us a project; and when it was done up, it would make a fantastic place to live, with the added bonus of making us a fair profit when we finally came to selling it. Deep down, I thought to myself, maybe the challenge of working together on the house, seeing the fruits of our labour, might bring us closer together; only time would tell.

We now had to get it. I phoned the agent and put in our offer; it was well below the asking price, due to the amount of work required. But to my utter dismay, but also my absolute delight, the agent phoned back about an hour later and said the vendors had accepted our offer. We both thought, maybe there was something wrong with the place, something terrible that we hadn't picked up on. It was too good to be true, wasn't it. Simon wanted to pull out, having second thoughts about the whole thing, but I knew we had to buy this house, deep in my heart, I felt it was the right thing to do the house had me in its spell, and there was no getting away from it!

Over the next week or so, I couldn't get the house out of my head. I woke up in the night, and all I could think about was the powerful feeling of 'the house calling me'; it was weird. It was like the house needed me, needed me to save it, perhaps, or was it me who needed saving. Oh my god, have I lost my mind, it was just a house, wasn't it! Anyway, over the next few days, Simon seemed to accept the inevitable and started to suggest things we might change in the house when we finally moved in. I was relieved, although I had a small inheritance which would pay a big chunk off the price, without his backing and desire to live in this old, ram-shackled unloved house; my dream of living in the country would be scuppered. We started receiving letters from the solicitors regarding the house, forms for this and that; and over the next seven weeks, after a couple more visits to the house, we finally got a completion date, 10th June. I was so excited, we would be in for my birthday; we could hold a party in the massive garden, and we could show all our friends what a beautiful spot we had found.

Chapter 3
Acceptance

We had been together for over 11 years now, and they had been amazing years. We still loved each other, I think, or were we just used to being with each other. We still looked after each other's interests, and I am sure Simon still loved me; he certainly told me enough. Every day when he left for work, he would kiss me on the forehead and say, "Love you, see you later."

I would always reply, "Love you too!"

But was this just polite rhetoric a habit. Did we mean what we were saying, was it sincere. When we went out with friends, we always looked like the perfect couple, holding hands, being affectionate, never arguing over stupid stuff. I'm sure all of our friends considered us as the forever couple, together until one of us died. But is anything forever; I'm not sure. When I was young, I thought that my parents were going to be there forever, but that wasn't true. My first love in junior school, Jason with the ginger hair, I was going to marry him and have children, a dog and live in a massive house in the country. Then during rehearsals for the Christmas nativity play, I caught him behind the stage with Katie Robinson, kissing her on the cheek. He broke my heart, big time.

If you could step back from your life and look in, I think you might see the complete picture. You might see things in perspective more focussed. When you lead a busy life, and you have been in someone's life for a long time, I think you lose track. You go with the flow, you don't want to upset the apple cart; 'as they say', anything for an easy life, but is it easy. When you're compromising all the time just to placate your partner, I don't know what the answer is, but for sure, it's easier to carry on as we all do, waving goodbye in the morning and getting on with your day. It sounds like I am dreadfully unhappy the way I'm going on, but I'm not. I just wish those early exciting years—when we were as one. We both loved the same things, we yearned the same goals, and sex was amazing—was upon us now.

If only we could 'Turn back the clock', what a stupid saying, you just have to make sure that you live your life the way you want to live it. Basically what I'm trying to say is, our life together had been amazing. We had travelled the world together, had fantastic experiences, seen and done things most couples would only dream about; and now after all these years, the spark had gone. No more fluttery feelings in the stomach when he pulled on the drive; just a cursory peck on the cheek when he walked through the door. Yes, he may still love me; but the sexual attraction, the passion, the lust had all but died. I'm not putting all the blame on Simon it takes two to tango, and I was just as guilty for letting things slip into what was now a loveless relationship, heading for the precipice of breakup. But after saying all of that, we were still together; it was easier; besides, we had just bought the house in the country, so we would have to stick together for that. 'Wouldn't we', and so it goes on, making the best of things but not actually living your life the way you would wish.

Chapter 4
The Big Move

The weeks running up to 'The Big Move', as we had nick named the move, into the country house were exciting but also stressful. Exciting because it was such an adventure for me; something I had wanted all my life. To live in a country house, with views, no neighbours, and with the added benefit of a large pond in the garden, the sound of ducks quacking and splashing in the water was marvellous but also stressful. Simon was getting more and more grumpy as each day passed, suggesting we should pull out of the sale, with only days to go before we exchanged contracts; I could have killed him. I should have listened to his concerns more. I was so wrapped up in my emotions that I thought he was just being awkward. I just hoped he would get over his insecurities regarding all the work the new house would cause.

Anyway, the big day arrived; we were moving into the house today. It was the 10th of June 1995; it was a sunny day, very warm, with a clear blue sky. I had butterflies in my stomach, and I couldn't wait for the removal van to arrive, so we could start loading the enormous amount of packed cardboard boxes out of our old house, ready to start the new adventure in our new old house in the country. I say boxes because there seemed more boxes than furniture. Most of our furniture was built in, apart from the beds, chairs, sofas, mirrors and pictures. We were leaving the carpets; they weren't brilliant; and besides, they wouldn't fit the larger rooms at the new house. Simon didn't seem too bad on the day; he must have accepted the challenges ahead, and when our friends turned up to help, he seemed quite chipper, making jokes about the hours of graft that lay before us, saying, "Onwards and upwards, and when it's done, the takeaways on me."

Tom and Chloe shouted out in unison, "How about the drinks."

"Oh! Those as well, of course." Shouted Simon as he lifted a rather heavy box off the floor.

The removal van driver had very skilfully reversed onto the drive, just brushing the leylandii trees that lined the edge of the tar macadam drive and was only feet away from the front door. This left us just a gentle slope up the ramp into the waiting hands of the second member of the removal team. So, has he expertly packed the contents into the available space, we systematically emptied each room, leaving the house sounding hollow. It also seemed strange; as I had left Roscoe the dog with another friend for the day, I thought it may be too unsettling for him. I had planned to have him dropped off later when all of our belongings were in the new house, so he had familiar smells around him.

Although we didn't seem to have a massive amount of belongings, it still took three and a half hours to empty the house, garden shed and the garage. When we finally finished, we were all totally knackered. As I walked around the empty house, to check nothing had been forgotten, I noticed the slightly darker patches on the walls where the pictures had once hung. Deprived of bleaching sunlight, the patterned wallpaper was like new compared with the rest of the wall. The house was silent; all the helping hands now outside, preparing to travel to the new house. I sat on the floor, having a moment to myself, thinking of the good and bad times we had had in this house. I was a little sad but was also excited at the same time. Then I heard Simon shouting, "Come on, Poppy. We are all dying for a cuppa, we need to go now." I had a last look around, quietly saying goodbye to the place. I know it sounds silly, but I would never step foot in this place again, and it represented a part of my life; sentimental I know, but that's just the way I am.

I heard the large removal van's engine start up; it was time to leave. I left a good luck card on the side for the incoming family, and for the last time, I pulled the front door closed behind me. As I turned, the removal van was just chugging up the road, grey smoke belching out of its exhaust pipe under the strain of gaining speed, with all the weight on board. Simon had started the engine in our car, and Tom and Chloe were sat in their car also, waiting for me. I looked back briefly, then jumped in the car and said, "OK, let's do it."

Simon snapped back, "About bloody time."

The first stop was the estate agents to drop off our keys and collect the new house keys. It was on the way, so we soon caught up with the removal van. As we followed the removal van, the atmosphere inside the car was a little strained. Simon seemed agitated, the realisation of the new house obviously bearing down on him. But I thought it was more than that; he seemed distant, and lately his affections had been scarce, to say the least. We hadn't had good sex in ages, and has we headed towards our new venture, I was living in hope that the all new and exciting times ahead would prove to be stimulating and rewarding for both of us. If not, I could see trouble ahead. With the van still in front, and Tom and Chloe following behind, we turned off the main road onto a narrow country lane. This would be interesting if we came across on-coming traffic. The van was brushing the hedges both sides as it was. We meandered along the lane for about two miles, it seemed like ten; then we turned a very tight corner and started climbing. The hill was so steep, our ears popped; then we reached the summit. The view was spectacular, you could see for miles. The fields were full of sheep, and I noticed above our heads the majestic flight of buzzards circling on warm thermals. We were in the country; I felt I had arrived home.

I say home, a little prematurely; we hadn't arrived yet. I wound down the window, so I could hear and smell the countryside. With just about a mile to go, the lane towards the house levelled out, with the occasional dirt track either side leading to other properties. I noticed busy sparrows darting in and out of the hedgerow. I loved the sound of sparrows; it reminded me of my childhood. The council house I grew up in always had loads of sparrows flying in and out of the eaves. Then I noticed the removal van brake lights come on; they were slowing down as they approached the entrance to the house. The driver's arm gesticulating through his window for us to overtake, I presumed he wanted us to lead the way up the drive first. I was so excited, we pulled into the gateway. I looked up to see the elegant house stood at the other end of the drive. I had butterflies in my stomach; I couldn't wait to get inside. Simon drove very slowly up the drive; Tom and Chloe following us. We passed the pond on our left; the ducks were making a right racket, like they were welcoming us to our new home.

We all jumped out of the two cars. Simon was moaning; he was thirsty and wanted a cuppa as soon as possible. Tom and Chloe were laughing and joking; they seemed like they were really in love.

"Come on, Poppy, open the door and get the kettle on," screamed Simon. Then the beeping started. The removal van was reversing up the drive, being careful not to back into the duck pond. Chloe shouted over,

"What a beautiful place; you're so lucky to live in such an idyllic spot." I already knew how lucky we were! I put the key in the door and turned it clockwise. The door swung open crikey; the heat hit you like a train. We soon discovered why the AGA was left on—that was the only way of cooking or boiling the kettle—so even in the summer, the AGA was on. Consequently, it was like a sauna as we entered; we might have to rethink that one. Simon opened all the windows to let in some breathable air. I filled the AGA kettle; it was very nice of them to leave it behind. I placed it on the very hot cooking plate; we would soon see how hot the AGA was; besides, our electric kettle was somewhere in the back of the now parked-up removal van.

While waiting for the kettle to boil, the other three went wondering around the gardens. I was itching to walk around the house. It seemed different now it was empty, but it still had a very friendly atmosphere. I don't know why, but the attic room was in the back of my head, so I quickly scaled the stairs arriving at the entrance to the room in the roof. I pushed open the squeaky door and entered, just the same as when we originally looked at it, still covered in thick cobwebs and dust, smelling a little frowsty. I looked at the black steel door set into the wall at the end of the room; it intrigued me. I walked over to the door and grabbed the handle, half-expecting it to move, but it was still solid. It must have been true what the old man had said—it was put hear as a joke.

I went to the window; I could see Simon, Tom and Chloe stood on the edge of the pond, looking at the vast amount of ducks swimming around. I twisted the rusty catch on the window; and to my surprise, it opened easily on its painted-over hinges. I shouted, "Ahoy over there, I'm up here in the roof." They all turned to see where I was shouting from. They spotted me, then waved.

Simon shouted again, "Is that tea ready yet." I thought to myself, *Cheeky so and so.* I closed the window, then looked around the room again. I felt at ease up here in the attic. It was going to make a perfect art stroke retreat room. I descended the stairs, and as I entered the kitchen, I could hear the whistle on the kettle screaming out. It had boiled quite quickly, but then I thought, we had no cups. Right at that moment, Jim, one of the removal guys, walked in with a box marked, 'Urgent tea supplies'.

"I thought you might need this box first," he said, probably hoping he would get a cuppa.

"Perfect timing, Jim. How do you both like your tea?"

"Strong and sweet for both of us."

He replied, with a strong brummie accent. I made a large pot of tea. The whole team were now in the sweltering kitchen, gasping for a well-deserved cuppa. After we polished off a second pot of tea and a packet of chocolate digestives, which I had packed into the emergency tea supplies box, we all got on with the task in hand of emptying the removal van. I had labelled each box with a letter. I then had corresponding sticky letters, which I stuck on the door of the room. I wanted each individual box to be placed in, so simple! They all thought I was a control freak, but it worked so well, the removal men said they would recommend the idea to all their clients. Simon was muttering something under his breath, it sounded like, "Bloody smart arse." He was only jealous because he hadn't thought of it himself, but you would think that he would be pleased, if it saved a lot of confusion and time, if the team didn't have to keep asking where to put what!

I could hear Jim and Pete, the removal men, struggling to get up the stairs with my easy chair. It was bulky and also very heavy, "Poppy," shouted a breathless Pete.

"I'm coming," I shouted as I climbed the stairs.

"Which bedroom do you want the chair in, my dear," Pete said, gasping for a breath. I was scared to tell them that the chair was destined for my art room, which meant another awkward flight of stairs up to the attic.

"I'm really sorry, but the chair is to go into the attic room, which means negotiating the dogleg staircase."

There were gasps of annoyance and negative feedback,

"I'm telling you now, young lady, this chair will not go up that staircase. It's far too big, and it's certainly too heavy to get around the handrail." Simon heard the commotion and came running up the stairs, "What's the problem now."

He seemed so grouchy today, he wasn't happy at all. I explained about the chair, "Poppy, why don't you just put the chair in our bedroom, problem solved."

"I want it in the art room."

I snapped back! The two removal men could see a domestic starting. Jim butted in, trying to calm things down,

"I wonder if the chair comes apart; they sometimes do."

He and Pete turned the chair over, and sure enough there were two catches,

"Aargh, there you go."

Jim said, with relief in his voice. Pete pressed them both in, and the back of the chair slid off the base,

"Hey Presto, we can get it up there now, young lady," exclaimed Jim. Simon turned, huffing and puffing and went back downstairs. I was so happy. I was looking forward to sitting in that chair, in my retreat room, looking out the window at the garden and pond. They still had a struggle getting around the dogleg in the staircase, but after a few minutes, they were asking where to place the chair. The base was placed by the window; then the back was slotted back on. I jumped on the chair, reclined the back; it was so comfy, and I could see through the window; it was perfect.

"Thank you, guys. You're the best."

They responded with, "Any chance of another cuppa."

The rest of the day passed without incident. Tom and Chloe were marvellous, working their socks off but still very entertaining, taking the Mick out of Simon because he was so grumpy, but they lifted everybody's spirit with their banter and laughter. About 4:30 p.m. and the van was empty, and it was time to wave goodbye to Jim and Pete. They pulled off the drive, shouting their goodbyes through the open window. Just after the van disappeared down the lane, another car appeared. It was Molly, who had kindly decided to deliver Roscoe the dog to his new home. He was so excited to see me, he ran around the house like something possessed. He went straight to his bed, which I had placed by the AGA for warmth through the night. I think Molly was after a nose around the house. It certainly gave me pleasure showing her around; she loved it; she kept saying,

"Oh! Wow. Oh! Wow! It's beautiful, Poppy."

After the tour, I invited her to the house warming come birthday party on the 18th. She said she would love to come; then she jumped in her car and sped off like a mad thing. We carried on for a couple of hours more; we were all very tired and needed something to eat, so it was decided that Simon and Tom would pop to the local town and get a take away and some booze. Chloe and me sorted out the cutlery and laid the table. We also made up the beds, so after our well-deserved supper, we could crash.

After the lads left, and we were on our own, Chloe looked me in the eye and said in a very soft voice,

"Poppy, I hope you don't mind me asking, but are you and Simon alright? You seem to have been bickering all day."

I just burst into tears; Chloe wrapped her arms around me and tried to comfort me.

"What the hell he has done? Is he having an affair? If he is, I will kill him."

"I don't know, he's been distant for a long time. I think it might be this place. I'm not sure it's what he wants."

"He loves you though, doesn't he, Poppy."

"Chloe, I really don't know any more. He says he does, but he certainly doesn't show it, and our sex life is almost non-existent."

"But he wouldn't have gone ahead with this place if he didn't want to be with you, surely."

"I don't know what to think anymore. Anyway, Chloe, thanks for asking and caring, you're a real friend. I don't know what I would do without you."

We heard the boys' car coming up the drive. I dried my eyes, and we made ourselves busy. Chloe squeezed my hand, then went to greet the boys, grabbing the wine as soon as they entered the kitchen. We all tucked into the Chinese; the boys drank beer, and Chloe and I finished off two bottles of Pino Grigio. It had been quite a day. We were all bushed and ready for bed; we said our good nights and headed for the bedrooms. We both undressed. I put on my Jim-jams; Simon always slept naked.

"Are we okay, Simon? You seem very quiet."

"Poppy, I'm really tired, and I need some sleep. Goodnight love."

I cuddled into him, but no response. I kissed him on the shoulder and said, "Goodnight."

I lay on my back in the dark; thinking to myself there must be someone else. He was acting so weird. I could feel my eyes closing, and I knew it wouldn't be long before I drifted off.

Chapter 5
Birthday Party

The following weekend after moving into the house, it was my birthday. Simon brought me tea in bed, with my birthday card and a separate envelope.

"Thank you, Simon, what's in the envelope; it feels bulky."

"Happy birthday, Poppy. I hope you like it."

I opened the envelope and inside was a set of keys, car keys!

"Oh Simon, I can't believe you've bought me a car."

Simon cleared his throat and said, "Not exactly a car."

"What do you mean, not exactly a car?"

"Well, you know I will be spending sometime away, and we are quite away from the nearest town; you will also need to fetch materials for the work on the house. Well, I thought this would be more appropriate."

"What will be more appropriate?" I said with intrigue.

"Poppy, if you look out of the window, you will see for yourself."

I bounded out of bed and looked out of the window. I couldn't believe it. Sat on the drive was a small white van, with an enormous ribbon wrapped around it. I squealed,

"Poppy, I'm sorry, I thought it might be more practical than a car."

"I'm not cross, Simon. It's perfect, I can use it for the house; I needed transport. Now we are living this far out, and it will be great for taking the dog out, I love it."

I quickly got dressed and ran outside clutching the keys to my new mode of transport. It wasn't new, but it was in fine condition. I jumped into the driver's seat and started the engine; it sounded dandy. Roscoe jumped straight on my lap. He seemed as excited as I was; he started licking the steering wheel.

"No! No! Roscoe, don't gob all over the cab."

I got out and went to the back of the vehicle. I wanted to see what the inside of the back looked like. It had two doors to the rear and a sliding door on the passenger side. It had been boarded out, so it was easy to keep clean. It was perfect!

Simon came outside, "What do you think, Poppy?"

"It's great, thank you so much, it's just what I needed."

I gave him a big snog, which he didn't seem to appreciate,

"As long as you like it, that's fine," he muttered as he walked away.

The rest of the day we spent getting ready for my birthday party. It was a beautiful day; the time just whizzed by, and before we knew it, the guests started to arrive. We were putting on a barbecue in the garden; it was the perfect setting. Simon was doing his 'He Man Thing' in-charge of the cooking; I was mingling and topping up everyone's glasses. Everyone seemed impressed with the house and the land it sat in, but seemed concerned with the amount of work involved to bring it up to a standard that all our friends knew we expected. I wasn't worrying at all; in fact I was looking forward to the challenge. I had so many ideas and plans for the place. I couldn't wait till Monday to get started.

The soirée went really well. Everyone seemed to enjoy themselves; some of the guests had far too much to drink, and you can guess what had happened next—things got out of hand. Some of the boys thought it might be funny to throw Simon in the pond. I wasn't sure if he was really mad, or he just accepted it as a bit of fun. It took at least four of the guys to overcome his determination to stop on dry land, but after a lot of swearing and laughter, he eventually succumbed to their superior strength, and they tossed him into the water; a cheer went up from all the guests. Simon disappeared under the water for a few seconds; and when he resurfaced, his face was covered in mud and pond weed. I was crying with laughter, and so was everyone else. The dog was going mental, running up and down the bank barking his head off. Tom shouted out to Simon,

"Do you fancy a drink Simon or have you had enough?"

I could see the look on Simon's face. He was sort of smiling, but I knew him better; he was angry.

"Very funny, you morons,"

Simon shouted back as he climbed out of the pond onto the grassy bank. Everyone kept their distance, in case Simon tried to get his own back, by pushing them in. I went up to him, trying to calm him down, "What a fantastic sport you are, Simon."

He glared at me; his eyes full of hate, "I suppose you thought it was funny, didn't you, Poppy."

Someone in the garden shouted, "At least you've christened the pond, Simon."

"I'm going to change my clothes, you imbeciles,"

Simon said, in a gruff voice. He disappeared into the house, and the party carried on. Chloe came over, "Is he alright, Poppy. He looked cross."

"I'm sure he will get over it, it's only a bit of fun after all."

Sure enough, about 20 minutes later, Simon came out of the house in clean attire, muttering, "If you try and throw me in again, you're dead."

I don't think anyone would have risked it after that comment.

The drinking continued into the night. The outside lights came on just after dusk, then I lit the chiminea. It was getting a little chilly. About midnight, most of our friends had gone home. There was just Tom and Chloe, Colin and Kim and ourselves sat around the fire. There's nothing like watching the flames licking and flickering through the burning logs giving warmth to your grateful chilled body, with a glass of wine in your hand, and great banter between such diverse people that were sat around the fire. Let me try and describe the characters sat around the fire; to my immediate right was Tom, about 30 years old, fun loving, very proud and sporty, hardworking and was a hairdresser by trade. Then we had Colin; a little older than Tom; he adored his partner Kim, loved a drink and worked as a decorator. Kim knew that Colin adored her and used that to her full advantage; she wore the trousers in their house. Next, my best friend Chloe—the kindest, most loving, caring person I knew—she was brilliant. She also liked a drink; she drank the same as me—Pino Grigio. Then, of course, last but not least, Simon. I wasn't sure about Simon, lately. He had always been loving and caring and great in bed, but over the last year, he had become distant, grumpy and more arrogant than ever before. It seemed like our life wasn't good enough for him anymore, and it wasn't just me he was curt with. He was just as short and snappy with all our friends, and it was getting to me.

I overheard Tom asking Simon if he wanted to go for a beer in the week, and I was curious to hear Simon say that he was away from Monday, so would have to decline. Simon looked at me as he said it, to see if I had been listening. I just stared at him; I would bring it up with him later when we were on our own. The amount of drink we had downed during the night was staggering, and it left its toll. We were all pissed and the conversations were getting louder, and more in your face, as the time went on. Colin and Simon were arguing the strengths and weaknesses of the Wolves defence. They both followed football, and even more sadly, followed Wolverhampton Wanderers. I was never into football. I thought footballers were overpaid prima donnas. Tom was feeling left out. Chloe and Kim were deep in conversation about the attributes of dildos verses vibrators, and we're in fits of laughter when Kim pulled a vibrator out of her handbag. It was black, about 6" long and shaped exactly like a penis. She thrust it between Chloe's legs and screamed, "Try a bit of that." Chloe pretended she was having an orgasm, shouting,

"Yes, Yes, Yes, harder, harder."

I went and sat next to Tom,

"What are they like, Tom?"

Tom replied, "As long as they are happy, they're harmless enough."

Tom was a gentle soul; he loved Chloe with all his heart. Deep down, I wished Simon loved me in that way. I looked down at my hand. We weren't engaged, but Simon had bought me a ring—not a diamond ring—a gold band with a mother of pearl stone in a claw set. When he had given it to me some years ago, he had looked me in the eye and said he would love me forever, and no one would ever come between us. I must have gone into a trance. I was suddenly aware that Tom was talking to me,

"Are you alright, Poppy? You seemed to drift away. Shall I get you a glass of water?"

"No, no, I'm fine, just thinking about things. It must be the drink; I've had far too much."

He was such a caring delightful man, then the girls started singing, let's raise a glass to the birthday girl,

"Happy birthday to you, happy birthday to you, happy birthday, dear Poppppppppeeey, happy birthday tooooooo youuu."

God, they were sloshed.

"Thank you all for a fantastic day, thank you for all my beautiful presents."

Kim burst out laughing, "You haven't opened my present yet. It will put Simon to shame."

I guessed straight away what she had bought me.

"Don't forget the batteries."

Was her flying volley before she slipped to the floor, incapable of sitting in her chair? Colin jumped up, lifted her up from the decking, held her in his arms and said,

"Is it alright if I take her up to bed?"

"Of course it is, all the beds are made up. I will follow you up with some water. I think she's going to need it."

I said, happy for the night to draw to an end.

"I will get the water." Chloe said, "I'm going up as well."

So the night came to an end. The fire had almost burnt out, so we turned the outside lights off and retired to the kitchen. Simon had popped the kettle onto the AGA and disappeared upstairs. I assumed he wanted me to make the drinks. Tom and Chloe just took water; they kissed me on the cheek, thanked me for a wonderful day and went to bed. I was now on my own, with my best friend Roscoe. I gave him a big cuddle, told him I loved him, put him in his warm cosy bed, then climbed the stairs with two drinks—coffee for Simon and tea for me. I put Simon's drink down on the bedside cabinet, then walked around my side of the bed, sipping my tea as I went. I sat up in bed with my tea in my hand, sipping it like nectar; there's nothing better than a nice cuppa. "I will be going away for a few days in the morning for work," Simon said, nonchalantly.

"Yes, I heard you saying to Tom you wouldn't be around. I wish you would discuss these things with me, Simon. It would just be nice to know these things in advance."

"Well, I'm telling you now, what's the problem?"

"It doesn't seem like we are a couple anymore. You don't talk to me, you don't touch me, Simon; what is the problem."

"There isn't a problem. I'm tired, and I need to go to sleep. I have to be up at 5:00 a.m."

Simon kissed me on the forehead, said goodnight and rolled over; and that was that.

"Thanks for my birthday present. Goodnight, Simon."

There was no reply. I turned the light off; and within a minute, Simon was snoring, and I was mulling over in my mind what the hell might be going on.

Chapter 6
Work Begins

Monday morning arrived with a cacophony of ducks quacking so loud, it woke me up. It took a few minutes for me to realise where I was. It was only a week since we moved here, so I was still getting used to the surroundings. I started thinking about the house, then I realised it still had no name. I thought of all sorts, but then as I saw a flock of ducks glide past my bedroom window all flapping and quacking prior to landing on the pond. It hit me, 'Ducklands House'; it was perfect. I would hand-paint a sign and fix it to the gate as soon as I had a chance. The sun was bouncing on the water of the pond and reflecting a dancing display of flashing light through the window and on to the ceiling of our bedroom. It was mesmerising and very pretty. I stretched my arm out in the direction of Simon. He wasn't there, only a folded piece of paper lay on his pillow, it read,

Poppy,
I didn't want to wake you, you were fast asleep. I will call you later from my hotel. I will be away until Friday x.

I read the note a couple of times. I couldn't believe he had gone without waking me, and why was he stopping away all week. I was upset; things seemed to be getting worse, and nothing I said made any difference. It was certainly coming to a head. I could see us having a massive row when he returned from where ever he was. I decided to get stuck into a project, to take my mind off our problems; but first things first, walk the dog, that always calmed me down, then back home for breakfast. I walked the dog along the edge of the field, next to our land. I could be confident Roscoe would be fine off his lead, and he would get a better walk that way. The only problem was, he had a passion for chasing squirrels and rabbits; as soon as he spotted one, he was off. It was a pure pleasure walking along the hedgerow; fresh air filling my lungs, and the birds were singing. I could hear a skylark in the distance warbling away. I could just see him about 30 feet up in the air, almost stationary, apart from the flutter of his wings. Then Roscoe started barking; he had spotted a rabbit further along the edge of the field. Then he was off, like a rocket on a mission. He disappeared through the edge. It was unlikely he would catch the poor thing; the rabbit had a good head start. Sure enough Roscoe reappeared a few minutes later, looking rather disappointed without a rabbit in his mouth. I was relieved; I didn't like him killing the wild life. We returned from the walk, ready for breakfast. I fed the dog first, then poached myself a couple of eggs—hard whites and runny yolks, just the way I liked them, with a couple of rounds of white bread toast and a dollop of brown source, washed down with a gulpy mug of tea.

There was a long list of work to be carried out on the house; some jobs with a greater urgency than others. The highest priority was the cellar; it had about a foot of muddy water covering the old brick set floor. Not an easy job, the plan was to sink a well in the floor, place a sump pump in the bottom, so as soon as the water reached a certain level, the pump would take over automatically and pump the water through a plastic pipe out of the building and into the lower field. This would ensure the water level never reached the floor of the cellar, allowing it to dry out and also letting us store stuff down there, like beer and wine. I didn't feel like starting this job today. Besides, I would have to purchase the pump and the plastic tank to house it in, so I decided to have a look in my attic art room instead. The room wasn't in as bad a state as I thought. A bit of filler and some paint, new carpet and a few pictures on the wall would make all the difference. The damp marks on the ceiling were caused by an old leak which, I believed, had been repaired a long time ago, so a few coats of paint should make them disappear. I think the hardest part of any job is getting started, so I rolled my sleeves up and got stuck in. After only a few hours of filling, rubbing down and getting the first coat of paint on, it made such a difference. I was so pleased with myself. I painted the false steel door black, with the rivets highlighted in gold paint; it looked quite impressive. By tomorrow, I would have all the gloss paint finished, leaving just the carpet to fit. Oh! Yes, I'd forgotten, I had to buy some carpet.

The next day I popped into the local town, Leyton-Somer; it was about 8 miles away. It was fun driving my own van. After parking, I asked a local if there were any carpet shops in the town. Apparently, there were a few shops selling cheap off-cuts of carpet. I needed a piece approximately 4 metres x 5 metres, then I had a moment! How would I get it home; even with the van, it would stick out a mile. The first shop I came to was quite small, but had quite a few off-cuts of good quality carpet. I found the perfect piece of carpet, then I told the man in the shop about my dilemma, how would I get it home. His name was Richard.

"Where do you live then, love?"

He said, in a friendly manner. I told him the address. I said the house with the pond. I would have to paint that sign for the gate. This was ridiculous calling it 'The House'. Anyway, the postcode was enough this time. Richard said he didn't live far away, so he would drop it off on his way home in his works van—problem solved. I chose a cream-coloured carpet, with the occasional leaf pattern. It would be perfect for the art room, and the beige reclining chair would go with it just nicely. I paid for the carpet and said to shop owner I would see him later. By the time Richard arrived with the carpet, all the painting was finished. Tomorrow, it would be dry enough for me to fit the carpet. Richard very kindly helped me drag the roll up the stairs. We had to bend it a lot to get it around the dogleg stairs, but after an exhausting effort and some choice words, it lay on the floor in the room. Richard looked around the room, "Nice view from up here," he said, peering out of the window. Then he turned, interested in the steel door at the end of the room.

"Wow, that's an impressive steel door. Do you keep the crown jewels in there?"

"Believe it or not, no, I don't. It's a false door put there for amusement I believe."

He scratched his head, looking puzzled, "Why would anybody go to so much trouble."

"I thought the same thing when I saw it for the first time."

"Weird, I must say," replied Richard, still scratching his head.

"I think you deserve a nice cuppa, Richard."

"I certainly do, my love," he replied, gratefully.

After we finished our tea, I was just waving goodbye when I heard my mobile ringing inside the kitchen. I looked at the screen, it was Simon. "Hello Simon, how are you."

"Hi Poppy, I'm fine, busy day today. I'm just about to go for dinner, thought I would catch up before I went out."

"You never said where you were stopping, and what you were working on."

Simon started talking; then in the background, I heard a female voice shouting,

"Come on, the taxi is waiting."

"Who is that, Simon?"

"Oh! It's just someone from the design team here at the head office. I have to go, I will call you tomorrow."

The line went dead—charming. I was still none the wiser, and he didn't even ask how I was getting on. I felt lonely and hurt. Thank god I had Roscoe to cuddle; he never ever let me down. I decided to have an early night. I filled a large glass with Pino and went to the bedroom. I had a quick slurp of wine; then jumped in the shower before retiring to my bed to read my book—probably a bad move. I was reading a love story, wishing that my love life was as exciting as the couple in the story. I soon finished my wine; the dog was snoring at the end of the bed, and after all the hard work I had done today, my eyes were drooping. It wouldn't be long before I was away with the fairies.

The next morning I woke up feeling quite positive. I was looking forward to fitting the carpet, hanging some pictures and finishing the attic room. It would be good to have at least one room completed where I could relax with no clutter all around me. I had a quick breakfast, fed Roscoe, found my carpet-laying tools and headed up to the attic. It was going to be awkward. I couldn't move the reclining chair out of the room. It was far too heavy, so I had to fit the carpet at one end of the room, then manhandle the chair over the roll of carpet. Then roll out the remaining carpet, then fit the other end; it was a bit of a faff, but it turned out okay. I replaced the reclining chair in the same position facing the window, just perfect for watching the ducks on the garden pond. I just needed to dress the room now; I placed the clock, so I could see it from my chair. I tended to lose myself when I was painting, so it was essential to keep track of time. Then I placed a small chest of draws to store my brushes, paints etc. next to my easel, with a bare canvas already clamped on. I lay a large rubber sheet under the easel to protect the new carpet from any unintended spillages. It was a shame there was no sink up here; it would have been more convenient for washing out my brushes. *Put it on the jobs list,* I thought to myself. I finished up with hanging my own art, on the walls—country scenes mainly and one portrait of Roscoe. I sat in the chair, feeling smug. Then I thought to myself, *just one thing missing, a radio*; so when I wasn't listening to the wild life outside, I could turn on the radio and listen to Radio Two or the play on Radio Four. I eventually found a radio, sat it on top of the chest of draws; luckily, the plug socket was near enough to plug it in. I tuned it into Radio Two, the record playing took me back to my student days; it was Tainted Love by Soft Sell. I lay in the chair, closed my eyes and let my mind wander. The music brought back so many memories; those first days with Simon, how happy we were together, the other opportunities turned down; if we hadn't met that fateful day, where would I be now. Did I believe in fate or is your destiny laid out for you. Or are you in control of the direction your life takes, I wasn't sure what to think. For instance just say, you were walking down the street, and you happened to lock eyes with a stranger, you start talking, and a friendship strikes up—that's one path. On the other hand, imagine you were walking down the road, and at the moment you were about to lock eyes with that stranger, your phone rang; or someone obstructs you, and you don't make that fateful connection, then your life might take a completely different path. My mind tussled with all the possibilities; and after quite some time, I was still no nearer to understanding what card you might be dealt in life. I must have drifted off into a deep sleep because I woke up in a start. The clock said 3:30 p.m. I had been asleep about 1 1/2 hours, I had been dreaming, but I couldn't remember exactly what it was about. I did know it was a happy dream. I had a lovely warm feeling deep inside. I just wished I could feel like it all the time. I then realised how low I was feeling about our relationship; something was wrong. I decided that when Simon came home this weekend, we would get to the bottom of it. To take my mind off my troubles, I went and found a piece of flat wood, about four inches deep by two feet long and approx. half an inch thick; it was the perfect size for the house name. I taped it to the easel, then painted it black; then carefully painted the name 'Ducklands House' in gold paint. As soon as it was dry, I headed down the drive. It was so satisfying screwing it to the top bar of the gate. I stood back to admire my work and thought to myself, *I bet Simon doesn't like it.*

Chapter 7
The Other Side

The next day, I decided that now my art room was finished. I would start a new painting. I had previously taken some very nice pictures of the ducks splashing around in the pond. The sun had been shining, and the light on the water droplets was stunning. If only I could capture the effect on canvas, I would give it my best shot. On the way up the stairs, I noticed on the hall table the unopened present that Kim had bought me for my birthday. With everything going on, I had forgotten to open it. I grabbed it and took it up to my art room with me. I sat in my wonderful chair, looking through the photos of the ducks and decided on an image I wanted to recreate with paint. I clipped the photo to my easel and started sketching in pencil on the canvas. It was imperative to get the perspective with the numerous ducks and the trees and scrub in the background. The time taken on this process always paid off with the finished painting, although I preferred the next step when I used the brush. I really felt at ease in this room. It inspired me, and I believed it would make a huge difference to the paintings I created from now on. I suppose only time would tell, and of course if I sold any. After about an hour sketching the layout of the new painting, I fancied a break, so I picked up the present that Kim gave me and sat in my comfy chair. It was very nicely wrapped, complete with a bow; the tag read, "Happy Birthday, Poppy. Love, Kim." I tore off the paper, inside was a blue, velour-covered box, approx. 6" long, 2" wide and 2" deep; a bit like a box a very nice pen set would come in. I opened the box to find a note; it read,

Pocket-sized, bullet-shaped friend.
Keeps going right to the end.
Multi-speed, perfect fit;
Twist the end and place on your clit.
When you're coming, think of me.
Who needs men when this is free.

I chuckled, trust Kim to write something like that; she was a little minx. I took the vibrator out of the tube-like velour bag. It was a bit like a small black rubber cock. I twisted the end but nothing happened; then I noticed the battery sitting in the box. I fitted it and tried again. My word, I nearly dropped it; it was vibrating so hard. I turned the end; it slowed to a reasonable speed. I couldn't resist trying my new toy, so I lifted my skirt. I was wearing white cotton pants. I held the end against my now-moist clitoris. Wow! What a fantastic sensation. I hadn't had sex in ages; I was so frustrated and turned on. Without thinking, I slipped off my pants. I wanted more; my imagination was going wild. I was thinking of a massive stiff cock penetrating my soaking wet vagina. I slipped the vibrator into my slit. OMG, I was coming already. My body went into spasm. I arched my back, trying to accommodate the fireworks going on inside me. My toes curled, and I let out a cry of sheer joy as I climaxed, still with my friend inside me. I twisted the end; the vibrations stopped. The sun was pouring into the room. I lay there sweating on my reclining chair; my body relaxed. I closed my eyes and let the endorphins flood through my veins. I was totally in a state of calm. I lay there, my heartbeat slowly getting back to normal rhythm; my eyes were closed. It was so quiet in this room, but then from behind my chair came a sound!

A clunking sound; a metallic sound, like a steel bolt being moved. I turned around, straining my neck. There was no one there. The noise seemed to emanate from the steel door, but I was alone in the house. I must be imagining things. I was curious, had something dropped onto the floor; I couldn't see anything. I walked over to the steel door. I nonchalantly tried the handle; and to my total amazement, the handle moved. I quickly retreated; this couldn't be possible. I had tried many times, since I had moved in, to pull the handle down, but always to no avail; and now it was loose. How could this be; this couldn't be happening. Why did I hear the clunking sound, had the lock suddenly become freed; maybe the temperature in the room had expanded the mechanism, and it had freed itself!

I looked around the room. The clock said 2:35 p.m., my pants were still on the floor, and my little friend lay on my chair. I don't know what I was looking for, inspiration maybe; should I try the handle again, I had no choice really. It definitely moved when I tried it, and I had certainly heard a clunking sound. I moved back to the door. I grasped the black steel handle. I held my breath; my grip tightened around the handle. I twisted anti-clockwise; the handle moved. I heard the sound of metal moving. I gently pulled the door; and to my surprise, a sound of air being released, like you would hear in a sci-fi movie when the air lock on a spacecraft had been opened. My heart was pounding, but this time I wasn't having an orgasm. I was petrified what might be behind the door. The door was now 90 degrees to the wall. There was a kind of a fog inside, and the air was cold. I couldn't see into the space; the fog was so dense. I called out, God knows why; there could only have been a brick wall behind the door. "Is anyone there," I said nervously, hoping that no reply came back. Nothing, no noise; just the cold swirling fog. I plucked up the courage and reached forward with my right hand. My left hand was clutching the handle on the door. My fingers probed into the fog; as soon as they did, I felt a calm feeling flowing through my body. It seemed to draw me in, like a drug taking over your senses. I released the door handle and moved my body further into the swirling fog. My face entered the fog, then the rest of my body. Was I mad; how about if I couldn't get back out. The surprising thing was, I wasn't frightened. It seemed like it was meant to happen. I was now fully immersed inside the space behind the door. The floor I was stood on felt solid, and there seemed like a glow coming from deep inside the fog. I gingerly took another step, then bang!! I felt the steel door slam shut behind me. I panicked. I turned, frantically feeling for the handle on the door. I found it by chance. My heart leapt; then the reality hit me like a train. The handle was solid, just like it had always been on the other side. I couldn't get out, and I couldn't see much due to the fog. I screamed out,

"Help, help me, please someone help me."

But it was useless; there was no one in the house, no one could hear me; I was doomed. I didn't even know if there was enough air in here for me to breathe. I started to cry; why, I don't know. I was normally level headed in stressful situations. I had to pull myself together. I knelt down and reached out with my hands. The floor seemed to carry on; there was no cavernous drop if only I could see. I might be able to find a way out. I turned my head all around. The emanating light appeared to be coming from one direction. I decided, may be foolishly, to walk towards the light; I had no other choice. With one foot nervously stepping in front of the other, and my arms reaching out, I crept towards the light. Strangely I began to hear sounds, which, in a strange sort of way, reassured me. I say in a strange way, because I could hear the sound of cars passing me, which I shouldn't be able to hear in my attic room.

The light was getting more and more intense, and the sound becoming louder and louder. Then the solid floor I was walking on disappeared from under my feet. I started falling, and then with a flash of bright white light, I was suddenly in a different place. It seemed familiar. I was walking on a path beside a road; traffic was passing me. These must have been the cars I could hear when in the fog, but something was weird. First of all, the cars were older than I was used to seeing, and the most astounding thing of all was my clothes. I was wearing a brown mottled woollen coat. The belt pulled tight around my waist. My waist was tiny; it hadn't been that slim for years. I was wearing dolly type shoes; I had a canvass-style bag around my shoulder, which was quite heavy; and to top it all, my hair was red. Then I reached to my face with my hands, and I noticed my ring. My mother of pearl ring that Simon had bought me was missing; then the reality and the magnitude of the situation hit me.

I remembered this exact location, I remembered my clothes, the colour of my hair, but it was impossible it wasn't now! It was about ten years ago. I had dyed my hair red and worn clothes like these when I was at uni. I certainly remembered this coat; I loved that—this coat. This was my route home; I used to walk this way on my way home from uni, on my way back to my flat, where Simon would be waiting for me. Have you ever had that déjà vu moment when you feel this has happened before? Well, this was one of those episodes. I knew what was going to happen next, because it had happened to me before. When I say before, I mean about nine or ten years back. I knew any moment; now a car would pull up next to me, and sure enough at that moment, a flash car pulled alongside me. The passenger side window wound down. I stooped down to look into the car; and there he was—big blue eyes and a wide grin on his face. I remembered exactly what happened next, but I went through the motions anyway, as no one would believe what was really happening. I thought maybe he was lost and expected him to ask the way to where ever, but no! He said, "Sorry to ask, but do you fancy going out for a drink sometime?"

I was completely taken a back. Well, it was the first time this happened. A total stranger, and he was asking me out. He could have been an axe murderer for all I knew, but I didn't think so; he was actually quite cute. "That's awfully kind of you."

I replied awkwardly. I really didn't know what to say, "I have a boyfriend."

I spluttered out nervously. The young man in the car replied instantly, with a smile on his face totally unfazed, "Well, he's not invited."

The cheeky so and so, I thought to myself, but also rather brave, just to ask a complete stranger in the street like that. Beep! Beep! The sound of car horns, blared out from frustrated drivers trying to get past the obstruction caused by this cocky young man, who was asking me out. "You had better move; you're creating quite a tailback of traffic."

I shouted through the window. He leant across from the driver's seat and passed me a piece of paper, pressing it into my hand.

"If you change your mind, give me a call."

He then sped off. A plume of white smoke billowing out of the twin exhaust pipes at the rear of his flash car; then he was gone.

I put the piece of paper in my coat pocket and tried to gather my thoughts. I knew my flat was just around the corner; but if I went there, and Simon was there, what the hell would I tell him. Hello Simon, I've just travelled back through time, and we are still together in ten years' time. Oh! And by the way a total stranger just asked me out for a drink. I was totally confused, and to be honest, a little scared. How would I get back to my time? Roscoe was on his own; and Simon was away; who would feed the dog? I started running towards the flat. I reached the gate at the end of the path. I looked up towards the front door, it was as I remembered it, black with a gold letter plate and a dolphin shaped door knocker. I approached the door; I was petrified. What might happen next, I stood at the door. My mind in a spiral of thoughts; then I thought about how I had got here. The black door in my attic room; the formidable black steel door that had refused to open for such a long time. I started to feel cold, the image of the flat door in front of me seemed to ripple in front of me; then a swirling fog engulfed me. I had the sense of falling; a flash of light, then my eyes opened. I was back in my attic room. I was laying in my reclining chair. I looked at the clock; it said 2:35 p.m. That couldn't be right. I felt like I had been 'There', where ever 'There' was! At least an hour, but the time hadn't shifted at all. I noticed my mother of pearl ring had reappeared on my finger. I jumped up and ran to the door. I grabbed the handle, expecting it to move; but it was as solid as ever. *Had I really been through the door and travelled back in time, don't be silly,* I thought to myself. I must have been dreaming. I picked up my pants off the floor where I had left them; then the present from Kim. It was certainly a hit with me. It had made me come so quickly. I placed it back in its pouch and put it in the back of a draw. It was sad that after all these years together with Simon, it had come to me frigging myself off with a vibrator. I then realised I was desperate for a cuppa, so I headed for the kitchen where Roscoe was waiting patiently for me. He was jumping up, trying to lick my face. I gave him a big squeeze, then popped the kettle onto the AGA.

While drinking the tea, my mind wandered over what had just happened or had it! Surely, it must have been a dream. I could remember the instance approximately ten years ago when this chappy had pulled up in his car and asked me out. At the time, I was in a relationship with Simon, so I had refused. I had always thought, if I had said yes to the cheeky so and so, how different things might have turned out. An image of the young man in the car exploded into my vision. It was so vivid, it made me jump! He was rather dishy, and those blue eyes were mesmerising. I wondered what his name was, but it was too late now; the chance had gone forever. I lay in bed that evening, thinking about all sorts. Simon was coming home tomorrow evening. We needed to have a serious discussion about us; something must be wrong. He had changed so much over the past few months. I tossed and turned for most of the night; the image of the man in the car kept popping into my thoughts. I just couldn't stop thinking about him.

Chapter 8
Revelations

The next day, the Friday, Simon would be home tonight. I was excited, as he had been away all week, yet nervous, because I didn't really understand how things had got so bad between us. Was I over-reacting; I suppose all couples go through patches where they don't seem as close as usual, but this seemed deeper than that. I just wanted things to be normal again. I spent the day sorting the house out, clearing some of the clutter, so the house felt homely; and I prepared a lasagne for our tea. All I had to do was bang it in the AGA about an hour before he arrived home. All through the day, my mind kept drifting back to yesterday. The man with the blue eyes and cheeky smile was haunting me. I don't know why, I didn't know him; I didn't even know his name. The other problem was how it could have happened. I must have been dreaming, but it felt so real—the door opening, the cold fog, my clothes. Then I remembered that he had passed me a piece of paper with his number on. I had put it in my pocket; then stupidly, I realised that when I came back to this time, I was wearing my now clothes, minus my pants. They had still been on the floor where I had left them. Throughout the day, I was thinking how stupid I must be to even consider the possibility of travelling through time. Then the next minute, thinking how perfectly reasonable it was to pass through a steel door in my attic and travel back ten years into my past. I must be losing my marbles. I decided to go for a long walk with Roscoe to clear my mind. We headed off across the fields; the dog was in heaven. How lovely it must be to be a dog—the only important things in life were companionship, food and a long walk. I'm definitely coming back as a dog. As we crossed the field on our return to the house, I noticed a car on the drive. It was Chloe. I could see her banging on the back door. I shouted,

"Chloe, we are here in the field."

She turned and waved. Roscoe shot off towards her, barking as he went. I was so pleased she was here. I needed to have a catch up with all the goings on. God knows what she would think about my time travel, would she believe me, or think I was off my rocker!

"How are you, my beautiful friend?"

She said as she hugged the life out of me.

"So! So! Come on in, let's have a coffee. I have something amazing to tell you."

We sat at the kitchen table with our cappuccino coffees and a slice of cake each.

"Come on then, Poppy, what's this amazing news."

Chloe seemed really excited, and I wished I hadn't said anything now; she would probably think I was crazy. I looked into her eyes, took a gulp of my coffee; then I started to tell her what had happened, not mentioning the bit about the vibrator—that was a bridge too far.

As I explained to her about the clonking sound coming from the door, and how I had opened it and gone inside, her eyes widened in utter astonishment. She took a slurp of her coffee. Her eyes transfixed on me; she lowered her cup onto the saucer, quietly whispering,

"No way! No! No way."

The whole episode of what had happened spilled out of my mouth, and the more I spoke of the incident, the quieter my voice became. In the end, I was whispering, as if I didn't want anyone to hear about the truly life-changing episode in my life. When I finished, Chloe was dumbstruck. She was just staring into my eyes, bewildered at what I had just told her.

"Well Chloe, say something, even if it's only bollocks."

"I don't know what to say, Poppy. Had you been drinking?"

I was now upset. If my best friend didn't believe me, no one would.

"Oh Chloe, please believe me, I promise you that's exactly what happened."

"I do believe you, Poppy, but you have to admit, it's a bit of a shock. I thought when you said you had an amazing news, you were going to say you had shagged the local farmer."

"I could do with a good shagging, but that's another story."

I said to Chloe. I then explained how Simon had been away all week, and how I had heard a women's voice on his phone. She was really protective of me, straight away saying she would cut his balls off if he had been screwing around.

"Well, he's home tonight, so hopefully we will get to the bottom of things."

After chatting for about an hour, it was time for Chloe to leave. Before she went through the door, she turned and said,

"I do believe you, Poppy; but next time you travel back in time, bring back some proof."

I just laughed and said, "I will see what I can do."

She kissed me on the cheek, hopped into her car and disappeared down the drive, tooting her horn as she turned onto the road. I was again on my own, apart from Roscoe the dog. I started thinking about what Chloe had said—bring back proof from the past—how could that be possible. When I travelled back, my ring had disappeared, and I was wearing clothes that I had worn then; and when I returned, I had the clothes on that I was wearing before I went through the door. It appeared that nothing could travel through time apart from my mind and body. My mobile phone started vibrating across the kitchen table. I looked at the screen; it was Simon. I answered, "Hello Simon, I've missed you, are you nearly home."

"Yes, about an hour away, stuck in traffic on the M1. I will see you later."

The phone went dead. He didn't even say he missed me or loved me. It was really concerning me now, had he fallen out of love with me. I popped the

39

lasagne into the AGA, then set the table. While I was waiting, I checked that his favourite beer was in the chiller; then went and sat next to the pool in the garden. The ducks were as noisy as usual, but after a while, I didn't hear them. My mind was going wild thinking about all the possible things that might be wrong. Had he met someone else, someone younger, prettier with a high-powered job. I always thought that he was disappointed in me because I was just an artist, with no guaranteed salary. Surely not, up until only a few months ago, our sex life was brilliant, and everything seemed perfect. We had just bought this house with the intention of being together forever, but now I wasn't so sure; deep down, I knew trouble was brewing.

I heard the slowing down of a vehicle in the lane. I looked up to see Simon's car just turning into the drive. He pulled up next to the back door. I ran over, pulled open the driver's door and hugged him.

"Give me a chance to get out, Poppy."

As he stood up next to the car, I wrapped my arms around him. I tried to kiss him, but he seemed awkward; he wasn't kissing me back. I was so excited, I had missed him terribly. I wanted sex; lustful sex may be on the kitchen table. I couldn't wait to get indoors, but he wasn't having any of it. "Poppy, let me get my things out of the car and get inside. You're like a dog on heat, what's the matter with you. I've only been away for five days."

I backed off, hurt at being rejected and disappointed that he didn't feel the same way towards me. We went inside. Simon shouted,

"I'm off upstairs for a shower."

I looked down at Roscoe. He hadn't even got out of his bed to greet Simon. Maybe the dog knew more than I did. I poured myself a large glass of wine. I thought to myself, *I think I'm going to need this.* The first sip was bliss, followed by a gulp. I was angry at the way he had acted. I dished up the meal, banging the plates down on the wooden kitchen table. I shouted up the stairs,

"The tea is on the table."

I poured a cold beer for Simon and refilled my glass with Pino, then sat down and started my meal. Simon came in,

"Starting without me; you must be hungry."

I looked at him, my blood boiling, "I'm not bloody hungry. I'm bloody angry; you've been away all week, and you haven't even kissed me since you got back; what the hell is wrong."

Simon stared at me; his eyes glaring at me as if he hated me; then he let rip, "I've worked my butt off all week, to come home to this, being cross examined, asking me what's wrong, not kissing you. I wish I had stopped away."

"You might as well have, you're acting like you don't even love me anymore. Simon, what is the problem; have you got someone else?"

"Don't be so bloody stupid, Poppy. Of course I haven't got someone else. When have I got the time to see someone else, I'm always at work."

He slammed down his beer glass. The beer spilled all over the table and his lasagne.

"Now look what you've made me do."

I jumped up, grabbed his plate and poured the beer off the plate into the sink, salvaging the remains of the meal. We ate the rest of the meal in silence. The only noise came from the dog, Roscoe, who was sitting next to me, looking up at me—his tail wagging, mouth salivating, hoping for a morsel of human food, which all dogs seemed to prefer.

After dinner, we retired to the lounge. I lit the log burner as it was a bit chilly in more ways than one. Simon was still sulking; I hated that emotion. It just wasted time instead of sorting out the problem and getting on with life; the problem just dragged on and on. Then you always ended up talking about the issue anyway, but hours or sometimes days later, so infuriating. I snuggled up to Simon on the green leather sofa, but Simon wasn't very accommodating. He seemed to pull away, said he was watching the TV. I gingerly rubbed his leg, then slowly moved my attention to between his legs and found his semi-hard cock being stifled in his denim jeans.

"What are you doing, Poppy? Can't we just relax in front of the telly, without resorting to sex."

I pulled away hurt, like a scolded child. I felt really upset!

"What the hell is wrong with you, Simon? You've been away all week, you didn't want to talk on the phone; and now your back home, you don't want to touch me. It seems like you hate me; what have I done wrong?"

"Nothing's wrong, Poppy. I'm just tired. It's been a busy week, then the drive home, Well, I'm just done in. I think I need an early night."

"Oh! No, you don't, Simon. We need to sort this out right now. Don't give me that rubbish, you're tired. I bet you had the energy when you went out with your female friend the other night."

Simon's face went cold. If looks could kill, I would be dead. He jumped up, stood there for a few seconds then turned towards me—a tirade of abuse erupted from his mouth. It was like he had been possessed by the devil. I was shocked and scared. I had never seen him like this in all the years we had been together.

"Poppy, you don't even know Lucy, so don't bring her into it!"

I stood up with the intention of leaving the room, but as the frustration grew, I turned and retorted!

"Oh Lucy is it, I suppose she's younger than me, prettier than me; and no doubt your shagging her, because your certainly not giving me any."

The taste was salty in my mouth; the smell of leather next to my face. I was face down leaning on the sofa. Simon had lunged out swiping me across the face; the force knocking me off balance. The salty taste was blood; he had split my lip open. This couldn't be happening; Simon would never hit me, but the reality was, he had!

"Poppy, I'm so sorry, I just lost it. I will never hit you again, I promise."

Simon attempted to embrace me. I pushed him off!

"I'm going to make a cup of tea; then I'm going to bed."

I sat up in bed, sipping my tea, contemplating what had just happened. The hot tea made my lip sting. Simon put his head through the door,

"Can I come in and sleep with you, Poppy?"

"You can if you promise to tell me the truth about how you feel. We can't go on like this anymore. It's absolutely ridiculous, and it's making me very unhappy."

Simon agreed to talk. He quickly got undressed and got into bed, stark naked as always. I finished my tea and turned out the bedside lamp. The full moon shone through the window, allowing just enough light to make out shapes in the room. We were both sat up, leaning against the leather headboard.

"Well, Simon, what the hell is going on? Tell me whatever it is. I would sooner know than go on like this."

There was silence for a couple of minutes, then a heavy sigh. I knew he was about to tell me something devastating. Did I really want to know; deep down I was scared, but I knew it had to be sorted out. I braced myself as Simon poured his heart out. I was quiet throughout, listening in disbelief. His voice seemed to stutter as he explained how he had fallen in love with a girl from work. Yes, it was Lucy; and he had been involved for about three months. He said he had tried hard to end the relationship, but after spending this week away with her, had succumbed and slept with her.

My heart sank. I knew as soon as he had admitted to sleeping with her, there was no going back. I felt tears running down my cheeks. They ran onto my split lip, smarting, reminding me what Simon had done in his frustration, but it was no excuse. There never was an excuse for a man to hit a woman. I thought the confession was over, but to my amazement, there was more to come!

"I've also been promoted, and I've accepted the position."

"Simon, I don't think that has any relevance to what you've just told me. I don't care that you've been promoted. I only care that you've shagged a girl at work."

"But Poppy, the promotion means I have to be based at the head office."

The realisation of what he had just said hit me. Not only was he in love with someone else, but he had already planned to move to London. "Poppy, I'm so sorry. I didn't mean any of this to happen; it just did. I won't see you stuck, I promise; and you can stop in the house until it's sold."

It then hit me like a ton of bricks, a freight train; a juggernaut smashing into my heart. This house that I loved, my relationship with my partner of almost ten years was over. The realisation overwhelming me, I began to sob my heart out. Simon attempted to console me. He put his arm around me; it repulsed me. I turned the light on, jumped out of the bed. I was now angry and coming to my senses.

"Don't you ever touch me again, you cheating, two-faced, cowardly bastard. If I hadn't pushed you and repeatedly asked you what was wrong, when were you going to tell me."

"Poppy, I tried. I tried many times, but I just couldn't find the courage. I didn't want to upset you."

"Upset me! We have just bought this house; and by the way, I also put money into it, so don't tell me I can stop in the house until it's sold. I will stop here as long as I like."

"Poppy, I need the money from this house to purchase the house in London."
Simon's voice was getting louder and angrier, but so was mine.

"I suppose you need a nice little house for you and that bitch to move in to,
very cosy!"

I grabbed my dressing gown. I wasn't going to sleep in the same bed as that
snake.

"Simon, I want you out of this house first thing in the morning. I'm going to
sleep in my studio, and I don't want you anywhere fucking near me."

I alighted the staircase, entered the attic room and bolted the door. I lay on
the reclining chair and covered myself with a throw, cuddling down, praying that
the steel door behind me would unlock; so I could escape this time and disappear
into the past.

Chapter 9
The Dawn

My eyes opened, I looked around. The events of the night before rushing back to me. My lip was still throbbing, focussing my mind on the reality of what had happened the night before. Not only had Simon told me he no longer loved me, but he was in love with someone else, and he had struck me in anger; and on top off all that, I was going to lose the home I loved. It couldn't get any worse, or could it! I got up out of the chair. It was unusually quiet, even the ducks on the pond were having a lie in. I was dreading talking to Simon. I descended the stairs heading for the kitchen; I was desperate for a cuppa. I opened the kitchen door, and immediately, Roscoe was all over me. I bent down to cuddle him. He went wild, as if he hadn't seen me for years. He licked my sore lip, as if to say, "Don't worry, I will look after you."

At least someone loved me, has I stood up, I happened to look out of the window. Something was missing; then it hit me that Simon's car was gone. I couldn't believe it. I know I said I wanted him out, he obviously couldn't wait to get away from me. I ran up the stairs shouting his name, "Simon, where are you."

But there was no answer, just silence. His suit bag, his away bag, and even some of his clothes from his wardrobe were missing. He had obviously gone to be with the bitch in London. Then I noticed a note on my pillow,

Dear Poppy,
I'm so sorry if I've hurt you. I never meant any of this to happen. I will always care for you. I will call you later in the week.
Take care of yourself!
Simon x.

Well, that was that. He had gone, out of my life, forever. The tears rolled down my face, and I cried uncontrollably, but there was no one to hear me. I felt so alone and very sad. These are the times when you would turn to your mum or dad, but they were sadly long gone, so I phoned Chloe and briefly told her what had happened. She was so supportive and willing to listen and arranged to come over as soon as she could escape work. I put the phone down, pleased that my friend would be here later, then went back to the kitchen to make the cup of tea I was so desperate for.

Throughout the day, my mind kept going over the past few months, trying to work out the time when Simon's mind was elsewhere. He had been a bit moody, even grumpy, for the past three months coinciding with the time he had been seeing Lucy. Why oh why had he committed to buying this house if he was in love with someone else, how stupid can you get. Maybe he thought he could be with me and see Lucy on the side until I pushed and pushed him to tell me the truth and forced his hand, and he realised I wouldn't put up with it. Anyway, the reality was he was gone. He had broken my heart, all I could do was pick myself up and get on with my life. It wasn't going to be easy. I was determined not to let him reduce me to a gibbering wreck. I was better than that, and I would prove to him that Poppy Day would survive the humiliation of being dumped for a younger model if indeed she was younger than me. I would come through this stronger and certainly wiser than before. I then curled into the foetal position on my bed and sobbed my heart out. I wasn't as strong as my mind portrayed to be.

I must have lay there most of the day, feeling sorry for myself; it was dead quiet in the house. Even the dog Roscoe wasn't bothering me for attention; he seemed to sense that something was upsetting me and just lay next to me with the occasional nudge of his wet nose into my chin, reassuring me that he was there if I needed him. His eyes full of love and wilfulness to please. If only I could find a man who had a fraction of this dedication to please, I would be a very lucky lady. I must have drifted off to sleep because a banging in the distance awoke me. At first, I wasn't sure where I was; then as my eyes focussed, Roscoe pounded off the bed, cascaded down the stairs, barking, excitedly heading for the noise. I then came to my senses and realised someone was knocking at the back door. I descended the stairs, half-hoping it was Simon coming back to beg me for forgiveness; but alas, it wasn't him. It was my best friend Chloe banging frantically at the door. As soon as I released the catch, the door flung open. Chloe grabbed me, frantically.

"I've been knocking for ages. I thought you had done something stupid."

"Oh my god, Chloe, how weak do you think I am. Do you really think I am that desperate that I can't live without Simon."

"Well, Poppy, after the call this morning, you were so upset, and I've called you at least six times today on your mobile, with no success. I started to panic."

"I'm so sorry, Chloe. I've slept most of the day, I didn't hear the phone, but really, I'm okay. I am upset, but I'm not going to let that fucking two-timing, lying, cheating excuse for a man reduce me to a broken-hearted, pathetic shadow of a women. I will show him I am strong. I don't need him, and he will regret the day he betrayed me!"

"Well, it's good to know you're fighting back, Poppy. If I see him first, I will screw his balls off."

"I don't think he's got balls, Chloe. If he had, he would have told me months ago before we bought this place."

"I've brought wine, Poppy. Do you fancy a glass or two?"

"Oh yes! I will just pop a pizza into the AGA, then we can get pissed and have a bite to eat while we slag the male race into oblivion."

Over the next couple of hours, we gulped our wine down, ate a pizza and generally tore Simon apart, calling him every despicable name we could think of and his precious Lucy. We hadn't even met her, but she was a slut, a whore and a first class bitch all rolled into one. I'm not sure this session made me feel any better, but it had to be done.

Having Chloe here supporting me made me feel so much stronger. I was determined to stay positive, to make a plan, to move on; and with friends like Chloe, I was sure to succeed.

"Poppy, how about your man in the past?"

"What do you mean?"

"Well, you need a man, you need a shag, go through the door and get him."

"Oh, you believe me now, now you're pissed, anyway what makes you think I fancied him."

"You know full well that you fancied him when you told me about how he stopped his car and asked you out. You were gushing, your eyes lit up, and your face coloured up, as if he had been sat next to us. You definitely had the hots for him."

"It all sounds great, but what if the door never opens again."

"Poppy, don't sound so negative. Retrace your steps, do exactly as you did the last time, and you might find the door will unlock, and you can travel back in time and find the man of your dreams."

If only she knew, the last time I had just frigged myself off with a vibrator, before the door opened, God forbid I have to have an orgasm each time I want to travel.

"Poppy! Let's go upstairs now. If the door opens, I will come with you, and I can vet this new man on the block."

I resisted profusely, but she practically dragged me up to the attic room. She was more pissed than I was. I sat on the reclining chair. Chloe sprawled across the carpet. She kept giggling, and I kept saying,

"Quiet, quiet."

Then she giggled more. We sat there for quite a while, waiting for the sound of the lock giving up its secret hold on the steel door, but nothing happened. After about an hour, we got bored and decided to go back to our wine. I for one was a little disappointed, but deep down, I thought maybe the 'Door' would only open for me.

As it was Saturday night, there was no work in the morning for either of us, so we set about another bottle of Pino, opened some nuts and talked our way through the night into the early hours of the Sunday morning. I wish we hadn't because when we finally woke up, I had the most horrendous headache I had ever had. Chloe looked ashen and kept disappearing to the loo; the sound of painful retching emanating from the bathroom door. Why oh why do we do this to our bodies. We know how we will feel the next day, and we still go ahead and blissfully down enough wine to float a small boat. Will I ever learn?

Chapter 10
Destiny

After we had had our breakfast, a bit of toast was sufficient. The thought of a cooked breakfast made my stomach churn, and Chloe only just managed to hold her tea down. About half an hour later, it was time for Chloe to leave for home. I was looking forward to some time on my own, time to reflect and plan the way forward—a way forward without Simon. After talking all night about the situation, I now had a sense of what I wanted to do; and oddly it involved the man from the past, that's if 'the door' would ever open for me again. Why the man in the past had such a pull on me, I had no idea. There was just something about him; I had the same feelings I had before buying this house, as if some greater power was controlling me.

I waved goodbye to Chloe; she tooted her horn as usual as she sped off down the drive. The ducks on the pond responded with an echo of competing quacks. I walked back into the house. Roscoe was close to my ankles. I was quite excited; the thought of seeing the man from the past gave me a warm glow in the pit of my stomach. That's if the 'Door' would look on me kindly and release its hold on my future, or should I say my past. Throughout the day, I was thinking about going through the 'Door' into my past. Would I be able to get back, the last time I travelled it only took me, to think of the 'Door'; and the shimmering started; and I was travelling back to my time, the future. Also the actual time I spent in the past seemed to be normal, but when I arrived back, no time had elapsed. I remember looking at the clock in my studio as soon as I arrived back; no time had elapsed. So I assumed if I went back again, I would arrive after the last visit; and so on, the time there would gradually catch up with the time zone I was in now 1995. This was really important because if I travelled back and was gone too long, who would feed Roscoe. I decided I would leave loads of food in the kitchen, just in case I was delayed. I would also call Chloe, and let her know if I didn't call her after 8 hours of absence, she would have to come to the rescue and look after Roscoe.

It's strange. Normally when you travel, you have the stress of packing all the right clothes, hair products, make up and so on. But with time travel, certainly in this case when I went back, only my body and mind travelled with me, so I couldn't stress about what to take. I decided I would attempt to travel the next morning. This would give me time to prepare myself and put into place back-up procedures, should I get stuck in the past. So I phoned Chloe and told her of my plans. I arranged to leave a key inside the well roof. The well was just outside the kitchen door. It was built with local stone—the same stone as part of the house was built with. It was round; the stone circular wall stood about three feet from the ground; then two wooden posts protruded out of the stone, which supported the slate roof and also supplied the supports for the central axle. The axle had rope wrapped around it; on the end of the rope hung a galvanised bucket. There was a winding handle at the end of the axle, which allowed you to wind the bucket back up after dropping it into the water. It was a lovely original feature of the house and certainly added character to the property. It also offered a great place to hide the house key, which I placed on a hook screwed to a rafter. So Roscoe was sorted; no worries there, but there was something niggling me at the back of my mind. I decided to make a cuppa and settle into a garden chair overlooking the pond. That would relax my mind, and maybe I might focus on what was bugging me.

It was such a beautiful day, very warm, clear blue sky. The birds were singing. In fact, there was a Robin above me on a branch, singing his heart out. How such a powerful sound came from such a small creature astounds me; it certainly lifted my heart. I used to be so happy, always having a laugh, playing jokes on my friends and always looking for an excuse to have sex. I really missed the excitement of doing it in different places; it didn't matter where, as long as it didn't offend anyone. But alas, I was now on my own, so the only sexual pleasure I was going to enjoy was going to be with my little bullet-shaped friend. It then popped into my mind—the niggle at the back of my mind. It was this, when I travelled back in time to meet the man in the car. What would I tell him, "Oh, I've just travelled through time to come and see you." He would think I was crazy. Also I would have to tell him that I was prepared to see him behind my boyfriend's back, because if I dumped Simon back in 1985, it would immediately change the future. Then I would be stuck in the past, because the 'Door' wouldn't exist, because we wouldn't have bought the country house in the future, with the 'Door' in the attic. God! The more I thought about it, the more complicated it proved to be. If, when I travelled back, I didn't live with Simon, how would I get my money from the bank without my bank card, clean clothes to wear, my passport, my student card. I couldn't take anything with me. So I would have to go back in time; then go home to Simon as if nothing had changed; then try to see the man in the car without Simon finding out. Also the man in the car, if he still wanted to see me, would have to put up with me living with Simon.

Then it occurred to me that I might bump into myself how does it work. Do I travel back into the person I was, or is there an extra person; I was so confused. I was beginning to think it was all too much trouble. Besides, when I travelled back, I might not even get to see the man in the car. He may be long gone, so all these tribulations and stress I was causing myself would be pointless. Then it hit me. If I was living with Simon, our sex life then was amazing. How would I explain why I didn't feel like having sex. I couldn't openly have sex with two men, or could I. The only way I could see this working was to travel back, but make sure that I never crossed paths with Simon. This way, I wouldn't have to explain. This left the problem of no money, but then a plan popped into my very confused mind. I planned to travel back, hopefully to arrive during the working day. Simon would be out at work. I could then attempt to get into the flat and take the things I needed. I could then hide my possessions somewhere safe. Then each time I travelled back to 1985, I could retrieve them.

My brain was hurting. I had been deliberating all day. I looked at the clock; amazingly it was gone 7:00 p.m. Roscoe was whining; he needed his walk and some tea—talking of tea. That was just what I needed, but first I couldn't ignore the dog any longer; so off we went across the fields. The dog was in heaven; I was in turmoil.

Chapter 11
1985 Here I Come

I woke early the next day, remarkably. I slept well, although feeling apprehensive about the day ahead. I also felt excited; my life recently had been testing to say the least, but the worst part was feeling unloved and having no fun. It made life laborious, dull, and it was turning me into a very different person. I used to be such a jovial, positive, naughty young lady; and I wanted her back. Look out, world, Poppy Day was coming back. The first job of the day was to spend a little time with my best friend. We had a lovely walk around the edge of the adjoining field. We kept to the edge, as the field was planted up with linseed rape. The smell was overwhelming, but the colour was a stunning vivid yellow—a site for sore eyes, as my mum would have said. I was so lucky to live in such a beautiful spot. I would fight tooth and nail to try and hold on to this place. I didn't know how, but I would find a way.

Roscoe seemed starving when we arrived back home. He couldn't wait to devour his breakfast; he polished it off in seconds. There was no way he could have tasted it. I filled up a large bowl with dry mix biscuits and topped up his water. The water wasn't really an issue, has he could get out of the dog flap and drink from the pond. I then had a quick shower, dressed in jeans and a blouse and set about locking the house up from the inside. Happy that the house was now secure, I climbed the stairs to the attic room; crikey it was hot up here. I lay in the reclining chair in the hope that the door would unlock. As I lay there, my mind was wandering from one thing to another; first Simon and then the house, back to Simon, and how things had all gone wrong; it was driving me mad. I kept looking at the clock; it said 10:20 a.m. It seemed like ages and still no noise from the door. The next time I looked at the clock, it said 10:58 a.m. I started to think that maybe the last time I travelled, I had been dreaming, or did I have to have an orgasm for the 'Door' to respond like the last time. I closed my eyes and started to think of the man in the past, his piercing blue eyes and cheeky smile. A few minutes later, I heard the clonking sound of the lock mechanism in the 'Door' releasing. It was time to go. I glanced at the clock; it read 11:25 p.m. I nervously approached the 'Door'.

I paused as my hand reached for the handle; was I certain that this was the right thing to do, would I be able to get back. I thought to myself, my life couldn't get much worse, so I grasped the handle and pressed it down. The 'Door' opened, has it had before; a release of cold air, and I was looking into a swirling fog. I stepped into the fog, this time knowing what to expect. The temperature was still a shock; it brought a shiver down my spine. After taking a step into the cold fog, there was a resounding thud of the 'Door' as it closed behind me. No need to panic; I had been here before. The white light ahead shone through the fog. I looked at it as a guiding light. I walked towards it, thinking to myself, *Well, it wasn't a dream; it's certainly happening for real, just like it did before.*

I could hear the voices of children playing. They got louder the more I walked into the fog. Then without warning, the solidness underfoot disappeared. I was falling through the fog; then a white flash of light, and I was walking along a pavement next to a park. The other side of the green metal fence between the path and the park were loads of children playing on the swings and slides, all competing with each other to be the loudest. I recognised my surroundings; this park was on my route home from uni to home. I must still have been at uni due to the way I was dressed. I still had my brown mottled coat and my multi-coloured canvas bag around my shoulder, but this time, I was sporting a blue and white floral dress, about knee-length, with white pumps and blue laces. *Very nautical,* I thought to myself. I attempted to pull my hair forward to see what colour it was. It wasn't red any more, it was Ginger; and again, I noticed my mother of pearl ring had disappeared from my right hand. I leant against the fence to gather my thoughts.

Since the last time I travelled, time had moved on. I remember I had dyed my hair Ginger in the last year of my course, so at least six months had elapsed from my last encounter; and I had dyed my hair at the same time I had been preparing my final display of art work for my degree. I now knew the time I had arrived back in. It was the latter end of 1985, and it appeared I was walking home from uni; the park was on my left hand side and the road on my right. Now what! I couldn't go home, as I had planned. It felt like late afternoon. The children were obviously out of school, so Simon might have come home from work. I decided I would walk in the direction of home and see if any bright ideas popped into my head.

As I was walking along the road, the weight of my multi-coloured canvas bag hanging around my neck was making my shoulder ache. I stopped walking and pulled the bag strap from around my head. I placed the bag on a low wall. I had stopped next to and opened it. I peered in, and OMG, I couldn't believe it. I opened my purse to find not only money but my bank cards, my student union card; also at the bottom of the bag, mixed in with art materials, pencils, was my diary and for some strange reason my passport. I couldn't think for the life of me why I was carrying my passport, but this was epic. It meant I didn't need to break into my flat and take these things. I was so happy; I placed the bag back around my neck and carried on walking. It was a beautiful sunny day, with scattered fluffy white clouds in the sky. I now had spring in my step.

After walking about 200 yards, I happened to slip my hands into my pockets. My fingers in my right pocket stumbled on a piece of paper. I retrieved it; it was folded in half. I then realised it was the piece of paper the man in the car gave me the last time I travelled. My heart missed a beat. I unfolded it; it had a phone number written on it. It was a local dialling code, so he wouldn't be far away.

This meant I could phone him to see if he was still interested in that drink he had offered me. The good news was, when I had opened my purse, I had noticed I had change; so if I could find a phone box—not many people had mobile phones in the 80s—I could give him a call. I set off looking for a phone box in earnest. It wasn't far down the road when I noticed a red phone box on the other side of the road. I felt a little nervous, has he now might not be interested.

As I attempted to cross the road to get to the phone, I stepped into the road, and there was an almighty blast of a car horn. I jumped back onto the path a little shaken; my heart was pounding. A large flash car pulled up next to me; the window wound down. I leant down, about to let rip at this inconsiderate driver. My mouth was wide open, expletives about to escape, when I realised it was him—the man in the car—big blue eyes, with that infectious smile.

"Do you need a lift, young lady," he said, in a friendly voice. I found it hard to speak. I was so taken aback, also shook up from the shock.

"You nearly killed me."

"I think you could do with a stiff drink," he replied, without hesitation. I thought to myself, *well, he's still interested*, but I wasn't going to make it too easy for him.

"I'm not sure. I don't even know you; you could be an axe murderer for all I know."

He chuckled; his blue eyes seemed brighter than normal.

"I'll tell you what if you come for one drink with me. I promise I won't murder you; and if you don't enjoy yourself, I won't accost you ever again."

He was certainly not one for giving up; I had to give him that. I just stood there, my mouth frozen. I must have looked gormless.

"We'll jump in then; we are holding the traffic up."

He had swung the door open, in anticipation, confident that I would succumb to his hypnotic blue eyes. I then found my voice. It just popped out,

"Okay, just a quick drink to settle me, after you scared me half to death."

He looked just like the cat that got the cream. I sank into the soft leather of the passenger seat; it felt luxurious. I pulled the car door; it clicked shut. He leant across me. I panicked. I thought he was going to kiss me. I felt my face turn red.

"Don't panic; just helping you with your seat belt."

I felt so stupid why would he try to kiss me, we had only just met. He pressed down on the accelerator. There was a roar from the powerful engine. I sank back in my seat from the force of the car shooting forward; then the ride settled as he achieved cruising speed,

"Sorry, I didn't want to slow the car coming up behind us."

I assumed he didn't want me to think he was showing off. There was a strange silence, which seemed to last forever. I started to speak at exactly the same time as he did, we both apologised at the same time, then both of us saying,

"You first."

We both burst out laughing. It certainly broke the ice.

"My name is Sam," he said, looking over at me.

"Mines Poppy,"

I replied. At last, I wouldn't have to refer to him as 'the man in the car' anymore.

"What a lovely name, Poppy,"

Sam said.

"Well, you won't believe this, Sam. I've always said if I had a son, I would name him Sam."

"You approve then, Poppy."

"I certainly do."

The car then changed direction. Heading out of town, he obviously had somewhere in mind for this quick drink. He kept staring at me.

"Do you think you could keep your eyes on the road Sam and not on me."

"I'm finding it difficult; you're so beautiful and lovely, and I'm really happy that you agreed to have a couple of drinks with me."

I felt myself flush; my face getting redder by the minute. Surely I was past that stage in my life when compliments embarrassed me. Then it registered,

"A couple of drinks, you said one quick drink."

He replied instantly, "What's a drink or two between friends."

He already considered us as friends, and we hadn't had the first drink yet. He was certainly a cocky so and so, but I have to admit I liked him. I liked him a lot.

The car started to slow. I could see a black and white place ahead. We were in the country a few miles from the local town. We pulled into the gravel car park and parked under the shade of an oak tree. Sam jumped out and ran around to my side, opening the passenger side door; he reached forward with his hand, grabbing mine. It was the first time we had touched. I felt a tingle deep in my stomach. Has I climbed out, clutching my bag, I stood next to Sam. I was surprised, he wasn't much taller than I was. I then heard the beep beep as Sam remotely locked the doors.

"Come on then, Poppy. Let's get that drink."

The gravelled car park made a crunchy noise as we walked to the entrance of the pub. The hanging sign above the door read

'The Chequer's Inn'. We entered through double, dark-oak-leaded light doors into a lovely oak-beamed lounge. The floor was laid with large, red, irregular-shaped stone slabs, and the room had a selection of eclectic soft sofas and chairs. Sam said,

"You grab a comfy seat, and I will bring the drinks over."

He then turned away, then turned back towards me, "Sorry, what would you like to drink."

May be he was suffering from nerves, but I doubted it.

"Just a small Pino for me, thanks Sam."

He scuttled off to the busy bar while I found us a nice quiet seat near a window overlooking the garden.

I sat there, looking around at the artwork on the uneven walls, criss-crossed with old split and bent oak beams. The artwork was mainly of country scenes and horses. I felt comfortable here; it was homely. At the end of the room stood a large fireplace, a stone hearth with a humongous firedog made up with dry logs, ready for the first chilly day to arrive. I didn't think that would be any time soon, as the sun rays were bursting through the leaded light windows. As I was scanning the room, I had this panicky feeling that I might see someone I knew. How would I explain that I was with a different chap. I then caught sight of Sam stood at the bar; he was wearing blue denim jeans and a white cotton, well-ironed shirt. I say well ironed, because it had the single pressing crease down the arms. I do like to see a man in a white crisp shirt. My eyes then moved down to his very muscular behind; he certainly looked after himself. At that moment, he turned. I looked away quickly. I didn't want him to think I was ogling him. He was cocky enough without that encouragement.

"There you go, young lady."

Sam placed the drinks on the table. Mine was not a small.

"Is that a large Pino, I asked for a small."

"Oh, sorry about that. The barmaid must have misheard me."

"Sam, you must think I'm stupid."

"It won't hurt, Poppy. You're safe with me."

Sam took a gulp of his lager, licking his lips with pleasure as the golden fluid quenched his thirst. My Pino was lovely; sometimes pubs served Pino which were acidic, but this one was very smooth. The next hour passed very quickly; we got on like a house on fire. The conversation flowed like we had known each other for years. I told him about my art course and about the end of year exhibition of all my work. He said he would love to see it, which sent bolts of panic down my spine; the girls at uni would wonder who the hell he was. Sam told me about his work. He was also a salesman, like Simon, but selling music equipment. I thought to myself, *he had the gift of the gab.*

Throughout the time we had sat together, he hadn't taken his eyes off me once. I have to admit his eyes melted my heart; it was so nice to be appreciated. I wondered to myself, does he fancy me. I certainly fancied him. Every time his hand touched my leg or my arm, as he gesticulated, I felt that tingle of joy shooting through my heart. I thought to myself how could we possibly make this work. Should I just come clean and tell him I was a 'time traveller' or just try to blag my way through. I would have to consider my options, but I did decide to remind him I was still in a relationship. After telling him about Simon, he also admitted to having a girlfriend, but said that he wasn't happy and was looking to move on. My heart sank; why did he ask me out if he was still involved with someone else. Then it dawned on me, I was no different. In this time zone, I was still living with Simon. It was a very complicated situation, but I didn't think it was the right time to discuss it.

"Poppy, let's just enjoy this drink and make the most of this time together."

"Sam, I agree things are complicated in lots of ways; we both have our reasons for being here."

We both finished our drinks and headed for the car. Sam, always the gentleman, opened my door first and closed it when I was settled into my seat. Sam got behind the wheel, buckled up and pulled slowly off the car park, heading back for the town.

"Poppy, would you like me to drop you home."

"Oh Sam, that's kind of you, but you better drop me off around the corner."

After a quiet drive back, I think both of us were in deep thought. Sam pulled the car over in a street, just around the corner from where my flat was. I looked at him; he looked at me.

"Poppy, I have to say something. I know you're not impressed that I have a girlfriend, but I genuinely like you a lot, and I would love to see you again."

"Sam, I feel the same, but I need to think about things. I will give you a call soon."

As I turned to climb out of the car, Sam caught hold of my arm and pulled me back towards him. He smelt divine. He kissed me ever so gently on the cheek,

"Take care, Poppy. Hope to see you soon."

I climbed out of the car, closed the car door and waved him goodbye. As he sped off away from me, I wondered if I would ever see him again. I stood there for a couple of minutes, thinking about our time together. God, he was lovely, but how on earth were we going to make this happen. I walked for a while, thinking how to get back to my time. I came across an alley where no one could see me. I stood there thinking about the 'Door', and sure enough my vision started to ripple just like before. There was a flash of light, I felt the cold fog, and I was in my reclining chair in my attic. I looked at the clock; it read 11:25 a.m.; no time had elapsed since I travelled.

Chapter 12
New Life

After gathering my thoughts, I got out of the chair and went downstairs. Roscoe was asleep in his basket; he hadn't even noticed I'd been away. Although I had been drinking with Sam, there was no effect what so ever on my body; which proved that when I travelled, there was no connection with the two time zones. Also when I travelled, time stood still in the future; but when in the past, time moved forward. So if I continued to visit the past, eventually the past would catch up with the future. I assumed then the 'Door' would refuse to open, and time travel would cease.

I spent the rest of the day cutting the grass, which was made easier due to the ride on mower, which the previous owners had left in the shed. They said they wouldn't need it in their new place. Then after a quick cuppa, I jumped in my van and visited the shops. I was desperate for groceries; and most important, I was running low on wine, which would be a tragedy if the girls turned up; I wouldn't hear the last of it. While out my mobile rang, I say rang, I had a ring tone of a dog barking, a 'no caller ID' came up on the screen. Bloody hell, it was probably a company phoning about insurance,

"Hello, Poppy speaking."

"It's me silly."

"Who's me?"

"It's Kim, sorry I've changed my phone. I'm just calling to give you my new number."

"I'm glad you've called Kim. Do you fancy going out for tea tonight? I was also going to ask Chloe."

"That would be great. We can try that new wine bar in town."

"I will arrange with Chloe, and I will take a taxi. I could do with few drinks. I have lots to tell you, see you at 7:30 tonight."

After I finished my shopping, I called Chloe, filling her in on our plans for the night ahead. She was always up for a girls' night out and agreed to meet up later. When I arrived home, I stopped at the end of the drive to collect the post. It was just a simple post box built into the stone wall next to the gate. The front was on hinges, so you could open it and grab the post, of which there seemed quite a handful today. The dry stone wall formed a low perimeter around the property, which also kept Roscoe from running out into the lane, providing one remembered to close the gate.

As soon as I got in the door, Roscoe was all over me, sniffing inside all the shopping bags which I had dropped on the floor.

"Oh! Roscoe, there's nothing in there for you. Get out, you little scamp."

After I walked and fed the dog, I decided to have a long soak in the bath and relax before hitting the town. Besides, it had been a long eventful day; time travel takes it out of you, you know. I had filled the bath so much that I could almost float, complete, with loads of bath suds; it was heaven. I lay there thinking about Sam; god, he was a hunk. His piercing blue eyes, blonde wavy hair, his cheeky grin and those muscles—he was a real turn on. I started to have disgusting thoughts about him; and before long, my fingers were slipping into my slit, finding my already aroused clit. I imagined Sam fingering me, occasionally sucking my erect stiff nipples. I must have really missed sex, because I could feel myself losing control. I arched my groin, so it was out of the water. My slit was slippery from the lust juice; I was almost there. I pinched my clit, just as I peaked, and a tumultuous orgasm ripped through my body. My back stiffened; my legs kicked out creating a tidal wave—a tsunami of hot soapy water cascading over the end of the bath—I didn't care; I was in heaven, and this was from just thinking about him. Imagine what the real thing would be like.

After cleaning up the soapy water all over the bathroom floor, I quickly got my hair done, put on a bit of lippy and slipped on a black, fairly tight fitting dress. No tights; it was far too muggy for them. Then while I waited for the taxi to arrive, I poured myself a large glass of wine. I locked the house up and sat by the pond. I had placed a small round table and a couple of chairs right next to the pond. It was a lovely place to sit and contemplate. I was thinking about Simon; he hadn't bothered to phone me since he left, and I have to admit I was hurt. I still couldn't get my head around what had transpired. We seemed so happy, we had bought this place together; and now it was all over. Was I so unbearable to live with, what had this Lucy got that I hadn't; I bet it was youth.

Just as I took the last sip of my wine, I heard a car slowing down. Yes, it was my taxi; he pulled up to the gate and pipped his horn. I waved and made my way down the drive, precariously though. I was sporting a pair of three-inch heels, which I had bought from a fabulous shoe shop in my local town. I pulled the gate back on its latch and slipped into the back seat of the taxi. The driver was dishevelled; his hair black and greasy. He turned to face me; his teeth were crooked and yellow. I assumed from smoking cigarettes.

"Where we going then, Bab?"

He said, in a strong black county accent. His breath stank of a mixture of garlic, cigarettes and mint. He had obviously popped a mint prior to me getting in, to try and mask his disgusting breath.

"Can you drop me in the centre of town, please?"

"Of course I can, Bab; off to see your fella, are you?"

"My husband is meeting me in town."

I lied; I didn't want him to think I was available. All the way there, the driver was chatting about this and that. I just nodded my head, to convince him I was listening, but in reality, I was miles away. I was thinking about Sam; I wondered what he might be doing and had he mustered up the courage to end his relationship with his girlfriend. I couldn't wait to travel back in time again to find out. It took about ten minutes to reach town. The driver pulled over in the pedestrian area, where all the bars and restaurants were situated. You couldn't get any more central.

"That will be £11.50, Bab. Shall I come back later to pick you up?"

"No thanks, my husband has his car with him."

I would sooner have walked back home than travel in that cab again. I paid the driver and left in the direction of the wine bar.

I soon came upon the bar; in fact, you couldn't miss it. The whole façade of the new bar was the green neck of a bottle of wine protruding out of the brickwork, with what appeared to be liquid shooting out. Obviously made from clear resin, but it was very authentic of wine spilling out. Underneath were the luminous letters spelling the name of the bar, 'Whino's'.

Brilliant, I thought to myself. It described me and my friends perfectly.

I entered through the rather unusual revolving doors into the maelstrom of revellers. It was rammed, and the music was quite loud. I wondered how I would find the girls; then I heard the wolf whistle. It emanated from the gallery that overlooked the bar area. I glanced up to see Kim and Chloe beckoning me to join them upstairs. I climbed the wide wooden staircase up to the next level. All around the balcony were quaint booths, with tables and bench seats, ideal for private get-togethers.

The girls greeted me with hugs and a large glass of Pino; then Kim shouted,

"Where did you get those heels? I love them."

"Yes, they are rather lush, aren't they? I bought them from that shop in town called Blunts Shoes."

Then Chloe pitched in,

"I go there all the time. They have a fantastic range of shoes, and upstairs they have a range of fetish footwear."

Both Kim and I looked at each other; then Kim said,

"Oh! So now she tells us, how long were you going to keep this little secret from us?"

We then all burst out laughing and sat down. I noticed another bottle in the ice bucket sat in the middle of the table. I think the girls had already polished off a bottle prior to me arriving,

"Sorry Poppy, we couldn't wait to get started."

"No worries, I started while waiting for the taxi."

I settled into the booth. Kim and Chloe sat opposite me. Chloe was wearing a white blouse, unbuttoned low to show off her impressive boob job. She wore a large pearl necklace around her neck, with a matching bracelet. She had a short black skirt on; she had magnificent legs, so why not show them off. Kim, on the other hand, was showing off her magnificent behind, in black leather trousers and a red knitted top. They were both showstoppers and attracted many a drooling look from men walking by. After going through the quite limited menu, we placed our order with the waitress that was servicing our booth; then got down to the serious business of catching up on the current gossip. Kim was also considering a boob job, which we both suggested wasn't necessary, but she insisted that bigger boobs would make her and her partner, Colin, much happier. Chloe was going for promotion at work, and she would probably get it. She was so focussed, they wouldn't dare give it to any of her colleagues. Then the attention turned to me; Chloe had already mentioned to Kim about my venture into the past. Kim was very cynical, asking me so many questions and hardly allowing me time to answer before asking the next question.

"Girls, I'm sorry, but I can see you don't believe a word of what I've told you and; it upsets me to think that my two best friends, who have known me for years, don't trust my word."

Kim dived in straight away, "You have to admit, it's a bit far-fetched; and what proof do you have to show that you've travelled back ten years. I love you, Poppy, but you are asking a lot."

Then it was Chloe's turn.

"Poppy, all you have to do is give us something. Anything that links you with this hunky guy Sam."

The problem was, the 'Door'—the time machine—didn't allow me to bring anything back, not even my clothes. Then the pressure was off, the food had arrived, and it looked delicious. We were all ravenous, so the talking stopped, and the eating began. Kim had ordered a meat feast pizza. Chloe was a little more health-conscious, so ordered the chicken salad, with a side of curly fries; and I had the beef lasagne, with a side of garlic bread. I topped all the empty glasses up and proposed a toast,

"Here's to your new boobs, Chloe. Cheers."

We all touched glasses, looked each other in the eye and shouted, "New boobs."

We had a few weird looks from the table next to us, but we didn't care. We had drunk too much to worry about what people thought of us. We then toasted prematurely for Chloe getting the promotion, and then Chloe held up her glass and shouted,

"Here's to Sam and Poppy."

We all burst out laughing. I thought to myself, *I will show them, they will laugh on the other side of their faces. I would find a way to prove to them that Sam was for real.*

By the end of the night, we were all slaughtered, but it was great to let my hair down and talk things over with the girls. It was tricky getting down the staircase from the booth area. We held on to each other and finally reached the exit—the revolving door. We ended up going around a couple of times before we fell into the street, laughing so much I nearly wet myself. The taxi rank was quite busy, but there was a long line of waiting cabs, so we didn't have to wait long to head home. We all hugged each other, said our goodbyes and headed in different directions. I made sure the cab I got into was not the one I had arrived in. The driver in this one was quite a dish, and he certainly smelt better. I gave him the address, and we were off. It didn't seem long before we arrived at the end of my drive.

I paid the driver, and he sped off to find another fare. As I turned, my heel caught in the rough tarmac drive, and I fell against the stone wall next to the post box. A couple of the stones fell to the ground, accompanied by my handbag. There were no street lights out here, but luckily, the moon was out, so I could just about see what I was doing. I gathered up the contents of my bag, then attempted to place the stones back in the wall. They went back in, but they didn't fit as well as before. I lay in bed; my cup of tea in my hand. Roscoe was asleep at the bottom of the duvet. My mind was dwelling over the day. Then a flash of inspiration hit me; it was brilliant! I was so excited, but would it work. The girls would be eating humble pie. 'The door' wouldn't allow me to bring anything back, but how about time itself delivering the proof. This was my plan; the next time I travelled back in time, I would travel to this house and place the proof. Whatever it might be into the gap behind the loosened stones in the garden wall. Then when I returned to this time, the evidence I had hidden in the wall should have stood the test of time and still be preserved behind the stones. The only problem was, if in the passing years, someone had rebuilt the wall, the evidence may have been removed.

Was it an accident when I stumbled out of that taxi tonight, knocking those stones out of the wall, or was it fate. I had a feeling that this mysterious house was helping me in my quest.

Chapter 13
Come Back to Mine

The next day I woke to heavy rain pounding against the window. The sash windows rattling in their runners has the wind buffeted and whistled around the house. I looked out the window towards the pond; even the ducks were taking shelter, most of them huddled together on the sloping bank, under the relative shade of a massive black poplar tree. I went down stairs and noticed the post still unopened on the kitchen table. In my hurry to get out last night, I had forgotten I had retrieved it from the post box. It looked like a lot of bills, but there was one handwritten envelope amongst them that caught my eye. I recognised the palette-shaped emblem on the front of the envelope. It was from a small art shop in my local town who displayed my artwork. It read!

Dear Poppy,
Good news, we have sold two of your paintings. The first one, Ducks Having Fun and also the fantasy painting, Black Leather Together. Please find enclosed a cheque for £850. We have taken our 10% commission as you instructed. Also, the person who bought the fantasy painting asked for your number. We obviously didn't give it to him, but if you would like to contact him, here is the number 0120 456 876. Oh! And his name is Sam Devere.
PS: Can you please let us have some more of your work to display!
Kind regards,
Catherine x

The name exploded off the paper—Sam—it couldn't be the same. *Sam, my Sam, don't be so ridiculous,* I thought to myself. Besides I didn't know his surname, and he wouldn't have known it was my painting because I always signed my work with a pseudonym, and the art shop were under strict instructions not to divulge my real name to anyone. I decided to put this connection out of my mind; it couldn't be my Sam. Sure enough inside the envelope was the cheque. I was so happy. A couple like that every month, and I would just about scrape by. Then I panicked; the shop wanted more work. I would have to get busy and produce a lot more, although I had some pieces in reserve. I couldn't let them down or myself. After I read all the mail, I did some chores around the house, then went to the attic to do some painting. If I was strict with myself and tried to do a couple of hours every day, I would soon have a collection of work to supply the art shop. Who knows I could try and find other outlets to sell my work, then I would be self-sufficient. I might even find a way of keeping this place.

After two and a half hours of painting, my mind started to wonder, Yes, you guessed it, back to Sam; and then the inevitable, the clonk of the 'Door' unlocking. As I ran to the 'Door', I glanced at the clock; it said 12:23 p.m. I entered into the swirling fog. I could feel goosebumps down my back from the drop in temperature. The 'Door' closed behind me. I ran to the light, not worried any more about falling.

I could hear people around me, and the occasional 'ding ding' of a familiar bell, strange! Then the scene around me unfolded. I was sat on the back seat of a bus. All the people were in front of me, so they wouldn't have seen me appear from nowhere. I was wearing white flared trousers, floral mules, a vivid yellow top with a blue denim jacket, with my canvas bag on my lap. The familiar sound of the bell was made by passengers, pressing the buzzer, requesting the bus to pull up at the next stop. I recognised the route. I used to catch this bus occasionally when I was late or tired, going home from uni. I sat there looking out of the window, clutching my trusty canvas bag, remembering the shops and buildings from all those years ago, when out of the corner of my eye, I caught the site of a flash car parked outside a cake shop. I recognised that car—it was Sam's. Then a second later, he walked out of a shop with what looked like a large sausage roll sticking out of a paper bag. I shouted 'Sam'; everyone on the bus looked around. They certainly heard me, but obviously Sam couldn't.

I ran to the front of the bus, pressing the 'buzzer' on the way. If I could stop the bus in time, I would be able to catch him. I reached the front; the bus came to a stop. The concertina doors opened, with a whooshing noise. I was just about to exit the bus when the sound of the driver filled my ears with,

"Just a minute, young lady, where's your ticket."

I froze. Of course, I hadn't bought a ticket. I had just appeared on the bus, and everyone was staring at me like I was a common thief.

"I'm sorry, but I have to go. I need to catch someone."

"You're going nowhere until you pay for your ticket, young lady."

I hurriedly delved into my bag, retrieving my purse, apologising profusely, trying to find the right change. I took a cursory glance over my shoulder to see Sam climbing into his car.

"Another ten pence please if you don't mind," piped up the driver. I slammed the ten pence coin into the drivers hand, closed my purse and ran out of the open door. By the time I reached the end of the bus and looked across the road, Sam had pulled into the traffic and was heading away from me; sod it! I shouted out several times, but he continued to drive away.

I was so hungry; I had to get something to eat. There was a great cake shop on my left if I could just find a parking space. Bingo, a car was just pulling out. *Sam, you're a jacksy devil,* I thought to myself. I nipped into the space with such expertise. As I ran into the shop, I remotely locked the car. A reassuring beeb, beeb sound emanated from the car, to let me know it was locked. I often drove down this road in the hope that I would bump into that delightful young girl,

Poppy. This was the road where I had seen her many times before. It was the road she must have taken from home to uni. Anyway, a quick cursory glance up and down the road proved unsuccessful. No Poppy today; back to the hunger problem. The counter was full of delicious cakes and sandwiches, but I was a sucker for hot sausage rolls, so I ordered a large one. No good for my waistline but damned tasty. The assistant put it in a paper bag, but it was so long, it protruded out about four inches. I paid over the money and left the shop. There was pandemonium on the street; a bus had pulled up, blocking the on-coming traffic. The sound of car horns from frustrated drivers was deafening. I jumped into my car and before pulling off, took a cheeky bite off the end of the of the sausage roll, wow! Crikey, it was hot. I put it down on the passenger seat while I put my seat belt on. I started the engine, wound my window down, cranked my head out of the open window to make sure nothing was coming and slowly pulled out into the chaotic traffic.

Has I drove slowly up the road towards some traffic lights, I was sure I could hear someone shouting my name. The radio was off, so it wasn't that. There it was again,

"Sam, Sam, wait for me."

I looked in the rear view mirror; and to my surprise amongst the throngs of people was this ginger-haired young lady running towards me, gesticulating with her arms and shouting my name,

"Sam, Sam, wait! It's me, Poppy."

God she was so beautiful and she was running towards me, I didn't blame her though, I was pretty irresistible. As I was stuck in slow moving traffic, she soon caught up with me. She ran up the near side of the car, opened the passenger door; and before I could say anything, she jumped in, straight on top of my opened sausage roll. I burst out laughing; she looked at me, bemused,

"What's so funny?"

I laughed again, "Well, you've just crushed my lunch."

"Oh! Sam, I'm so sorry."

I then felt the crinkly paper wrapped around the sausage roll under my bottom, and soon felt the heat of the sausage meat penetrating my pants. Sam was in stitches; he thought it was hilarious. The thing was I had white trousers on, and I could just imagine the mess. Not only my clothes, but the plush velour car seat. I was so embarrassed; I arched upwards off the seat and retrieved the mangled mess from between my legs. Sam was choking with laughter,

"It's not that funny, Sam."

He had difficulty keeping the car in a straight line,

"Sam, I think you better pull over."

We pulled over into a lay-by. I jumped out. Sam was still laughing. He shouted out to me,

"Poppy! Bend over and show me my lunch."

I then also started to see the funny side of things. I bent over; my backside was now facing Sam,

"Oh my god, it looks like you were caught short."

Then Sam looked at the car seat. The greasy pastry had left a large stain on the fabric, with streaks of meat spread in all directions. I thought he would go mad, but all he said was there are some wipes in the glove compartment—a quick rub, and it will be like new. I was taken aback; he was so relaxed about it. If it had been Simon's car, he would have hit the roof and sulked for days. It was so nice to be with someone who was so chilled, "Poppy, I think I should use one of those wipes to rub the mess from your bottom."

"You can forget that Sam you just want to touch me up."

"Well, that's true, also I was just trying to be helpful."

"But seriously, why don't you come back to mine, so we can sort your trousers out."

I thought about Sam's offer for a couple of minutes. Then realised, it wouldn't do any arm, so I bit the bullet and said, "Sam, that would be great if you don't mind, but what will your girlfriend think."

"Girlfriend, what girlfriend, she moved out a couple of weeks ago."

I hope my face didn't show it, but my heart missed a beat when he told me she had gone from his life. Sam turned the radio on. I couldn't believe it. The record playing was, 'I ran' by 'A Flock of Seagulls'. It was definitely a sign. I loved this record. Then Sam asked,

"Poppy, do you like this; it's one of my favourites."

I knew then, this was meant to be. Somehow fate had brought us together, and I was convinced the house had some influence over the way my life was panning out. As we drove towards Sam's flat, I had a glow in my heart.

Chapter 14
The Flat

I felt at ease and safe in Sam's company. He was a joy to be with. The conversation never appeared strained; we just got on together. It was like a match made in heaven as they say. It only took about ten minutes to reach Sam's place. We swung off the road into the parking area at the rear of the quite swanky looking flats. There were about 30 in total, set in very nicely tendered gardens. The flats were set over three floors. Sam pointed up,
"Mine's the one at the top, on the end of this block."
There were no lifts, so we climbed the stairs. Sam flew up them; he was obviously fitter than I was. Coming here made the travelling back in time very real somehow. It was like having a different life but in another time zone, and I still wasn't decided whether to tell Sam the truth about the 'Door'.

We arrived on the top floor, outside No10. The door was shiny, red in colour, with a brass letter plate and lock. I noticed a spyglass in the door, "Come on in then, Poppy; welcome to my humble abode."

Sam led the way, past the small kitchen and into the lounge. It was about 20 feet long and 15 feet wide, with a massive window, which spanned from the floor right up to the ceiling. The glass in the lower part being obscure to allow some privacy from nosey neighbours in the house's opposite. The room boasted a brown leather, three-piece suite, complete with a few chenille cushions, a glass unit holding what looked like a very expensive music system; and at each end of the window, sat very large speakers; in the corner sat the television. The walls were painted in magnolia, the curtains and carpet were beige; there was one large picture on the end wall, depicting a beautiful sunset seen from a palm-tree-lined golden beach. While I had been taking in the room, Sam had popped out, reappearing with a blue dressing gown in his hand, "Here you are, Poppy. If you pop your clothes off, I will put them in the wash."

I just stared at him, then replied,
"In your dreams, sunshine."
Sam just smiled,
"Oh sorry, Poppy, the bathrooms by the front door."

The bathroom was compact but functional—a white suite, with marble like tiles floor to ceiling. I took off my trousers and wrapped the lush dressing gown around me. I could smell aftershave on it. It smelt of pine needles, very nice too. There was a knock at the door,

"Poppy, if you pass your trousers out through the door, I will put them on a quick wash."

I passed them out, then thought how thoughtful he was, and how domesticated he was, I don't think I ever saw Simon using our washing machine at home. As I walked out of the bathroom and into the kitchen, I heard the slamming of the door on the washing machine,

"Just a short wash, Poppy, as we have to dry them after."

"Thanks so much, Sam."

"It's a pleasure, Poppy. It's so nice to have you here. In fact, I haven't stopped thinking about you since we had that drink together."

I glowed inside. We must both feel the same way about each other.

"Sam, me too, I've thought of nothing else. I just couldn't wait to travel back again, to see you."

"Travel back again, what do you mean? Have you been away?"

Oh shit, I thought to myself. It just slipped out. That's the trouble with lies; they always catch you out.

"Oh yes, I've been to see friends up north."

I could feel my face going red; he must have known I was fibbing. I would have to tell him soon. I couldn't go on like this.

We looked into each other's eyes. We both smiled; we were about two feet away from each other. My heart was pounding in my chest. He must surely have heard it thumping away; then he moved closer. Sam embraced me, and we started kissing passionately. I had a tingling sensation right down into my stomach.

Kissing Poppy made me feel like a stallion. She was so beautiful; she smelt divine, and her eyes melted my heart. I pulled her ever closer, wrapping my arms around her, so she couldn't escape; then I felt my manhood appreciating this sexy body next to me.

"Pleased to see me, are we, Sam?"

She had obviously felt my erection through my bulging trousers, but she didn't seem fazed. She just had a glint in her eyes. Then to my total dismay, she started rubbing my swelling cock,

"Sam, you are a naughty boy; what are we going to do with this bad boy."

As soon as I said it, I couldn't believe it had come from my mouth. I was acting like my old self, but I had only just met Sam. What he must have thought of me, I dreaded to think. I have to admit I was so turned on, my juices were flowing.

"Poppy, I know what I would like to do with it. You're so sexy, you're driving me wild with lust."

Sam's hands were now all over me. He was thrusting his groin against my very moist tush. Then I felt his hands inside the dressing gown. There was no stopping him now. In a flash, his hands were grabbing my buttocks, pulling me onto his throbbing cock.

"Poppy, I so want to have you."

"Ditto Sam, I want you, I want you inside me."

As soon as I said it, Sam undid his belt. His trousers dropped to the floor. His erect cock was sticking out the top of his boxers. I grabbed it, at the same time ripping his shorts off. He reciprocated by pulling my pants down. I felt the warmth of the hot washing machine on my buttocks, and the gentle sway as the machine went through its cycle of washing my clothes. In seconds, we were both stark naked; then I felt his stiff wet cock slip inside me. It felt good to feel wanted, but that wasn't enough for him. Sam started sucking on my stiff nipples, burying his face into my breasts. It was shear lust; we were like rampant, sex-starved teenagers.

I couldn't believe I was having sex with her; she was so out of my league. Her breasts were to die for and her body…well, she was so sexy, I didn't think I would last long. She was sat on the front of the washing machine, legs wide open. Each time I thrust my lusting cock into her, she screamed with pleasure,

"Fuck me, Sam, fuck me harder."

She was like a women possessed. I was out of breath, but I couldn't let her down. I had to satisfy her; each time I thrust my aching cock into her, her breasts moved in unison towards me. My mouth wrapped around her nipples, sucking them in turn.

I felt the machine slow down. It made a clicking sound, then it was quiet. Had it finished its cycle, no! It then clicked again and started its spin cycle. The vibration reverberated through to my clit. Sam's hard cock pounding me, and the vibration of the machine, it was just too much. I couldn't hold on any longer. Sam was there too, I could tell. His penis seemed to swell inside me; and from the look on his face, he was about to explode.

"Poppy, I'm coming. I can't stop aargh!"

As soon as he said it, it was all over for me too. My orgasm was wreaking havoc through my grateful body. My legs wrapped around Sam so tight, he grimaced, or was it because he'd just shot his hot cum into my slit. His face filled with pleasure. We held each other; our heart beats throbbing through our soaking wet skin. At the same time, the spinning drum had also reached its climax of spinning and slowed. Its cycle over; it came to an eventual stop.

"Poppy, you're amazing."

"Sam, I'm so sorry, I don't know what came over me."

"Don't worry, Poppy. It's probably my magnetic charm. I have this effect on women. They just find me irresistible."

"Oh stop it, Sam, your incorrigible."

"Yes, and you're beautiful and sexy, and you're in my flat; how lucky am I."

I picked up the dressing gown from the floor and covered up. Sam just stood there naked, not ashamed at all.

"Would you like a cup of tea, young lady?"

"I would love one. Can I take a shower while you make it?"

"You know where the bathroom is, just make yourself at home."

The thing was that I did feel at home. I hadn't known Sam very long; we had just had sex, and it all felt perfectly normal. I hadn't given Simon a second thought. I popped off to the bathroom quite at ease. After showering, I put the dressing gown back on; and as I turned, I noticed a framed certificate on the wall; at the top in gold letters were the letters,

P A D Y. I knew this had something to do with Scuba Diving, then I looked at the name of the recipient, awarded to Samuel Devere. My god, it was the same name as the person who had bought my painting in the future—the fantasy piece, *Leather Together*. I was totally confused; I didn't understand the connection. I decided to put it to the back of my mind and went back to the kitchen. Sam wasn't there; then I heard him calling, "Poppy, I'm in the bedroom. Come on in, the tea's going to get cold."

I entered the bedroom. It was fairly compact, about 12 feet square. The curtains were open; you could see into the gardens, but the room wasn't overlooked. The bed had a padded brown leather headboard, with a sumptuous burgundy-coloured duvet. At the opposite end of the bed was a bank of mirrored wardrobes. Sam was sat up in bed; the tea cups sat on bedside tables on either side, still steaming, with each cuppa was a chocolate mini roll.

"Come on Poppy, hop in, I won't bite."

As he said it, he tapped the bed with the flat of his hand as if to encourage me. I didn't need any encouragement. I was quite happy to jump into bed with him. I pulled the duvet back and was about to climb in when Sam piped up with,

"I don't think so, young lady. It's against the rules to wear dressing gowns in bed. Look at me, I'm starkers."

He lifted the duvet to expose himself. He didn't give a hoot about flashing his bits. We had just had wonderful sex, so I suppose it didn't really matter. I let the dressing gown slip to the floor and jumped in,

"Come here, gorgeous."

Sam said as he wrapped his strong arms around me, pulling me into his warm muscular body. He kissed me gently on the forehead, then said, "Ready for a cuppa and a chocolate roll."

We sat up in bed and tucked into our chocolate rolls, washed down with hot tea, like we had been together for ever. It was the happiest I had been in a long time, and I didn't want it to end. After we finished our little snack, I lay my head on Sam's bare chest. He wasn't hairy at all, unlike Simon who had a chest like a gorilla. I could see us in the mirrored wardrobes. Sam had his eyes closed, I was staring at us; it was like a dream; was it really happening. I could feel the powerful solid beating of Sam's heart, and my mind started to wonder. How the hell was I going to tell him that I was a time traveller; he would think I was mad. I couldn't bear to lose him now; it all felt so damned right. As my mind meandered, going through all the options of how to handle the very complicated issues, I heard Sam's breathing change. I couldn't believe it; he had gone into a deep sleep, then the snoring began, not too loud just a reassuring rasp of air with every breath. He was obviously very relaxed with the situation, just to drop off like that. Me on the other hand, wide awake, torturing myself over my dilemma.

My thoughts changed to Roscoe. I hoped he was alright. It seemed like ages since I had seen him; then stupidly, I thought of the house, then the attic room, then the 'Door'. Oh my god the 'Door'; the vision around me started to ripple. I tried frantically to think of something else, but it was too late. The rippling vision got worse. I knew what was happening; I was going back. The temperature dropped; a swirling fog appeared from nowhere. I felt like I was falling, then a flash of light; I couldn't stop it.

I opened my eyes. I was back in my attic room, lay in my reclining chair. I looked at the clock, it read 12:23 p.m. No time had elapsed at this end; time had certainly moved on in the past. Then it hit me; what the hell would Sam think when he woke up. We had just had sex together; we had been enjoying each other's company in bed. Sam had fallen asleep completely relaxed, believing we were both into each other; now he would wake up to find me gone. No explanation as to where I had gone, not able to contact me; and worse, I didn't know how long the time lapse would be before I eventually travelled back. It could be months; what would Sam think of me, disappearing like that, especially after being intimate; god only knows. I began to cry; I was so upset, I hated the idea of Sam waking up to think I would just go and not even leave a note. He would be so upset with me; it wouldn't surprise me if he decided never to see me again.

Chapter 15
Not as You Think

I sat in the chair in my attic room, gathering my thoughts. Sam would definitely be upset when he awoke to find me gone, with no explanation as to where or why I had disappeared. The problem now was, when I went back the next time, I didn't know how much time might have elapsed since I was last there. If it turned out to be months, he would certainly take the hump, and I stood the chance of losing him. If on the other hand, only a few days had passed, I might be able to convince him that I was serious about our relationship; but one thing for certain, I was going to have to tell him about my time travel. As no time had elapsed in the present, the day was still young; so after walking the dog, I decided to get on with some painting. After a few hours I finished the pond landscape, which pleased me intensely. That was another one ready to deliver to the art shop for them to sell. After my very recent sexual endeavours, I felt invigorated, fulfilled and naughty; just like the old days, which put me in the mood for painting something a little more risqué.

I decided to paint a fantasy piece. I say fantasy, it wasn't really a fantasy; more like real life. I thought I would paint a scene of a couple having sex on a washing machine, who knows it might float someone's boat; it had certainly floated mine. My mind drifted back to Sam's flat, and how exhilarating sex on a washing machine was, especially when it was on a full-spin cycle. The thought sent a peculiar tingle down my pubic area. I decided I would paint the bodies as they should be, but to disguise the faces of the copulating couple, I didn't want anyone recognising me. I had a real sense of excitement, and I couldn't wait to start sketching out the scene. In fact, it made me feel closer to Sam, as I drew the basic outline of the couple getting it together on the washing machine.

I was so engrossed in the painting, I hadn't noticed the time. I glanced through the window to see darkness. I couldn't believe it; where had the time gone. I looked at the clock; 9:15 pm, no wonder my stomach was complaining. It was time for some food; and of course, the obligatory glass of Pinot, but first feed Roscoe. After all, he couldn't help himself, could he! After we were both fed, and the Pinot was taking affect, I lit the log burner, turned on the television, dimmed the lights and relaxed on the sofa. Roscoe was quick to join me; he lay across my lap, staring at the flames, content. I thought it was time I updated Chloe, so I phoned her on my mobile,

"Hi Chloe, how are you."

"Never mind me, what's been occurring. Come on, I want all the gossip."

I told her about what had happened, the stain on my clothes, the flat, glossing over the washing machine incident, getting into bed, then the untimely return to the future, leaving Sam without an explanation.

"Don't worry, Poppy. If he's into you, he will forgive you."

"I'm not so sure, Chloe. Just disappearing like that, god knows what he's thinking of me."

"Poppy, stop worrying, it will be fine. I will pop over tomorrow when I've finished work, about seven-ish, love you. Oh! And I will bring a take away and the wine."

The phone went dead; she was gone. The fire was crackling; the red glow from the embers was dancing around the room. I didn't really notice what was on the TV. My mind was in melt down thinking about Sam.

I must have nodded off. Luckily my glass of wine was wedged between my legs, so it didn't spill. Then I was woken by the phone ringing. I looked at the screen; it was Simon. Oh my god, he did realise I was still alive. "Hello Simon, what do you want at this time of night?"

He didn't even ask if I was okay.

"Poppy, I'm sending the estate agent around tomorrow to value the property. We need to get things moving."

"Over your dead body, Simon. Don't you think we need to discuss this; where do you think I'm going to live."

"Poppy, I need the money from the house to finance the property in London."

"Tough shit, Simon. You need to get your ass away from your bit of stuff and come home and discuss this with me. Oh! And I won't be showing any estate agents around till hell freezes over."

The phone went dead. Roscoe looked at me; my raised voice had unsettled him. He could always tell when I was upset. He started whining and attempted to lick my face, I guess to calm me, like he would a puppy. I wasn't into dogs slobbering in my mouth, so I pushed him away. "Come on Roscoe, let's go to bed."

He knew exactly what that meant. He darted up the stairs before I had even got off the sofa. Before getting into bed, I made a cuppa and took it upstairs. I thought I would just glance over the painting I had been working on. I was pleased how much I had achieved, another session and it would be finished. I glanced at the clock; it read 11:45 p.m. I sat on my recliner to drink my tea, and my mind started to wander. I heard the lock clonk on the 'Door'. I turned the handle and entered the swirling fog; strange, it wasn't cold. I walked towards the distant light. I began to fall has I had before; then in an instant, I was in a dark, enclosed space. A vertical narrow beam of light was just in front of my face. I could hear voices—female and male—it wasn't a normal conversation; it was erotic. It sounded like a women in the final throws of an orgasm. I focussed my eyes on the slit of light in front of my face. I was mortified, shocked and hurt. It took my breath away; the slit I was gazing through was the gap between the mirror wardrobe doors at the bottom of Sam's bed.

The scene, that my unbelieving eyes were peering into, was too much to take in. I felt like only a few hours had passed since I was in that bed with Sam. Now he was being pleasured by a blonde—long-legged beautiful woman—who couldn't seem to get enough of Sam's cock down her throat, with the occasional verbal encouragement to cum in her mouth. Sam was lay on his back; I couldn't see his face, just the curvaceous arse of a long, dark-haired woman; she was sat on his face shouting,

"Sam, I'm cumming, lick my clit harder."

I gasped in horror. They obviously heard me. The blonde girl exclaimed, "Sam, you naughty boy, you have someone else here to join us."

The blonde girl let go of Sam's erect cock and turned towards the wardrobe. Her fingers grabbed the two doors and yanked them sideways, exposing me for all to see. Sam pushed the dark-haired girl off to one side,

"Poppy, do you fancy joining us."

Before I could muster an answer, the blonde girl grabbed me and pulled me onto the bed. I was on my back; I shouted,

"Sam, stop her, I don't want this."

"I think you protest too much," said the dark-haired woman.

"Come on, Poppy. Let the girl have a bit of fun."

Then Sam held my arms down, while the blonde girl straddled me. She was smiling, licking her lips as she leant down, millimetres from my face, "I want to lick your face, you naughty girl."

My only escape was to travel back to the future. I thought of the 'Door', praying for a shimmering vision—the start of my escape. She dangled her breasts above me, begging me to suck her nipples; then her tongue was in my mouth, saliva dripping all over my face.

I screamed. I managed to free my hands and forced her tongue away from my face. The shimmering vision started. I was going back, thank god! Then, I was back in my attic room on the reclining chair. Roscoe was sat on me, licking my face; I was covered in slobber. Oh my god, had I been dreaming. I looked at the clock; it read 3:00 a.m. I couldn't have travelled; the time had moved on by hours.

I was so relieved. I just couldn't imagine Sam being like that. Deep down, though my mind must have been in turmoil, wandering what Sam might be up to!

I went to bed, fretting about the situation, worrying about the estate agents turning up tomorrow. I was so unsettled; I would be amazed if I got any sleep.

Chapter 16
Girl Power

I woke up with a determination to sort out all the problems in my life. I was going to come up with a plan to pay Simon off. I wasn't going to lose this place now; I had it, and also I was going to tell Sam the truth about my time travel, and he would have to accept it or walk away. I popped up to the attic room to sign the *Pond Landscape*. I had forgotten the day before. I always signed in silver paint; it was distinctive and easy to read. I used a special silver pen, easier than a brush, and signed the name 'Tony Le Meros'. No one would ever guess it was me; first of all, they would think it was a man, possibly a Spanish man; and with the fantasy art pictures, I didn't want customers to think I was up for anything kinky, so all of my paintings carried this name, the landscapes and the fantasy stuff.

I wrapped the painting in bubble wrap, jumped in my van and headed off to the art shop. The art shop was in a small town called Leyton-Somer. It was about 8 miles away from where I lived. Although the shop was small, they did very well, promoting sales by featuring local artists—not me of course—I preferred to be anonymous. They also advertised in all of the popular arty magazines and were well known by the art fraternity. They also had a catchy business name, 'ART in your HEART'. When delivering paintings, I always pulled up at the back of the shop. I didn't want any one connecting me with the paintings. The shop-owner knew the drill; if anyone was in the shop, she was always discreet.

"Morning, Poppy. Lovely to see you; would you like a coffee?"

"I would love a cup of tea if that's okay, Catherine."

Catherine was in her 40s, quite trim and trendy. She had blonde hair and a good eye for what would sell. She couldn't wait to see my latest offering. There was no one in the shop, so I unwrapped it while she sorted out the tea. Catherine entered the shop, carrying two mugs of tea. She glanced at the painting which I had placed on an easel.

"Oh! Poppy, that's fantastic. The way you've expressed the light bursting through the leaf cover, then dancing on the water of the pond, it's magical."

"Do you think it will sell then?"

"Without a doubt, Poppy. In fact I have someone in mind, he will just love it."

It felt good to be praised. Simon had never really appreciated my work. The good news was, she thought it would sell.

"Poppy, do you have any more fantasy art. They seem to be building in popularity at the moment."

"As a matter of fact, I'm working on one at the moment. It should be ready by the weekend."

After we drank our tea, I was about to leave when Catherine asked about the young man who bought the picture *Black Leather Together.*

"Did you get in touch; he seemed really keen to meet you."

"You didn't tell him I was female, or my real name, did you?"

"No! I just said I would pass his comments onto the artist."

"What was he like Catherine; not creepy I hope."

"Not at all, quite the opposite actually."

She described the man; piercing blue eyes, a shock of blonde hair sweeping across his cheeky face, even what he was wearing right down to his shoes; it was Sam down to a tee! I couldn't understand why a person called Sam would be buying my paintings and also asking about me. I then brushed off the subject. I would have to think long and hard about the situation. It was more complicated than I first thought. I thanked Catherine for the tea and said goodbye. I got into the van and drove home. I have to admit, I can't remember the journey home. My mind was busy mulling over the intricacies of time travel. At least, Chloe was coming to see me tonight. I could run a few things past her to see what her thoughts were.

As I approached the house, I noticed a car pulled up on the verge near the gate to my drive. I pulled up to the gate, got out to open the long, five-bar gate when a man jumped out of the car and came towards me.

"Hello! Are you Poppy Day?"

"Who wants to know?"

I responded in a less-than-polite manner. Deep down, I knew who it was likely to be.

"David Grant, Herbert Grant estate agents. Mr Simon Bridges instructed me to value Ducklands Farmhouse."

"Did he know? Well, I also own this house, and I'm telling you now, it's not for sale."

"Well, Miss Day, I have a letter here, authorising me to value this property, signed by Simon Bridges."

I was so angry, I jumped in my van, drove onto the drive; just enough as to allow me to close the gate, I then locked the gate. I leant over the gate and shouted!

"Now listen to me, Mr David Grant. Take your letter and tell Simon Bridges to 'stick it where the sun don't shine', and get your car off my verge before I call the police."

The estate agent looked a little taken aback. I don't think he expected the welcome he got. He was muttering under his breath as he retired to his car. He turned and retorted,

"I will be phoning Mr Bridges as soon as I get back to the office."

"Bully for you."

I shouted back, trying not to show how upset I was. I parked the van near the back door; and as soon as I opened the van door, I was greeted by Roscoe, trying to lick me all over,

"Hello, my beautiful friend, have you missed me."

I didn't know what I would do without him; he was such good company. Then his ears pricked up. I turned to see about a dozen waggling ducks coming towards me; they often came to the kitchen door for bread. Roscoe was off, like a shot. Fortunately for the ducks, they had wings, so they escaped the jaws of Roscoe. But in Roscoe's heroic attempt to have a free dinner, he ended up in the pond. The ducks scattered; all quacking at the same time. Roscoe doggy paddled back to the bank, got out with a disappointed look on his face, then went into a spasm; flicking dirty pond water, from his saturated body, all over the place. "Come on, Roscoe; let's get you dried off by the AGA."

The rest of the day went without drama. I decided to get on with my fantasy painting. My mind flitting back to the washing machine frolics with Sam. I missed him more than I was letting on. I just hoped he was missing me. I was just signing the finished painting when my phone rang. I picked it up and saw the caller's name; it was Simon. I guessed what this was about.

"Poppy for Christ's sake, why did you turn away the estate agent?"

"Simon, I told you to come home and discuss selling the house with me, so you just decided in your own arrogant way to send around some toffee-nosed estate agent to value the house. Now get this straight in your head. I own a percentage of this house, and I will buy your share as soon as I get the money."

I could hear him scoffing down the phone.

"What are you laughing at? You jumped up, two-timing twat."

The phone went dead. One thing Simon couldn't accept was someone taking a stand against him. Basically, he was a spoiled brat; and if he didn't get his own way, he threw his dummy out of the pram. It's amazing, how when in a relationship, you know about all the negatives and annoying traits of your life partner, but you tend to ignore them for the sake of an easier life. Why I spent so long with Simon, I will never know. There was no way I would ever go back there.

It was about seven o'clock when I heard a car pipping at the end of the drive. It was Chloe. In my anger earlier, I had forgotten to unlock the gate. I ran down the drive to greet her. Chloe was leaning over the gate, shouting,

"What's this Fort Knox, when did you start locking the gate."

"I'm sorry, Chloe. I will explain later."

I undid the gate and pulled it open. Chloe drove past me and parked next to my van. She jumped out as jolly as you like,

"I have food and wine, who's the mummy."

It was so good to see her. I couldn't wait to tell her about everything that had happened. While I dished up the take away, Chloe poured the wine; we sat at the kitchen table. It was warm and cosy near the AGA. I let her go first with her gossip; first of all, she brought me up to speed with what our circle of friends had been up to, then she filled me in with what was going on at her office. It was good to hear about other people's problems, instead of wallowing in my own car crash of a life.

"Well, Poppy, what's been happening in the life of a time traveller."

"Very funny, Chloe, I haven't been back since I spoke to you. First, I need to run a few things past you, to see what your thoughts are, before I make any decisions. First of all, Simon wants this place sold. He even sent an estate agent here today to measure the place up, that's why the gate was locked."

"You're joking."

"I wish I was. I told him I would buy him out."

"How are you going to do that?"

"I haven't got a clue."

We both started laughing; then took another gulp of wine. I then got down to the complications of time travel.

"These are the issues, Chloe, now concentrate."

I then proceeded to try and explain the issues that were bothering me. I told her that when I travelled back, I didn't know where I would appear, or how much time had elapsed since I last travelled. Also that I could bump into myself back in 1985, because I was still there living my life with Simon; and if I did anything that changed what happened since 1985, while I was back in 1985, it would change the future. Chloe was looking me right in the eye, concentrating, but I could see she was struggling, trying to compute the information I was giving her. For instance, if I were to bump into Simon while I was with Sam, and Simon dumps me, then that will stop us buying this house in 1995. Chloe looked perplexed,

"Does it matter if you don't buy this house? There are lots of other houses."

I looked at Chloe in amazement,

"Don't you see Chloe; if we don't buy this house in the future, and I'm back in 1985, I can't get back. Don't you see, I would never had seen the 'Door', and time travel wouldn't be an option."

"Oh!"

She said as if she understood. I've also thought why don't I just find Sam now, in 1995 and start from now. The problem is, we fell for each other in 1985; ten years have passed, and he is probably married with children now. The only way to stop that process is to continue seeing Sam, so that he doesn't have the opportunity to fall for anyone else, the problem with that theory is? I looked Chloe in the eye, waiting for her reply.

"Poppy, I haven't got a clue, you've completely lost me."

"The problem is I either have to stop back in 1985 with Sam until the date reaches now, 1995, but I have no control over the 'Door' calling me back at any time. Or I explain to Sam about the situation and hope he wants me enough to suffer a precarious, sporadic relationship, seeing me each time I travel back. The only problem with that is, I have no idea of the duration of time between each visit. It might be days, it might be months; why man in his right mind would put up with that."

"Poppy, take a breath and eat your take away; it will get cold."

We both had another gulp of wine. It was time to open another bottle. Between us, we could certainly put it away.

While we both digested all the ins and outs of time travel, we both went quiet while we tucked into our food. After finishing our meal, we retired to the lounge. I had lit the fire before Chloe had arrived, so the room was well cosy. I sat on one end of the leather sofa; Chloe on the other.

"I think the best thing to do, Poppy, is tell Sam everything; all the problems you've just outlined to me; and I think if it's meant to be, he will go for the only option."

"Which is?"

"To see you each time you travel back, until the time catches up with 1995."

I felt a sense of relief, to hear Chloe say it. It made me feel like a great weight had been lifted from my shoulders.

"You're right; it's the only way and the best way. It's down to Sam now; let's hope he goes for it."

"He will, Poppy. He's not going to risk losing you, unless he's a complete schmuck."

After polishing off three bottles between us, putting the world of time travel to rights, we were both tired and quite squiffy. It was obvious that Chloe would have to stop over. There was no way she could drive in her state.

"Poppy, can I sleep with you tonight. It's awfully spooky in that back bedroom."

I laughed out loud,

"You little baby, are you scared on your little lonesome."

I shouldn't have mocked her really; I just thought it was funny. All the time I had spent on my own in this house, I had never felt scared or perturbed in the slightest.

"Of course you can, Chloe, but you do realise there will be three in the bed, don't you."

Chloe's face was a picture; a big smile spreading across her drunken face. You just knew something rude was coming.

"You kinky so and so, you've arranged for a hunky man to entertain the two of us; haven't you."

"Well, Chloe, he is rather handsome, but also quite hairy, and he answers to the name of Roscoe."

"Oh you tease, Poppy, I was getting quite excited then."

We both settled into bed. Roscoe stretched out between us. I turned out the light. It was comforting to have someone else in the bed with me, "Good night, Chloe." There was no reply; she was in the land of nod, and it wasn't long before I joined her.

Chapter 17
Coming Clean

As soon as Chloe had driven down the drive, and I was on my own, I ran up to the attic room. I was desperate to get back to Sam. I didn't have to wait long, just a few minutes walking around the attic room, and I heard the clonk of the lock in the 'Door'. I was keen to get back and find Sam, to see if he still wanted a relationship with me after the sequence of events the last time I travelled. I yanked down on the handle. The lock released, and the 'Door' swung open. The cold fog swirled out through the opening. I jumped in; the 'Door' automatically closed behind me, and I headed towards the distant light. As I approached the light in the swirling fog, the ground under my feet disappeared. I began tumbling downwards. I wasn't too alarmed. I knew it would be alright; well, it had been before.

I could hear a creaking noise; then the sound of someone's voice—a ladies voice.

"Doors closing, stand clear, doors closing."

There was a flash of light, and I had arrived. I looked around; there wasn't a lot to see, although it seemed familiar. I was in a confined space. I then realised I was in a lift, and it felt like it was descending. I looked at the lighted panel next to the chrome doors. Yes, the numbers were decreasing, 6, 5, 4, 3… then the lift slowed down,

"Doors opening, stand clear, doors opening."

Oh my god, someone was about to enter the lift. I just hoped it was no one I knew; the doors opened. I was faced with a lot of young people, students actually. I was in the uni lift. I pushed past them in a hurry; I was petrified someone would know me. I noticed a sign on the wall indicating the stairs. I ran down the stairs two at a time. I entered the lobby; it was busy with throngs of students making their way to lessons. Luckily, I didn't recognise any of the students; strange though because I knew everyone on our course. I caught sight of the exit doors and made a beeline for them. My heart was beating faster and faster. The scene seemed to move in slow motion; people's voices were slurred and echoey. I arrived at the exit door. I reached out with my hand to push the door open when I heard a voice, crystal clear,

"Hello Poppy, what are you doing back here."

I turned to see my course tutor. I stood there, dumbstruck. What did she mean 'back here'; she couldn't know I'd just travelled back in time,

"Sorry Mrs Bowcher, what do you mean 'back here'?"

"Well, Poppy, it's been six months or more since you graduated. Have you signed up for another course?"

Oh my god, my mind was now in overdrive. The last time I travelled, I was wearing student clothes, so I must have been at uni. I looked down at my clothes; I was quite smartly dressed, not student clothes, far from it; my trusty canvas bag was on my arm. Then I realised Mrs Bowcher was waiting for an answer. It must have looked like I was on something. "Are you alright Poppy, you seem flustered."

"Yes, I'm fine, thank you; no, I haven't signed for another course. I was just passing and thought I would just pop my head in. I spent some happy years here."

"Well, Poppy, it's great to see you. I wished the students on this course showed the same commitment and talent that you had. I can't see any of them achieving a 2:1 degree, like you did."

"I'm sure you will knock them into shape Mrs Bowcher."

"What's this Mrs Bowcher business? You always called me Lynne when you were a student."

The truth was, I couldn't remember her first name; only her surname. It had been ten years, for some reason. Mrs Bowcher had stuck in my mind.

"Anyway Lynne, I must be going, lovely to see you. Bye, bye."

She just stood there; her mouth open as if she was about to speak, bewildered as to why I was in such a hurry. I ran out of the door and down the street towards the town. Crikey, it was cold outside. It felt like winter; my brain was computing the information it had just received.

The devastating realisation was that the last time I saw Sam, I was at uni. Lynne had just informed me that my course had finished at least six months ago, and my clothes backed up that theory, because I remember wearing clothes like this when I worked in my first job as a designer, after graduating. It started to sink in. The last time I saw Sam, we had sex and I disappeared; that was at least six months ago. There was no way Sam would accept me back now, would he! I decided I would go straight to Sam's and ask him. I checked my purse to see if I had enough money; then jumped on the No 8 bus which would take me almost all the way to Sam's flat. I sat on the bus, watching the world go by; my mind was in turmoil.

After Poppy disappeared that day, all those weeks ago, I began to lose hope that I would see her ever again. At first after she left, I was quite angry, just to vanish into thin air; not even leaving a note to say why. Then my feelings turned. I was hurt but also sad. I really felt that she was serious about me, and we had a future together. About two weeks after she left, I was walking down the high street, and I happened to glance across the road. At first I thought I was imagining things, but alas, I wasn't, it was definitely Poppy.

Poppy was holding hands with some guy, and they seemed very happy together. I couldn't resist it; I wolf-whistled her. They both stopped and looked across the road. Poppy definitely clocked me; she looked me straight in the eye, then turned and carried on walking hand in hand with her man. Well, that was that. I came to the conclusion that Poppy and I were not going to happen; it was such a shame. She was attractive, funny, a great sense of humour; you couldn't want a better body. She had more curves than a bowl of cherries. Sex with her was amazing; she was exciting, naughty, and her sexual appetite, I could tell, was yet to be discovered. It was such a shame how things had panned out. I was convinced she was into me; why the hell she had gone back to her bloke, god only knew.

The bus pulled up at the stop I needed. I was the only one to alight the vehicle; the driver shouted 'Thank You'. I heard the swish of the bus doors close behind me; then it slowly pulled off; black fumes bellowing everywhere. I felt the heat from the engine bleaching out of vents at the back of the bus as it passed me, which reminded me how cold I was. It wasn't far to Sam's flat from here. My stomach was in turmoil as I walked the few hundred yards, to where I would find out my fate. I was sure that telling him the truth was the right thing to do. I approached the flat with immense trepidation. If he rejected me, I would be inconsolable. I walked to the back of the flats, where Sam and I had parked the car the last time. As I entered the parking area, a car had just pulled up, and a young lady got out. I quickly retreated behind a wall for cover; then I heard Sam shouting down. He was hanging out of his bedroom window, "Hi Sally, come on up, the kettle is on."

Well, that was that. Sam had obviously found someone else. He hadn't wasted any time finding a new conquest to warm his bed. I leant against the wall; tears rolling down my face. That stupid 'Door'… why didn't it bring me back sooner. I might have been able to save the situation, but no, it brought me back six months later. Obviously it was too much to ask for Sam to wait for me; he had soon replaced me. I turned on my heels and headed away from the car park. I then turned left and started walking on the path in front of the flats; then my ears were treated to a very loud wolf whistle. I wasn't sure where it came from, except it seemed to be above me. I looked up to see Sam hanging out of his lounge window, "Poppy, where are you going, where have you been."

I stood there in disbelief. I knew he had another woman up there in his flat, and he had the audacity to whistle me and ask where I was going—just no respect. I was so angry, I shouted back in an unlady-like manner, "You have some nerve, Samuel Devere; not happy with one woman, you want two."

I turned and briskly walked away. I could hear Sam protesting out of the window, pleading with me to listen, but I was upset and a little jealous of the woman who was now with Sam. I quickened my step, with the intention of getting as far away from Sam as soon as possible, but I soon heard footsteps behind me, and the breathless voice of Sam demanding that I stop and listen.

"Poppy, please stop and listen, let me explain to you."

I twisted around to see Sam running, at quite a lick, towards me. His arms flailing in the air because I had stopped in my tracks. Sam had difficulty in slowing down on the cold and slippery path. He crashed into me, knocking me off my feet. I ended up flat on my back, with Sam on top of me, looking into my eyes with a big grin on his face.

"We will have to stop meeting like this, Poppy."

"Sam, get off me. You have a lady waiting in your flat, or have you forgotten."

"Poppy, I'm so glad to see you. I thought you had gone off with that lanky bloke, with the attitude."

I looked around, and quite a few people had gathered, wondering why this guy was on top of me,

"Are you alright, young lady?"

One by-stander said, obviously worried about my welfare.

"Yes, I'm fine thank you; if this idiot would get off me."

"Ooohh! Idiot is it, says the girl who just disappeared without a trace."

"Sam I can explain why I had to do that, but not here."

"Look Poppy, come back to the flat, have a cuppa and let's talk."

I was surprised at his invitation, considering he had company, but I was angry, so I agreed. *Let's see him wriggle out of this one,* I thought to myself. We didn't speak as we climbed the stairs. His front door was open; in his dash to catch me, he had left it open. He told me to make myself at home while he put the kettle on, so I entered the lounge, thinking I would be alone.

"Hello, I'm Sally. I'm Sam's sister. You must be Poppy; he's told me all about you."

I felt my face flush with embarrassment. She must have heard me causing a scene outside his flat window.

"Nice to meet you, Sally. I apologise for my behaviour just now. I thought Sam had forsaken me for someone else."

"Just between the two of us, Poppy, Sam is into you big time, but don't let on, I told you so."

"Thanks for that, Sally, I think I'm going to like you."

Sam walked into the room with a tray of tea and cake,

"You've introduced yourselves then, who's for cake."

I was so relaxed in Sally's company. It was like I had known her for years. There was something about her. I just couldn't put my finger on.

After we polished off the tea and cake, Sally made an excuse to leave. She knew Sam and I had things to talk about. She gave me a wink as she said goodbye. She made her own way out and left us to sort out our differences. We were both sat on the sofa. Sam was smiling; he looked into my eyes and said,

"Poppy, I know your secret."

My heart missed a beat. How the hell did he know; I hadn't given any clues as far as I could remember!

"Okay Sam, I admit I'm a time traveller, but how did you find out."

Sam started laughing,

"A time traveller, of course you are, what I meant was, Poppy I know your still seeing that gorky boyfriend of yours, even though you said you had split up."

"What makes you think I would lie to you, Sam?"

"About two weeks after you visited me last time, and you disappeared without trace, I was walking up the high street when I saw you walking hand in hand with him. When I wolf-whistled you, you turned towards me, recognised me, then turned away and carried on as if I was nothing."

"Sam, please sit and listen and wait until I've finished explaining the whole complicated issues of my life as a time traveller. It's hard to believe, but everything I'm about to tell you is the truth. You may well have seen Poppy in the high street with her boyfriend, but it wasn't me; well, it was me, but me in 1985."

"Poppy, it's 1986 now."

I then realised I had been away for over six months, so technically it was 1986 now.

"I am from 1995, and I travel back to this time, via a 'Door' in my attic; so the person you saw was me but not me. I am with Simon in 1986, but we split up in 1995. I am from the future, and I have definitely parted company with Simon; so when I told you we had finished our relationship, I was telling you the truth."

"That's a relief, I thought you were two-timing me,"

Sam said, flippantly. I spent the next two hours trying to explain all that had happened since the first time I had travelled. Sam was quiet throughout, occasionally scratching his head in bewilderment. Then to my amazement, he held my hand, looked me in the eye and said,

"So the reason you just disappeared out of my bed, after we had sex, was the time machine calling you back, and you have no control over its actions."

"Yes, I've just explained to you. I could just disappear while I'm talking to you now. If you can't accept it, there's no way we can have a relationship."

Unknown to Poppy while she had been talking to me, I had been listening, but my heart had been dancing. It all seemed difficult to believe, but the only thing I was really interested in was her. She was so beautiful, her skin was like a fresh peach, and her eyes melted my soul; just the mere touch of her hand sent a tingle down my spine. She was exciting and so alive, and now she was talking about us having a relationship. Could life get any better, I didn't think so; and if being with Poppy meant she might disappear occasionally, so be it!

"Sam, you don't seem fazed about what I've just told you. Most people would scoff or think it totally ridiculous if their girlfriend told them they were from the future."

"Poppy, I don't know how much I buy into this time travel thing, but if it explains why you vanished into thin air the last time I saw you, and if it means being with you most of the time, then count me in."

"Sam, you do realise it will be difficult, and I won't be able to work, due to disappearing from time to time; although I could try and sell some artwork. I will have to crash here when I travel back, and we have to make sure I don't bump into myself or Simon, because if I do, it might change the future, then all will be lost."

Sam looked a little bewildered; then he pondered for a moment, then he said,

"Poppy, when will things be normal if we go down this route?"

"If I've worked things out right, just over nine years, and we can live as a normal couple."

"So Poppy, what do we do for the next nine years."

"Just live, love and make the most of the time we can spend together and make the most of this opportunity to be with each other."

Chapter 18
Coming Together

"This calls for a celebration, Poppy. How about we have a glass of fizz."

"That would be just dandy, young man."

While Sam went off to the kitchen, I thought to myself, *just over nine years to get to know one another, would we make it.* It was going to be tricky, but I would certainly give it a go. It was now February 1986, and I was excited for our future together. Sam entered the room with a bottle of Prosecco and two glasses,

"You do the honours, Poppy. I'm sure you've opened a few of these in your time."

"Moi, I don't think so, it's very rare I have a drink."

"Yes right, I had your measure. The first time I met you, I thought I might have my work cut out keeping up with you."

The truth was, in 1986, I was only 21 years old, and I definitely didn't drink as much as I did in 1995, so I would have to take it steady and slowly work up to the 1995 levels. The conversation flowed, and so did the bottle; it was soon empty, and we were both more at ease with each other. Sam's eyes were all over me, you could tell; he was undressing me in his mind. I have to admit my thoughts weren't pure; in fact they were disgusting. I wanted him bad, and I didn't have to wait long before he made the first move.

I was nervous, god knows why. The fact was, she had ten years more experience than me, or did she. Now she had travelled back, she was only 21, wasn't she, or was her mind and life experiences ten years older than her body. I was still new at this time travel thing, and it took some working out. As I looked into her eyes, my heart raced. Her teeth were perfect, her lips wet. I wanted to kiss her, to put my tongue into her mouth; she was like an aphrodisiac, a drug, which I was delirious on. My balls were aching; I wanted her so bad.

"Sam, why don't you put some music on; anything will do; I'm sure we have similar taste."

I stood up to switch on the Hi-Fi. My growing erection in my boxers caused some discomfort, and it didn't go unnoticed. Poppy had clocked it. I noticed her gaze was drawn to the ever-growing bulge that betrayed my inner thoughts of lust, growing in my loins.

"Trousers a bit tight, are they, Sam."

I grinned; she had a naughty sense of humour, and I loved it.

"It's alright for women; it's not quite as obvious when you get turned on."

If only he knew how turned on I was, I wanted to rip his stiff cock out of his trousers and give it a damn good sucking. Instead, I was a little more subtle and gently rubbed his swelling cock through his trousers. The music started playing, and we both burst out laughing. We looked at each other; then started singing the lyrics to the song that the DJ had decided to play. I want to break free by Queen; very apt for the moment and also appropriate as I unzipped his fly; his massive hard penis popped out.

"Poppy, you seemed such a quiet girl. Well, you had me fooled. I wouldn't normally be attracted to a woman who devour one's manhood, but as you have me over-powered, there's not a lot I can do."

Poppy had de-bagged me; my trousers and boxers were gone. Poppy's mouth had closed around the end of my grateful cock. Her head was moving up and down, occasionally coming off and spitting on the end. There was no need, I was soaking wet.

"Come on, big boy, let's have what you've got."

She was quite something when she got aroused. I have to admit it was a bit of a shock; not only was she gorgeous, but also very naughty. She seemed to lose all her inhibitions when it came to sex. I had dreamt of meeting someone like her for years. I thought to myself, had I died and gone to heaven.

I was on my knees. Sam stood, with just his shirt on; his cock down my throat. He forced me back onto the leather sofa,

"Okay young lady, you want to play rough, do you."

"Oh Sam, I'm so scared, you're not going to shag me, are you."

Sam smiled. I smiled. He then ripped off my blouse, exposed my breasts, leaving my bra on. My nipples were erect; he sucked them, licking and biting them in turn; god, he was good.

I felt guilty. I was like an animal possessed; the more I touched her, the more she wanted. I stripped the rest of her clothes off; she was so fit. I kissed my way down from her breasts to her pussy. She obviously approved; her legs stretched apart even further. I felt her grab my hair and pull my face into her throbbing slit,

"Lick my clit, lick my clit, harder Sam, aarrgghh."

She certainly loved being licked; she tasted divine. I playfully bit her clit, then thrust my tongue into her; she writhed in ecstasy.

I didn't think I could last much longer. Each time he sank his wet tongue into my tush, it pushed me closer to oblivion. I felt the orgasm build to a crescendo. I couldn't halt the flow of pleasure rippling through my selfish body; nothing on earth was going to stop the inevitable. The drug of lust took over. My back arched, my breathing was laboured; my heart was banging like a drum.

I thought Poppy was going to pull my hair clean from my head. She shouted,

"I'm cumming, don't stop, don't stop, aargh aargh."

Her pubic area lifted into the air. She went rigid, pressing her head hard into the leather sofa. Her skin seemed to take on a beautiful glow as if pure pleasure was flowing through her whole body, and she was more beautiful than ever when she came.

"Sam, I want you inside me."

She exclaimed, in a whispered voice. I didn't need asking twice. I cupped her bare buttocks with both hands and gently slipped my wet hard cock into her as far as it would go. She sighed with pleasure,

"That feels good, Sam, now fill me with love."

As I gyrated up and down, her bare breasts still cupped by her black lacy bra flowed forwards, then backwards; it really turned me on.

"Sam, snog me please."

Her mouth was wet. She licked her lips seductively; our mouths met, the kiss was electric. I felt my balls tighten; there was no going back now, "Poppy, I'm cumming."

"I want to see it," she said excitedly.

"What do you mean, you want to see it?"

"Shoot your cum all over me, please Sam."

It was almost too late. I pulled out just in time. I felt the rush through my penis. I squeezed it just before I ejaculated. Poppy was wide-eyed, as cum shot out all over her pubes, stomach and breasts. The feeling was out of this world. I leant towards Poppy; we kissed passionately. I looked into her blue eyes and said, "You're such a naughty girl."

"And you're a dirty boy. I think we are going to make a lovely couple."

After showering, we decided to have a cuddle in bed. It was so cosy, I felt really wanted and safe. We talked about all sorts. Sam told me all about his job in the music industry. He wasn't an artist; he sold music equipment for one of the giants—a Japanese company. He was mainly based in the local town, but occasionally travelled throughout the UK, hence the flash car.

I explained to him that in the future, I was a self-employed struggling artist, selling mainly country scenes, but I also dabbled in the erotic fantasy market.

"That figures with you, Poppy. I think you are a dark horse when it comes to sex, after today's session."

"Are you telling me, Sam, that you're not up for kinky sex; you shock me."

I said jokingly. I was sure he was just as adventurous as I was.

"Well, Poppy, if you need a model for your erotic fantasy market, I'm sure I could oblige. I might even be able to sell them through people at work."

"That would be great, Sam. I could earn some money to help with my keep. Oh! I couldn't sign them as mine though, it might change the future."

"I could say they were my paintings and sign them Sam Devere. I can set you up a studio in the spare room; it would be perfect, wouldn't it."

"As long as you kept me in plentiful supply of tea, I think it could work."

We both laughed and snuggled in for a cuddle; then Sam seemed serious.

"How long will it be before you will be called back?"

"I just don't know. It might be in a few minutes. It might be next year I have no idea what triggers the 'Door'."

We must have drifted off to sleep, because when we came to, it was dark outside. The good news was, I hadn't disappeared this time.

"Poppy, how do you fancy a take away for tea tonight. I know the best Chinese, and it's just around the corner."

"I love Chinese take away; can I come with you to fetch it."

"Of course, you can. Then I was thinking, as tomorrow is Saturday, I think we had better go shopping for some new clothes for you. If you're stopping, you can't go on wearing the same clothes."

I hadn't even thought about my clothes. The other problem was, I couldn't take money from my bank account to pay for them; otherwise, the '1986 Poppy' might wonder where the money had gone; so the plan to sell my paintings turned out to be the best option.

"I will pay you back as soon as my paintings start to sell. I promise."

"Poppy, don't be silly, it will all work out in the end, so don't worry about the money."

We got dressed; unfortunately my clothes looked a little creased after being strewn all over the floor in Sam's haste to get me naked, but I had no back up, so they had to do. Sam's car was luxurious and very quiet, much nicer than my van. The engine purred as Sam hit the accelerator; then a thought hit me.

"Stop Sam! Stop."

"What's the matter, Poppy?"

"Have you forgotten, we have been drinking."

"Poppy, I only had one glass, you drank the rest."

"Did I?"

I was now a little embarrassed. I hadn't realised I had drank most of the bottle,

"Oh! Sorry Sam."

"No worries, I can't stand the stuff. I prefer a nice beer; that bubbly stuff gives me wind."

"Best you stick to the beer then."

There were no hairs and graces with Sam. He just said what he thought; and he was a breath of fresh air after stuck-up Simon. Sam found a parking space about 50 yards from the Chinese; it was called 'King Wah Chinese Take away'. I had been here before with Simon,

"Good choice, Sam; I've had food from here before."

We stood outside the shop. The menu was stuck to the window, so we were going down the list to see what we fancied. I happened to glance up and into the shop. I thought my heart would stop; I was in total shock. The blood drained from my head, I went white, I couldn't speak; I was gasping for breath. Sam carried on talking to me, not realising I had frozen in time; then he looked at me and realised something was wrong. "What's the matter, Poppy, do you have asthma?"

I managed to point into the shop. Sam turned to follow my pointing finger,

"No way! My god, it's you and that guy with the attitude."

It then hit me like a ton of bricks. Poppy was from the future. She was stood next to me, but she was also in the Chinese. Everything she had told me was true; there was no doubting it now.

"Sam, we must go now; if they see us, it's all over. Please, let's get away."

We ran back to the car. Thankfully they were still in the shop as we drove past. We sped away up the road, to get as far away from them as possible.

Chapter 19
Soap Stars

After the Chinese take away incident, we decided to keep a low profile in the local town, just in case. The next day, the Saturday, Sam and I went shopping. We decided to go to a town about 15 miles away; that way, we could relax and enjoy being a normal couple if it was ever possible to be normal when one of you was a time traveller. This was the first time I had stopped over night without the 'Door' calling me back. I suppose I wasn't stressed, and I wasn't thinking of the 'Door'; maybe, that was the secret. I also wondered, if I managed to stop here longer, would it affect the duration of time in the future. If so, I had a problem—how about Roscoe? Then I remembered the plan that I set up with Chloe; if I didn't answer my phone over a 12-hour period, she would go the house and feed the dog. After reassuring myself that all would be okay at home, I started to enjoy our day out together. Sam drove into the car park. It was a pay and display, just off the main shopping area. The time on the ticket said 10:26 a.m.

"Poppy, I've bought eight hours; do you think that's enough."

"What sort of women have you been shopping with; that's more than plenty of time."

"I think there's a posh clothes shop near the river."

Sam pointed towards where he thought the shop was.

"Sam, what would I want a posh clothes shop for?"

"I thought we were going to get you fitted out with a new wardrobe."

"We are, silly, but there's no need to spend loads of money."

Sam looked at me, gone out,

"What are you planning to do then; steal them?"

"Don't forget, Sam, I lived as a student with next to no money for years, follow me!"

We walked hand in hand along the street until I saw what I was looking for,

"Here we are, perfect."

"It's a charity shop."

"Well, what's the problem?"

"You can't buy second hand clothes; there's no need."

"There's very much a need, Sam. I have no money, and I can guarantee I will find just what I need in the next six charity shops that we go in."

"Six, really! Do we have too?"

"Trust me, Sam; you will be amazed what bargains you can find in these type of shops."

"Okay Poppy, promise me one thing, let me buy your underwear from a proper shop."

"Okay, it's a deal."

In the very first shop, I found two dresses—four tops, a jumper and a bandana for the measly sum of £16.50. Then in the second shop, a shop raising money for Staffies—a charity close to my heart because I love dogs—I noticed a very long pair of shiny patent ladies boots, with 4" heels and a silver steel zip running from the sole to the top; and they were my size, size 5. Sam's eyes perked up,

"Wow, I like those."

"Oh, it's alright to shop here now; is it. What do you think, Sam?"

"Do you think you could walk in them; the heels are rather high."

I looked at him mischievously and quietly whispered,

"They're for the bedroom only."

"Oh right. Yes, yes, I think you should take them."

He replied rather sheepishly. Sam seemed to get into the spirit after the boot episode and took an active role in looking for clothes that were a little more risqué. In the 'Air Ambulance' Shop, he found me a very nice black leather jacket, complete with soft black leather skin hugging trousers, which I thought were fantastic and also very poignant, considering he had never seen my painting *Black Leather Together.*

At first, I was reticent to shop in charity shops, but Poppy soon had me converted. There were certainly bargains to be had, and when she started picking up kinky stuff, I was sold on the idea. When I held up the black leather items and Poppy said,

"Shall I try them on," I couldn't believe my luck.

"I think you should, we don't want to have to bring it back, do we."

I waited outside the changing rooms. The excitement was building inside me. I could feel my boxers getting tighter. I discretely had to rearrange my tackle, to avoid strangulation. Then the curtain swooshed open. Poppy didn't come out; she invited me in,

"What do you think, Sam?"

I was speechless. The black leather trousers looked like they had been sprayed on to her perfectly shaped behind. She bent over to accentuate the curve of her bottom. I playfully patted her arse.

"Steady on, big boy; don't touch what you can't afford."

I replied quickly,

"I'm saving as you speak."

I said, with a quiver in my voice. Then she straightened and turned. Well, I was dumbstruck. She had the leather jacket on, which fitted like a glove. She pulled the zipper down slowly; and to my astonishment, she was naked underneath. Her breasts were swelling against the fit of the jacket. I reacted in an instant, pulling the changing room curtain across, first of all to stop people seeing, but then to suck on her nipples.

"Oh Sam! Do you think black suits me?"

I withdrew my head which was buried in her chest.

"God Poppy! What are you like," I said, in a nervous hushed voice. She grabbed my dick through my jeans,

"I think you like me in black. Well, your cock seems to."

Poppy said, in a husky voice.

I kissed Sam. I was really turned on, but I could see Sam was panicking.

"Shall we take it then, Sam; it's only £15.00."

I retreated backwards out through the curtain; an assistant gave me a long stare.

"Just helping her with the zip; it was a bit stiff," I shouted across the shop. The assistant pulled a face; then went about her business. A couple of minutes later, Poppy appeared from the cubicle with the trousers and jacket draped across her arm. She had a silly grin on her face, like a naughty schoolgirl, who had been caught snogging behind the bike-sheds. We paid the inquisitive assistant, then left the shop, carrying a growing number of shopping bags. We now had the makings of a new wardrobe for me, but before we did any more shopping, it was time for lunch.

The cafe was set right next to the river. We had a choice of sitting outside, but it was far too chilly, so we chose a window table on the first floor. The view took in the fast flowing river, and the rather quaint sandstone bridge that spanned the water. There were very low beams in the ceiling, and the uneven floor creaked with every step you made. The windows were Georgian sash, with panes of floated glass, so thin that you could feel the cold air from outside. Each little square table boasted a table lamp, with a frilly lampshade, a menu and a brass table number inserted into the dark oak tabletop. There was a distinct smell of roasted coffee beans drifting up the stairs. The kitchen was noisy, trying to cope with the copious amounts of orders from the constant flow of hungry customers. The place seemed full of young waitresses dashing around like busy bees, trying to keep everyone happy. It only seemed like a minute after sitting that a young, very attractive girl, notebook in hand, appeared at the table. She had long blonde hair tied into a ponytail, with a bright red band,

"Hello, I'm Holly, what can I get you?"

We hadn't really had time to read the menu, but Sam asked me if a Tuna and cheese Panini and coffee would suffice.

"Just what I would have ordered, Sam, how did you guess?"

Before he could respond, the waitress was hotfooting her way to the kitchen, with the scribbled note. Unfortunately, she didn't ask what sort of coffee we required, so Sam had to nip down the stairs to make sure we got one latte and a cappuccino for me. While he was away, it gave me time to reflect on the day. So far, it had been so much fun. Sam had been attentive; showing a true caring affection for me. Even with the waitress not bothering to ask what type of coffee we wanted didn't annoy him. He simply got up and went to rectify it. If that had been Simon, he would have made a scene. Before long, our lunch arrived; it was delicious and just enough. We laughed about the incident in the changing room. Sam said,

"Poppy, you really are the most extraordinary lady. I have ever met, would you have gone further if I hadn't chickened out."

"Sam, I just find it a real turn on getting up to mischief in places where you might get caught."

"Me too, Poppy, but I don't have the bottle you have, that's for sure."

"Don't worry, Sam. We have plenty of time to practise, and you know what practise makes! 'Practise makes perfect' as my dad used to say."

I was very excited about the rest of the day. It was now time to find the lingerie shop to buy Poppy's underwear. I settled the bill, and we headed back to the shops. For some reason, Poppy wouldn't let me see the lingerie she tried on. She said she had to keep some surprises for me, so after trying three shops, she had a selection of day-to-day underwear and a select range for special occasions. On the way back to the car, struggling with all the bags, Poppy grabbed my arm,

"Look Sam, just what I need."

In the window of another charity shop, that we hadn't been in, was an artist's easel, complete with paints, brushes and a selection of stretched canvases—a bargain at £20.00.

"Oh! Sam, I feel so guilty; you having to pay for everything today. I promise you, as soon as I sell a painting, I will pay you back with interest."

"Poppy, stop worrying about money. It only cost a fraction of what I was expecting to spend today, thanks to you and your charity shops."

By the time we arrived home and walked through the front door, it was gone 6:30 p.m.

"Shall I put the kettle on, Sam, I could murder a cuppa."

"That would be lovely, Poppy; you need to find your way around the kitchen, so you can cook dinner tonight."

He said it, with tongue in cheek, but I really didn't mind; it would make me feel more at home.

"Sam, before I make dinner, would it be okay if I had a bath."

"Poppy, certainly not! But it would be okay if we had a bath."

"Well, Sam, I'm feeling rather dirty; so may be, you could scrub my back."

"It's a deal. I will start running the bath."

Before I could move, Sam was off like a whippet, straight to the bathroom. I heard the taps flowing, and Sam singing; he was like a child in a sweet shop. I was also excited, but I was playing it cool. I opened the door to the bathroom, and I was met by a mist of steamy air; the rush of water cascading into the bath and the smell of bananas.

"Sam, I don't believe it, you have banana-scented bath soap."

"Sorry! I have to admit it, yes it's banana, but I didn't buy them. It was a Christmas present from a so-called friend."

I stood in the bathroom. Sam was prostrate in the bath, with a massive stiffy.

"Room for a little one," I said, knowing what the answer would be.

"What are you waiting for?"

I dropped my clothes where I stood. Sam just stared, as if in a trance, "What's the matter, have you never seen a naked women before?"

"Not as beautiful as you," he replied. I stepped into the bath; it was surprisingly hot. Sam was smiling like a Cheshire cat, as I lowered myself on to him. The water level raised considerably, luckily, not over the edge of the bath. He kissed me ever so gently on the lips,

"Hello, my lovely friend," he said, in a very sensitive tone.

"Thank you, Sam, for making me feel wanted. It means a lot."

"Poppy."

He stopped speaking, as if to think deeply about what he was about to say,

"Poppy, I'm not sure how to say this, but, but, I think I've left the soap on the basin."

"You're such a tease, Samuel Devere, but just remember, who's on top!"

I pushed hard on his head; then he was under, "Who's the boss now, smart-arse."

Bubbles rose from his submerged mouth, as he tried to answer me! The water in the bath was like a tidal wave, heaving too and throw, with our bodies acting like giant paddles pushing the soapy water from one end to the other. Sam surfaced; his bright blue eyes covered in soap. As I fought to hold him down, my elbow knocked the open bottle of bath soap into the water. By the time I managed to grab it, it being so slippery, the whole contents of the bottle had leaked out into the bath. We were both hysterical with laughter. The more we thrashed about, created more and more bubbles. Sam grabbed my buttocks and pulled me on to his erect slippery cock. He slid into me, almost covertly; it was that quick. I leant over him, offering my nipples to his open mouth. He licked them, spitting out the soap that was everywhere,

"Spit on me, would you, you dirty boy."

I filled my mouth with soapy water and squirted it all over his face; it was hilarious. Sam thrust his ever-wanting cock harder into me; it felt good with him inside me. I changed position slightly. I was now on my knees, but still impaled on his erect cock. Now I could gyrate up and down; I was now in control.

I lay there. Poppy was sat on me, jumping up and down on my lustful dick. Her breasts, shiny and slippery, were bouncing in my face. She rested her hands on my shoulders, desperate to get a grip, as she rode me like a stallion.

"Poppy, if you keep going like that, I'm going to come."

"Me too, big boy, I'm almost there; cum inside me, Sam."

Her face glowed with pleasure. Her neck flushed red. She was panting, trying to get her breath.

"Oh Sam! Fuck me! Fuck me! Give it to me!"

It really turned me on when Poppy used the F word, and that was the catalyst. Her rhythmic gymnastics had worked their magic. I felt the rush, as the hot cum accelerated towards the end of my knob!

"Poppy, it's all over."

The grimace on Sam's face told the story. I felt his penis explode inside me, filling me with molten hot cum. My vagina contracted, gripping his swollen cock like a vice. My orgasm took me to a heavenly place; the drug of sex flowing through my veins. I collapsed onto Sam's heaving chest, kissing his neck with gratitude.

"Poppy, you're an animal. I feel like I've been raped."

"You could have said no! If you had wanted."

"You're joking, Poppy! You're the best shag I've ever had."

"Thank you, my lovely Samuel. I love you so much."

"Oh my god, Poppy, you wait till you turn around."

"What's the problem, Sam?"

When I turned around, I couldn't see anything. Well, I could, but just bubbles. The room was filled with yellow bubbles, right up to the ceiling; you could cut patterns with your hands in the wall of bubbles—it was incredible. We couldn't stop laughing. It was like a banana massacre—the smell was intense. I climbed off Sam and put my foot down towards the invisible floor,

"Sam, the floor is soaked."

In our moment of passionate frenzy, we had whipped the spilt bath soap into a right lather, producing tons of bubbles, and the momentum of our competing bodies had forced the bath water over the edge of the bath and all over the floor.

"Don't worry, Poppy; it will soon dry out. Just throw the towels on the floor when we're dry."

Nothing ever seemed to faze Sam. He was so easy going; it was just a pleasure spending time with him. You never had to worry about him hitting the roof over something trivial.

After we got our dressing gowns on, well mine was an old one of Sam's, it was one thing we forgot to buy from the shops today. I then prepared our tea. It would have been Salmon and salad, but it was frozen, so no time to defrost it; so we had chicken and pineapple pizza. It was a hit with both of us; we're so peckish after our nautical escapades. We sat on the sofa, watching TV. Sam swigging beer and me drinking wine. I rested my head on Sam's chest and said,

"Sam, are you sure this is what you want, because I don't want it to end. I've loved today, and I just want to make sure we are on the same page."

"Stop fretting, Poppy; you worry far too much. Things will be fine; and if I get fed up with you, I will tell you."

He kissed me on the head and rubbed my back as if to reassure me. I was so happy!

Chapter 20
Alfresco, June 1987

The longer I remained with Sam in 1986, the more settled I became. During the following weeks, you could feel a bond growing between us. While Sam was out at work in the day, I would attempt to paint a masterpiece. We had had some success. Sam had already sold one painting which brought in £200. I was also busy keeping the flat tidy, doing the washing and ironing and, of course, the cooking; although Sam did like to keep his hand in with certain meals. I felt like I was earning my keep by doing the chores, as I was still uncomfortable with Sam having to keep me. Over the weeks, we had prepared for my departure. We didn't know when, but it was inevitable that the 'Door' at some time would call me back to the future. I now felt confident that our relationship was strong enough to stand being apart, for however long the 'Door' decided.

In our preparation for me disappearing, we now had a key to the flat hidden in the garden, so if I turned up and Sam was away, I could still get in. We also placed a calendar on the wall in the kitchen. Every day I was there, I would sign a P for Poppy across the date; then if I disappeared, when I came back, I would see instantly how long I had been absent. I also planned to get one for the 'Ducklands', just to double check that no time had elapsed when I travelled back to the future. I had been in the past now for several months, and it would soon be my birthday. Sam said he had something planned, so I was hoping that I would still be here. In saying that, I was really missing Roscoe, Chloe and the house. I assumed that in the future, no time had elapsed, and Roscoe hadn't even notice that I had disappeared. Deep down, I wondered if something had happened in the future. Why hadn't the 'Door' called me back; was it that I was settled and not stressed, or I hadn't thought about the 'Door', or had some catastrophic event occurred in the future, disabling the time machine to function; if so, I could be stuck here for years.

I decided not to worry about it and get on with my day. Sam was at work, and I was halfway through a painting. It was a fantasy piece, depicting a scene of a couple having sex on the bonnet of a car. The girl was lay on her back naked; apart from a very long pair of black shiny boots, the man stood with his pants around his ankles. I wasn't sure why I felt compelled to paint such scenes. May be, it was a secret desire buried deep in my psyche, and it was a way of memorising them until they were played out in real life; if so, look out Samuel.

The days passed quickly. You know what they say, 'time flies when you're having a good time'. This day in particular had flown by before I knew it. I heard the key in the door, and Sam was home from work.

"Hello Poppy, my little sex bomb, how's your day gone."

"Pretty busy, and the painting is almost finished; what do you think."

Sam looked at the painting and said,

"Aren't those the same boots we bought from the charity shop; and that car, it's the same as mine."

Sam had a wicked grin on his face,

"Does this mean this is a fantasy you want to play out?"

"It might be," I said, with a glint in my eye.

"Poppy, it's a lovely evening. Why don't we go to that pub in the country we once went to, for tea; remember the one with the beams."

That would be great; no cooking tonight, I thought to myself. Then a thought popped into my mind, "Sam, you don't have an ulterior motive, do you?"

"I don't know what you mean, Poppy, but you could wear those long boots if you wanted."

I put my arms around his neck and kissed him, "You're such a naughty boy, sometimes, Sam. I think I might have to spank you later."

"Oh! No!"

Sam replied, insincerely. After showering, Sam was the first to get dressed, while he waited for me. He went into the lounge to play some music, while I decided what to wear.

I was always quicker to get ready than Poppy. Denim jeans and a short-sleeved shirt, a quick flick of the hair, and I was done. While I was waiting, I thought I would play some music. I loved music with a good beat; music I could dance to; so I put on Don't Leave Me This Way by the Communards. Such a great beat and certainly a piece of music that I found difficult not to dance to. I was well into my moves when the door opened, and Poppy walked in. Oh My God!! She looked stunning. Her hair was swept back, held in place by a bandanna. She wore a white cotton blouse, which was fighting a battle with her breasts. The buttons were straining under the pressure, just awarding a glimpse of her red and black bra, which had the enviable task of containing her voluptuous breasts. She wore a short white flouncy skirt with red poppy's printed on it; and if that wasn't enough to blow your mind, she had the skin hugging long boots on—the ones we got from the charity shop.

"I love what you're playing Sam, great to dance to,"

Poppy said, in a raised voice, as it was so loud.

"And I love what you're wearing, Poppy. You look amazing."

"Well, thank you, Sam. You can buy me dinner if you like."

We skipped down the stairs, both excited about eating out in the country. It was a beautiful evening, as we sped towards The Chequer's Inn. I opened the windows, letting a nice cool breeze into the car. Sam's hair was swishing around, and occasionally the breeze lifted my skirt—much to Sam's liking. The record playing on the radio was Just Can't Get Enough' by Depeche Mode. I looked at

Sam and thought to myself, I couldn't get enough of him, he was truly wonderful. I just hoped he felt the same about me, I feared I was falling in Love with this lovely man and l wondered if my heart was going to be broken all over again.

I don't think Poppy realised what she was doing to me. Every time the breeze blew her skirt up in the air, I had a glimpse of her lily-white thighs. She kept grabbing at the skirt to try and hold it down, each time with an excited squeal. Then she reached across and touched me.

"You soon reacted; you randy devil."

"Poppy, what do you expect, those boots up to your knees and your skirt flying around."

She then started to unzip my fly!

"Poppy, you can't do that while I'm driving. We will end up in the hedge."

"I'm just relieving the pressure, you concentrate on the driving."

Sam's cock was so hard that it stuck upright out of his fly. I wrapped my hand around it and gripped it firmly, then proceeded to wank him off. "Poppy! Stop it. I'm going to crash the car if you don't."

I couldn't believe Sam's reaction, but before I stopped, I leant over and engulfed his wet cock into my mouth, whipping my searching tongue around his foreskin. He tasted spunky; never mind, I would have him later.

As we pulled into the car park, I noticed Sam's cock still standing firm, still protruding out of his fly.

"I suggest you put that weapon away before we go in to the pub."

I said, with a naughty grin on my face. Sam climbed out of the car, facing away from the pub and attempted to get his erect cock back into his trousers. He pulled up his zip, but you could still see a distinct bulge in his pants. I was in hysterics.

"Poppy, it's your fault, you sex maniac. If you hadn't attacked me in the first place, I wouldn't be in this position."

Sam was jesting, and he loved it really. I knew what his next line would be!

"Poppy, you're so naughty. After we have had tea, I'm going to sort you out."

"Oh! Really, I will look forward to that."

I replied, with excitement building in my tummy. As it was a glorious evening, we chose to take a table outside in the garden. It was quite busy, as everyone else had the same idea. The garden was mainly set to lawn with scattered shrubs, as you walked out under the cover of sprawling Clematis, mauve in colour, climbing across a rickety arched pergola. You were drawn to a blazing yellow Acer Japonica standing proud in the far corner. In contrast, in the opposite corner was a berberis, with deep purple foliage. Then next to the table, we sat at, were pink lilacs which gave off the most gorgeous sweet scent.

"What a delightful garden, Sam, isn't it just lovely."

"It will be even better when I get a drink, the usual, Poppy."

"Yes, please, a large one please; I like large ones."

As I spoke, I stared at his groin,

"Oh! Very funny, Poppy, you just wait."

While he was away, I sat with the sun bearing down on my face. My eyes closed, thinking about my life and how extraordinary the changes had been, when I felt the touch of someone's hand on my shoulder.

"Poppy, how lovely to see ya."

My heart missed a beat. I kept my eyes closed, thinking that if I didn't open them, she might disappear, but that didn't work! I knew who it was; I didn't have to see her. She had the most telling Birmingham accent ever. It was my dear uni friend Laverne, and I hadn't seen her since leaving uni, years ago. She was originally from the Caribbean, but her family moved to the UK in the '60s. Her arms engulfed me; she started screeching with happy laughter, then asking questions ten to the dozen. What was I going to do? I was with Simon when she knew me before, but before I could think what to say to her, Sam turned up with the drinks in both hands, and the menu tucked under his arm. Sam put the drinks down on the table, placed the menu down; then without hesitation, thrust his hand out towards Laverne.

"Hi, I'm Sam, a work colleague of Poppy, nice to meet you."

Laverne just looked at me, then towards Sam, still holding his hand, "Very nice to meet you, Sam," she replied, with a big smile on her face; her gleaming white teeth accentuating her lust for life. Sam then made the excuse, that he needed the toilet and shot off in the direction of the loos. Laverne looked at me, then screamed,

"He's hot, better than that other guy you were with; what was his name, Simon? His eyes were far too close together; and if you don't mind me saying, he was punching way above his weight going out with you, Poppy."

She never changed; she always spoke her mind, and she had seen right through Sam's attempt to put her off the scent.

"Don't worry, Poppy; your secret is safe with me."

I was dumbstruck. I just stared at her; she leaned over and pressed a business card into my hand,

"Give me a call sometime. I have to rush. My man's waiting in the car park. I only came back into the garden because I left my hat."

Then she was gone. It had been a shock, but also, it had been great to see her again. I looked down at the card she had pressed into my hand; it read, Laverne Lucerne, wedding planner extraordinaire; then the telephone number. I popped it into my trusty bag. Sam reappeared, "Well, has she gone."

"She has, bless her, but she saw right through you, thought we were a couple."

"No way! How did she do that?"

"That's Laverne, she's a right card."

I took a gulp of my wine, I needed it; we then looked through the menu and ordered our food. Sam had steak and chips with pepper sauce, and I ordered sea bass with a green salad. The food was outstanding; no wonder the place was busy. While eating our food, the conversation got around to the fantasy painting I had been working on. Sam had ideas of re-enacting the scene.

"Well Sam, if you feel like you're up to it, bring it on."

On the way out of the pub, I used the ladies, topped up my lippy and checked for debris in my teeth. It was strange looking in the mirror and seeing myself so young. Anyway the man of my dreams was outside, waiting for me, and I have to admit I was really excited. As I walked out the main door, I heard the purr of the powerful engine of Sam's car. He had pulled up next to the entrance. The passenger window was down, and I heard him shout,

"Hello darling, do you fancy a ride."

I undid the top button of my blouse, allowing a full view of my cleavage, leant into the car window and replied,

"Sorry, my dad told me not to go off with strangers."

Then turned and started walking away, casually looking over my shoulder, as if to tease him even more. About 20 yards away, I popped up my thumb as if hitch hiking. The car approached, the throb of the engine, like the echo of his passion to have his wicked way with me. I couldn't resist any longer and jumped into the car laughing.

Sam turned out of the pub the opposite way to the way we came in,

"Why this way, Sam."

"This road goes deeper into the countryside; more chance of privacy if you know what I'm saying."

Sam winked at me with a grin on his face and a glint in his eye. I felt a surge of naughtiness flush through my tush,

"Sam, what makes you think I'm the sort of person who would have sex out in the open."

"It was your fantasy, that's why you painted the scene."

Sam was obviously turned on; there was a giveaway bulge in his trousers. I thought I might tease him a little, so I opened my legs a little wider. I put my hand up my skirt and started to finger myself. I was surprised how wet I was. I licked my lips seductively; my tongue wet, spreading the saliva along my top lip. I made the sound of the final throws of sex, as if my orgasm was upon me,

"Oh yes! Oh yes, aarrrgghh."

"Poppy, you're such a tease. You wait till I stop this car; you're going to get a right seeing to."

"What are you waiting for, big boy?"

As I said it, the car took a sharp turn into an entrance to a field. The large double gate had been left open. I think the farmer had recently been in with a combine, because there were loads of bales of hay scattered around the field. The throb of the engine subsided. It was now quiet, apart from the sound of skylarks high in the sky singing their hearts out, and the sound of a distant tractor in a faraway field. Sam was upon me in seconds, kissing me passionately; his tongue was in my mouth, then his hand up my skirt,

"You dirty bitch, you've got no knickers on."

I laughed out loud,

"I thought it might make your job a little easier."

"So you planned this when we were back in the flat!"

"Of course, I did, silly."

She was such a tease. I just wanted her so badly; my fingers found her clitoris, soaking with lust. I fingered her, rubbing her wanting clit, causing her to squeal with pleasure. My mouth moved down to her chest, pulling her blouse open with my teeth. Poppy helped by pulling her bra down, exposing her tits. I didn't waste any time; my mouth sucked on her brown stiff nipples.

"I want your cock, Sam! And I want it now!"

"Don't worry, my little sex bomb, you're going to get it, alright, but not here."

"What do you mean, not here, I need you now."

"Not in the car! You're going to get it across the bonnet, just like in the painting."

We both jumped out of the car, full of anticipation. The bonnet of the car was facing into the field, so if any passing cars were to pass, we were fairly well shielded. I pushed Sam against the bonnet of the car, undid his leather belt and took out his very erect penis. He was so wet; I suppose I had been teasing him for the past few hours. Sam's trousers dropped to the floor. I then took him in my mouth; he groaned in pleasure as I licked the end of his massive dick.

"Oh Poppy, you're so beautiful. I can't wait any longer; I have to have you now."

I lifted her up onto the bonnet, so she was facing me. Her bulging breasts sat proud, her legs akimbo; black boots up to her knees, then pink flesh. She had pulled her skirt up over her waist, exposing her neatly groomed pussy. I stood there, my pants around my ankles.

"Come on, Sam, what are you waiting for, I want your cock."

He grabbed me by the hips and pulled me on to his hard cock. It slipped into me, filling me with such pleasure,

"I told you I was going to give you a good shagging for teasing me," he said, slightly short of breath. I kept slipping down the shiny bonnet, but then I was shoved back up by the force of his thrust. Each time his balls banged against me as he brought me to orgasm. There was a creaking from the car suspension. I was panting for breath, I could see Sam was close, the veins in his neck enlarged,

"Where do you want it?" he said desperately.

I was there. My body was alive with electricity culminating in a thunderbolt of pure heaven in my stomach. Before I could relax, I needed to pleasure Sam. I slid off the bonnet, took him into my mouth, just in time to feel the powerful ejaculation, as he shot his load down my throat. He held me by the hair; the bandana fell to the floor, as he emptied his cum into my mouth. He tasted salty. I licked his cock clean before retiring into the car. After rearranging our clothes, we cuddled in the front seat,

"Sam, you really are wonderful, sex with you is amazing; and deep down, I'm falling for you in a big way."

"I feel the same way, Poppy, and I have to say, I think I've fallen in love with you!"

I felt my heart miss a beat. He did feel the same way about me, as I did for him; but to my horror, the scene around me started to ripple. The temperature dropped and a fog descended,

"Sam, I love you too."

I shouted in desperation. There was a flash of light, and I was on my way back to 1995.

I sat there in shock. The temperature in the car had dropped by at least 20 degrees, and there was a strange mist in the air. All I remember was Poppy telling me she loved me; then her vision seemed to shimmer, then a bright flash of light, and she was gone. I sat there for quite a while; the reality of what just happened slowly sinking in. I wondered if she was okay, and when I might see her again, I guess there was nothing I could do but wait for her return, whenever that might be.

Chapter 21
Ultimatum

I sat in the chair slightly confused. One minute I was in the arms of the man I was in love with, and it seemed that he also loved me. The next minute, I was back in the future, not knowing whether he had heard what I had shouted before I had been unceremoniously transported back to 1995. I had been back with Sam for several months, and it felt like I had been away for ages. I assumed that time here had stood still, and no time had elapsed at all. That was another reason why I needed a calendar in the attic room, so as soon as I arrived back, I could see at a glance how much time, if any, had passed. First thing first, was Roscoe okay? I ran down the stairs calling his name; no response, god. I hope he was okay. I bounded into the kitchen, and to my great relief, he was curled up in his basket asleep. I knelt down next to him; I had missed him terribly. It had been months since I had seen him, but to him, it had only been a few minutes since I had fed him. He looked up at me, nonchalantly, as if to say,

"Go away, I'm sleeping."

I made myself a nice cuppa and sat at the kitchen table, pondering about all sorts of stuff. I wondered why, when I travelled back into the past, the time had always moved on, sometimes by a small amount and other times by months. Was it dependent on how long I spent in 1995 before I went back through the 'Door'? That was something out of my control, as I had to wait for the 'Door' to unlock. Then I thought, if I went back upstairs now and waited for the door to open after only spending a short time here, would it return me to the car where Sam had just declared his love for me. The problem was I might be waiting for days for the 'Door' to open. After gulping down my tea, I decided to carry on as normal, allowing the 'Door' to dictate when I could travel back. One thing I could do to help me keep track was to go and buy a calendar, so I could see in an instant how long I'd been away.

"Come on, Roscoe, we are off to the shops."

Roscoe's ear's popped up, alert to the chance to get out. As soon as I opened the van door, he darted in, up on to the passenger seat with his paws leaning on the dash.

As I drove down the lanes, Roscoe was so excited, moving from the dash, to the side window, in a frenzy, not wanting to miss anything, occasionally yapping when we passed horses or sheep in the fields. I needed a few provisions, something for tea, dog food, a calendar, assorted tubes of watercolours and of course some wine. I parked in a pay and display car park. I bought a ticket for two hours—that would be plenty of time. I checked my pockets for doggy bags, just in case. I put Roscoe's lead on and set off. Roscoe was so well behaved, never pulling on the lead, just keeping my pace apart from the occasional stopping for a sniff of the remnants of another dog's visit to the numerous lampposts and corners of buildings that we passed on our way. I soon got all the provisions, apart from the calendar; most shops put out there calendars at Christmas. Eventually I found a shopkeeper prepared to look in his stockroom to see if he had any left over from the previous Christmas. Bingo, he found two; one with racing cars on and another with scenes from around the UK. I chose the latter.

"Thank you so much for looking. That was very kind of you. Can I have the one with UK scenes on please."

"Of course you can, my dear, no charge though, just put something in the charity box." next to the till was a red charity box, with a picture of the Air Ambulance on—a charity close to my heart. I slid a load of change into the slot; it must have been at least three pounds, which I thought was fare. Before we headed home, I passed a coffee shop. It had several free tables outside on the pavement, and also it was dog friendly as it had a bowl of drinking water next to the door, with a sign saying, 'Dogs Very Welcome'.

We sat at one of the tables near the shop entrance. I ordered cappuccino with a slice of coffee cake, and Roscoe had water. I couldn't resist his big brown eyes looking up at me, so I broke a bit of cake off and gave it to him. It was gone in a second. He licked his lips, readying himself for more.

"You're not having any more, you little scamp."

I rubbed his head; squeezing one of his ears. They were so floppy and nice to rub. As I straightened from leaning down, I glanced across the street, and I was sure I saw Simon. He had his back to me, and he was walking with a blonde woman; and I noticed they were holding hands. *It couldn't be, he was in London,* I told myself; then I just discarded the thought and got stuck into my coffee. After enjoying the coffee and cake and sitting there people watching, the time was about to run out on the parking ticket; so I gathered all the bags, and we set off to the car.

I arrived home to find a car parked at the top of the drive. I didn't recognise it; it was new and expensive. I parked the van and went across to the car. It was empty, apart from suit bags hanging in the back seats, one either side of the car. *Strange,* I thought to myself. I entered the house; the door was unlocked and sat at the kitchen table was Simon,

"Oh! It's you. You've changed your car then."

"Yes, it was part of the package, with the promotion."

The atmosphere was very frosty. Simon seemed on edge, and I wasn't that friendly.

"You said you wanted to talk, talk about selling the house, remember."

"I am not selling the house. I said I would find another way."

"Oh! Poppy, get real, how the hell are you going to find the money to buy my half share out. Have you sold a painting this year?"

My blood was boiling. He always tried to put me down, belittling me and my skill as an artist.

"I have actually, several paintings, not that it's any of your business."

"Poppy, it is my business. I need the money for our, I mean my place in London."

I was getting very upset now. He made me so angry, my voice was getting louder and louder, and it was upsetting the dog. Roscoe disappeared through the dog flap.

"I see! Our place, you mean you and the bit of stuff you've probably been knocking off for years."

"Poppy, calm down."

"Where is she then?"

"Who do you mean?"

"You know full well who I mean. I saw you and her in town today; and there are two lots of clothes hanging in your car. Do you think I'm stupid?"

Simon looked dumbstruck. His mouth open, not knowing what to say. "Well, what have you got to say for yourself, as the cat got your tongue; you're not normally stuck for words."

"Look Poppy, you have to accept it. I'm with someone else now. I won't be coming back to you."

I started to laugh. It was comical. Simon actually thought I still wanted him. As far as he was concerned, we had only split up a few weeks ago, but unknown to him, I had been with Sam for months, and I was well over him.

"What are you laughing for? I understand you must be missing me, and you think we still have a chance but…"

"Stop right there, you arrogant twat. First of all, I don't want you back; and no, I'm not missing you. In fact, I can't stand the sight of you."

"Why are you getting so upset then, Poppy?"

"Because I don't want to lose this place, and it's quite obvious that you've been seeing the bimbo for longer than you're admitting to."

Simon's face changed. I could tell he was lying, and why had he brought her with him if he was simply coming to discuss selling the house.

"Why have you brought her with you, and where do you think you're stopping; you're definitely not stopping in our bed tonight."

"Lucy wanted to visit her family while we were up this way."

"So she's local then; I thought you met her at your head office."

"No, she used to live near here, but she now works in London."

"So you were screwing her when you were with me; and for Christ's sake, why did you buy this place if you weren't in love with me."

Simon closed his eyes and held his head in both hands, sighing loudly. "Poppy I'm so sorry! I didn't mean for any of this to work out like it has. When Lucy started working for us as a rep, we were just good friends, but then things progressed when we were away at the sale's conference; and I just couldn't bring myself to telling you."

"Simon, you're so stupid. Now we have this mess to sort out, and I don't know where I'm going to get my share to pay you off, but I will!"

"Poppy, I can't wait forever. I will need it by the end of next month at the latest, sorry! If I don't put the deposit down, then I will lose the property I'm after."

"Do you think I'm bothered if you lose your love nest with the bimbo?"

"Will you stop calling her a bimbo, you don't even know her; she's quite intelligent actually."

"Simon, just get out of my site; you make me sick, and you can tell the bimbo to look out if I ever see her."

"Alright I'm going, but I need to get the rest of my things before I do; and Poppy, I will carry on paying my half of the mortgage but only until the end of next month."

He then got up from the table and went upstairs to get the rest of his things. I wasn't bothered at all. I was only thinking about where to get the money to pay him off. I had roughly seven weeks, or I could lose the 'Door'. I thought I might sit in the attic room while Simon gathered his things. I felt closer to Sam there, even though he had never been there. The unfinished painting of us having sex on the washing machine stood on the easel, waiting for me to finish it. I lay in my reclining chair, mulling over the past few months, trying to remember when it all went wrong. I could hear Simon opening and closing wardrobe doors downstairs. Our bedroom was literally underneath the attic room. He must have made several trips up and down the stairs; and about half an hour later, I heard Simon shout up the stairs,

"I'm finished down here; whatever's left, could you just box up, and I will collect when the house is sold."

I didn't answer. He was still convinced that I wouldn't be able to raise the money, but I would show him. I was absolutely determined. I heard the back door slam shut. I got up from the chair and looked out of the window, in time to see his car pull off the drive and roar down the lane. I had only been back in 1995 for a day, and I was so missing Sam. To take my mind off the situation, I thought I would complete the painting. I had decided to call it *In a Spin*. Just as I was signing the painting with the silver pen, there was a resounding clonk from the lock mechanism in the 'Door'.

Oh! My god, I was on my way back to 1987. "Sam, here I come," I shouted with glee. I ran to the 'Door', turned the handle and literally ran inside. As per usual, the door closed behind me; and in seconds, I was falling through the cold fog. The strange thing was, this time there was no light to guide me. It was pitch black, with an eerie sound of a distant snoring.

Chapter 22
Close Encounters

I was falling into darkness. Normally, there would be light; this time, just sound—the sound of snoring. I had arrived. It was very warm and cosy, the surface soft; my head was resting on what seemed like a pillow. It was dark, I couldn't see much. I soon realised I was in a bed with someone, and I was stark naked. Not to worry, it would be a nice surprise for Sam when he woke up. I reached over to touch him. *Oh! My God* His back was hairy; Sam wasn't hairy! This wasn't Sam!

I was in bed with Simon, how could this be, where was Poppy. If I bumped into her, it would all be over. I had to get out of here fast.

My eyes were slowly adjusting to the darkness. I could just make out shapes in the room. If Simon woke up, I didn't know what I would do. I lifted the quilt slowly and slid to the edge of the bed, dropping my bare foot to the carpet. Now with both feet on the floor, I stood up slowly. I tiptoed naked towards the bedroom door. I could just make out a dressing gown hanging on the back of the door. I slipped it on, it swamped me; it must have been Simon's. I didn't care; at least I wasn't naked now. If I could just escape out of the house, I turned the handle on the door and thought, *yes, I'm out of here*, but as I pulled the door open, there was a loud creaking from the hinges. Then from the darkness came,

"Is that you, Poppy? I thought you were stopping at Lavern's in Birmingham."

So that was why he was sleeping on his own. At least I wouldn't bump into myself. I didn't answer him. I spirited myself down the stairs as quiet as a mouse, arriving at the front door. It was locked, but believe it or not, I remembered that we always left the key on the coat hook next to the door.

I put the key in the lock and turned. The door was now unlocked; as I opened it, the freezing cold hair hit me in the face. I was bare foot. I couldn't go out in the freezing cold, with nothing on my feet; next to the entrance, there was a line of footwear. I grabbed a pair of pink wellies; they must have been mine; well, they fitted anyway, gosh! They were cold; I stepped outside and very carefully pulled the door closed behind me. Thankfully, I had successfully escaped without being caught. I ran down the street, wanting to put as much distance between me and Simon's place, as quickly as possible. It was tricky, as the path was like an ice rink. My brain was working overtime; the last time I was here it was summer; it definitely wasn't now. My pace slowed, in contrast to my heart. I hadn't realised how fast I'd been running. My chest was thumping, and you could see my breath condensing in the freezing air. How the hell I was going to explain my attire if I bumped into anyone; I didn't know! Then it dawned on me, lots of the houses I was passing had wreaths hanging on their front doors, and some had Christmas trees in their front gardens. It was sometime in December. I was praying it was December 1987.

It was obviously the middle of the night; I guessed maybe 3:00 a.m. There was no one about apart from the occasional tomcat on the prowl, which was good for me. Sam's flat was about a mile away from where I was, and it wasn't easy walking in wellies. I was doing quite well negotiating the streets, but I was absolutely freezing. Then I heard a car coming along the road behind me. I carried on walking, hoping that it would just pass, but it didn't. I heard it slow down; then it pulled up next to me. I ignored it; then I heard the window wind down. I turned around to see a police car, with the bobby in the passenger side, leaning his head out of the window,

"Are you alright, young lady, off home are we."

"Yes officer, not far now, thanks for asking though."

"It's just that you seem to be in your night clothes, are you sure you're alright."

I had to think quick.

"I've been to a pyjama party, and I didn't think it would be this cold walking home."

The officer laughed, said something to the driver, then said,

"As it's Christmas, we will drop you home if you like, you look perished; but don't tell our sergeant. We're not supposed to pick up passengers unless we're taking them back to the nick."

The bobby jumped out of the car, opened the back door and said,

"Get in then, you're under arrest."

They both started laughing, and so did I. I don't know why!

"Only joking, it's been a long night. Anyway, what's the address where you want dropping?"

I panicked; I could remember the number of the flat, but my mind went blank, and I couldn't for the life of me think of the name of the road where Sam's flat was.

"No worries, I will direct you," I said quickly, recovering from my embarrassment.

I'd never been in a police car before; it was incredibly warm. There were bags of shopping on the back seat. I suppose they were only human the same as us. The officer who was driving was about in his late 30s; the other one a lot younger. I'd say about 25, and as it happens, quite cute.

"If you go straight up this road for about a quarter of a mile, and then turn left at the Running Horse Pub. Do you know it?"

"We certainly do, they provide us with plenty of work on a Friday night."

"It's a bit rough then."

"It's all the silly offers they have on drink; once the lads have a few sherbets, they want to fight the world."

We turned left at the pub,

"Okay, follow this road until you come to the chip shop; then turn right, and I'm just down there on the right. Drop me by the phone box if you like."

A couple of minutes later, the car pulled up. I thanked the officers for their kindness, wished them a Merry Christmas and got out into the freezing cold. They returned the festive greetings and went off into the night. I was outside the flats; everything was in darkness, and there was a deathly silence. I walked around the rear to where the car park was. I remembered the key to the flat was hidden under the base of a stone cat that was sited near the garden entrance to the flats. Sure enough, when I lifted the cat, the plastic box we had secreted the key in was still there—much to my relief. I retrieved the key and repositioned the cat, then quietly alighted the staircase to Sam's flat.

I have to admit I was a little nervous about entering the flat, but also excited to see Sam. The problem was, I had been away at least six months; and for all I knew, Sam might have moved on. I arrived at the door number ten. There was a small light built into the door buzzer, so it illuminated where to put the key. I pushed the key into the lock and turned. Well, I tried to turn the key, but it was solid. The dead lock was on, so it meant there was someone in the flat, but I would have to ring the bell. I pressed the bell, hoping it wouldn't make too much noise. All I could hear was the sound of a dog barking inside the flat, which was weird, as Sam didn't have a dog. I waited for a minute, then I saw a light shine through the spyglass in the door; someone was coming to the door. I heard the lock turn and a chain being undone; then the door opened. Sam stood there in his dressing gown, with a massive grin on his face,

"Poppy, I can't believe your back. I missed you so much."

He grabbed me with both arms and pulled me to his chest, hugging the life out of me. He then kissed me so passionately, my legs went wobbly. Sam then started laughing; he took a step back and said,

"What the hell have you got on; you must be freezing to death."

"Well Sam, do you think I could come in."

"I'm so sorry, silly me, come on in, Poppy."

Once I was inside the flat, Sam locked up; then he made some hot tea. "Shall we drink it in bed, Poppy, then you can bring me up to speed on the latest fashion."

"Very funny, I'm sure; let's go to bed, and I will tell you all about it."

I abandoned the dressing gown and was stood there naked, apart from the wellies, when Sam said,

"Very nice, very fetching."

"Oh! Aren't you the funny one?"

I quipped as I jumped into the bed after we finished our tea. I started filling Sam in on the night's events. He couldn't believe I'd returned from the future and ended up in Simon's bed; then having such a narrow escape getting out of the house. He then understood why I was wearing a very large dressing gown and pink wellies. His eyes widened when he heard about the police car.

"Absolutely brilliant, Poppy, coming up with the pyjama party idea, you must have been thinking on your wellies! I mean your feet."

"You're such a funny man, 'Devere'."

We then hugged each other really hard, as if to make sure we couldn't be parted. Sam then kissed me on the lips, then so sincerely, he said, "Poppy Day, I love you so much, you best not leave me again or else…"

"Or else what, Mr Devere."

"Or else, you get a good spanking of your arse to start with."

"That sounds rather nice, not much of a deterrent if you ask me."

"Oh, we have a sadist in our midst, do we?"

We both laughed. My head was on Sam's chest, not a hair in sight. Then I thought about hairy Simon, and what he might think when he woke up in the morning. Thinking back, I vaguely remember the conversation I had when I returned from Laverne's the next day, all those years ago. Simon insisted that I had been in the bedroom the night before, and then there was the mystery of his missing dressing gown, which he seemed to go over the top about. It was just a dressing gown after all, wasn't it? Then when I challenged him for not locking the front door, that added even more intrigue, he insisted that he had locked the door before he went to bed. Then came the intruder theory, maybe someone broke in and stole his dressing gown. If I remember right, I did, at the time, wonder where my pink wellies had disappeared to.

My mind then flicked back to reality. I was in the arms of a lovely man, naked and wanting. Sam had left the bedside lamps on, allowing me to see the man I loved.

"Sam, remember when I disappeared from the car, the first time you ever saw me travel back."

"Yes, it's etched in my mind, forever. I certainly didn't have any doubts about you being a time traveller after that."

"Well, as I was about to disappear I shouted something, did you hear what I said."

"No! What did you shout!"

He smiled as he said it. He had heard me, he just wanted me to say it again.

"Sam Devere, I love you with all my heart."

"Ditto."

I couldn't believe she was back. The last six months had been difficult to say the least. I'd missed her so much, and I had doubted that she would ever reappear, but she was back. She was in my bed, and she loved me; what else could I wish for. She smelt divine, her skin as soft as a peach, her hair as silky as silk itself. I kissed the nape of her neck, licking her skin up to her ear. I breathed into her ear,

"I love You, Poppy Day."

Her open moist mouth married with mine; our tongues entwined as if we were one.

"Sam! Make love to me please."

My manhood was ahead of the game, already proud and wet, looking to please. My fingers found Poppy; wetter than me, her clitoris swollen, awaiting my tongue. Her legs opened wide, allowing me in; she purred with pleasure as I licked her clit. She tasted of nectar—the elixir of life.

Sam was such an attentive lover, his tongue darting into my grateful slit, bringing me ever closer to orgasm. His attention moved to my stomach, kissing it ever so delicately, while tenderly stroking my arms; then my stiff nipples were the subject of his next endeavour, sucking them both in turn. I was desperate for him to have me.

I couldn't wait any longer. I had to be inside her. I rose up, looked into her eyes, cupped her buttocks with both hands and pulled her onto my erect penis.

He entered me with such force, filling me with such joy; he felt hot as he repeatedly rammed his penis up me, filling my pussy full.

"Come on big boy, give me more."

I shouted out, scared he might stop, but there was no danger of that, "Poppy I'm coming; sorry, I can't hold on any longer."

We were both out of breath, panting like we had just run a marathon. Sam's thrusting slowed as he neared the ultimate goal; he was close to cumming, as was I. The power of orgasm ran through my body, gripping me with such an overwhelming tirade of emotion. I had tears in my eyes.

I felt the rush deep in my balls. There was no going back now; my groin aching, the hot cum speeding its way into Poppy. As my ejaculation exploded from the end of my penis, I lowered down to kiss Poppy. Our lips wet, our bodies sweaty as I collapsed, our bodies coming together in a heap on the creaking bed. It was the early hours of the night; and after our escapades in bed, we were both spent. We lay on our backs, holding hands. Sam switched off the light, and we drifted off into a deep satisfying sleep.

The next morning, although Sam should have been at work, he phoned in saying he had a family emergency. He had missed me so much, he wanted to spend some time with me, which I greatly appreciated. I heard him shout from the kitchen,

"Red or brown sauce on your bacon sandwich?"

I bobbed my head around the door and said,

"Red on one half and brown on the other if you don't mind."

"No probs, Poppy, come and sit down; I need to talk to you."

Just before sitting down at the kitchen table, I glanced at the calendar. I had to fold several pages back before I spotted the letter P written across a date. It read the 10th of June 1987.

"What's the date today, Sam?"

"Poppy, it's a very special day today."

"Oh! Yes, and what's that?"

"It's my birthday today. December the 18th."

"No! You're joking, you're not joking, are you. Oh! Sam, come here."

Poppy kissed me, then sang Happy Birthday.

"Sam, I will bake you a cake later, and I will cook you dinner tonight."

"Okay! That's fantastic. Oh! Why did you want to know the date?"

"Sam, did you realise I've been away six months, and you still waited for me."

Sam just looked at me, bewildered,

"Poppy, why wouldn't I wait for you; I love you. If you look at the calendar, you will see a tick on every day you weren't here. I was counting the days and now your back."

The breakfast was wonderful; sitting together, just like a normal couple, chatting away and drinking loads of tea.

"You said you wanted to talk to me about something, Sam."

"Well, I've been thinking, I'm doing okay at work, the business is growing, so I thought it might be a good time to move to a bigger place and wondered if you would help me. I realise you might disappear occasionally, but you always come back; what do you think."

"Sam, that's fantastic news, I would love to. Can we start looking today?"

"We sure can, partner."

"One other thing, Sam. When I rang the bell yesterday, all I could hear was a barking dog."

Sam started laughing; then explained!

"Well, Poppy, I've always wanted a dog, but as I live in a flat, first of all, it's not allowed; and secondly, it wouldn't be fair to the dog. So when we find a house with a garden, I can get a dog."

"It sounds good to me. We had better find a house, pronto,"

I said with glee, as this meant Sam was serious about us, and it meant our future was more secure.

Chapter 23
City Slickers

After breakfast, I got dressed in my own clothes, jeans and a thick jumper, which we had bought from the charity shop. Then I had a horrible thought. When I came back this time, I was naked, so my trusty bag with all my things in did not appear. The next second, Sam walked into the bedroom, "Oh! By the way, Poppy, when you disappeared last time, the strange thing was, after you were gone, I sat there for a while in the car, when I noticed your shoulder bag on the floor."

"Really! I was only just thinking about that, how weird."

Well, that was good news but strange. Previously when I travelled, everything I had with me disappeared. Anyway, the good news was my trusty bag was safe. I could now look forward to the day with Sam on the hunt for a new house. During the morning, we visited several estate agents, collecting loads of house details. We also managed to see a couple of houses, but they were so run down or overlooked or overpriced that we thought we would stop and have lunch.

"Poppy, I think we are going to have to widen our search area, maybe as far as Toddminster." Alarm bells started ringing in my head; this area was near to the Ducklands, and I had never told Sam exactly where I lived; because if ever there was a connection, it might change the future, and it would destroy all of our plans.

"Don't give up that easily, Sam. It would mean a longer commute for work; and you wouldn't be able to pop home for lunch, and I would miss that little treat."

"You're probably right, you normally are, okay let's carry on regardless."

Sam carried on looking through the piles of details on the table. I was relieved to say the least.

After lunch, we were reinvigorated. We both had a sense of purpose and got stuck into the challenge. While driving back towards Sam's flat, I noticed a new development being built.

"Sam, pull in there, it's worth a look."

We pulled up to the site office car park and went into the show home sales office. A very bubbly lady, wearing a dark blue two-piece suit, a tight pencil skirt with three inch high heels; her neck adorned with a large pearl necklace. She approached us; her perfume was over-powering. She was full of herself, and in a false posh voice, she introduced herself, "Good afternoon, I'm Pamela, can I be of any assistance; I'm the sales manager for 'Pawson Homes'."

Sam spoke,

"Hello, I'm Sam Devere, and this is my partner Poppy."

I had a lovely warm feeling in my stomach when Sam said I was his partner. It made me feel happy and secure.

"We are looking for a three or four bedroom house, with a decent-sized garden, do you have anything available."

In the middle of the office was a large glass box; inside was a model layout of the site. Each model house had a number printed on its roof, "It's your lucky day, believe it or not. We have had a cancellation in today on a four-bed property; the only problem is, you won't get to pick the finish, as the original buyers picked the finish months ago."

"What do you mean the finish?"

I said, curiously. Pamela went into her selling mode, explaining that the finish meant the choice of tiles, the carpets and curtains and the style of kitchen. The good news was the price was reduced due to the original buyers, having to forfeit their deposit. When we looked at the choice on the finish, the colours picked were pretty neutral. The carpets were mottled creams and browns, so they wouldn't show the marks and the kitchen doors had a natural wooden finish. The thing was would we both like the house.

"Okay Pamela, shall we view the house to see if it's what we're looking for."

Pamela offered us the keys and pointed to the house through the window,

"Take as long as you need; just bring back the keys when you've finished."

We walked around the house with an open mind. We kept looking at each other to see if we were on the same page; we definitely were. We walked back to the sales office. Pamela was waiting for us, with a big beaming smile on her face,

"What did you think, are you interested?"

I was just about to say how lovely it was when Sam piped in,

"It's alright but not what we really wanted." I looked at him with a puzzled look on my face. I thought he loved it. We were just going through the door when Pamela shouted,

"We may be able to throw in the white goods if that would help. Fridge, Dishwasher, Washing Machine."

"Thank you, Pamela, but the garden is a little small, and the en suite in the master bedroom was cramped. I feel the price is a little ambitious. I'm afraid it's not for us."

"Mr Devere, I'm sure we can compromise on the price; what would you think if we shaved 5% of the bottom line."

Sam went quiet for quite a while, then he replied,

"I will tell you what. If you can stretch the compromise to 10% plus, what you've just offered I might be interested!"

Sam then just thrust his hand forward and went dead quiet. Pamela stared into Sam's eyes, Sam stared back; there was no sound. I nearly said something but decided against it. It seemed like forever before the silence was broken. It wasn't Sam who spoke first; Pamela grasped Sam's hand and said,

"Deal, Mr Devere, you have a deal."

It was incredible the way Sam negotiated that deal, and it was Sam who got what he wanted. Pamela acted smug, but she had nothing to feel smug about. I was so proud of Sam but also excited. The house was perfect, and I knew we would be very happy there. After Sam signed loads of paperwork, we jumped into the car and headed off. Sam looked at me and said,

"Did we just buy a house?"

"Sam, I think you did."

"Poppy, we are a team now, we just bought a house."

That made me feel really special; Sam confirming that we were a team.

The rest of the journey back home, we spent laughing and joking. We were so happy and couldn't wait to move into the new house. The garden was massive, and it backed onto woodland. It would be perfect for the new dog.

"Poppy, I have to ask you a favour."

"Sam, absolutely anything for you, what can I do?"

"The thing is, we have just bought a new house, but we have to sell the flat first. Do you think you can work your magic on my bachelor flat, so someone might like to buy it."

"Of course I will. Give me a few days, and you will have offers coming out of your ears."

A few minutes later, we pulled into the car park at the flat. We both jumped out; I ran ahead towards the entrance,

"Come on slow, coach. I'll race you to the front door."

I didn't hear footsteps behind me, so I turned, but Sam wasn't following me. He was stood near one of the many garages.

"Poppy, come here, I've got something to show you."

I was intrigued. I walked over to him. He was stood in front of a blue garage door; it had the number 10 on it,

"You want to show me your garage door."

I said a little puzzled,

"Not exactly, I wanted to show you what's inside."

"More like you want to have sex in your garage, you dirty boy."

Sam opened the up and over door, revealing a bright red Ford Fiesta car. I looked at Sam as if to say "well, why do you have another car in your garage".

"Well, Poppy, what do you think. I know it's not new, but my sister was selling it, and I thought you might need transport; and I actually bought it for your birthday, but then you disappeared."

I was absolutely gob smacked. I remembered Sam saying he had organised something for my birthday, but then, after going back to the future for six months, I had forgotten all about it.

"Sam, it's fantastic, it's so shiny, can I drive it."

"Of course, you can drive it. I've put it on my insurance, with you as a named driver. The only problem is, if you get pulled for speeding, the summons will go to where your licence is registered to, and the 1987 Poppy will get the fine."

I thought about it for a while; then realised, I couldn't ever remember getting a fine through the post, so I assumed it would be alright,

"It will be okay, Sam. My licence is clean now, and it always was."

Sam looked at me as if to say "goody two shoes".

"Here are the keys, Poppy; shall we have a spin around the block."

I flung my arms around him and snogged his face off,

"Sam, you're such a wonderful man. I love you, love you, love you."

I was so excited; more excited than when Simon had bought me the van. I squeezed into the car; garages are never really wide enough to open the car doors. Even with this being a small car, it was a struggle. It was lovely to drive; it had a CD player, electric windows, even a leather steering wheel.

I was so impressed; she had never driven this car before. She had jumped in, found the controls in seconds and was off. There was no stopping her; she was so capable, she was a breath of fresh air, totally different to previous girlfriends, and I loved the ground she walked on. After a quick spin around the block, I parked up in the car park,

"What a day, Simon; first we buy a house, then you give me a car. It can't get much better than that."

"Well, Poppy, there's one more surprise."

I looked at him. I had no idea what was coming next,

"I don't think I can take any more surprises."

"Well, the good news is, you don't have to cook dinner for my birthday tonight."

"Why, are we going out for dinner, the pub in the country, maybe."

"Yes, we are going out for dinner, but not the country pub. We are going for dinner in a posh hotel in London; it's my company's Christmas party tomorrow night, so I thought we could go down a night early and celebrate my birthday in style, what do you think!"

"Oh! Sam, life's never boring with you, is it. It's terribly exciting; I can't wait. Oh Sam, what will I wear. If it's that posh, and I'm nervous about meeting all your work colleagues."

"Calm down, Poppy; first of all, you have something you can wear to a restaurant tonight. Then tomorrow, after we have breakfast in bed at the hotel, we can go shopping and buy you a party frock, so chill out. We need to pack an overnight bag and get on the road, it's already three o'clock."

It didn't take long to throw a few things into a couple of bags. Simon supplied the brown leather bags, one slightly bigger that the other. His suit for the evening soirée went into a very plush suit carrier, green in colour with a gold zip.

"Poppy, if I drop the bags down to the car, would you put the kettle on, so we can have a brew before we head off."

"Great idea, I'm on it."

Sam disappeared with the bags. I popped the kettle on; and while I was waiting for it to boil, I thought I would just scoot around and tidy up a little. In the bedroom, I noticed the dressing gown I had worn the night before. Simon's dressing gown was still on the floor where I had discarded it. I could never give it back, so I thought I would wash it and take it to a charity shop. Some poor devil would appreciate it. As I picked it up, it must have been upside down, because something fell out of the pocket. Strange because I hadn't felt anything in the pockets on my fretful journey back to Sam's flat the night before. I bent down to retrieve it; it was a crinkled piece of paper. I unfolded it; it was a small square receipt. At the top was the name of the business The Coffee Cabin. The receipt was for one cappuccino, one latte and one slice of walnut cake, then the price

£2.75. Weird, because I had never been to that coffee shop, and I certainly didn't like Walnut cake. I then noticed the date; it read the 9th of December 1987, just over a week ago. It couldn't have been Simon's receipt; he wasn't keen on coffee shops. He always said, "I could have a cheaper cup at home." So I decided to put it in the bin. As it fell from my fingers towards the bin, it seemed to flutter as if in slow motion. As it fell, it turned, and I noticed writing on the reverse side of the printed side. It landed print side up. I bent down to retrieve it from the bin. I turned it over, and in blue ink it read,

Simon,
Call me! Or visit me.
17 Acacia Close,
Chatterton,
Worcs
Tel. 0253 7769
Lucy xx

I fell backwards onto the bed, holding the receipt in my hand. I sat there in shock, seeing that name, Lucy. It couldn't be the same Lucy, surely. He said he hadn't known her long, that it had only been a few months; but if this was the same Lucy, he had lied, and he had known her for years. I thought we had been happy and settled in 1987, but why had he been in a coffee shop, which he hated, with this Lucy, if he wasn't messing around behind my back. My mind was in overdrive, thinking back over the years. There had been times when Simon had been missing for a while, or had been vacant. When I'd asked him where he'd been, I never ever thought anything sinister might be going on. Maybe it was a different Lucy; and okay, he might have had a coffee with her, and that had been the end of it. That must be the case, because I would have known, wouldn't I! I heard the front door open; Sam was back from the car,

"Are you ready, Pops?"

I smiled; he'd never called me Pops before. I slipped the piece of paper into my pocket. I didn't want any secrets from him, but the less he knew about Simon and the future, the less chance of haltering the passage of time.

"Yes, I'm ready and waiting, birthday boy."

We quickly drank our tea, locked the flat and got in the car.

The journey down to the Big Smoke, as people called it, went quickly; the conversation never stopped. It was a cold day, but at least it wasn't raining. We had the radio on low, but then turned it up every time a tune came on that we liked. Sam was trying to fill me in on his colleagues. There was Bob the senior engineer, always playing jokes on people; then there was Pete the perv, always flirting with the girls. "Can't wait to meet him, Sam; see what chat up lines he's got."

Sam just laughed; no sign of jealousy at all. Simon would have retorted, "You keep away from him," always the control freak. After going through most of the local staff and all their fables, Sam explained that the London office had about 60 staff, so the party would be quite lively.

The trip down took two hours, including a short pit stop for a quick coffee and a toilet break, and then we were in the gridlock of the city; we had arrived at rush hour on a Friday night. There were lines of stationary traffic, red double decker buses churning out plumes of black putrid smoke, and what seemed like thousands of black Cabs; their brakes screeching, each time they slowed for the inevitable red traffic lights, dotted along the road. Sam took it all in his stride, not stressing at all; just taking in the sights, with the occasional short commentary on buildings he knew. It was so exciting. You can't beat a bustling city, especially when most of the buildings were covered in sparkling Christmas lights, all competing for the gaze of passers-by, busy in their mission to get the best bargains for their loved ones.

While driving down to London, the feeling inside me was amazing. With Poppy sat next to me, I felt the happiest I had ever been. We jelled so well, being with her was effortless; and to top all that, I would be sharing a bed with her tonight. She put her hand on my thigh and started rubbing the inside of my leg. I could feel an erection coming on. I looked at her and smiled, she said,

"You just wait until I get you in that hotel bedroom and give you your birthday present."

I couldn't wait, I knew what she meant; she had that naughty look in her eyes. The trip down went without incident, and the traffic was minimal. Poppy got quite excited when we reached the city; she kept pointing to things.

"Look at that, wow! Simon can you see that, aargh, look at the building lit up in green. Wow. My! Look at the size of that Christmas tree."

We were passing Trafalgar Square. The Christmas tree was massive. It must have been 30 feet tall and very impressive. There were thousands of people milling around; all we needed now was snow.

"How much longer before we arrive at the hotel."

"It's just beyond the next set of traffic lights; a couple of minutes, and we will be there."

I hadn't got a clue where we were stopping. Sam kept it as a surprise, but when we pulled up next to the entrance. I was delighted; the lit up sign read 'The Hilton'; and in smaller writing underneath, it read Hyde Park. At the front entrance stood the doormen, dressed in burgundy coats, braided in gold, topped with splendid top hats boasting the emblem of the hotel. They were there to greet and assist the visitors to the hotel; but as the car park to the hotel was underground, we had to drive past them. We went down quite a steep ramp to the very cramped and badly lit concrete car park. I was glad Sam was driving, as the parking spaces were very tight, and dotted all over the place was concrete pillars.

"Sam, I'm so excited. I've never stopped in a Hilton Hotel before; it must be very expensive."

"You're worth it, Poppy, only the best for my girl.

Besides, the company is paying the bill," Sam laughed out loud. After Sam had parked, we then realised just how small the spaces were. It was difficult to open the doors wide enough to climb out. It was easier for me being smaller, but I could hear Sam cursing under his breath, trying to extricate his backside through the gap.

"Are you okay, tubs?"

"Very funny, Poppy."

We eventually extricated our bags and suit bag from the car and made our way to the lift, which took us up to the opulent reception. There were luxurious soft furnishings scattered around the spacious gold-themed entrance hall, with massive wall hangings depicting winter scenes. The background music was Christmas-themed. Over, in the far corner stood the most beautifully decorated Christmas tree I have ever seen, adorned with hundreds of twinkling white lights,

"Oh Sam, isn't it just beautiful. I absolutely love this place."

"And I absolutely love you, Poppy. Shall we get booked into our room, then we can have a look around the hotel facilities."

We stood at the reception; the lady had a lovely smile, she asked,

"Can I help you, sir?"

I guessed she was Italian from her accent.

"Yes, I have a room booked for two nights."

"And the name, sir."

"Oh yes, of course, Devere, Mr And Mrs Devere."

I looked at Sam, surprised; he looked back with such a cheeky grin and said,

"Yes, we're here to celebrate my birthday, and my wife insists on the best hotels."

"Well sir, I'm sure your wife deserves the best, I think she will love the room you're in. It's on the 17th floor, and it looks over Hyde Park."

Sam thanked the receptionist, taking the key from the desk. As we turned, the porter was there,

"This way, sir, allow me."

He grabbed the bags and headed for the lifts.

"You're first time staying with us," he asked, trying to be friendly.

"It is for my wife, Poppy. I've been here before; though, it's been a few years since the last visit."

The porter pressed the button for our floor, then turned, thrusting his hand towards Sam,

"I'm James, yours."

"I'm Sam, and this is…"

Before he could finish, James said,

"And this is, Poppy. Very nice to be of service, and I hope you enjoy your stay."

The lift doors opened. They were very elegant, covered in brass filigree, with a dark blue glass infill. We stepped into the spacious car. I looked up to see a reflection of the three of us, in the mirrored ceiling. I noticed that James had a bald patch on top of his head. The lift was so quiet but also slow; it seemed to take ages to reach the 17th floor. The doors opened, James stepped ahead, carrying the bags.

"Follow me, guys; it's just up here on the left."

He opened the door, placed the bags inside the doorway and turned to leave. Sam reached into his pocket and brought out a note. He pressed it into James hand and thanked him for his service; then we were on our own. I ran to the window to take in the view, but to my surprise, it was pitch black outside. I would have to wait till morning to see the view. I turned my attention to the room,

"Sam, will you just look at that."

There was a massive sumptuous double bed, with loads of puffed up pillows stacked up against the leather headboard. I took a running dive onto the bed, like a silly child. I couldn't resist it,

"Come on Sam, try the bed, it's so comfy."

Sam jumped on, molesting me,

"Come here, you gorgeous creature. I can't wait any longer."

"You're joking, Sam. I need to check out the rest of the room."

Sam laughed, then replied,

"Alright, you fill your boots, and I will make the tea."

I then checked out the bathroom. Wow! A massive free standing bath, with gold taps; his and hers sinks, with a mirror that covered the whole wall, luxurious towels, and of course, on the back of the door hung two white dressing gowns, with the hotel emblem embroidered on the lapels.

"Sam, you've got to see this."

I shouted excitedly, but he seemed a bit blasé about the whole thing. I guess he was used to it, and he had stopped here before.

"You like the room then."

Sam said, sarcastically,

"You bet, Sam, it's the best hotel I've ever been in."

At the other end of the room was a three-piece suite, a coffee table and a large television. It was amazing.

"Poppy! Tea up! Chocolate hobnobs or short bread slices."

"Chocolate hobnobs, all day long."

We sat and ate our biscuits, washed down with tea; then, I turned my attention to the birthday boy.

Sam was sat on the sofa, leaning back relaxed. I knelt in front of him, snuggling in between his legs. He looked down at me and smiled. I think he had an incline that my motives weren't exactly innocent. I rubbed his growing cock through his denim jeans,

"What have we here then, Mr Devere; you seem to be pleased to see me."

"I'm always pleased to see you, Mrs Devere," he said laughing out loud,

"You didn't mind, did you."

"There's nothing wrong with a bit of intrigue."

I replied. I undid his black leather belt, pulled it through its carriers and threw it on the floor; then I slowly pulled down his zipper. He was wearing white cotton boxers; the bulge of his swelling tool stretching the cotton. I released the pressure by whipping down his boxers. He now sat there with his jeans and boxers around his ankles; one thing for sure, he wouldn't be able to run away. His cock stood proud; he boasted a jacket. I always thought it was better than a circumcised cock. I pulled the skin back, and the juices were already flowing from the pink hole at the end of penis. I held him firmly in my right hand, bent closer and spit onto the head of his erect rod. Sam pushed his head back into the lush sofa and exclaimed,

"Poppy, you're such a dirty bitch, suck me off now or else…"

"Sam, remember who's the boss. I'm in control, not you; now sit back and take it like a man."

I took him in my mouth. I have to say, it was quite a mouthful. Sam squirmed a little, in pleasure of course.

She was amazing; one minute, quite the lady, but then as soon as she was aroused, there was no stopping her. She absolutely loved sex and unselfishly loved to give pleasure. I asked myself, had I died and gone to heaven. The image of her shiny red lipstick lips, around the end of my dick, sent me wild; there couldn't be a better feeling. Then the *pièce de résistance*, she took off her jumper, unclipped her black lacy bra, then squeezed her full breasts around my throbbing cock,

"Come on Sam, fuck my tits now."

The juice from my wanting cock glistened on her milky white breasts. Each time she lifted her breasts with my cock sandwiched between them, she licked the end. It was just too much for any man to take. In fact, I couldn't take any more.

"Poppy, you're going to get it all over your face if you don't stop."

"Stop! You must be joking. I want your cum all over my tits or else!"

That was the catalyst. As soon as she said tits, it was all over. I felt the avalanche of hot cum speeding from my balls and out of my cock, like an erupting volcano.

"Happy birthday, Sam. That's a good boy; give me all you've got."

Sam seemed to go into a spasm. His body went rigid, his mouth open, groaning in pleasure as hot spunk shot out with great force all over my breasts. I just loved watching him come.

"Poppy, how about you, how about I pleasure you."

"No, it's alright Sam, I just wanted to do something for your birthday; anyway, there's always later."

She kissed me on the lips and said she loved me, picked up her discarded clothing, then ran towards the bathroom shouting,

"Let's try out that massive bath. I'll start running it while you get yourself together."

Chapter 24
Flaked Out

"Poppy, the table's booked for 7.30; it's now 6:50."

Poppy had been in the bathroom. She erupted into the bedroom; her arms in the air whilst pirouetting to show off her dress. It was the dress we bought in the charity shop all those months ago.

"Sam, what do you think? Will I do?"

"You certainly will, you look amazing; but, you will have to wear a coat because the restaurant is about a ten minute walk from the hotel."

"Okay no problem! What's the restaurant called?"

"Giuseppe's, arrgghh, and now I've spoiled the surprise."

"Why have you."

"Well, it's not going to be a Chinese or Mexican, is it; with a name like 'Giuseppe's', it has to be Italian; and now you know, so I've spoiled the surprise."

"Bellissimo, I love Italian food. Oh! I can't wait, come on let's get off, I'm starving."

I helped Poppy on with her coat!

"Gratsie, signore."

I laughed; she was such a card.

"I'll race you to the lift, Devere."

She darted off, like a hare out of its trap; she was so competitive.

"Come on then, slow, coach."

She shouted excitedly. Even though I was fit, I didn't stand a chance; before I had put the door key in my pocket, she was almost at the lift door. The people coming up the corridor the other way must have thought she had been on the hard stuff, but she didn't have a care in the world; bidding them a good evening as they brushed past her. I heard the chime emanate from the lift, announcing that it had arrived. Poppy had a wide grin on her face,

"Oh, you've decided to join me then."

"Oh, very funny, Poppy. I had to squeeze past those people; it slowed me down."

"Yeah sure."

We entered the lift. There were already people in there. We were squashed at the front. Poppy in front of me; her nose quite close to the doors. I had my arms wrapped around her body. A man in the other corner stood next to the elevator buttons, piped up!

"Which floor would you like?"

"Oh! The lobby please, thank you!"

The lift was slow and very creaky; especially as it was full of bodies, everyone trying not to make eye contact. I nuzzled into Poppy's hair; it smelt of peaches. I kissed her gently. Then to my horror, the little monkey reached backwards with her hand, grabbing my cock through my trousers. I withdrew in shock, not expecting the advance and pushed my bum into the lady behind, thinking on my feet. I exclaimed,

"I'm so sorry, my dear. I had a right twinge in my back."

I heard Poppy snigger,

"It's alright, no problem, no harm done."

The lady replied. I whispered into Poppy's ear,

"You wait till I get you outside."

"Promises, promises, I can't wait."

Then the chime from the lift sounded; a slight bump as the lift car came to a halt, a few seconds delay, then the doors opened and a melee of people came into view. We all spilled out, making the situation even worse. It was obviously a very busy time in reception. Above the noise of excited conversation, you could just hear the Christmas music in the background. Someone called out,

"Sam, Poppy, good evening! Would you like me to get you a cab?"

It was James from concierge—the man who had taken us to our room earlier. How he remembered all the guests' names was a mystery. I was terrible with names, good with faces. Sam spoke to him,

"You're so kind James, but we're walking; the restaurant is literally ten minutes' walk."

"I will get you an umbrella, just a second."

He ran off in the direction of the Concierge desk and was back in a jiffy, "Is it raining heavily, then, James."

Sam asked!

"Oh! It's not raining, sir. It's been snowing heavily for at least an hour."

Poppy squealed with excitement,

"I love the snow. Come on, Sam, let's get outside and see."

I'd never seen anyone get so excited over a bit of snow. We both thanked James for his help and headed for the door. We pushed our way through the revolving doors. Well, what greeted us was such a surprise. When we had arrived earlier, nothing; now everything was covered in fluffy white snow. Large flakes of snow were falling all around; it was so pretty.

"Sam, isn't it just so beautiful, don't you just love it."

I have to admit, Sam didn't seem as excited as I was. He stood there holding the brolly, looking at me, as if I had lost the plot.

"Poppy, I had no idea that you loved the snow so much. Shall we make tracks; I'm looking forward to some food."

I nuzzled into Sam under the brolly, he felt warm and safe, and I don't think I had felt this happy in ages. It took approximately ten minutes to walk to the restaurant, but I loved every minute of it. Sam slowed up, saying,

"Here we are."

I looked up at the rather grand frontage, in large golden letters, the name 'Giuseppe's', set inside a Roman-looking roof section, being supported either side by Corinthian pillars.

"Sam, it looks rather posh, and I bet it's expensive."

"Don't worry yourself, Poppy. It is my birthday after all."

We were approached by a person dressed in black—a bit like a bouncer but a lot friendlier,

"*Buon giorno.*"

"Hey *ciao.*"

Sam, being the more confident out of the two of us replied,

"Good evening, we have a reservation booked for 7:30. The name is Devere."

"My name is Gerardo Come on in. You must be freezing."

He held the door open,

"Ladies first."

As I walked through the door, I felt the warm air float over my grateful body. The doorman took the umbrella from Sam and beckoned him towards me. He then took our coats and handed them to a person at the entrance to a cloakroom. I tried to straighten up my dishevelled clothes, and when I looked down at our feet, I was shocked. Unfortunately we weren't wearing the right footwear for the weather, and the snow had marked our shoes, with what looked like a white tide mark across the black leather. I glanced at Sam, then averted my gaze towards our shoes. Sam just laughed,

"Not to worry, our feet will be under the table. No one will see them."

I thought to myself, *does anything ever faze this guy.*

Gerardo raised his hand in the air and clicked his fingers. Within seconds, a second person was on the scene. This time, a young, dark-haired, beautiful young lady. Gerardo whispered something into her ear; she turned towards us and spoke in a deep Italian accent,

"Welcome, welcome, my name is Sofia. I will be looking after you both tonight, please follow me, your table is ready."

She walked quite quickly, and to my surprise, she entered a spiral staircase which stood in the middle of the very busy restaurant; she kept looking back to make sure we were with her. She led us to a table right next to the window. It was candle lit, with a crisp white linen tablecloth and silver cutlery. She pulled my chair to allow me to sit, then did the same for Sam.

"Can I get you any drinks while you peruse the menu?"

Sam looked at me,

"Would you like Prosecco Poppy or Pino Grigio or something different?"

"Sam, I would love Prosecco if that's okay."

"You can have whatever you like Pops."

"Sofia, can we have a bottle of Prosecco and a pint of Morretti beer please."

"Coming right up, sir."

The waitress disappeared to get the drinks. We were on our own at last. "Sam, this place is perfect and look at the view out of the window; the snow, the Christmas lights twinkling."

Sam reached across the table and cupped his hands around mine and responded with,

"It's perfect, Poppy, because you're here with me. I couldn't wish for anyone more beautiful than you, to share this birthday celebration with. I love you so much."

My heart missed a beat; was this really happening to me. Sam was the perfect man. I was so happy, deep down I prayed that the 'Door' wouldn't be so unkind and call me back to the future. I leant across the table and kissed Sam on the lips,

"Sam, I love you too, you've saved my life."

We both looked longingly into each other's eyes, then Sam said,

"Shall we look at the menu, what do you fancy?"

Sofia arrived with the drinks. She placed Sam's pint on the table, then poured me a glass of Prosecco and placed the bottle in a silver ice bucket next to the table; then another waiter turned up with mixed olives, marinated in Parsley and Garlic,

"Compliments of the house while you decide what to order."

"Thank you so much. I love olives; do you, Sam?"

"Not really my cup of tea, Poppy, but I'm sure you will enjoy them."

Sofia asked,

"Are you ready to order, or do you need a little more time."

"Could we have a few more minutes, please?"

Sam said, politely; she scooted off.

"Poppy, I need meat. I will have the polpette, pork and beef meatballs in tomato sauce for starters, and to follow, I think more meat—the lamb rosmarino."

Then it was my turn. There was so much on the menu, it was difficult to choose. In the end, I decided on the Funghi Arrosto, baked mushrooms in creamy mascarpone and spinach sauce to start, followed by pollo milanese, chicken on a bed of polenta mash with tomato, onion and rocket.

We placed the order for our food. Sofia explained that all the food was cooked from fresh, so there might be a delay before it arrived. It didn't matter. The conversation was flowing, and so was the alcohol. By the time starters arrived, Sam was on his second beer, and I had finished the first bottle of Prosecco. Sam, being the attentive sort, had already noticed and ordered another bottle. The atmosphere in the restaurant was just lovely. Each table had a flickering candle, the background music was so romantic, the snow outside was still falling and was getting thicker on the window ledge. It was truly a night to remember; by the time we had finished our sweet, we were both stuffed and very pissed.

Poppy was slurring her words, and I could certainly tell I had had quite a few beers. I called for the bill, and with it came a silver platter, with an assortment of chocolate truffles. The look on Poppy's face when one melted in her mouth, she looked like she was experiencing a wonderful orgasm,

"That hit the spot, by the look on your face, Poppy."

"It sure did, Sam."

As I looked at her, her face was glowing with hidden pleasure, with chocolate spread around her sensual lips. I realised how much I loved her. How lucky was I, to have a girlfriend like Poppy, I was certainly punching above my weight. After settling the tab, Poppy thanked me for treating her, then said,

"I hope you haven't had too much beer, Sam. I was hoping to take advantage of you later."

I really wasn't sure whether I would be up to it, because as I stood up, the room was spinning, and my legs were quite shaky. That Italian beer carried quite a punch. It was going to be interesting walking back in the snow, that was for sure.

I could see that Sam was a little unsteady on his feet when he stood up, and so was I. I had drunk two bottles of bubbly and had baileys, so we were both in the same state. I clung onto him, with four legs between us. We stood more of a chance of escaping the restaurant without embarrassing ourselves. I can tell you, the spiral staircase was quite a challenge; we were both in stitches. I couldn't stop giggling. What we must have looked like, leading each other down the stairs, is anyone's guess. Anyway, we managed to reach the entrance where Gerardo helped us on with our coats, gave us our brolly, then proudly produced a single red rose, which he gave to me, saying,

"And this is for the beautiful young lady. Thank you both for eating at Giuseppe's and have a safe journey back to your hotel."

We thanked him for such a wonderful night and made our way into the snow-covered street. It must have been at least four inches deep. There was that strange eerie atmosphere when snow falls. The normal sound seemed muffled, deadened by the layer of cushioning snow, with that crunchy thud as your shoes trod down into the virgin white snow. I was surprised at how little traffic there was. Being London, I suppose the snow had fallen so quickly, it had taken the council by surprise; and as no salt had been spread, I guess the roads had been impossible to navigate. Consequently, people were walking in the middle of the road without a care in the world, certainly a rare sight in the capital.

As we neared the hotel, Poppy was getting more like a playful child; she ran ahead, shouting,

"Come on, Devere, what's your shot like."

And with that, a tirade of well-compacted snowballs rained down on me; and with some success, I have to admit, one of them landing on top of my head. Poppy burst out laughing, celebrating her success with an 'air pump' and shouting,

"What a shot."

I ran towards her, intent on revenge, but with limited control due to the drink, I lost my footing and ended up prostrate on my back in the snow. The next thing I heard was a blood-curdling, excited scream. Poppy was on the attack; she dived on top of me, pushing loads of snow into my face. She thought it was hilarious. Then I felt her warm tongue enter my mouth. She spoke,

"I love you, Samuel Devere, but remember, I am the snow queen."

I pulled her closer with both arms; her warm breath condensing in the cold air. Our lips met, and we kissed passionately. I would never forget this snowy night in the city.

A by-passer stepped around us, looking at us like we were mad. Well, we were mad, madly in love; that was for sure. We entered the bedroom completely exhausted, and the snow that had covered us had melted in the warm air of the hotel, leaving us soaked to the skin. We both ran to the bathroom and stripped naked, throwing the soaking clothes into the bath tub,

"We can sort those out in the morning, Poppy."

Sam said while he wrapped me in a massive warm towel from the radiator. It felt divine. I then wrapped the towel around both of us; it was so warm and cosy.

"Sam, are you ready for bed, I'm knackered."

"Oh! Poppy, does that mean no sex tonight? I am so disappointed in you; you've really let me down, it being my birthday and all."

Sam started laughing. He was winding me up. He wasn't up for a shag, any more than I was,

"You, little so and so, I thought you were serious then."

"Poppy, I'm pooped. I have to admit, it's been a long day; and with all the beer I've drunk, I honestly don't think my cock is up to it." We both got into bed and cuddled. Sam turned the lights off, and we both drifted off into a blissful dreamy sleep.

Chapter 25
The Penny Drops

We both woke up with a hangover; not surprising, considering the copious amount of alcohol we had consumed. Sam was flat on his back. I was lay with my head on his chest, looking towards the window. We had left the curtains open the night before, so the light was streaming into the room. It must have been getting on, at least after nine. Oh my god, we might miss breakfast.

"Sam, Sam, wake up, it's late; and we are going to miss breaky."

Sam stirred, scratching his head, then stretching his arms in the air, he said,

"Don't worry yourself about breakfast. A full English, times two, will be delivered to the room at 9:30 exactly."

I looked at my watch; it read 9:25 a.m. I slid out of the bed and went to the bathroom. I wrapped the soft dressing gown around me, then ran to the window to look at the view,

"Sam, you have to see the view, it's amazing. You wouldn't think we were in London. All you can see is snow-covered trees, people playing in the snow, dogs running all over the place and a few high rise buildings in the background."

"Poppy, what time is it? I could murder bacon and egg."

As he spoke, there was a knock at the door. I opened the door; a porter stood there with a trolley topped with silver platters.

"Good morning, ma'am, may I come in. I have breakfast for you."

"You certainly may, I'm starving."

The porter parked the trolley next to the table near the window. He turned and spoke,

"Two full English breakfasts, white and brown toast, coffee, a pot of tea and fresh orange juice; is there anything else you require, ma'am."

"No, that will be just fine, thank you."

The porter excused himself and was off like a rocket. He obviously had a lot of breakfasts to serve. Sam got out of bed, made himself decent and joined me at the window table,

"My god! That looks good, but first things first."

"I know what you're going to say Sam—tea."

I poured Sam a cuppa, from the large white china teapot and topped up my cup, which I had already downed. It was English breakfast tea, and it hit the spot. We were both very quiet while we tucked into the delicious bacon, poached eggs, yummy sausages, baked beans and several slices of toast. I don't know how, but it sorted out the hangover.

"Poppy, that was fabulous, that should see us through to dinner tonight."

"I should say so, I feel absolutely stuffed, Sam."

"Right the plan today, Pops. We need to find a party dress for you and a nice new tie for me."

"Sam, I feel so guilty with you having to pay for everything. I promise when things become normal, I will always pay my share."

"Poppy, as far as I'm concerned, we are a team, a partnership, a couple. It's only money; what's more important to me is us, being together. You're the best thing that has ever happened to me, so stop harping on about the money."

The way Sam spoke, with such sincerity and honesty, made me feel warm inside,

"Sam, I'm sorry! I'm just not used to such generosity and being made to feel so special. I will try not to mention that dreaded word again."

"What word is that, Poppy?"

"Mmm, arrggh! I nearly said it then."

We both burst out laughing,

"Sam, let's get dressed and go and hit the town, partner."

We walked up the street holding hands. The snow was crunchy under foot, the air was freezing, but I was so excited. Shopping in London, it's not something I've done that many times in my life. There were so many shops to look in, from the large department stores right down to the smaller independent shops, trying to be different by selling very unusual one-off items. London was such a cosmopolitan place, it seemed like the people were from every country you could imagine; but in saying that, everyone just jelled, as if to say, 'We are in London, and we are all Londoners'. The atmosphere that day will stop with me forever; being with Sam, the snow, the people and the noise—just delightful.

We came across a ladies clothes shop, with a fantastic display of party frocks, gowns and handbags. The window display was quite lovely, with silver and gold Christmas trees mixed in with the array of window dummies, displaying their wares. The floor was covered in fake snow, and the trees adorned with hundreds of twinkling white and cherry red lights. The display had obviously worked; it had stopped us in our tracks.

"Poppy, I can just see you in that blue dress there."

Sam pointed towards a dress. It was mainly blue, with beige and white flowers, edged in gold printed on it. It had puffed up short sleeves, a scalloped lacy neckline, which allowed a view of one's cleavage, a fitted bodice; then from the waistline, it opened up, finishing at knee level. I was surprised at Sam's choice, it was very me; it was unusual for a man to know what would suit a lady, but he was certainly tuned into me.

"I love it, Sam, but it looks expensive."

Sam gave me a stern look. I decided to be quiet; he grabbed my arm and led me into the entrance of the shop. Inside, it looked more like a boutique affair. There was music playing in the background; the walls were covered in scenes from around the world—Pretty paintings of back streets in Paris, couples drinking wine at candle lit tables, the skyline of New York and the idyllic panoramic views across the vineyards in Tuscany and so many more. I think they were trying to appeal to the vast number of foreign visitors to the city. It certainly had a charm to it.

We were approached by a young lady, with a French accent and a sweet smile,

"*Bonjour*, can I be of assistance, sir, *madame*."

It was pleasing that she addressed the both of us, not just assuming that the man was in charge. Sam pointed to the dress that we spotted in the window. She looked at me, measuring me up with her eyes,

"Size 10, I think, *madame*."

I was flattered, but normally a size 12 was about right.

"Can I try the 10 and the 12 if you don't mind, thank you."

She hurried off to the stock room and returned a few minute later, holding two dresses. I was so pleased they had the stock. So often I've seen something I liked in a shop, but to find they hadn't got my size. The assistant pointed me towards the changing rooms. They even had soft furnishings outside for the man in waiting to rest his weary legs, which pleased Sam. I pulled the curtains across and stripped off. I couldn't help having a laugh though. I dropped the cup on my bra, exposing one of my breasts, then tentatively held the curtains where they were pulled together, just opening them enough to see who was outside the cubicle. It was just Sam sat waiting patiently for me to appear. I squeezed my breast through the gap between the curtains and quietly said,

"What do you think of this, Samuel?"

I heard him jump up from the chair, pressing his face into the gap of the curtains, blocking off the view of my protruding breast and in a rather sheepish voice said,

"Poppy, stop it! You are going to get us thrown out."

He was laughing as he said it, but you could tell he was rather flustered.

"Oh Sam, no one saw, it was just a bit of fun."

"I will give you fun, young lady. You just wait till I get you back to the hotel; you're going to get a damned good spanking."

I felt a twinge inside my tush. He turned me on so much when he dominated me.

"Oh Samuel, I can't wait."

Sam laughed, then, with his face pressing through the gap in the curtains, he said,

"Poppy, you're incorrigible, only you could expose yourself in a London store. You must be the naughtiest person I have ever met."

"Sam, are you going to let me try this dress on instead of perving through the curtain."

Sam sat down, tutting under his breath, and I got back to trying on the dress. I didn't bother with the size 10. I knew it would be too small. I got into the size 12; it fitted perfectly, but I couldn't manage to pull up the zipper which ran up the back.

"Sam, could you help me with the zipper please."

Sam responded, rather sarcastically,

"Do you really expect me to fall for that one, Poppy? I bet you're as naked as a jay bird."

I laughed; he was so nervous that I would try something else on him, "Sam I'm serious, I can't reach the zip, honest."

The curtains opened, Sam looked at me and said,

"Poppy, it's perfect, you look amazing."

"Sam, can you pull up the zip, so I can see if it fits."

He did so, and it did fit; it felt comfy. I looked in the mirror; it was rather nice. Sam's face was peering over my shoulder,

"I think we should take it, Poppy, unless you would like to try some more."

"No! I love it, shall we take it then, Sam."

"Poppy, whip it off, and I will go and pay for it while you get dressed."

I took the dress to the counter; a much older lady greeted me,

"Oh! A very beautiful dress for a beautiful, mischievous lady."

She smiled. I felt my face get a little redder. She must have seen Poppy flash through the curtains.

"It really is, isn't it; and yes, she is rather mischievous, sorry!"

"Sir, don't apologise for being with a soul who loves life. Look after her, she will make you very happy."

I looked at her; her eyes focussed on mine, as if she knew Poppy was special. I withdrew my card from the machine. She handed me the receipt but held onto my hand and said,

"You will make beautiful babies, have a good life."

As I turned I thought to myself, *what a weird thing to say.* Maybe she was a gipsy, and she could look into the future, a bit like the old gipsy lady calling at your door, selling pegs and putting a spell on you if you didn't buy any. I picked up the rather posh bag holding the dress. Poppy joined me, and we left the store; we felt the cold air hit us.

"Sam, thank you so much, how much was the dress."

I hadn't even asked. I had no idea. I pulled the receipt from my pocket and read it,

"Well! Sam, how much was it!"

I couldn't tell Poppy how much it cost. She would have insisted that we return it. All I can say is, it took my breath away when I read the amount at the bottom of the receipt, but she was worth it. I would be proud to walk into the room tonight and show off Poppy in all her glory. I told Poppy that the dress was a bargain, but refrained from telling her what the old lady had said about the babies and Poppy's indiscretion.

It was now time to find a cafe for a heart-warming coffee. Just a few yards up the road, we stumbled upon a quaint deli that served, and I quote 'The best cake and coffee in the City'. I pushed the door open, allowing Poppy to enter first; the sound of a bell rang out. There must have been a trigger on the door to alert the owner that customers had arrived. Poppy seemed excited, then I realised she had clocked the cake's on display inside the curved glass counter. She leant over the counter, as if she was bowing to the cakes in adoration of their splendour. "Oh Sam, just look at the cakes. My mouth is watering just looking at them; which one do you fancy."

I have to admit; they were quite special, and the choice was fantastic. "Poppy, do you mind if I share some of yours. I'm still full from breakfast."

Poppy's eyes widened as if I had offended her. With both of her hands clutching her chest, she stared at me and replied, in an over-acting stern voice,

"Share! Share! You can have my belongings, you can have my body, but never expect this girl to share her cake."

She burst out laughing, realising that people in the cafe were all looking at her. Someone shouted out,

"Go on, girl! You tell him, expecting you to share your cake, who does he think he is."

There was a roar of laughter from other customers in the cafe; then the sound of a cockney geezer asking,

"What can I get ya! My dear!"

Poppy replied, in her faint feminine voice,

"Can we have one cappuccino, one single shot latte and a slice of the double chocolate sponge, with the squirty cream topping, please."

We were told to take a seat, and our order would be brought to us, so we found a table near the window. I had to rub the condensation off the window, so we could see outside. I guess with all the customers and the steam from the kitchen, the glass kept misting up. The order soon came; a short stumpy lady, with very rosie red cheeks, placed the coffees down. Why her cheeks were so red, I wasn't sure. It was either she had been outside in the cold, or she had been at the bottle. She then asked who the cake was for; I soon piped up,

"The cake is for me, thank you very much."

Sam interjected, rather hastily, "Can I have another fork, so I can have a little taste."

The short stumpy lady looked at me, as if to get my permission,

"Yes! It's okay for him to try a little," I joked.

I was rather glad that Sam helped me with the cake. It was delicious but also very sickly. After we had finished, Sam was sorting out the bill when I glanced out of the steamy window. I noticed across the road, a strange black-fronted shop. When I say black-fronted, I mean black; even the glass was black. Above the facade, in silver letters read,

SECRET PLEASURES.

We thanked the staff for the lovely cake and coffee and left the cafe. I was clutching onto my dress; then Sam reminded me that he needed to buy a tie.

"Sam, before we find a tie, what do you think that shop is across the road."

Sam looked across, then started laughing,

"Poppy, you know full well what sort of shop that is."

"Sam, honestly, I haven't got a clue, but it sounds intriguing with a name like that, Secret Pleasures."

"Poppy, why do you think it's all blacked out, so you can't see the people inside or the produce they're selling."

"Sam, you mean!"

"Yes, I mean sex toys, pornographic magazines, films."

I felt such a fool. I honestly had never seen a sex shop; I certainly had never been in one. I always thought they were down back streets and really seedy, not on the high street with high quality signage. I know Kim had bought me a vibrator back in the future, but I hadn't thought about where she might have bought it from.

"Oh Sam! We have to take a look. I've never been inside one before, I'm curious."

"Really! Poppy! You want to go inside."

"Yes please, Sam, if you don't mind!"

This girl never stopped amazing me. She asked, if I minded going in. I have to admit, it rather turned me on to think she wanted to go in and explore the goodies on sale.

"Well, Poppy, as it's you, I will go in against all of my principles, to make sure you're safe inside the den of iniquity, come on then."

We ran across the road, swerving between the slowed down traffic, slipping from time to time on lumps of ice. Arriving at the entrance, a little out of breath, I looked at Poppy to see if she was still up for going inside, but she was ahead of me and pushing the black door inwards, tittering, like a schoolgirl, as she entered the shop.

It wasn't at all like I expected. I thought it would be quite smelly, with dimmed lighting and dirty old men in raincoats skulking in the corners, peering into porn magazines, but it wasn't anything like that. First of all, it was brightly lit, and it smelled of violets; it had plush carpet, and the fixtures were quite smart. All of the products were set out in categories, with signs above each area to help you find what you wanted. Also the clientele, mostly men were dressed in suits and not at all dirty old men. A lady approached me to ask if I needed help finding what I was looking for, but I declined, saying that we were just browsing. I was holding Sam's hand; we were in front of the lube section. I had no idea that you could buy so many creams to aid smooth intercourse. Sam pulled me towards another section; we both burst out laughing. It was full of bondage products—rubber masks, rubber suits, with holes in strategic places, whips, handcuffs. Sam looked at me and whispered,

"Remember I said I was going to spank you when we got back to the hotel; well, those handcuffs might come in handy."

I have to admit, the thought of Sam spanking me while being restrained sent a quiver of pleasure through my veins, but I wasn't going to let him know my inner thoughts.

"Dream on, Sam. If anyone will be wearing cuffs, it will be you, chained to the head board while I devour your big wet cock."

"Poppy, stop it, you're giving me an erection."

She was such a tease, I could feel my trousers getting tighter as my cock stiffened. The lustful thoughts were flying through my mind.

Something caught my eye, in the next section were an array of dildos and vibrators. Some were massive and looked very real; you could actually see veins embossed on them, like real penis; but next to them were a selection of smaller vibrators. I hadn't told Sam that in the future I had owned one, but he seemed to lock on to my interest very quickly.

"Poppy, how about as a memento of our trip to London, I buy you one of those vibrators."

Sam pointed towards them, suggesting the model called the 'bullet'. It was almost identical to the one that Kim had bought me. I felt excited inside and thought about the fun we might have using it on each other, but didn't like to appear too keen.

"Well Sam, if you think we will use it, then yes, let's try it."

Before we knew it, the sales lady who had obviously been listening to our conversation was on us, like a shot.

"Hello there. Would you like to see anything? I can open up the cabinet if you like."

Sam asked to purchase the product called the 'bullet', in quite a refrained voice. The lady, not being very sensitive, replied in a raised voice,

"Excellent choice. If you don't mind me saying, sir, one of our best sellers; would you like me to show you how it works."

Sam looked a little embarrassed; he just wanted to pay for it and get out of the shop.

"No thanks! If you could just wrap it, please. Oh! Can I pay on credit card?"

"Of course you can, sir. Would you like anything else today, sir. Porn films, magazines, K Y jelly."

Sam was getting more and more flustered. I put my arm around him to let him know I was feeling his awkwardness. At last, we were out of the shop, both in fits of laughter,

"Oh my god, Sam, I didn't think she was ever going to shut up, and she was so loud."

"Poppy! The things I do for you, you drag me into sex shops; what next, a strip joint?"

Sam was obviously winding me up. I think, deep down, he was more than happy that we had experienced the sex shop; that was for sure. It wasn't long before we found a man's outfitters and got the last thing on our shopping list; a very nice blue and black tie, which would go very well with the blue evening suit that Sam was wearing tonight.

We arrived back at the hotel about three o'clock, so it left plenty of time to get ready for tonight's Christmas party. I hung my dress up to allow any creases to drop out, laid out my shoes, underwear and bag, so everything was ready for tonight. Sam did the same with his suit, shirt, tie and shoes; now we could relax before the big event. I was still a little nervous at the thought of meeting all of

Sam's work colleagues, but it had to be done. Sam was sat on the sofa near the window. He called me over, in a rather strict, like teacher's voice,

"Poppy, come here, young lady. I think we have that small business of you being very naughty this morning to sort out."

"Who me!" I replied, in a very innocent tone.

"You know full well what you did earlier, and can you remember what I said what would happen when we got back to the hotel."

"I can't remember, sir."

I said, with excitement building inside me. I knew what was coming, and I was getting quite moist down below.

"Oh! I think you do, now come here immediately."

I stood in front of Sam. I couldn't help but laugh; he was really acting like a teacher, about to punish a student for bad behaviour.

"Do you accept that you misbehaved earlier today and that naughty girls must be punished."

"I do, sir."

"Right then, undo your jeans and pull them down as far as your knees."

I stood there, my jeans at half-mast, boasting just a pair of white cotton panties. Sam pulled me towards him, bending me over his knee. I squealed,

"Please sir, don't spank me too hard. I will be a good girl from now on."

Poppy was certainly acting the part, and I just knew she was as turned on as I was. I slipped my hand inside her panties; she had the peachiest soft cheeks you could ever imagine. I felt my penis grow. My fingers searched between the crack of her beautiful arse, moving towards her wet pussy. Poppy sighed with pleasure as my finger rubbed gently against her bulging clitoris. I then pulled her panties down exposing her glorious arse in all its beauty,

"Poppy! Who's the boss and think carefully about your answer."

Poppy replied, without delay,

"I am, of course."

In a split second, Sam responded. I felt his large flat hand connect with my bottom, and it stung.

Poppy squealed, in excited pleasure,

"Poppy, would you like to rethink your answer."

"Not really, you know I'm the boss."

I now knew she wanted more, a simple answer of 'you are' would have stopped the spanking, but she was defiant and knew the resulting response. I hate to admit the pleasure it brought me, as my hand came down on her lily-white cheeks. They sort of quivered, like a jelly, as the force of the slap reverberated through the cheeks of her bottom. She reacted by reaching backwards with her hand, to ward off the onslaught of the slaps, but I grabbed her by the wrist and held her arm up her back. There was no escape; then came the surrendering squeaky retort of, "Okay! Okay, Sam, you're the boss."

"At last, Poppy, the right answer."

The slapping stopped, but I was so turned on, I wanted Sam's cock, then Sam spoke,

"Poppy as you're now a good girl, it's time for a little massage."

I wondered what he meant, but my curiosity was soon satisfied. Sam fumbled in his pocket, then I heard a vibrating sound, I squealed with anticipation, as Sam stroked the inside of my thighs with the bullet vibrator, slowly moving towards the erogenous zone around my clit. I was in heaven.

"What do you think Poppy, does it feel nice."

I didn't have the heart to tell him that this wasn't the first time I had been at the mercy of a sex toy.

"Sam, you're going to make me come if you don't slow down."

"Me too, Poppy, it's such a turn on spanking you."

I then felt the bullet enter my slit. Sam slowly pushed it up me. It was just too much. There was no way of stopping the cataclysmic orgasm that tore throughout my body. My face buried into the fabric of the sofa, my free hand gripping the cushion; I screamed in ecstasy as the drug of sex ran through my veins. My beating heart was throbbing through my face. "Poppy I want you, I want you now."

I jumped up, throwing the rest of my clothes on to the floor. Sam did the same; we were both stark naked.

"Poppy, I'm not going to last long."

Sam pushed me onto the sofa facing the window. I could clearly see the people on the terrace below. I held firmly onto the back of the sofa. Sam was behind me, holding me by the hips,

"Poppy, I want to fuck you from behind while you look through the window."

"Sam! You really are a kinky so and so, aren't you."

"You make me like this, Poppy; you're so sexy, you drive me wild."

I felt his massive erect penis enter me, repeatedly ramming me. His balls smacked against my bare arse every time he thrust forwards. He was like a man possessed. I imagined someone on the terrace looking up and seeing my head bobbing up and down, not realising that a rampant virile guy was shagging me so hard from behind.

"Poppy, I'm coming, I can't hold it any longer."

"Same here, big boy."

I orgasmed for the second time, this time biting into the top of the sofa; then to my amazement, Sam pulled out.

"Sam, what are you doing, I thought you were there."

Before he could explain, I felt a gush of hot spunk splash all over my buttocks.

"Sorry Poppy, I just had to do that, sorry!"

"Don't worry, Sam, whatever floats your boat as long as you enjoyed yourself."

She was just amazing; nothing shocked her. She seemed up for anything. God, I loved her. I discreetly used my shirt to wipe away the cum that covered her arse; then we collapsed in a heap on the sofa. "Poppy, I just want to say, I realise the sex we just had wasn't the most tender, but you have to believe me, my love for you couldn't get any greater, and I love you dearly."

"Sam, you don't have to apologise. I loved it as much as you did. Oh! And by the way, yes, I am still the boss."

Sam burst out laughing; we lay there naked for ages, just cuddling, then we realised it was time to get ready for the big party.

Sam looked so smart in his blue suit, a white shirt set off his new tie and of course shiny black Oxford toecap shoes. Sam said, he insisted on leather soles, saying it was impossible to dance in rubber soles. I was proud to be his chaperone, but also nervous to meet all of his work colleagues.

Poppy was actually ready before I was. Even though she had to curl her silky brown hair, the dress we had bought earlier looked amazing. I believed she had stockings on, I guess I might find out later; and a pair of three-inch heels to finish off; but what stood out for me was the bright red lipstick she decided to wear. I absolutely loved to see ladies that wore red lipstick. It always reminded me of the war films I used to watch when I was younger; the ladies always wore stockings, fairly tight-fitting skirts and bright red lipstick. I feel it really accentuates and signals that these lips are for kissing.

"Poppy, you look great, and I have to say, I'm loving the lipstick. I can't wait to show you off to all of my colleagues."

"Well Sam, I'm feeling rather nervous, I'm dreading it."

"What have you got to be nervous about, you're great with people."

"Yes, I am, but just say if someone there knows me, they might know me and Simon as a couple."

"Well, Poppy, think about it! When you were with Simon back in the '80s, can you remember knowing anyone that worked for my company."

"No, I can't. Sorry Sam, I'm just scared; if the time line is broken, it will change everything."

"Don't worry, Poppy. It will be fine. I promise you. Let me get you a drink from the mini bar."

Sam quickly knocked up two large gin and tonics with ice. He passed me one, then raised his glass and made a toast,

"Here's to us, 'Poppy and Sam'."

We chinked glasses, then tipped them back. The strong gin certainly hit the spot, and I felt more relaxed in no time.

"Lovely, lovely Sam, I'm feeling better already."

"Yes, Poppy, it's because you're an alcoholic, and you needed a drink."

"Very funny, Sam, and you're not."

"Who, me?"

Sam picked up a couple of tickets and slipped them into his suit pocket. He grabbed the room key, then came over to me and kissed me on the lips,

"Shall we go then, sexy?"

We held hands as we walked to the lift. I could smell Sam's aftershave—Old Spice if I was correct. Sam pressed the button to call the lift. We could hear it creaking as it climbed up the shaft towards us. The doors opened. The car was empty; we jumped in, and Sam pressed the button for the first floor. It was labelled 'The Banqueting Suite'.

As the lift was so slow, an idea came into my mind.

Poppy had that look in her eye—the look of naughtiness. I had seen it many times, and it usually meant trouble, and I was right. As soon as the lift doors closed, she sprang into action. She pushed me against the back wall of the lift car and dropped to her knees in front of me.

"Poppy, what are you doing, people might get in any minute."

She didn't answer, but in a flash, she had pulled down my zipper and extricated my cock from my boxers. Without hesitation, her mouth was wrapped around the end of my semi-hard penis.

"Come on, Sam, aren't you pleased to see me; you're not very hard."

"Poppy, that's because I'm petrified that my boss might get in on the next floor."

She continued to suck me off; her tongue driving me wild. I had visions of her red lipstick all around the end of my knob. Then the inevitable—the chime of the lift announcing that the lift doors would be opening at the next floor. I panicked, unceremoniously pulling my cock from Poppy's mouth,

"Charming, I must say."

Poppy said, sarcastically, laughing out loud.

"Quick, Poppy, straighten up."

I hurriedly put my cock away and zipped up my fly. Poppy leant into me affectionately, placing her arm through mine. The door opened, and to my utter amazement, who should be stood there. Yes, you've guessed it—my boss and his wife.

"Good evening, Mike. Jane, this is Poppy."

After the introductions, the lift stopped and the doors opened. My boss and his wife left first, saying they would see us at the bar. I looked into Poppy's eyes and burst out laughing.

"God, that was close, Poppy. Another couple of seconds, and they would have had a right surprise."

We arrived at the entrance to the party room. Sam handed over the tickets, and the young lady handed us a package each.

"What's this, a Christmas present?"

Sam asked.

"No! They are masks for the night; everyone will be wearing them. It just adds a little intrigue to the night."

They weren't full masks; mine was gold in colour and covered my eyes and nose. It had purple feathers pointing up from the corners, and it fitted very well. Sam's was more like a Batman mask—black and shiny and no feathers. We donned the masks; they were held on with elastic bands which stretched around the back of your head. A little uncomfortable, but we didn't want to buck the trend—everyone in the room was wearing them.

Just inside the entrance was an easel, with the table legend printed on it. I couldn't believe how many tables there were.

"Sam, how many people work for you, there seems to be so many tables."

Sam looked at the legend, then turned and said,

"I see what they've done. Our sister company are here as well. I suppose it saves money to use the same venue."

"So Sam! Your company are into music, what about your sister company?"

"Oh! Not music, they're into security systems."

"Oh right."

I thought no more about it, and we headed for the bar, to get the drinks. I have to admit, I felt a lot less nervous with the mask on. I felt like I could talk to anyone, as no one could recognise me. Sam made a special effort to include me in conversation, so as I didn't feel ignored. The room was set out with round tables, all with candelabras, name places and silver cutlery and, of course, the obligatory Christmas crackers. The tables were surrounding the dance floor, and at the head of the room was the stage and the band, who were about to strike up any minute. We took our seats. Sam introduced me to the other guests; then the food started arriving; and before long, the night was rocking.

Sam and I had just danced the worst 'rock and roll' ever, we returned to our seats breathless and in fits of laughter, when, as Sam pulled his seat out to sit down, he accidentally bumped into the person on the next table. Sam apologised profusely, but when the person turned around to respond, I could have died. I recognised his voice.

"It's no problem, mate, we are all part of the same team."

He then turned around and started talking to his partner. I grabbed Sam's arm and whispered in his ear,

"We have to leave, and we have to leave now."

"Poppy, what's the problem; surely you don't feel up for it so soon."

"Sam, I'm serious, we have to go now!"

Sam pulled off his mask and then went to remove mine,

"Sam, I mean it! Put your mask back on; we've got to go now!"

We both stood up to leave. I grabbed my bag, then turned to leave, when I heard the guy say to Sam,

"We wish you and your misses a happy Christmas."

He thrust his hand forward to shake Sam's hand. Sam responded, grabbing his hand,

"I'm Sam Devere; this is Mrs Devere."

"Well, I'm Simon, and this is my girlfriend Lucy."

"Nice to meet you both, have a great Christmas. We have to leave. The baby sitter called; some crisis with a teddy bear or something."

I practically ran out of the room. My mind was in turmoil. I just couldn't believe that Simon was there and with Lucy. Was it the same Lucy from the future, I was in shock. We got back to the room; Sam poured me a drink.

"Sam, do you realise that was Simon, my Simon."

"Well, who was he with; that wasn't you, was it."

"No! It wasn't, that must have been his bit of stuff."

I think it must have sunk in how serious it really was, because Sam suggested that we pack our bags and get out of there, but then it dawned on him that we had both been drinking. We decided we would leave at first light; no one from the party would be up early, judging from the amount of free drink on the tables. Sam turned out the lights; and before long, he was away with the fairies. I lay there thinking, I hadn't told Sam about the piece of paper, with her name on, that I had found in Simon's dressing gown. It was starting to sink in that Simon had been seeing Lucy for years. Was I stupid; how could I have missed all the signs over the years, and how could Simon be such a shit.

Chapter 26
Undercover Cop

The return trip from London went very quickly. We left at first light; the motorway was clear all the way back home. Sam was quiet, and so was I. I kept thinking about last night; if they hadn't given us masks to wear, it could have been a disaster. I might have bumped into Simon face to face, and then it would have been game over. Then, if I hadn't seen him with Lucy, I wouldn't have known what a total shit he had been for all those years. He must have been living a double life all that time, and I hadn't had a clue. Sam looked over and said,

"Poppy, I'm so sorry you had to find out about Simon the way you did. I had no idea who he was, or, he even worked for our sister company. At least you know, I love you, and I would never be such a cad."

"Thanks Sam, I love you too, but it makes me so angry that he could lie to me, and I also feel totally stupid that I didn't see through his countless lies, over so many years."

"At least, we have each other now, Poppy; and we have the future to look forward to."

He was such a lovely man, trying to make me feel better about myself, but deep down I felt humiliated and hurt; and the next time I saw Simon, he was going to get both barrels. My thoughts turned to Roscoe. It seemed like months since I had seen him. I hoped he was alright, and I knew deep down that he was probably asleep in his basket, completely unaware that I had disappeared again. The longer I was in the past, the sooner time would catch up with the future, and the sooner Sam and I could get on with our lives, like a normal couple.

The next few months went by very quickly; and before we realised, it was time to move into the new house. After I had spent time preparing the flat for sale, it had been snapped up by a young couple, paying the full asking price, which had pleased Sam no end. The new house was such a joy, so much more room than before; plus we had the garden to enjoy. Sam concentrated on the lawn; he was so fussy about weeds. I looked after the borders. I planted all sorts of shrubs, including buddleia, to attract butterflies in to the garden, also varieties of clematis to give a range of colour and, of course, roses; you can't beat roses for their scent. In between the shrubs, I mixed in my favourite flowers—Fuchsias in all their glory, so many colours and variations in size, just beautiful. During the summer of that year, Sam built a barbecue on the patio area and also a pergola surrounding the patio doors. This was directly under our bedroom window and a perfect place to plant a passionflower, which, I realised, would take some time before it produced its beautiful waxy looking flowers, but it would be worth it in the long run. Working together, we furnished the house just the way we liked it. Sam was fairly easygoing, letting me pick the style of the furniture and the colour of the rooms. It seemed, as long as we were together, he was happy; and I have to say, I had never been happier.

As we now had four bedrooms, we turned one of the smaller rooms into my art studio; the room faced over the back garden with a view of the woods. The sales of paintings were growing very well, especially the fantasy pieces. Sam did well, selling through his work colleagues, and their families and I had made a contact in a local coffee shop who displayed my work on the shop wall, gaining even more sales. I felt so much happier, being able to pay towards my upkeep. We continued the practise of keeping a calendar in the kitchen, writing a capital P on each day that I was there. Today was 16 June, and I noticed Sam had already written 'Poppy's Birthday' on the calendar on the 18th. I remember the previous year I had been called back by the 'Door' and had missed sharing my birthday with Sam. Fingers crossed, I would see this one, back in 1986 and celebrate it together.

Sure enough, my birthday was spent in the garden. We had a barbecue with Sam's sister Sally and her partner Robert. I got on so well with Sally, it was like we had known each other for years. Sally was not privy to me being a time traveller. Each time I disappeared, Sam told her I was visiting family. He hated telling her lies, but thought she would never believe the truth. The week after my birthday, I was on my own at home. Sam was at work. I decided to sort out my wardrobe; some of the clothes needed ironing, some went in the wash basket. I was checking the pockets on a pair of jeans when I came across the piece of paper I had found months ago in Simon's dressing gown pocket. I remembered, at the time I had originally read it, we were just off to London, so I put it away and forgot about it. I hadn't mentioned it to Sam at the time, but after seeing Simon and Lucy in London at the Christmas party, it was now time to follow it up.

I pulled off the drive, with butterflies in my stomach. I hadn't a clue where the address was, but I would soon find it. I was determined to find out for sure that Simon had been seeing this Lucy for all these years. As I neared the town, I noticed I needed fuel, so I called at a garage to fill up. When I paid at the kiosk, I asked the lady if she knew where the address was. She wasn't sure, so she shouted to her colleague who was working out the back of the shop.

"Natalie, do you know where 'Acacia Close' is."

"Yes! Isn't it up that road behind the football stadium?"

"Oh yes, I know, didn't Harold who used to work here lives up there."

I was thinking. I wish they would be a bit quieter about it. I was trying to be discreet.

"Yes love, do you know where the football ground is."

"I think so, is it near the end of the Ring Road."

"Yes, my love, turn off there, and it's the first right. Follow that road for about half a mile, then turn left, it takes you behind the stadium; the place you're looking for is around there." I paid for the petrol and set off in search of the address, not really knowing what I would do when I got there. It only took about ten minutes to find the close I was looking for. I drove slowly up the road, looking for the number 17. The odds were on my side—13, 15; there it was, number 17—a semi-detached dorma bungalow, nicely painted, with a tidy front garden; the drive was empty. I drove past, not really knowing what to do next. At the end of the close was a turning point, so I turned around and headed back towards number 17. Just before reaching the house, on the opposite side of the road, was a pull-in by some garages, with a row of silver birch trees edging the road. I pulled over and switched off the engine. The trees allowed me to sit and wait without looking quite so obvious. I felt like an undercover cop on a stake out, but probably not as confident. The time was about 4:00 p.m., I thought I would give it ten minutes, just to see if I could spot this elusive Lucy, but then I realised I didn't know what she looked like. When I saw her with Simon in London, she had been wearing a mask. I decided it was all a waste of time. If I saw her, I couldn't recognise her; and if I did, I couldn't challenge her because it might change the future.

I was about to turn the key to start the engine when a bright blue swanky car pulled onto the drive of number 17. I crouched down into my seat, trying to be invisible. A middle-aged man, in a posh suit, jumped out with a brown leather briefcase in hand. He locked the car, had a cursory look round; then he disappeared into the house. I thought to myself, *this is a complete waste of time. I should go home and prepare the tea. Sam would be home by 6:00.* Then without warning, another car appeared; not quite as swanky but somehow familiar. It was a green Vauxhall, and yes, I did remember that car. After all, I had been a passenger in it many times in the past. The windows were down and loud music was blearing out. I could see that two people were in the car, a man driving and a long-haired blonde in the passenger seat. They seemed to be eating each other. I could just make out their heads very close together, like they were snogging each other's faces off. Deep down I knew it had to be Simon; after all, it was definitely his car. I didn't have to wait long. The music came to an abrupt end. The car's door flung open and out jumped Simon, then on the other side of the car appeared a long-haired blonde, with a figure to die for. They were both laughing and oblivious to anything around them. She ran around the car and wrapped herself around Simon, kissing him passionately, like they were so much in love. I just stared in amazement, dumbstruck. Back in 1986, I thought we were deeply in love. How could Simon have been the way he was with me and been carrying on with this Lucy character. I wondered to myself, did this Lucy know about me, or had he deceived both of us. They both disappeared into the house. I sat there, staring at the space they had just occupied; my mind in turmoil at what had just happened. I can't remember driving back home; I just appeared on the drive. Sam wasn't home, so I quickly prepared the tea. I laid the table, poured myself a glass of wine and sat in a chair on the patio, pondering about what had transpired. I decided not to tell Sam. Then I heard a car door slam; Sam was home—time to tuck into a lovely chicken curry, rice and garlic naan bread.

Poppy had seemed a little distant off lately, and I was concerned she wasn't happy. I needed to get to the bottom of it.

"Poppy, be honest, do you still love me; you seem out of sorts lately. I know something is bothering you, please tell me, whatever it is, we can sort it out."

Poppy looked at me with those beautiful blue eyes, and I could tell her mind was all over the place. She started to speak, then stopped, as if she was afraid to tell me something.

"Come on, Poppy, you can tell me anything; you must know that, surely."

"First of all, Samuel, don't ever think I don't love you, you are my life, I love you to the moon and back!"

She then explained how upset she had been after seeing her ex with his piece on the side, feeling used and stupid that it had been going on so long. I had thought she had accepted it after seeing the pair together in London, but she was obviously more upset about it than first appeared. "The thing is Sam, it means I've wasted the past ten years of my life believing that the person I was sharing those years with loved me and me only."

"Poppy, you seem to be forgetting something, think about it logically."

Poppy looked at me with tears in her eyes. I hated to see her hurting, and I just wanted to catch hold of her ex and give him a damn good smacking.

"Right, Poppy, this is the way I see it. Now listen to what I've got to say and let it sink in. I then believe you will feel a whole lot better about the situation."

"Yes master, you're holy one, please make me feel better."

I held Poppy's hand, then tried to explain to her how I felt about the situation we were in.

"Okay, the ten years you believe you have wasted, weren't wasted."

"How do you mean?"

"If you hadn't had those ten years with Simon, you wouldn't have bought the house where the time machine was."

"True."

"Then, you wouldn't have travelled back in time, and we wouldn't have met and fallen in love."

"Mmmmm, I see."

"Although you think those years with Simon were wasted, you're now reliving those ten years with me, so essentially you're getting an extra ten years of life. Most people would love an extra ten years on this planet."

"I get it now, Sam. I was getting upset with myself because I had been so dumb. I can't believe I hadn't noticed what Simon had been getting up to."

"Poppy! He is obviously an accomplished liar, with no conscience; and I truly believe that what goes around, comes around; and one day, he will get his comeuppance."

From that moment on, I never let what had happened with Simon affect me ever again. That night, Sam made love to me so gently and passionately as if to reassure me that I was loved. I knew as long as I was with this wonderful man, life would be great. I fell asleep completely relaxed and without a care in the world. The next morning, I woke up before Sam. We always slept with the curtains open. I was lay there looking through the window; raindrops were chasing each other. In wiggly lines down the windowpane, the silver birch trees were swaying in the breeze. I could hear Sam breathing, but there was something else in the background. I lifted my head off the pillow. Yes! There was another noise, like a faint whimpering,

"Sam, Sam! Can you hear that noise?"

Sam stirred, bleary eyed and raised up from the bed,

"What noise, Poppy, I can't hear anything."

"Shush! Listen, there did you hear that, like a baby crying."

We both went silent, looking at each other, waiting for the sound; then we both heard it, like a high-pitched whine.

"Sam! It's coming from downstairs."

We both donned our dressing gowns and descended the stairs, arriving in the hallway. Just as the noise happened again, we looked at each other, and both looked towards the front door,

"What could it be, Sam."

"Simple way to find out, Poppy."

Sam opened the front door. We looked out; no one there. Then we looked down; curled up in a tight ball, on the doormat, was a small black and tan dog, shaking and whimpering at the same time.

"Oh! My god, it's a puppy, and he's soaking wet."

I leant down and stroked the dog's head. His head turned, and he licked my hand.

"He seems friendly enough, Sam; the poor thing, and look how skinny he is."

"Poppy, what makes you think it's a he!"

"I don't know, to be honest, Sam, what do you think."

Sam turned the dog on its back.

"There you go; it's certainly not a he. It's definitely a girl."

The dog didn't have a collar on, so it might have been a stray, but she was beautiful. She looked like a miniature Alsatian. Sam passed me a towel off the radiator in the kitchen,

"Wrap her in this, it's nice and warm."

She snuggled into the towel. Her eyes were looking at me as if to say thanks. I carried her into the house,

"Oh Sam, isn't she beautiful; can we keep her. You said you wanted a dog, and she's obviously been abandoned."

"Poppy, you don't know that, there might be someone frantically looking for her as we speak."

"Poppy, I have to go to work. I think the best thing to do is take her to the vet's and see if she's been chipped; then, if she is a stray, maybe we can consider taking her on."

While Sam went to get ready for work, I looked through the food cupboard to see if I could find something for her to eat. The best thing I could find was a tin of stew; it would have to do. I opened it and poured the contents into a dish and placed it on the floor. As soon as she smelt it, her nose started twitching. She gulped the whole dish full down in a few seconds, licking the dish shiny clean; even her tail started to wag, bless her. Sam appeared, ready for work, jangling his car keys.

"No time for toast now, Poppy. I will see you at lunch time; let me know how you get on at the vet's."

Sam stroked the dog, then kissed me on the lips,

"Love you, sweetheart."

Then he was gone, and I was on my own with my newfound friend, "What shall we call you then, you little ball of friendliness."

I started going through loads of names. Barney, no that was a boy's name; Lucy, definitely not Lucy, that was the tart's name; Bella, that was a nice name. I decided to wait to see if she was chipped; no point getting attached to her if she belonged to someone else. I called the vet's and explained the situation. They told me to pop her down, and they would run the scanner across her. I quickly got dressed; and as I turned from the basin after cleaning my teeth, the dog was sat on the bed, looking at me; her tail wagging.

"You little tinker, it didn't take you long to find me, did it."

I couldn't believe the dog had come looking for me. I had only been gone a couple of minutes. I now had to get her in the car. I had no lead or car cage for her, but it turned out alright. I opened the car door, and she jumped straight in and curled up on the passenger seat, like she was used to it. We arrived at the vet's, and I have to admit I was a little apprehensive. If they found a chip, I would have to give her up to her rightful owner. The young receptionist greeted us, asking the dog's name. I explained I didn't know it, so she registered her in my name. She wrote the name down and told us to take a seat. I held the dog on my lap, as I had no lead, but she was so well behaved, it wasn't a problem. Her ear's pricked up each time another pet came through the door, but she didn't attempt to jump off and chase. Occasionally, the vet's door would open, and pet's name was called out, requesting the next patient. I was the only one sat there when the vet's door opened, and the vet shouted out,

"Polly please, Polly."

I looked around confused; the vet looked at me confused.

"That's you, my dear, Polly."

"Oh! I'm sorry, my name is Poppy."

The lady laughed, then took another look at the piece of paper in her hand.

"Oh! Yes, sorry. It's the way it's written. I thought it said Polly. Come on in, Poppy."

I carried the dog into the room and placed her on the examination table. "So what have we here then, Poppy; the notes say she's a stray."

I went through the story of how we had found the dog, explaining that if she wasn't chipped, we were prepared to give the dog a home. The vet grabbed the scanner and approached the dog. I was anxious, hoping not to hear the tell-tale beep of an implanted chip.

"Good news, my dear! There's no chip on this dog, but I do suggest you put a notice in the local paper with a picture, just to give a potential owner the chance to recover their lost pet."

"Of course, I will do that, now I know that there's no chip."

Just as I was leaving, the vet spoke.

"I hope you don't find the owner. This dog is malnourished. She needs feeding up; and I'm sure you will give her the care she needs."

"Oh! Thanks. Don't worry, we will look after her. She will become part of the family."

I went to the desk to settle the bill and was told that there was no charge, due to the fact that I was rescuing the animal. On the drive home, I called at the pet shop and bought a collar, a lead, a dog bed and some food. I had no intention of placing an ad in the paper. Whoever this dog belonged to wasn't fit to keep animals. How anyone could let a dog get into such a state didn't deserve to own such a loving creature. I thought about what had happened at the vet's, with the mix up with names, and I thought it was an omen; so I decided to call the dog Polly.

"What do you think, Polly, is that okay if we call you Polly."

The dog just looked at me—her tongue out; her tail wagging. I think that was a yes from the dog. I just had to tell Sam now that there were now three in our relationship.

Sam arrived home from work. Polly ran to the door to greet him. Sam bent down to stroke her.

"So you're still here then, you little beauty."

"Sam, meet Polly; she found us, and now we are three."

Chapter 27
Daymare

Over the next few months, I have to be honest, I was really missing Roscoe; and on occasions, had thought strongly about the 'Door' willing it to call me back to 1995. It wasn't that I wasn't happy, because I was. I loved Sam with all my heart, and Polly was never far from my side. This time-travel episode had been the longest period I had ever stayed away. It was now February 1989, so I must have been here for almost two years. Even Sam seemed to accept that I was here for good. He even booked a holiday for the coming summer to a Greek island. God knows what would happen if I disappeared while on the aircraft. Try explaining that to the crew, one passenger down on arrival in Greece; it didn't bare thinking about.

I had been away in London on business. Our sister company were trying to get our music shops to stock a range of their security products in store; and to be honest, I wasn't a fan of the idea. We had spent three days going over all the positives and negatives, but I still wasn't convinced, so I decided to do more research when I got back home. I had really missed Poppy. Three nights without her had been difficult; no cuddles, no sex, and I hadn't slept very well without her, thinking about her being on her own. The only saving grace was, she had Polly to protect her. Before I set off home, I called the house phone to let her know I was on the way back, but there was no answer. The drive home was tedious—loads of traffic, stop start on the motorway, and I was really tired, so I pulled into the services for a cuppa. It was about lunchtime, the sun was shining through the car window and the warmth hit my face, it was lovely.

I don't know where the time had gone, but before I knew it, I was pulling onto the drive at home. Poppy's car was on the drive but also another car, which I didn't recognise. I thought to myself, *weird, she hadn't said the night before when we spoke that she was expecting any visitors.* I jumped out of my car, curious, who it might be. I pushed the front door key into the lock, but it wouldn't open; the dead lock had been applied. *Strange*, I thought to myself. I tapped on the door, but to no avail. I decided to go around the back to see if she was in the garden, but still no Poppy. Then it dawned on me, she must be in the woods, walking Polly. I sat on one of the patio chairs and waited for her to return. It was really quiet; the sun was out, but it was quite cold. Then, from above me, I heard a squeal; it came from our bedroom. I shouted,

"Poppy, I'm down here, let me in."

But there was no answer, just more shrieks of excited laughter; what the hell was going on. I banged on the patio window. The anxiety growing inside me, she wasn't expecting me home this early, but surely not, not Poppy, no, it couldn't be! In desperation, I climbed up the pergola; it was covered in the growth of last year's passionflower. My suit was covered in green stain, but I didn't care. I needed to find out what was going on. It took some effort to pull myself up; there were no footholds to climb on. I was out of breath when I finally reached the bearers directly under our bedroom window. I was on my knees, and I could hear voices from inside the room. As I raised up, level with the window, I almost fell off the pergola in utter shock. The scene that hit my unbelieving eyes shot through me like an ice-cold dagger.

I could not believe what I was witnessing, not my Poppy. She wouldn't do it to me, she loved me; I was so shocked, I froze. I tried to call out; my mouth opened but no sound came out. Poppy was on the bed, stark naked on all fours. Stood at the end of the bed was a naked guy, very muscular, with a stupid grin on his face. He was holding Poppy by the hair, pulling her face onto his massive erect cock. Poppy seemed to be smiling; she was certainly enjoying herself. Behind Poppy, on his knees was another guy. He was holding her by her thighs, thrusting his penis up her and occasionally slapping her arse, shouting,

"Come on, you dirty bitch."

I couldn't take it anymore; I started to bang on the window, shouting out in anger,

"Stop it! Stop it! Poppy, stop it!"

But they just carried on, oblivious to the noise I was making. They must have heard me; my fist was pounding the glass, but they totally ignored me,

"Bang! Bang! Bang!"

The sound of banging got louder, becoming real. I was confused; the banging continued. Then I became aware of glass next to my face. The glass was misted up; someone was banging on the window. I looked around, not sure where I was. I was in my car; there were people all around the vehicle. I pressed the button to wind the window down. A police officer stared back at me and said,

"Are you alright, sir? These people were worried about you, you've been here for hours; they thought you were dead."

"I'm fine, thank you, officer. I must have dropped off to sleep. Sorry if I've caused any upset."

"As long as you're okay, sir, I'm glad you woke up when you did though. I was about to put the window in."

I was so glad that I woke up when I did, also relieved that it was a dream. Poppy would never do anything like that. Why I would dream such a thing, God only knows.

I spent the rest of the journey home contemplating what had happened. The only reason I could think of, that would make me dream such a thing, was a comment Poppy made once when we were making love. She admitted to having a fantasy—a fantasy I'm sure lots of women have—to have two men in bed with her, so she had two cocks to play with. It had obviously lodged into my brain and manifested itself in a dream. I was in no doubt that Poppy was a loyal, loving partner and would never betray me, especially after what had happened to her with Simon. The rest of the trip home went without incident. I was so excited to arrive home; I had really missed Poppy. I pulled onto the drive. Poppy's car was on the drive, and I'm glad to say no other car was present. I grabbed my case from the car and entered the house. Polly was all over me, like she had really missed me. I called out,

"Poppy! I'm home, come here. I've missed you so much."

But there was no reply, just silence. I thought maybe she was hiding, that was the sort of thing she would do. She was probably waiting for me to walk past the wardrobe, and she would jump out to try and startle me. But there was no surprise. I looked in all the rooms; Poppy was nowhere to be seen. The other clue that something was up was when I fed Polly. She was ravenous, like she hadn't been fed for days. I went straight to the calendar, and then it hit me. The last time a letter P had been written on the calendar was yesterday. Poppy must have been called back to the future; that's why she hadn't answered the phone when I had called earlier this morning. I was gutted; she had been here for such a long time, I had got used to her always being around. Now she was gone, and I didn't know how long she would be away for. Polly looked lost; she kept whimpering. She just didn't understand where her friend had disappeared to. I just had to accept that Poppy had gone back to the future and look forward to her reappearing soon.

The 'Door' calling me back came as such a shock. I was sat on the sofa, drinking a cup of coffee. Polly was sat on my lap, she started whining; she knew something was up. She ran around the room barking. Then the temperature dropped, and I knew it was time to travel; and before I knew it, I was sat in my reclining chair in the attic in 1995.

Chapter 28
Turned to Stone

Although I hated leaving Sam, back in 1989, and Polly, of course, I was also very happy to be back in 1995. I had been away almost two years, and I had missed Roscoe so much, not to mention Chloe and Kim. I lay in the chair, gathering my thoughts. I had even missed this house; it was such a lovely place to live, and I hoped that one day Sam and I could live here together if I ever worked out how to pay Simon off. Just the thought of him made me angry; and although I wanted to tell him, I had seen him with the bitch Lucy, all those years ago. I couldn't; could I.

It was totally quiet in the attic room, you could have heard a pin drop; the only sound came from the sporadic sound of ducks quacking on the pond outside. I even recognised the smell. I looked at the clock, but couldn't tell if time had moved on since I had travelled. Simply because I had been away for so long, that I couldn't remember what time it had been when I had gone through the 'Door'. I'm sure that no time had elapsed; it had never done before when I had travelled. I ran downstairs, and sure enough Roscoe was in his basket sleeping. I gave him such a fuss; I had missed him so much. I opened the fridge to get the milk out for a cup of tea, and it was fresh, which proved no time had elapsed.

After the tea and a slice of toast, I called Chloe, then Kim and arranged to meet up later to bring them up to speed with all that had transpired since I last saw them. I was so excited when Chloe answered the phone. I hadn't heard her voice for almost two years, but for her, it had only been a few days.

"Hello, my darling friend, how are you?"

Chloe answered, in a rather confused voice,

"I'm fine, Poppy, why shouldn't I be."

"Oh! Nothing, it's just been a long time since we shared a glass of wine together."

"Poppy, my dear, it was only last week that we decimated two bottles together."

"Chloe, I will explain when I see you; see you later at 7:30-ish."

I put the phone down. They just didn't understand how weird it was, living in the past, with time slowly catching up with the future, but absolutely no time moving on in the present. I, for one, would be extremely happy when the two time zones caught up with each other, and I could live a normal life. I spent the rest of the day sorting the house out, then had a stroll around the fields with Roscoe. I wondered if when we all got together, Roscoe and Polly would get on together; that's if Roscoe was still alive in six years' time. My mind drifted back to when I first got Roscoe. She was now six years old, so when both time zones, the past and the future eventually married together, she would be approximately 12 years old; so she should make it. On the other hand, Polly was just a puppy, so I had no doubt that these two dogs would eventually become friends.

It was so frustrating living the life of a time traveller. I was already missing Sam, wondering what he was up to, and how he felt when he arrived home to find me gone, and how would Polly cope. I spent so much time with her while Sam was at work; she would be so stressed on her own in the house. I was actually tempted to go and try to find Sam in 1995 and try and skip the time difference, but there were still six years to catch up on; and anything might happen that would change the future, then I could lose everything. When I left Sam this time, it was 1989, so if I went straight to him now, in real time, six years would have passed since I last saw him. Anything could have happened in that time, so he might not even be single. No, I just had to wait for the time difference to catch up; there was no way around it. I just had to keep travelling back through the 'Door' until both time zones matched.

After I showered and got dressed, I was looking in the mirror, doing my make-up, when I realised what a difference of six years made to my skin. It certainly looked older than when I was with Sam. After laying on the war paint, I nipped downstairs to feed Roscoe. It was almost time when the girls would arrive with wine and a take away. I was so hungry, I couldn't wait. I was just putting the plates on the AGA to warm when my phone began to ring. I looked at the screen. Oh my god, it was Simon. I felt the blood drain from my head, I so wanted to let him know what I knew, but I had to keep my cool; so I decided to bite my lip and kept quiet for now.

"Hello, Poppy speaking, who is it."

"You know full well who it is, Poppy, don't be stupid."

I pressed the red button, and the phone went dead. Silly I know, but I was so angry with him, I just couldn't bring myself to speak to him. The phone rang again, and yes, it was Simon; but I just ignored it, and eventually it stopped ringing. I bet he was seething; I could just imagine his reaction. I bet he was swearing his head off. I just chuckled to myself, *Sod him, I would talk to him when I was good and ready.*

I heard the screech of the bolt being drawn across on the gate. The girls were here. Roscoe disappeared down the drive to greet them. I also went outside, excited to see my friends.

Kim and Chloe both jumped out of the car and hugged me,

"Oh girls! It's just great to see you both. I've missed you so much."

Kim was carrying a carrier bag; the bottles chinking away inside.

"Do you think four bottles will do the trick," she said, with a large grin on her face.

Chloe, piped up,

"I should think so; I can only have a couple of glasses. I'm driving, don't forget."

"That just means more for me and Poppy then."

Chloe was clutching a bag with the take away in, which I took off her. It smelled delicious. It had been a long time since I had tasted a curry from my favourite local takeaway. It was a well-oiled drill, while Kim sorted the drinks. Chloe and I dished up the grub. We sat around the kitchen table; we all raised our glasses and proposed a toast.

"Here's to the three musketeers."

We all touched glasses and repeated,

"The three musketeers."

"Oh girls, I've missed you so much. It's so nice to see you, to be together."

They both stared at me gone out; then Kim spoke,

"Poppy, it's been two weeks max since I saw you and probably less for Chloe. I don't understand."

"Kim, I thought I had explained how my time travel worked. When I go back, the time here stands still; but while I'm back in the past, time moves on."

Both the girls' eyes were staring straight at me, as if they were being told off.

"Now believe it or not, this time I travelled back, two years have elapsed; so when I say I missed you, I really have missed you."

I burst into tears; the whole situation overwhelming me.

"Oh Poppy! We are so sorry. We just didn't realise you had been away for so long."

Then Chloe chipped in, excitedly,

"That means you must have loads of gossip to fill us in on. Come on, Poppy, spill the beans."

Over the next two hours or so, I relayed all that had transpired over the past two years, when they heard about Simon and his bit of stuff. There was talk of castration, mainly from Chloe who was so protective of me. They were both desperate to see a picture of Sam and, of course, Polly the dog. Also, they were very curious about my sex life.

"So, Poppy, what's he like in the sack," Chloe asked; then Kim started,

"Out of ten, where does he score? Is he better than Simon?"

I giggled nervously, and I could feel myself going red. I didn't really think it was right to discuss our sex life, but they wouldn't stop going on about it; then in the end, I just blurted it out,

"He's amazing in bed; and yes, he's far better a lover than Simon ever was."

There were roars of laughter, and the girls raised their glasses. Kim leading the charge,

"Here's to Sam, the man who can."

It seemed at last, they both believed that I really was a time traveller, and I have to admit, I felt a lot better knowing I had the support of two people who were watching my back.

The plates were clean, and the bottles were empty; our stomachs full. Kim and I were a little tipsy; poor old Chloe who had only had one glass of wine was sober, but she had to drive back, so *c'est la vie.*

"So Poppy, when you go back, what year is it now."

"Well, Chloe, when I left, it was the summer of 1989, but when I travel back the next time, who knows, it might be the same time, or time might have moved on months or even years."

Then Kim interjected,

"So it's 1995 here, and the goal is for the past to catch up with the future, right."

"Yes!" I said with relief that they were now beginning to grasp the logistics of my dilemma.

"So another six years in the past, and we will finally get to meet Sam the man," Chloe said, with a big grin on her face.

"But before that, Poppy, you still need to find a way of proving to the both of us that you really are having a second life without us."

I grinned, but thought to myself, *easier said than done.*

"I will work on it, I promise," I replied to placate her.

After we had coffee, and we had said our goodbyes, it was well after 12 o'clock. I locked up and headed up the stairs to bed. Roscoe was close at my heels all the way up the stairs. I felt lonely laying in the bed on my own, apart from the little scamp who was nuzzled up to me. I could feel the warmth from his body through the duvet; my hand gently playing with his ears, while contemplating how I was going to pay off Simon, and a myriad of other problems flying around in my head. I woke up confused. I had been dreaming of Sam and was convinced I was still with him; so when it dawned on me I was in 1995 without him, my mood slumped. Then I had an idea, but it was risky and stupid, but I so wanted to see Sam. I thought I would drive the 30 miles to where Sam and I lived back in 1989, to see if I could get a glimpse of the man I was in love with.

After walking Roscoe, I had a quick breakfast of toast and tea and set off in my van. Roscoe was really excited; he loved going out in the van. As usual, he sat on the passenger seat with his front paws on the dash, his tail wagging and his tongue out, occasionally barking as we passed sheep or horses in the fields. What I was doing went against all common sense; and if I got caught, well, it wasn't worth contemplating. It could spoil everything.

I finally reached the road where the house was. I drove past and pulled into a lay-by opposite the wood, which stood at the back of the house. The plan was to enter the woods behind the house, sneak up to the back fence and peak through any gap I could find and hopefully see Sam or Polly. As I left the van, Roscoe wasn't happy. He kept barking and scratching at the side window. I felt bad about leaving him. In fact he made so much noise, I had no choice but to go back and get him. As soon as I put his lead on, and he realised he was coming with me, he went as quiet as a mouse.

"You little scamp, Roscoe, you always get your own way."

I scrunched his little face between both hands and kissed his nose, then set off towards the woods. It was awkward climbing over the fence and trying to keep hold of Roscoe's lead, so I let him go through a gap at the bottom. I told him to sit, which he did, while I climbed over the top, dropping unceremoniously on to the bracken. I lay there, feeling a little stupid; then Roscoe was on me, slobbering his wet tongue all over my face.

"Get off, Roscoe, arrgghh!!!"

As I got up off the ground, Roscoe started barking. He kept running towards me, then jumping back, like it was some sort of game,

"Quiet Roscoe, quiet."

As I leant down to grab his lead, he was off like a shot. His lead was trailing behind him; then he was gone. The bracken was taller than the dog, so all you could see was a ripple of movement, wherever he ran. This was the last thing I wanted. If anybody else was walking in the woods, it would just draw unwanted attention. I frantically ran after him, calling his name; but after a few minutes, I realised the woods were quiet apart from the staccato call of foraging magpies. Roscoe must have got the scent of a squirrel; that would be the most likely reason he had bolted. In the distance, I could hear the vague barking of a dog—it had to be Roscoe. I decided to leave him to his own devices while I sneaked up to the fence of Sam's house. At least, I could get a look without worrying that Roscoe would start barking.

It was around 12-ish, so I might be lucky to get a glimpse of Sam if he had come home for lunch. I eventually found my way to the back fence. It was quite a struggle as the undergrowth was like a jungle. It was a 6ft larch lap fence, so I wouldn't be able to peer over the top. Luckily, I saw a burst of concentrated light, like a laser piercing through the fence into the dark shadows of the wood. I made my way to where the light emanated. Luckily for me, a knot in the wood had fallen out, leaving a hole the size of my thumb, allowing the bright sunshine to stream through. I pressed my face against the hole, the sunlight blinding my sight for a couple of seconds; then the view opened up. I must have been at the wrong house. Although it was familiar, there was a pagoda under the bedroom window, but the garden was so overgrown. The oak tree that stood in the middle of the garden seemed so much taller, the shrubs that I had planted were massive, and the passionflower on the pagoda had grown as tall as the eaves on the house. The most outstanding thing that struck me—and it was so out of character for Sam—was the total neglect of the garden. Sam would never let the lawn get into such a state, but it was. I was confused; then the penny dropped. It was 1995; I was thinking that I was looking into 1989 when I had last left—that was six years ago. This was the garden six years on from then, but why hadn't Sam tended the garden. Then I thought to myself, *Sam doesn't live here anymore. We must have moved again, that's why it's in such a mess. The new people were obviously not into gardening.* I was just accepting this concept into my befuddled brain when I heard the patio doors slide open. I pressed my eye hard up to the hole and focussed on the patio doors. My heart missed a beat, a cold shiver ran down my back; I froze. What happened next will remain stuck in my mind for ever.

Chapter 29
Fait Accompli

The image that arrived with such an impact on my retina will stick with me for the rest of my life. I couldn't believe what I was seeing. The patio door was fully open, and what filled the opening was unbelievable. I had to pinch myself several times before I would accept what I was witnessing. There was a man in a wheel chair, wearing pyjamas and a dressing gown. He looked very stiff, no facial movement, and his head was held in a brace to support it. I looked hard at his face; the tears ran down my cheeks, and my heart was broken.

It was Sam. He looked a lot older than the last time I had seen him, even allowing for the six-year difference in time zones. He seemed expressionless, like he wasn't there. I pulled away from the fence, holding my head in my hands and sobbed my heart out. I slumped to the floor; my whole world crashing in on me. What the hell could have happened; he was fine when I left him. All sorts of scenarios went through my mind. Had he been in an accident, had he had a stroke; whatever had happened to him, it had left him crippled and in a wheel chair. I reappeared at the hole, hoping that I had been seeing things; but as I feared, Sam was still there in his chair. I noticed a small ramp had been built next to the door to allow access onto the patio.

A rather stern-looking lady was in control of the chair, manoeuvring him carefully through the opening and onto the patio. I guessed she must be his carer or a nurse. She pushed him across the patio to where there were some chairs and a table. She then swivelled him around to face the sun. He always did love the sun on his face. She then disappeared into the house, and Sam was left on his own. I felt like climbing the fence and going to hug him, but that wasn't an option. A couple of minutes later, the nurse came through the doorway, holding two glasses of drinks, which looked like orange juice; and then to my utter surprise, following her was a dog. It was Polly; she ran straight over to Sam, burying her head in his lap, her tail wagging; but the strange thing was, Sam didn't attempt to stroke her. Although I could hear Sam saying something to her, his arms remained next to his side. I assumed he was unable to move them. The nurse placed the drinks down on the table and then proceeded to raise one of the glasses to Sam's mouth to allow him to have a drink. He was obviously paralysed from the neck down. The tears were still streaming down my face, when the 'nurse' then leant towards Sam and kissed him on the lips. I then realised she wasn't a nurse at all; she was Sam's partner. I again pulled away from the hole in shock. I needed to take stock of the situation, so much must have happened in the past six years.

I then heard a rustling in the bushes. Roscoe had finally given up on the squirrels and decided to join me. He was so excited to find me, he started yelping with pleasure. I tried to stop him, but he just carried on. I peered through the hole, and to my dread, Polly's ears were pricked up alert to the sound. Then the lady stood up and looked towards the fence; it was time to get out of there. Unknown to me, Roscoe had other ideas. He had found a hole under the fence and was off like a rocket, into the garden towards Polly. He ran straight at Polly, then they started chasing each other around the garden. The lady shouted out,

"Polly, come here at once."

She wasn't amused. The two dogs were having so much fun; they seemed to love each other. I couldn't shout out or call for Roscoe to come back for fear of being recognised by Sam. Then to my complete surprise, both dogs came shooting through the hole in the fence. Roscoe was rolling over in the bracken, obviously in love. Polly, on the other hand, came through all excited, but when she saw me, she stopped in her tracks. She started whining. I could hear the lady calling her,

"Polly, are you alright, come back here, that's a good girl."

Polly was very hesitant. She slowly moved towards me, smelling me; then all hell let loose. She jumped on me, licking me to death. She was so excited, she wet herself; then Roscoe joined in. God knows what the lady on the other side of the fence thought was going on; there was such a commotion. I realised I needed to end the situation before the fence got knocked down and Sam saw me. I grabbed hold of Polly and forced her through the hole, I then put my boot in the way until I heard the lady catch the dog by the collar and lead her away. It was now time to grab Roscoe's lead and get out of there.

I ran all the way back to the van, Roscoe in tow. I cried the whole time while driving back home. I just couldn't believe what had happened to my lovely Sam. To see him like that broke my heart, I thought to myself, *it was my fault. If I hadn't disappeared back to the future, it might not have happened.* I pulled onto the drive, absolutely devastated. There had to be away to change what had caused this tragedy to Sam. I parked the van and went inside. I sat at the kitchen table with a cup of tea, thinking what I could do. Then I decided to have a long soak in a hot bath and run over all of my options. The bathroom was bathed in sunlight. There was clear glass in the window to allow a good view over the fields. Besides, there were no neighbours to look back at you. While the bath filled, steam filled the air. I dropped my clothes to the floor, poured some eucalyptus bath soap into the water and immersed myself in to the pleasure-giving water. I then started going through what might have happened, and how I might be able to change the past, to influence the future. The exact thing I had strived not to do since I had first travelled. The first thing to do was find out the facts. I couldn't go and ask Sam when it occurred. If I travelled back to before the accident happened, we wouldn't be any the wiser. I then had a thought. I had seen on the TV, when people were researching something, they went to the library where you could look into a machine and study old newspaper cuttings. I was now excited. If I could find out the date of the accident, I might be able to travel back to before it happened and make sure it never happens. The problem was, I couldn't guarantee that when I travelled back the next time that I would arrive before the fateful day.

I quickly got out of the bath. It was only 12:30 p.m. The library would be open until 4:30 p.m. at least. I arrived at the local library. I looked at the clock that hung above the reception desk. It read 1:29 p.m. The young lady on reception looked up from her work and spoke,

"Good afternoon, can I help you."

"Oh yes, please. I'm hoping to look through some old newspaper reports for the local area, would that be possible."

The young lady looked over her dark-rimmed glasses. I expected her to say something like "This is a library, we only have books", but to my surprise, she replied,

"Of course, you want to use the Microfiche machine, what dates were you interested in."

I was a bit taken aback, but also in a dilemma. I had no idea when the accident may have happened.

"Well, I'm afraid it's a little vague. What I do know is that the event I'm looking for happened after 1989 and before 1995."

"Okay."

The lady replied, nonchalantly,

"I know I'm not being very helpful, but this is all I know. It was probably a road traffic accident, and it happened to a local man between those dates I've just mentioned, and I'm hoping that it was reported in one of the local papers."

The lady smiled and asked me to follow her. She led me to an area of the library where there stood three quite large square metal boxes, with like-glass screens at the front. Each one sat on a desk, with a swivel chair pushed underneath. Two of the machines had people sat at them. Their heads quite close to the screens, obviously perusing through their chosen files.

"If you make yourself comfortable, give me a few minutes, and I will get the files you've requested."

Then she was gone. I sat at the machine, and about 15 minutes later, the lady came back with a very small box of what looked like sheets of plastic. She proceeded to load one into the machine. She then showed me how to move through the files by moving a toggle arm at the front of the machine. I started off with quite a lot of enthusiasm but after about an hour of trolling through thousands of pages of news stories, I have to admit my patience was wearing thin. Each plastic film contained thousands of excerpts from each individual newspaper. It was like looking for a needle in a haystack. My mind was becoming blank, and I feared I might have passed the article without noticing it. After two hours without success, my spirit was diminishing,

I was about to give up, when I scroll past a picture of a man's face, which jolted my subconscious. I moved the picture back into view; my heart rate quickened, and my hands went cold and clammy. The face looking at me from inside the machine was Sam's face. The headline above the picture read,

"Local man, Thanks Air Ambulance for saving his life."

Oh! My God, I had found the report. I read on, transfixed by the story.

Local man, Samuel Devere, was rescued by The Air Ambulance service today when he fell 20 feet from rigging on to the stage at a music concert. The company he worked for were contracted to supply the lighting and sound systems for a series of concerts around the country. This particular concert in Manchester was the opening venue in a string of concerts aimed at raising money for a cancer charity. Thirty one-year-old project manager Samuel Devere was inspecting the lighting rig when it collapsed, fell 20 feet on to the stage below. He was taken to hospital with a suspected broken back; and due to the severity of his injuries, it was decided to use the Air Ambulance service to expedite a speedy transfer to the spinal unit, some 30 miles away.

As the story unfolded, the tears rolled down my face. Imagining the pain and suffering that Sam must have gone through broke my heart. I looked through my bag for a pen and paper, then looked to the top of the page for the date of the report. It read the 19th May 1993. I carefully wrote down all the relevant facts. These I would have to commit to memory, so that the next time I travelled back, I could relay the story to Sam. I just preyed that when I went back, I arrive before the 19th of May 1993. That was the only chance I had of preventing Sam being crippled for life.

I was so desperate to travel back to warn Sam of the impending danger ahead that I decided to work in the attic, so if the 'Door' did decide to open, I would be ready. I was working on an oil painting. It depicted a country scene, looking across the valley at the distant hills—the impact of the piece being the sky. There were dark clouds building, edged brightly by the powerful sun fighting to drench the fields below with its life-giving rays. It brought a smile to my face, thinking about it. It was a little like the situation I was in. The 'Door' being the dark clouds, preventing me the sun from getting through to Sam to give him life-changing information. Next to the easel was the piece of paper which I had written all the facts about Sam's accident. The most important fact being the date, then the place, the name of the concert and the injuries he would sustain if I didn't forewarn him of the dangers ahead. I made sure the facts were well and truly in my memory. I knew I could take nothing through the 'Door' except myself.

Chapter 30
Distant Shores

I had only been back in 1995 for two days, but I was desperate for the 'Door' to open, so I could see Sam and Polly again. I painted all of that day and the following day, constantly staring at the 'Door', willing it to open, but nothing. I wondered to myself, *what the hell it was that triggered it to open.* I thought about all the times when it had opened, but couldn't come up with anything in my mind that might have been relevant. Was it temperature, the weather, my mind willing it to open; was it something in the past that caused it to open—god, I was so frustrated. I ran at the 'Door' and kicked it really hard. That was a big mistake. The steel door didn't yield, but my big toe did. It felt like I had broken it. I could feel it swelling up inside my trainer. I lay on the floor in agony, swearing like a trooper. I took my trainer off; the pain was intense. Just to pull my sock off was agony; my big toe was swollen and very red. I limped to my reclining chair and sat down. I needed painkillers but they were in the kitchen draw, two flights of stairs down below.

Then as I lay back into the chair, there was a resounding clonk. The 'Door' decided to open. I got up as quickly as I could and hobbled towards the 'Door'. I pressed down on the handle and sure enough the 'Door' opened. There was the familiar sound of cold air escaping; a fog drifted into the room, and the temperature dropped considerably. I managed to get inside, though the pain was excruciating. The 'Door' slammed behind me. I went down onto my hands and knees and crawled towards the light in the distance; it was less painful that way. I could hear birds singing and a dog barking. I reached into the light, but then started falling through the thick fog. This time the fall seemed longer than before. Then a cataclysmic flash of bright white light, and I was sat on lush green grass, in the shade of a tree.

Before I could even get my bearings, the dog that I had heard barking was on me—a slobbering, wet, frenzied tongue searched out every orifice it could find. My mouth, ears, nose were covered in slobber, but I didn't mind at all—it was Polly. I had returned to the past and arrived in the garden of our house under the oak tree,

"Hello Polly, have you missed me."

She was whining in pleasure. She smelt just as I remembered her to smell. I stood up and realised my big toe didn't hurt any more. I was wearing sandals, a short skirt and a tea shirt, so it must be the summer months, but what year was it.

I looked towards the house, in particular the patio doors. To my great relief, there was no ramp leading onto the patio. I must have arrived before the accident in May 1993. Then from above the pagoda came the sound of a window being opened. I looked up to see Sam bare-chested, hanging out the window. I shouted up to him,

"Oh, my precious Sam, I've missed you so much. I'm coming up, wait there."

I ran to the patio doors and yanked on the handle; they were open. I ran through the house and into the hall, then up the stairs, screaming all the time,

"Oh Sam, I love you, I've missed you."

I burst through the bedroom door, and stood there completely naked was Sam; and what a body he had. I launched myself so hard towards him, we both ended up on the bed.

"Oh Sam, I've missed you so much, how long have I been away this time."

Sam started kissing me. He had tears in his eyes. He held me so tight, I could hardly breathe—well Sam, how long.

"Poppy, let's just say it's been so long that I thought I would never see you again."

"Sam, what do you mean, it was summer when I left, and it's summer now by the state of the weather."

"Yes, Poppy, it is summer, but it's now 1990; you've been away for just over a year."

I was stunned, not only about the length of time but also that Sam had waited for all that time without giving up on me, or had he.

"Sam, please tell me you still love me, and you haven't found someone else."

His face went deadly serious. He gulped like he dreaded what he was about to say, then he spoke,

"Poppy, you've been absent for over a year; all men have needs."

I knew what he was about to say, that he couldn't wait that long for a shag, so he had found someone else.

"I know what you're going to say, Sam."

"Let me finish, Poppy.

"What I was about to say was, all men have needs, and I've waited over a year for this; so if you don't mind, I want sex right now."

We both started laughing. I was so relieved that Sam had been true to his word. When he said he would always wait for me to return, then I felt evidence of his intentions. I could feel his cock getting ever harder. I was lying on top of him, but I only had a short, thin skirt on, so it was quite apparent that his lustful thoughts were having an effect on his manhood. Sam expertly stripped me off my pants, leaving my skirt on; then my tea shirt flew across the room, and before it landed, my breasts were swinging freely. Sam lifted me up and slowly sat me on his very stiff wet cock. As he entered me, the feeling of him inside me filled me with such pleasure, I sighed with satisfaction. I leant forward to kiss him; my breasts just touching his masculine chest.

"Poppy Day, I love you with all my heart. Don't you ever leave me again."

Our lips met; I slipped my tongue into Sam's mouth. He was wet with wanting. I gyrated up and down on his massive tool, filling my pussy with his lusting throbbing penis.

"Sam! Fuck me, fuck me harder. I want your cum, and I want it now."

I loved it when Poppy used that expression 'Fuck me'. It really turned me on. In fact, everything about her turned me on; she was a sex bomb waiting to go off. She was bobbing up and down on my cock so sensually that it wouldn't be long before I came. She lowered towards me, pushing her tits in my face. I gently licked her nipples; they became as stiff as my cock. I was holding her by the cheeks of her gorgeous arse, pulling her on to my pulsing dick; my balls were about to explode. It had been a while since I had relieved myself, so my balls were ready to deliver my message of love. She licked my nipples; then started biting them. This sent me over the edge.

"Poppy, it's all over, I can't stop it."

"Don't worry, babe, I'm there too."

Poppy got quite physical when she came; her nails digging into my shoulders, her face contorted, almost like she was in pain.

"Sam, I love you so much."

She was so out of breath. She could hardly talk. There were beads of sweat running down her neck. I knew Sam was about to come. His cock seemed to swell inside me; then his eyes rolled. He gripped me even harder; then I felt his hot spunk filling my pussy. Sam groaned, "Aaaarrrgghhhhh, I love you Pops."

After our shenanigans in the bedroom, we cuddled for a while; then we both showered. Sam put the kettle on, and I made an entry on the calendar in the kitchen. I put a P on the day marked 25th August 1990. We sat at the table and began to catch up on all the gossip since I'd been away.

"Sam, I really do appreciate you waiting for me all that time. Weren't you tempted to see someone else."

I looked at him. He looked hesitant to answer. He smiled, and then said,

"Well, I do have an admirer—a lady at work. She's a little older than me; she asked me out for a drink."

"Well, did you, I wouldn't blame you, honest."

"To be honest, yes, I did go for a drink with her, but I explained that I was in love with you, and we could only be friends. Besides, she is attractive but very stern and scary."

I instantly thought about the 'nurse' who was looking after him in 1995. I wondered if she was the same lady. I suppose if I had disappeared for six years, Sam's loyalty may have wavered.

"The main thing is this Sam, you did wait for me, and you still love me; and if you want to be friends with this cougar, that's fine by me."

Sam whipped me, with the tea towel.

"She's not a cougar, just a work colleague, so please don't worry about her."

I thought it best not to broach the subject of the future accident right at that moment, because deep down I knew, this mystery woman was somehow connected.

Over the next couple of weeks, things between us settled down. We got back into the normal routine—Sam going to work in the morning and me keeping the house running smoothly, whilst still finding time to paint. I don't know why, but now I was back with Sam, and our sex life was torrid, all I wanted to paint was fantasy sex scenes. We were so alike, in our everyday life, we both were attentive, loving and passionate with each other; but as soon as we were aroused and up for a shag, we both turned into depraved sex monsters. The unusual trait that Sam possessed was, he loved to watch porn, but only with me. He said it turned him on, watching me watch porn, and I believed him when he said he never watched porn on his own. That night after we had eaten our tea, Sam placed an envelope on my lap and said,

"Surprise, I hope you like it."

"What is it, Sam?"

"Well, Poppy, open it, and you will find out."

I was so excited; I ripped open the envelope and inside was what looked like airline tickets. I looked up at Sam.

"Where are we going, Sam, and when?"

"Polly, read the tickets."

I scrutinised the tickets and read the destination. It read, 'Zante Greece'. I was so excited. Then I looked at the date; we were flying in two days' time.

"Oh, Sam! You're so good to me, but two days to pack my case, it's going to be a challenge."

"Well, I've booked half a day off work tomorrow, so we can go and get anything you might need; maybe a nice bikini and some sun glasses."

Then the panic set in. What if the 'Door' called me back while we were in mid-flight. The press would have a field day, 'Passenger disappears off jet liner while in flight'. Try explaining that one to the authorities; it would be in all the papers, even on the news headlines. I tried to explain to Sam how much trouble it could cause, but he didn't seem perturbed at all. He just brushed it off, saying,

"Poppy, it's very unlikely that you will be called back. It's only a four hour flight, I'm sure we will be fine."

I so wanted to go away that I decided to trust Sam's judgement and risk it anyway. Deep down, I just prayed that the 'Door' would leave me alone, at least for the next week or so. The next thing I heard was the dog flap. Polly came bounding in. I looked at Sam, and Sam looked at me.

"Who's going to look after Polly," I asked Sam.

"You know what, I hadn't even thought about the dog."

"You are joking, Sam."

"Of course, I am, Sally has offered to look after her; she loves Polly."

"Talking about your sister, what did you tell her about my disappearance."

"Well! I thought the best option was honesty, so I told her you were a time traveller."

Although he was smiling when he said it, I just knew he was telling the truth.

"Sam, my god, what did you do that for, and what the hell did she say?"

"It was really strange. Her reaction baffled me, she replied with, I always knew there was something special about that girl', just as if it was normal; then she said, make sure you don't lose that one."

I really liked Sam's sister Sally. From the first time we had met, we had got on like a house on fire. It was nice to know that she was on my side.

The following day we went shopping as planned. Sam bought a new pair of shorts, and I had some sunglasses and two bikinis—one was black with white flashes on; the other was canary yellow. That night we had a takeaway and spent nearly all night sorting out what to pack. Sam's case closed without any effort; mine on the other hand was never going to close, so we had to transfer some of my things into Sam's case. "Poppy, why are you taking so much stuff; do you really need so many outfits, and why so many shoes."

"Sam! You just don't understand, women like to be prepared, just in case."
Sam started laughing,
"Just in case? In case of what? That we get stuck in Greece for six months."
"Oh Sam! Stop picking on me, you want me to look beautiful, don't you?"
"Poppy, you are beautiful. Even if you were dressed in a sack cloth, you would look amazing."

With the cases both shut, our travelling clothes in two neat piles at the end of the bed, passports and tickets on the dressing table, we went to bed excited. Polly was asleep at the end of the bed, and it wasn't long before we joined her. The next morning, Sally arrived at the house quite early to collect Polly. I was a little apprehensive at meeting her now. Sam had decided to tell her I was a time traveller. I couldn't believe that Sally was so *blasé* about the whole thing. We sat and drank our tea around the kitchen table,

"Poppy, Sam tells me you're a time traveller; that would explain your untimely disappearances. I was concerned at first that you would break Sam's heart, but now with this information, I'm more confident that you will work it out."

I was completely got smacked, why would she just accept it. No normal person would; they would just assume you were mad. There must be a reason, and I was determined to find out why. After we finished our tea and toast and hugs all around, especially Polly, we said goodbye. As Sally backed off the drive, she shouted through the window,

"Have a lovely holiday both, especially you TT."
Sam and I looked at each other confused; then I shouted back, "TT!"
Sally replied, "Time Traveller."

Then curiously, she winked at me; then she was gone. Not long after, we set off to Birmingham Airport. It only took about 40 minutes to get there. As we got nearer, we could see approaching aircraft bringing back holidaymakers; their holidays coming to a rapid end. I don't really think the holiday starts until the car is parked, your bags have been weighed in, and you're sat in the bar with a nice drink, waiting to be called for your flight. You can then start relaxing; if you've forgotten something at this stage, it's too late, so all there is to do is relax and enjoy your drink.

After Sam had downed two pints, and I finished my large glass of Pino, the screens were flashing. Our flight had been called, and it was time to head towards Gate 28. It was quite some walk, but we were chilled, holding hands and extremely happy. After all, this was the first time we had been abroad together. I just love that moment when your plane is sat at the end of the runway, waiting for clearance to take off. The engine noise builds to a crescendo; you feel the brake being released, and the plane starts moving slowly at first; then the plane quickly accelerates towards the end of the runway. You turn to your loved one and hold hands; you both know deep down this is the crucial moment, but, alas, the aircraft reaches its desired speed; and hey presto, the hundred tonne plane lifts off into the cloudy sky. As you push through the blanket of fluffy grey cloud, the bright uninterrupted sunlight penetrates the cabin, and you feel instantly that you're in a different world.

I was sat next to the window, Sam was in the middle seat and sat next to him was a very slim, attractive young girl. Her skin quite tanned, she was adorned with gold jewellery, and what looked like a very expensive watch. She seemed like a person who could have anything she wanted in life, as long as she kept her eyes off my Sam. *My god, what was wrong with me. I wasn't a jealous person; why would I even think that,* I thought to myself, *Poppy Day, snap out of it; you silly, silly girl.*

Sam clutched my hand and kissed it, as if to reassure me, like he knew my thoughts.

"I love You, Poppy Day. I'm so looking forward to spending the next seven days and nights with you, thank you for coming back."

"Sam, there's nothing in the world that would keep me away from you." He kissed me again. Then the air hostess arrived with our lunch. There was a choice of cottage pie or a chicken dinner; we both had a chicken dinner with ice cream to follow. I absolutely love aeroplane food, especially when it's washed down with a nice glass. Well, a plastic glass of Pino, which I had. Sam took a nice cold beer.

The four-hour flight went without a hitch. No shimmering vision or a drop in temperature, so the 'Door' was leaving me alone. Our ears began to pop as the plane descended down towards the island of Zakinthos, or Zante, as most people called it. We both caught a glimpse of a long golden beach as we approached rapidly from the sea, then across the arid sun burnt land of this small Greek island. There was a short screech of tyres as the wheels hit the hot tarmac. We taxied for about half a mile; then the plane came to an abrupt stop. The seat belt sign lit up, then the deafening sound of hundreds of passengers releasing themselves from the bondage of their belts. Why such a rush, I have no idea, because it's always ages before the ground crew on these small islands get the stairs to the aircraft. Then the mad rush of hundreds of passengers getting into the aisles, in a bid to be the first off the plane. Why, you can't go anywhere, you just have to wait your turn. Then the moment when you know you're not at home any more, is when the aircraft door is opened, and the searing hot air rushes in.

The terminal building wasn't really up to much, quite sparse, with a few ceiling fans spinning in a desperate attempt to cool the hot putrid air. Hundreds of excited passengers all rushing to passport control, with only a couple of officer's to check off the passports, a quick cursory glance then a nod of the head giving permission to continue to the baggage hall. We found our position next to the carousel, both of us focussed on the rubber flaps covering the entrance, where the bags would mysteriously appear. But you guessed it; things in these hot countries didn't happen very quickly. Sam very thoughtfully started fanning me with his hat; then the sound of the buzzer warning of the start-up of the conveyor belt. Everyone looking towards the hole where hopefully your case would appear; some of the cases looked the worst for wear, with clear plastic tape holding them together after being thrown uncaringly from the bowels of the aeroplane.

There was a coach waiting to take us to our hotel, and I couldn't wait to arrive. I was so thirsty, the transfer took over an hour, and we hadn't thought to carry water with us. But when we arrived, we were so happy. The hotel was beautiful, and then we opened the door to our room; the air con was on full blast, and the cold air like an elixir for life. Sam ran to the window; the curtains were drawn to stop the sun from warming the room. He pulled back the drapes to expose an amazing view over the sea. We walked out onto the spacious balcony,

"Oh Sam! Just look at the view, it's beautiful."

"It certainly is, isn't it, Poppy."

Sam hugged me, kissed me gently on the back of my neck and whispered in my ear,

"I think we are going to be very happy here, Poppy."

"Oh Sam, thank you so much for bringing me. I love you."

We spent the rest of the time available unpacking; and before we went down for dinner, I took advantage of the very comfy bed for a well-earned snooze.

There were two restaurants to choose from. Once we ordered from a menu—quite formal—we chose to eat in the Terrace Restaurant, all the tables were set on a beautiful terrace, overlooking the sea. This was a 'help yourself from a buffet' restaurant, which suited both of us, as we could try all sorts of things and eat as much as we wanted. Several waiters were running around, serving drinks—a service that we used several times that night. Just as we were finishing our sweet, the sun was just dropping into the sea on the horizon. It was the most amazing, romantic sunset I had ever seen. The whole sky turned from deep blue to a crimson orange. I took so many pictures with Sam's camera. I just prayed I would get the perfect shot, so I could use it in a painting.

After dinner, we went inside the hotel. We found a comfy seat in the bar area, where there was a young lady singer entertaining the guests. Sam ordered a large beer, and I had a large glass of Pino. I looked at Sam; he was really enjoying the entertainment; he was singing along quite merry. At some stage during this holiday, I had to talk to him about the future accident, and how to prevent it happening.

"Sam, would you like a dance and let all these people know what a mover you are."

Sam laughed,

"Very funny, Pops. I'd love to, but I think I've had rather too much beer, I might just make a pratt of myself."

"No change there then."

I replied, laughing out loud.

"Right then. Come on, you cheeky sod, I'll show you I've still got the moves I had when I was a teenager."

We helped each other up and stumbled towards the small dance area. Unfortunately, the singer decided to announce our arrival. All eyes were now on us—how embarrassing. Then she started singing a slow ballad; thank god, it wasn't a fast one; it meant I could hang onto Sam and save my blushes.

"Poppy, I will never forget this dance with you. You look fantastic. I must be the luckiest guy alive. I love you, Pops."

Sam's speech was slurred. I suppose we had been drinking all day, starting at the airport, then on the plane, plus what we had knocked back tonight,

"Sam, how do you fancy going to bed. I'm quite tired."

"Count me in, boss."

We entered our room. We had left the air con on, so it was lovely and cool. I bagged the bathroom first; I was desperate for the loo. When I came out, I found Sam crashed out on the bed, still in his clothes, snoring his head off. I'd never known anyone who could fall asleep faster than him. There was no chance of any passion tonight, so I struggled to undress him, got him under the covers, cuddled up and before long was away with the fairies.

Chapter 31
The Baptism

I woke up the next morning; and at first, I wondered where the hell I was. I felt really cold, and the room was dark, then it dawned on me, we were in Greece. I jumped out of bed and first, pulled the drapes; the sunlight hit me like a train, but wow, what a lovely feeling. I opened the patio doors and ran out onto the terrace; that was a big mistake. I was barefoot, and the stone floor was red hot from the incessant sun beating down on it. I couldn't believe how hot it was. I must have looked like one of those lizards you see on nature programmes, running across burning hot desert sands, trying not to leave their feet down for too long. I made it back inside, with both my feet feeling burnt. My screams must have woken Sam,

"Poppy! Are you alright, what's all the screaming about?"

"It's the patio! It's bloody hot, I've burnt my feet."

Instead of feeling sorry for me, he took the mick and started laughing. I was not impressed.

"You dipstick, did you go outside without your flip flops on."

"Yes, I did, and a bit of sympathy would be nice."

I jumped on the bed and straddled Sam; then I caught both of his ears in my hands and pulled them. He was laughing.

"How do you fancy a bit of pain, Samuel Devere?"

"I surrender, Poppy. Sorry, I mocked you; you're hurting my ears, please let go."

"First of all, who's the boss, Samuel. Come on, who is it."

"You are Poppy, Poppy Sir, you are."

I kissed him on the lips and let go of his ears,

"Good morning, my beautiful girlfriend. Are your feet really hurting you."

"The pains slowly fading, but they were stinging when I came back in."

"So it was a bit of fuss over nothing, just an excuse to beat me up. I see, Poppy Day."

She was sat across me, staring into my eyes. I couldn't believe how beautiful she was. All she had on was a flimsy tee shirt; her bulging breasts pressing against the thin fabric. She leant forward again; her lips met mine. She kissed me passionately, then said,

"How do you fancy?"

I interrupted her,

"How do you fancy a shag?"

"No! How do you fancy going down for breakfast."

"Aarrgghh, you're such a tease. Alright, give me five minutes to freshen up, and I'm with you."

A few minutes later, we entered the reception. One of the friendly female staff on the desk spotted us straight away. They were so attentive.

"Good morning to you both. Follow me, and I will show you where we serve breakfast."

We followed the young lady out of reception and onto the terrace outside; the view was amazing. There were a lot of people already eating breakfast.

"Just sit at any free table, and someone will be with you shortly, enjoy!"

Then she was off back to reception, leaving us to settle down to our first breakfast at this wonderful hotel.

"Oh! Sam, what a beautiful place to eat breakfast. Look at the view, it's stunning!"

The hotel was set on the side of a hill, so we were slightly elevated giving us an uninterrupted view across the sea. There were several ships making their way in lots of different directions, leaving their tell-tale, white, churned-up wakes in their trail. We chose a table for two next to a low stone wall; and within seconds, a rather handsome, dark-haired young man was at the table.

"Good morning, my name is Spiros. I will be looking after you this morning. Would you like tea or coffee, may be some toast."

Sam ordered tea and toast; then introduced us. He always liked to get on first name terms with people he met, and it certainly made things a lot easier when you knew people's names.

"Very nice to meet you, Spiros. I'm Sam, and this is Poppy."

Spiros looked at both of us, repeating our names as if to reconfirm in his mind the names. He looked me in the eye and said,

"Poppy! Isn't that the name of a flower?"

"Yes, Spiros, the red poppy."

"Well, Poppy, it's a beautiful name for a beautiful lady."

I felt myself going red, my face flushing. I don't know why; may be because Sam was sat there, smiling.

"Okay! Sam and Poppy, I will fetch you your tea and toast. Help yourself to our buffet breakfast; it's all laid out under the canopy over there."

He pointed towards an area where a lot of people were milling around, and the staff were all wearing full whites with chef hats on. The reason it was all set out under the canopy was to protect the food from the onslaught of the overpowering sun. Even at this time in the morning, it packed quite a punch. The choice of food was extensive. I went for fruit juice and cereal, with a good dollop of Greek yoghurt on top. Sam attempted to make up a cooked breakfast; the Greek bacon was very streaky, two fried eggs, a very thin long sausage and some mushrooms. He looked quite pleased with himself when he arrived back at the table, with a bulging plate. We both really enjoyed our breakfast, and after washing it down with several cups of tea and toast, we were both stuffed, both of us vowed not to eat again until dinner tonight. After gorging ourselves, we went back to the room to get our swimming costumes on and decided to spend the first day by the pool. That way, we could settle ourselves in; and by talking to other guests, we would find out what was hot on the list for a visit.

Poppy looked great in her black and white bikini. She had a fabulous body, and she was mine. I noticed other men around the pool glancing over, quickly looking away when they saw me staring back. Poppy's skin was like a peach, hardly a blemish anywhere; but she was so white, she had obviously not been in the sun for a long time.

"Poppy! I think it might be wise to go easy today. The sun is really overpowering, let me cream you up!"

"Oh! Sam! Can't you wait till later, you naughty boy."

"Poppy, you know what I mean—sun cream—your skin is so pale, you will end up with sun stroke."

"Okay, Sam, if you don't mind, I have some factor 40 that should do the trick."

Poppy lay on her front, on the sun bed. I squirted a load of cream across the top of her legs. I had to smile.

"Oh yes, Poppy, very nice."

"What do you mean, Sam?"

"Oh! It doesn't matter, Poppy. I was just being disgusting."

"What, Sam, what do you mean."

I leant in towards Poppy's ear and whispered,

"The cream looks just like cum, and it looks like I've just jizzed all over your legs."

"Sam, you're a bit randy for this time in the morning, aren't you; wait till later, and you can jizz anywhere you want."

"I will keep you to that, Poppy."

My hand stroked the cream all over her legs, her skin was hot, the cream made my hands very slippery, I massaged the cream, slipping in between her legs and gently rubbing her tush as I did so,

"Sam! Keep to the plan; it's the bare skin that needs the cream."

I worked down her firm legs, but when I touched her feet, she squealed so loud that everyone looked around.

"Don't touch my feet, they are really ticklish."

"That's worth-knowing, Poppy. The next time you have me pinned down, I will know how to retaliate."

"Sam, if you have any sense, you better not. It drives me absolutely wild."

I sniggered under my breath. At least now, I had one weapon against Poppy, which might render her incapable of fighting back, the next time we had a sex tussle. Unfortunately, Poppy refused to let me put cream on her front side, saying she couldn't trust me to behave—she was probably right. After about 40 minutes of sunning ourselves, we couldn't bare the heat any longer, so we jumped into the pool to cool off. It was so satisfying, and I couldn't resist swimming up behind Sam and grabbing his cock through his trunks. He was a little surprised, but he soon turned around, pulled me into him and snogged me.

"Poppy, I love you so much."

"You too, my muscular hunk."

I could feel his cock getting ever bigger under the water. I reached down, slipping my hand into his trunks; he laughed nervously. He slipped his hands down my bikini bottoms, cupping my buttocks; he nuzzled into my ear,

"Poppy, I'm going to fuck you so hard when we get back to the room; you won't know what's hit you."

I started laughing,

"What's so funny, poppy."

"Well, Sam, I was just wondering how you are going to get out of the pool, with that massive hard on bursting out of your trunks."

"Oh shit, Poppy, stop touching me; it might go down in a minute, it's not funny."

"Oh yes, it is, you thought it was funny to tickle my feet; now it's my turn."

I slipped my hand around his cock and started to wank him off. I couldn't stop laughing; then he saw the funny side. We both laughed like silly little kids playing in the pool.

"Look, Poppy, there's a swim-up pool side bar over there. Let's swim up and have a beer, and may be my manhood will calm down a bit."

We swam up to the bar; there were plastic seats just protruding out of the water for bar guests to sit on. The bar was semi-circular, with a thatched roof to protect from the ever-searing sun and very lively music playing in the background. It was a great atmosphere. There were several couples sat around the bar; some were more inebriated than others. This was an all-inclusive hotel, and some of the less-concerning guests were pushing the boundaries when it came to 'drink as much as you like' policy! The very-friendly barman approached,

"Hi guys, what I can get you."

Sam was off again.

"Hi, I'm Sam; this is my girlfriend, Poppy. What's your name?"

"Hello there, I'm Christian. I'm the bar man of all bar men, and I can see we're going to get on like family; what is it that I can get you! Poppy and Sam."

Sam ordered a beer, and I asked for Christian's special cocktail. All he would tell me about the cocktail was that it was Gin-based. Sam and I sat at the bar, holding hands, looking into each other's eyes, like love-sick school children. I had to keep pinching myself. I just couldn't believe how my life had changed. If it hadn't been for the 'Door', I would never have had the chance to spend my life with Sam.

"Sam! How's it going?"

I glanced down towards his embarrassment.

"I think the cool water is helping, but it's still uncomfortable in my shorts. Don't talk about it, and it might go away."

We both laughed, just as Christian arrived with the drinks.

"What's so funny, guys? Come on, let me in on the secret."

Sam responded quickly,

"Oh! It's nothing. We were just laughing about Poppy burning her feet on the patio this morning."

"Not you as well! A lot of the guests forget how warm it is out here, and the marble floor gets very hot."

Sam's large beer was so chilled, it had ice on the outside of the glass. He took a swig, followed by a sigh of pleasure,

"Aarrgghh, god, that's good, just like nectar."

I tried my drink; it was a long drink, orange in colour, with fruit hooked around the top of the glass, with a fancy bird-shaped brolly sticking out of the top. I sipped it through the fruit. Crikey, it had a kick.

"Christian! How much Gin is in here; it's really strong."

Christian laughed,

"Don't be such a lightweight and enjoy."

After a couple of drinks at the bar and trying out the local ouzo, I was feeling a little tipsy, and Sam's problem had well and truly subsided, so we made our way back to the sun bed for an afternoon nap. I reapplied the sun cream layback on the bed; my sunglasses on and drifted off into a wonderful sleep.

I lay on the bed, looking at Poppy. She was fast asleep. The cocktails must have knocked her out. She was so beautiful, I realised deep down that this was the girl for me, for the rest of my life, and decided there and then to ask her to marry me. I would pick my moment carefully, but would have to wait until we got home, so I could buy the perfect engagement ring.

I woke up to see Sam downing another beer. I was running with sweat,

"Here Poppy, have some beer while I get you a cold drink."

Sam passed me his beer, then ran off towards the bar. He soon came back with a tall glass of lemonade and another beer.

"I didn't think you would want another cocktail, so I got you lemonade and a menu for lunch."

"Sam, I thought we were going to wait for dinner tonight, after such a large breakfast."

"Well, Poppy, it must be the alcohol. I'm feeling quite peckish."

"To be honest Sam, so am I, what shall we have?"

We both ordered a burger and chips, with a tzatziki side dish to dip the chips in. It was delicious, but I was worried if I carried on like this, the rest of the holiday, I wouldn't fit in my costume.

"Poppy, I will have to start calling you 'chunky' if you carry on like this."

"You cheeky sod, Samuel Devere."

I pinched the fat around his stomach.

"What's this then, porky."

Sam pulled me on top of him,

"I'm only joking, my lovely. You have the most perfect body ever, and I love you to the moon and back."

We started kissing and cuddling, then the dreaded happened again. Sam's cock was on the rampage again, I just couldn't stop laughing. "Sam, do you think we should do something about it; you're obviously pent up and ready to shoot."

"Yes please, Poppy, but how am I going to get up and walk past all these people."

"Don't worry, Sam. I will get all the stuff together; then you wrap a towel around yourself and walk behind me."

"Good plan, Poppy, let's go then."

We arrived back at the room. The air con had been left on, so the room was chilled. It was just a pleasure to behold. Sam opened the curtains, and the sunlight burst in. I lay on the bed, stretched out, enjoying the cool air. Sam stood at the end of the bed in his shorts; he still had an impressive swelling, which he was holding with his right hand.

"Right then, Poppy, what did I say you were going to get when we come back to the room."

I looked at Sam innocently and replied in a child-like voice,

"I'm not sure. Was it a cup of tea."

We both laughed. Sam dropped his shorts, exposing his massive hard on; he held his dick in his hand and said,

"I don't think it was a cup of tea. I think it was more like a good shagging, and you said I could jizz all over you."

I slipped my fingers into my bikini bottoms and fingered my clit, at the same time, seductively licking my lips,

"Well if that's what I said, Sam, I suppose you had better shag me then; if you think you're man enough to pleasure me."

Sam jumped on the bed, ripped off my bikini, parted my legs and attacked my wet clitoris with his tongue. Each time his warm wet tongue darted into my slit, it sent an electric shock through me. He was like a man on a mission. I held his head by his hair, pulling him harder on to my clit.

"Well, Sam, are you going to fuck me or what, give me some cock."

Before I'd finished talking, I felt his huge wet cock enter my vagina; it filled me with such pleasure. He rammed it up me so hard, it felt like it was in my stomach. He kissed me so tenderly on the lips, all the time banging away. His balls were slapping against me, each time he thrust his dick up me.

"Come on, Poppy, you said you wanted cock; is that hard enough for you."

"Is that the best you can do, Sam, I said fuck me, not tickle me."

That sent Sam wild. He fucked me so hard that the bed was banging against the wall. Sam was gasping for air; our hearts pounding. I could feel the inevitable orgasm building inside me. My clit was on fire; it couldn't stand much more.

"Sam, I'm coming, don't stop; give it to me. Aarrgghh, oh fuck! Oh fuck! Fuck, fuck! Fuck!"

My body went into a spasm. My toes curled, my back arched; the feeling of ecstasy shot through my whole body. There is no better feeling. Then it was Sam's turn; he pulled his tool out of me, held it in his hand and gently squeezed the end. His eye's bulged; I knew what was coming. He released the pressure on the end of his throbbing cock and ejaculated his hot spunk all over my belly and breasts; some of the cum even reached my face. My grateful tongue licked it off my lips.

"Oh, Sam, you were desperate to cum, weren't you; that's a good boy. Come on, give me all you've got."

Sam collapsed onto me; his sweaty torso sticking to mine; the spunk acting like sticky glue.

"Poppy, I love you, you beautiful creature, please don't ever leave me."

"Sam, I'm never going to leave you, you are my life; why would you even think it."

We held each other so close and eventually fell into a deep sleep—two as one.

The next day, we took a stroll into the local town. It was quite quaint; most of the buildings were painted white with blue windows and doors. There were a few fishing boats moored up in the small harbour; their catches already sent to the local hotels and restaurants in the area. There were numerous cafes and bars scattered about the waterfront, and the gift shops were busy with tourists looking for that special gift to take back to their loved ones. We found a nice bar right on the edge of the seafront and ordered a couple of beers. We kept our hats on as the sun was relentless. I was already feeling a little sore from the time we spent in the sun yesterday. The beers arrived, delivered by an old man. His face was covered in deep wrinkles, his teeth were hit and miss, and I don't think he had shaved for a while, but he was still very friendly, "English. Yes! Manchester United."

Why people abroad always thought you were into football I had no idea, but Sam was on the case.

"Yes, we are English. I'm Sam, and this is Poppy. We are stopping in the hotel just up the road. Do you know where we can hire a car?"

As Sam spoke, he put his hands up as if holding a steering wheel. It was unnecessary, as the man had a good grasp of English and responded quickly, by pointing up the street.

"Yes, yes, my brother; his garage just up the road. Ask for Dimitri, tell him that Anatolia sent you; he will give you a good deal."

The man then went back into the bar and left us to enjoy our drinks. I thought it might be a good time to broach the subject of the accident, but I had no idea how to start the conversation. I took a swig of beer and took the bull by the horns and just came out with it.

"Sam, there's something I've been meaning to talk to you about, and it's very important that you listen carefully and take heed of what I'm about to tell you."

Sam took a gulp of his beer, then looked me right in the eye and said, "This sounds ominous; it's not going to threaten our future together is it."

"Well, Sam, it could, that's why it's important that we tackle it now and make sure that the terrible event never takes place."

Over the next half an hour, I explained to Sam how I had visited him in the future, how I had looked through the fence and seen the devastating scene of him in a wheel chair and being cared for by the stern women. Then how I had researched the accident and found out about the charity music concert in Manchester where he had fallen and broken his back, leaving him paralysed and in a wheelchair for the rest of his life. Sam went very quiet, swallowed heavily; then took another gulp of his beer. He obviously knew from the seriousness of my voice that I wasn't joking; then he spoke,

"Poppy, is it definitely going to happen, and does it mean we won't be together in the future."

"Sam, no! It doesn't mean that! We can change the future, so that this terrible accident never happens. The fact that we know how and where it happens means that we can change the outcome, and we will be together forever."

Sam wrapped his arms around me, squeezing me so hard that it hurt, "Poppy! I couldn't bear not to be with you. We must make sure that this accident never happens, now what do we have to do."

"Well, Sam, the accident happens on the 19th May 1993. It's now only August 1990, so we have three years to make sure you never plan a concert in Manchester, then it just can't happen."

"But Poppy, you have always said that we mustn't change the past, or it might stop us being together in the future."

"I know what I said Sam, but what choice do we have; do you want to end up in a wheel chair?"

We just looked at each other, knowing full well we had no other options. So when the 19th May 1993 approached, we would have to change history and hope that it didn't change the timeline and prevent us being together in the future.

"Poppy! Shall we go and hire a car and get on with our holiday."

The garage was quite run down, and the hire cars weren't in tiptop condition; but Sam said he preferred to support the locals, so we found Dimitri told him that his brother had sent us.

"You have come to the right place. Anatolia, bless him, always sends his customers to me. I will give you the best deal on the island."

All of the cars had scratches and dents in them; some were worse than others. We decided to go for a Suzuki open top jeep. It was yellow with a black interior and covered in a coating of sand. After the formalities of checking Sam's driving license, which was just a cursory glance, Dimitri took Sam's money, thrust a basic map into Sam's hand, and we were off. As we sped off up the bumpy road, free to go wherever we wanted, the feeling of adventure created butterflies in my stomach.

"Well, Poppy, where shall we go; we have the whole island to explore."

"Sam, I think we better go back to the hotel to get our swimming stuff, towels to lie on, the camera and some water; then we can head off to the unknown."

"Poppy, you're so sensible; it's a good job one of us is."

"You said it, Sam!"

If you have ever visited the Greek islands, you will know how bad the roads are and trying to follow a map is almost impossible, especially if you leave the main roads, which is what we did. Sam insisted on finding a beach that no one else could get to; he said because we had four-wheel drive, it would be fine. Although the map showed a beach at the end of the road, we were attempting to navigate. The road seemed to disappear, turning into a craggy, pot-holed, overgrown track.

"Sam, do you think we should turn around. We could get totally stuck and who would find us out here."

"Poppy, stop worrying; we won't get stuck; and besides, I have my mobile with me; so if things go pear-shaped, I can call for help."

"Sam! Do you really think that you will get a signal out here? You must be having a laugh."

"Poppy, I will have a bet with you. When we stop at the beach, if we find it, and I get a signal on my phone, you will have to do a dare."

"Okay, Sam! But if you don't get a signal, you will have to do a dare, deal."

Sam started laughing, like he knew he was going to win, or did he know something I didn't.

The road was absolutely terrible, no wonder the hire vehicles are bashed around; but after about 40 minutes of being shaken to bits, we came to a peak; then the road started to drop away sharply. We pulled over and jumped out. It was deathly quiet, apart from the sound of crickets who were gathered in the olive trees. We looked down, and the sandy track led to a beautiful, secluded sandy beach, and there was no sign of any other vehicles; we had found our deserted beach. The track down to the beach was a little scary, mainly loose sand with copious amounts of boulders strewn all over the place, but Sam was determined to achieve his goal and achieve it—he did. We parked the car under the shade of some olive trees, grabbed our stuff and walked towards the sea. We were gobsmacked, we both looked at each other in amazement; we just couldn't believe it. About 20 yards from the beach, amongst the shade of some trees stood a hut—a sign above the opening said 'Stavros's Bar'.

We were both in stitches. After the journey we had had, we thought we wouldn't see a soul; now right in front of us was a bar—truly amazing. We approached, thinking the bar would be deserted; but to our surprise, came the sound of a welcome.

"Good day, my friends. My name is Stavros. Do you fancy a nice cold beer?"

Sam replied,

"Does the Pope have a balcony?"

Stavros didn't seem to get the joke, but still put two cold beers on the bar. I have to admit the pleasure from that first cold beer was almost as satisfying as sex; it went down without touching the sides. While we drank our beer, Sam opened our beach bag and retrieved his phone. He looked at the screen, and his face lit up.

"What are you looking so smug about?"

I said, knowing full well that Sam had got a signal on his mobile phone. "Well, Poppy, remember that wager we had. 'If I got a signal on my phone, you had to do a forfeit'. Well, look at that!"

Sam pushed the phone towards me, so I could see the screen; the signal strength was at two bars.

"Okay Sam, you win, I owe you a forfeit."

Then Stavros explained to us that he hadn't seen many people arrive in a vehicle to this beach, and that most people arrived by boat. He then went on to say that Sam must be a wicked driver to navigate over the mountain on such an atrocious road. Sam seemed proud of himself.

"I told you, Poppy, we would make it and look at the amazing beach I've found you, who's the daddy."

"Okay Sam, don't get too carried away; we have to get home yet, but before we do, can we have a dip in the sea."

We paid for the beers; then found a secluded spot in the sand dunes near the edge of the water. After a quick dip to cool down, we lay on our towels with our eyes closed. All you could hear was the sound of the water lapping up against the rocks—it was heaven. We were lay there on our backs, soaking up the sun. Poppy had slipped her bikini top off; her magnificent firm breasts defying gravity and proudly pointing up towards the clear blue sky. There were grains of damp sand stuck to her nipples; and as the sun dried them, the grains fell away.

"Poppy, shall I put some cream on you? You're going to burn; it's a right sun trap in this sand dune."

"Yes please, Sam, I can feel my skin burning already, and we have only been here about an hour."

Bingo! I thought to myself, *now I get the chance to touch her.* I started with her arms, then her shoulders, moving down to her voluptuous breasts. She smiled,

"Sam, that's really nice."

Before soaking her nipples in sun cream, I sucked them. They were as stiff as pencils; she sighed with pleasure. I then worked the cream into her belly, moving down to her legs. She very kindly opened them; it was such a turn on rubbing the inside of her thighs. I couldn't help myself any longer. I pulled her bikini bottoms over and slipped my finger into her moist crack. Poppy didn't object; in fact, she encouraged me,

"Sam, that feels good, please don't stop."

I thought to myself, *no chance of that.* My cock was as hard as a truncheon, and I knew what I wanted.

"Turn over, Poppy, and I will cream your back."

She turned over but stopped on her knees. I couldn't resist any longer, so I pulled her bikini bottoms down and off. She was on all fours and as naked as a Jaybird. Her breasts were swinging under her, and her full beautiful arse was facing me. You could just see her moist vagina between the crease of her buttocks. That was it; I couldn't hold back any longer. I sank my eager tongue straight in to her wet pussy. She gasped, "Oh Sam! That feels great, don't stop, please."

Her head dropped down on to the towel; her hands flat on the sand as if to support herself while I pleasured her clit with my tongue.

"Sam, take off your shorts. I want your cock."

Before I could react, Poppy had turned around, whipped off my shorts. Then, she lay on her back. I then straddled her; my hard wet cock went straight in her mouth. My face was between her legs. I didn't need an invitation; my tongue soon found her soaking wet clit. Poppy was so good with her tongue, licking the end of my cock; she would ram it in her mouth so hard, I thought she was going to choke. This couldn't go on much longer. I could feel the lust building in my balls,

"Poppy, can I cum inside you, I'm really close."

I spun around to face her and opened her legs wide; the wetness on her pubes glistening in the sunlight. I knelt in front of her, then plunged my tool into her hot wet fanny. I felt her warm breasts touch my heaving chest as I bent down to kiss her beautiful face. She whispered in my ear,

"Sam Devere, I fucking love you, you dirty boy."

As I thrust myself into her, in and out, in and out, the sun burning my back, I couldn't delay it any longer. Poppy dug her nails in my back. She was there and so was I—we came together. The relief was immense as my load filled her pussy with love. I collapsed on top of her; we were soaked in sweat. I rolled off her, landing on the hot sand. Oh! My god! I jumped up so fast to escape the burning sand that I hadn't realised I was exposing myself to a load of tourists who had just arrived by boat. I dropped down like I had been shot.

"What on earths the matter with you, Sam; dropping down like that, you look like you've just seen a ghost."

"Not exactly, Poppy, but I have just seen a load of people getting off a boat."

"Yeah right, Sam, you don't get me that easy; you know there is no one on this beach except us and the barman."

Then we both heard the excited chatter of people who must have just spotted the bar, so we quickly got our costumes back on and went to join them. After a quick refreshing cool beer, we got back in the jeep and started the arduous journey back to the hotel.

Negotiating the mountain track was quite a challenge, but as usual trusty Sam didn't let me down; and before we knew it, we were back on the tarmac of the main road. We sped up, and the cool breeze was so welcome to our sunburnt shoulders. I turned the radio on, and we both loved the track that was playing— I Can't Help Falling in Love with You by Elvis Presley. We both looked at each other; we both knew this was the real thing. We were very much in love.

The rest of that week went by so quickly, it was just a blur. Each morning, we would explore the island in our rusty jeep; then in the afternoons, we crashed by the pool—sunbathing, reading and, of course, drinking. By the end of the week, we were both as brown as chocolate, with the obligatory white bits where our swimwear had been. Sam looked so handsome, his muscular chest bronzed in the sun, his teeth looked even whiter than usual; then those beautiful blue eyes. I was so lucky to have found him.

"Poppy, why are you staring at me, you look like you're in a trance."

"Oh! Sorry Sam, I was just thinking how much weight you've put on this week."

"You cheeky so and so, come here."

Sam lunged towards me. He went straight for my feet. I quickly got up and ran towards the pool, screaming like an excited child. I dived in to the pool, to escape his grabbing hands. Sam was on me in a second; I surfaced, gasping for air. I was laughing so much that I kept taking in water. "Sam, I was only joking! Honestly!"

He grabbed me by the buttocks and pulled me into him,

"Come here, you gorgeous creature. I'm going to smack your bare arse when we get back to the room."

"Sam, you're such a pervert, but I like it. I like it a lot."

Then out of the blue, the scene in front of me started to shimmer. The temperature all around me dropped. Oh! My god, the 'Door' was calling me back!

"Sam, help me. 'The Door', it's calling me back."

"Hold on, Poppy, concentrate on me. Look me in the eye, think about us."

Sam was gripping my shoulders and shouting encouragement at me, desperate to prevent me going, but still, the shimmering persisted. I felt my body slipping into the clutches of the all-powerful 'Door'.

The last thing I heard Sam shout was,

"Get under the water."

Then he pushed down on my shoulders. I just managed to take in a big breath before I was submerged. I had my eyes open under water. Sam's face was right in front of mine. He pushed me onto the floor of the swimming pool; all the time he was trying to reassure me by sticking his thumb up in front of me. To my utter dismay, the water around me started to warm up and the vision of Sam; although we were under water, it wasn't as shimmery as it was. I couldn't hold my breath any longer; my lungs were bursting. I pushed hard for the surface, as soon as my head was out of the water. I took an almighty gulp of air; my heart was pounding from the lack of oxygen. The good news was, the shimmering had stopped, and the temperature had returned to normal; then Sam surfaced, not quite as erratic as I did. He looked at me and smiled, then spoke,

"We stopped it! Wow! We stopped the 'Door' calling you back."

"Well, it looks that way, Sam, but for how long. I have to get on that plane tomorrow."

"Don't worry, Poppy. We will be alright. I just know it!"

That night after we had a few drinks and said our goodbyes to people we had made friends with, we got into bed. We were all packed up and ready to go first thing in the morning. We both lay there thinking, obviously about the same thing, because we turned to each other at the same time and said,

"Do you think it was the water that stopped the 'Door' from working?"

"Well, Sam, that was the first time ever, that once the process started, I didn't end up travelling, so I definitely think that being under water stopped the 'Door' working."

"Well, Poppy, let's hope that the flight home tomorrow is uneventful, because there won't be a pool we can jump in to on the plane."

Neither of us slept particularly well that night; obviously concerned about the flight home in the morning, but there was absolutely nothing we could do to influence what the 'Door' might do.

We were both a little anxious as we boarded the flight, but there was nothing we could do, other than go through the motions and hope that the 'Door' would leave me alone at least until we arrived home. The good news was that, the seat next to Sam was free, so we had three seats between us, so we could stretch out a bit. After we had lunch and a glass of wine, Sam was getting a bit frisky. I had a blanket on my lap, and he kept trying to slip his hand under it to try and touch me up.

"Sam, stop it! You're so naughty, behave yourself!"

"Look, Poppy, if you're not careful, I will have to invoke the forfeit."

"What forfeit."

"Poppy, do you remember the phone signal."

"Oh yeah."

"Yes! So you're in my debt, so I request you to follow me to the toilet and…"

Before I could finish, Poppy burst out with,

"You can forget that! If you think I'm going to join the 'Mile High Club' today, you can forget it."

"Poppy! I never had you down as a chicken; certainly not a person to go back on a deal—a deal is a deal."

"Yes, Sam, a deal, but you never said I had to shag you on a plane."

"Who said a shag; it might just be a kiss."

"Yeah, right! Come on then, Sam, let's go; but I'm not shagging you in the toilet, and I mean it!"

We made our way to the back of the plane. There were two toilets, one opposite the other. No one was waiting, so we entered the cubicle and locked the door. Poppy was laughing, and so was I. I was only winding her up about the forfeit, just to see if she would honour her commitment; but then to my surprise, she undid her blouse and got her tits out,

"Well Sam, would you like to cum on my boobs."

To be honest, there really wasn't room for a shag but a blowjob, absolutely. My cock was out in a jiffy, and Poppy had her wet mouth wrapped around the end before I could say yes. She was sat on the toilet. I was stood in front of her. It was such a turn on seeing her with my cock in her mouth, and her firm breasts on full display. I pulled her head up, kissed her passionately on the lips and said,

"Poppy, you never cease to amaze me; you are one in a million."

"Yes, I know Sam, now stick your wet cock between my tits."

She grabbed her breasts and pushed them on to my cock, then proceeded to wank me off, using her breasts as hands! It was amazing, and I couldn't believe how quick I was ready to cum.

"Poppy! You won't believe this, but I'm there."

As I spoke, the sound of the door lock clicked as a passenger tried to get in. I panicked and withdrew from the comfort of Poppy's breasts. Poppy just grabbed my dick and started to wank me off.

"You're not going anywhere till you've jizzed on me."

Within a minute, my hot cum shot all over her tits. She was smiling, and so was I.

"I will start calling you Dirty Devere from now on, Sam."

"You can talk, Poppy. I will call you 'Poppy is Porn'."

After making ourselves decent, we were both very dubious to open the door; we felt sure we would have a welcoming committee waiting for us. I slid the bolt across and gingerly opened the cubicle door. To our delight, no one was waiting outside, so we scuttled back to our seats, relieved that we had gotten away with it. The rest of the flight went without incident, just time to reflect on the magnificent holiday we had spent on a Greek island. The wonderful people, the beautiful beaches, the splendid vibrant colours of the Bougainvillea—it had been just perfect; and before we knew it, we had arrived back at Birmingham Airport. The only thing I could think about as we drove down the motorway towards home was Polly the dog. I just couldn't wait to see her.

Chapter 32
Not to Be!

It was great to be home. We had both missed Polly the dog. Sam had phoned his sister, Sally, from the airport to tell her we would be home in an hour, so when we arrived on the drive, Sally and Polly were waiting for us. Polly went absolutely bonkers; she didn't know which one of us to lick first, so she went from me to Sam, then Sam back to me, yelping in pleasure.

"I think she's missed you both, the way she's reacting."

Sally piped up!

After we got our bags in the house and drank several decent cups of tea— 'you just couldn't have a good cup of tea abroad'—we filled Sally in on the holiday. Then it was time to bid her farewell; she sped off the drive like she was on a mission.

It's great to have a holiday, but I just love coming home to familiar smells, and the most important thing is your own bed. We soon got back into the normal routine; Sam off to work every day, and me running the house. I got stuck in to producing some paintings to sell, and I was particularly pleased with the painting I was working on at the moment. It was a scene with a couple getting amorous in the sand dunes. The colours were amazing, the sunlight so intense that the shadows were almost black, the sand almost white, the skin tones were coffee-coloured and the sky a deep blue. I was going to call the piece *Beach Buddies.*

Each day I awoke, I thought about Roscoe waiting at home for me. I would then go to the calendar in the kitchen and write a capital P on the day in question; they soon added up; and before we knew it, another year had passed. In fact, I was beginning to think that after we had thwarted the 'Door' from calling me back, by being submerged under the water the last time, that we had, we stopped it working. So it was now July 1991, only four years to go before Sam and I could have a normal life without any more time travel, and I couldn't wait to introduce Sam to the girls.

I was at work. Poppy had just phoned from home to ask me what I would like for lunch, but I had to decline. There was so much work coming in that I couldn't justify leaving work for an hour or so. I was also a little nervous about going home; because it was the day I had planned to ask Poppy to marry me. I wasn't nervous about asking her; it was her reply that worried me. What if she said no, or hesitated, she might not want to get engaged until everything was normal. That's why I had delayed and delayed asking her. After all, I had decided last year on our holiday to ask her to marry me. Time and time again, I had planned a romantic place, fancy restaurants, but when the moment arrived, I chickened out. The one time I was sure Poppy had noticed the bulge in my pocket, where I had secreted the ring. Poppy had said nothing, so it went on; but tonight when I got home, I would definitely ask her. The plan was, to take home a large bottle of fizz, which was cooling in the work's fridge right at this moment; and then I would ask her to marry me, under the oak tree in the back garden.

I was disappointed that Sam couldn't make lunch. It was quite lonely working at home most of the time; never mind it was only a few hours before he would arrive home. Besides, I had a painting on the go, so I settled down and concentrated on getting it finished. While painting, my mind drifted from one thing to the next; strangely my mind focussed on an episode in my life that I tried to forget. All those years ago when I had received a call to say my mum had been rushed to hospital, and I should get to her as soon as possible. Sadly, I didn't make it, and that troubled me for years that I didn't get to say goodbye. If I had just been near home when she was taken sick, I would have been there; how cruel life could be. What I would give to see her face once again, to hold her, to nuzzle into her neck and smell her and get that feeling that all was well.

I pulled onto the drive full of anticipation. I checked the ring was in my pocket, but left the fizz in the car. I didn't want to alert Poppy what was about to happen. I was greeted at the door by Polly; she seemed so excited to see me. Then Poppy flung her arms around me, kissing me profusely, like we hadn't seen each other for weeks.

"How would you like a nice cold beer, my lovely man?"

"That would be great, Poppy; why don't you grab a glass of wine. We could enjoy it in the garden, as it's such a lovely evening."

While Poppy was retrieving the drinks from the fridge, I nervously made my way into the garden, constantly checking the ring box was in my pocket; a bit like the 'pat down' on the way to the airport, making sure you have your passport. I stood under the Oak tree, pretending to admire the sun light bursting through the gaps in the leaves. Poppy approached with the drinks, followed by the dog— I felt my heart miss a beat.

"There you go, handsome."

Poppy passed me the beer; we both took a swig from our glasses.

"Well, Sam, are we going to sit down."

Poppy started to walk away,

"No wait! I have something I wanted to say, Poppy."

Poppy turned and looked me straight in the eye,

"Yes, Sam, I love you too."

Poppy said, with a big grin on her face.

I kissed her, passionately. I put my hand in to my pocket to retrieve the ring. Sam seemed to be acting a little odd. He seemed nervous about something.

"Are you alright, Sam; you seem a little preoccupied."

I didn't answer; then just as I pulled out the boxed ring from my pocket, Poppy dropped her glass of wine. She exclaimed, frantically,

"Oh! No, Sam. The 'Door', it's taking me."

Before I could even say anything the image of Poppy shimmered, the surrounding air turned icy cold. There was a flash of a very bright light, and she was gone. The dog was not amused. She kept running around, barking profusely, looking for Poppy, but alas, she was gone; and once again, I didn't get the chance to ask her to marry me. I was bloody annoyed, I started swearing,

"Fuck! Fuck! Why did the 'Door' have to take her tonight, just as I was about to propose to her. Fucking hell." And now I had no idea how long it would be before I would see her again.

"Shit! Shit! Fucking shit!!!"

The dog was bemused; she just sat staring at me, trying to understand why I was so angry.

"Don't worry, Polly. I'm not angry at you; it's that fucking 'Door' I'm cross with."

I gave her a reassuring stroke, then downed my beer, then headed for the kitchen to get another. As I walked into the kitchen, the oven timer started beeping. Bless her cotton socks, Poppy had prepared tea, which I would now have to eat on my own. In the oven were two breasts of seasoned chicken, and ready on the side were two plates of freshly cut salad. I sat at the kitchen table to eat my tea. I gave Polly the other chicken breast, which she devoured without tasting it. I was so sad and lonely, and I had no idea how long she would be gone. The last time she travelled, she was away for almost a year. I couldn't bear the thought, so I decided to have a few drinks to numb my feelings. Over the next hour or so, I drank a few more beers; and all the time, I kept staring at the open ring box that lay before me. Would I ever get to ask Poppy to marry me?

Over the next few months, I got back into a routine of a single man—going to work, coming home, walking the dog, talking to the dog, cooking my tea. I really missed Poppy; so much in fact, that I even considered trying to find her in her time zone; but I kept hearing Poppy in my head, saying that if we ever attempted to do that, it might change the future, and it could jeopardise our future together. I decided to hold tight and be patient and hoped that Poppy would appear back in my life sooner rather than later. Sally my sister was a great help, because she knew about Poppy. I still didn't know why she was so understanding, but at least, I could talk to her without loads of awkward questions about where she had disappeared to. While Poppy had been with me, I had neglected my friends. Not because I didn't want to spend time with them, just that the time we had together was precious, with not knowing when she would leave. So once a week, I would meet up with them for a couple of beers. They had obviously met Poppy, I just told them she was visiting family up north. I also thought I had better keep fit and look my best for when Poppy came back, so I played Squash every week with my mate Tim. It was so satisfying to take out all my frustrations on the ball, imagining it was the 'Door' who took my Poppy away. Tim must have wondered where my aggression was coming from; anyway, it certainly helped me win a few games.

It was Monday morning, and I had just arrived at work when I heard my boss call me from his office.

184

"Sam, I've got some good news, more work to tender for, and it's a big one, so I want you on this. We can't afford to lose such a prestigious job as this."

Bob passed me the paperwork. He beckoned me to sit. As I opened the paper work, I read the job name, and the blood drained from my head. It read, 'Beat Fest Manchester'.

"It's not until May 93, but it's a big job, so loads of planning."

I thought to myself, *this must be the concert where I would fall and cripple myself for the rest of my life; the one that Poppy said to avoid at all cost.*

"Sam, I know it's just over a year before the concert, but there's so much to tender for. We have to get this right, so take as much time as you need to get this contract."

"But Bob! You have much better people than me for this job, why don't you get Mike to do it!"

"Sam! What's the matter with you; this is right up your street. No! I don't want Mike, I want you on this. You're the man for the job!"

It didn't matter what I said. He was adamant that I do the job. I left his office in a right state, thinking to myself, *how the hell I was going to get out of this one.*

Chapter 33
Sanctuary

I opened my eyes. I was back in my attic room; then it hit me, the excruciating pain in my big toe. I looked down; it was swollen, throbbing and very red. I tried to stand on it, but it was just too painful. Roscoe came bounding in and licked it. As I pulled my foot away, I banged it against the chair. I thought I might pass out with the stinging pain. I had to get it seen to. I looked around for my phone; maybe Chloe could come and take me to the local A&E department. I couldn't see my phone anywhere. I must have left it in the kitchen when I had breakfast. It took such an effort going down the stairs on my bottom, desperate not to knock my big toe against the bannisters; but eventually, I reached the kitchen, and my phone was on the worktop.

"Hello Chloe, could you please come and help me; I'm in so much pain."

"Poppy! What the hell have you done, has someone hurt you."

"No! No one has hurt me. I lost my temper and kicked a door, and I think I've broken my toe."

I could hear laughing at the other end of the phone.

"It's not funny, Chloe, it's really painful."

"Well, if you kicked a door, it is funny. Why the hell did you do that?"

"Never mind that, Chloe, can you help me."

"Well, I'm on a day off, doing paperwork today; so I will head straight over to you as soon as I get finished."

"Thank you so much, Chloe, see you then."

While I was waiting, I made a cup of tea and made sure Roscoe wasn't hungry—stupid me—Roscoe was always hungry. As soon as I put the food in his dish, he woofed it down. After unlocking the back door, I then settled down in a soft chair. I drank my tea while gazing out of the window; the lounge window overlooked the drive and front garden, so I would see when Chloe arrived. As usual, I had really missed Chloe. I had been away a long time. Each time I came back, the house looked different. Thinking about it, I had spent more time at the other house, together with Sam, than the time I had spent here. In fact, I had been with Sam for several years, but had only spent a few weeks in the country house. My mind was wondering all over the place. I was already missing Sam and thinking what he might be doing, was he missing me, how much time had passed since I left. Then Simon popped into my thoughts. He would be onto me soon about selling this place or paying him the money.

Then I heard the gate bolt being pulled; she was here. I looked out to see Chloe picking up the post from the box, then jumping back in her car and shooting up the drive.

Within seconds, she entered the room. She threw the post onto the sideboard, which was highly polished; and unknown to both of us, one of the letters slipped off the top and down the back of the unit. She then spoke,

"What the hell have you been up to, kicking a door, more to the point, why!"

She was laughing as she spoke.

"It's not funny, Chloe. I think it's broken."

Chloe looked at my foot; her face changed.

"It does look rather angry and swollen. I think we better get to the A&E Department ASAP."

We sat in the waiting room for what seemed like hours, and I don't think we stopped talking for a second. I brought her up to speed with everything that had happened while I was away with Sam; then I heard my name being called.

"Poppy Day, please! Poppy Day!"

Chloe was being a tart. The doctor was rather dishy, quite young, about in his late 20s, dark hair, dark brown eyes, with a foreign accent; maybe French. She was drooling all over him; it was embarrassing. I kept cutting her dagger looks, but she ignored me.

Then the doctor spoke,

"We need an X-ray. I think it might be broken. My colleague will take you to the X-ray department."

After waiting another hour, we were sat back with the doctor. He put the X-ray onto a light box on the wall. He hummed and arrhhd then, with what seemed like gusto. He exclaimed,

"Dislocated! We will have to put it back."

"What do you mean, put it back," I replied.

"Put it back where it should be. I will manipulate your toe back into its right position."

I went white with shock, the thought of anyone touching my toe, let alone manipulating it, made me feel sick.

"But Doctor! It's so painful."

"Do not worry, *madame*. I will use a local anaesthetic; you won't feel a thing."

Chloe grabbed my hand in support. The doctor injected the base of my big toe. The pain from the needle was bad enough, but after a few minutes, the throbbing subsided. The doctor took one more look at the X-ray on the wall, then held my foot with one hand and pulled my big toe with the other. There was a small click as the bones were realigned. I screamed like a baby; it was so painful. Then I noticed a slight grin on Chloe's face.

"What are you smiling about, Chloe. Do you realise how painful this is?"

"I'm so sorry, Poppy, but you have to admit, it is funny; it just creases me hearing you screaming like that."

Then I saw the funny side and started laughing as well. The doctor looked at us, like we were mad, then said,

"Okay, all done. Your toe is back where it should be. It will be a bit sore for a few days, but it will be fine."

We thanked the lush doctor and made our way to the car. Chloe went to the ticket machine; I could hear her cursing from the car.

"I don't bloody believe it; £6.85 for the pleasure, day-light bloody robbery."

"Chloe, I will give you the money."

"I will tell you what; you can buy me a glass of wine, a large glass."

We went straight to a wine bar, in a village near my house, and ordered two large glasses of Pino. We sat at the first seat available, as walking was still painful. Within seconds, Kim appeared. Chloe had phoned her from the hospital, to let her know what was going on.

"So, what have you been up to?"

She said, trying not to laugh!

"Not you as well, Kim; it's not funny. It really hurts."

"Well, it's not a good idea going around kicking steel doors, is it," she replied, sarcastically.

Chloe fetched another glass of Pino for Kim. Chloe proposed a toast, "Here's to all the lush doctors looking for a good time."

We all chinked glasses,

"To all the lush doctors."

Chloe started telling Kim about the doctor, and how sexy he was. They were like two schoolchildren giggling, you wouldn't have thought they were in long-term relationships the way they went on. When they settled down, I brought them up-to-date with my life in the past. They both seemed to accept the fact that I was a time traveller, but still wanted me to provide solid proof. They couldn't believe that I had risked travelling on a plane, not knowing if the 'Door' would call me back. Then Chloe asked why I hadn't got a tan if I had been to Greece. I just looked at her and said arrgghh!

"First of all, it was over a year ago; and secondly, when I come back through time, I bring nothing with me, not even a tan."

"Oh yes, I forgot the intricacies of time travel."

Chloe said, sarcastically.

"You can both snigger. I already have a plan that will prove that I go back in time, and I have a gorgeous lover called Sam."

"Oh great! When are we going to see this proof?" exclaimed Kim.

"I'm not entirely sure, but maybe when I go back next time, I will try to set the plan in action."

The girls seemed satisfied with my offering of proof, and now it was time to go. Easier said than done; as soon as I put weight on my poor foot, the pain returned.

"Come on, you cripple, let me try and support you,"

Chloe said, in a sympathetic voice. They then both took an arm each, like human crutches, and propelled me towards the door. I was not impressed with Kim, because as we passed some people by the door, she shouted out,

"Make way, please, she just can't handle her drink."

Chloe burst out laughing, and so did Kim. The people by the door must have thought I was a wino.

"Kim, do you have to try and embarrass me in my hour of need."

"I certainly do!" she replied, in a jovial retort.

After the girls manhandled me into Chloe's car, Kim bid us farewell, and we set off for home.

"I'm sorry to be such a burden, Chloe. I could get a taxi home to save you the trouble."

"Don't be so stupid, Poppy, as if I would let you go home on your own."

It wasn't long before we were driving along the lane towards the house. My mind was wandering. It had only been a few weeks since we were following the removal van, and everything seemed normal. We pulled on the drive. Strangely, the gate was open; I remember we had closed it when we left for the hospital.

"Poppy, there's a posh car parked at the top of the drive."

"Yes, I can see it."

My heart sank. I recognised the car; it was Simon's.

"Oh, bloody hell, it's Simon; and I can guess what he's after. He will want the money for this place, and I just haven't got it."

"Poppy! Stop stressing. We will find a way. I think he's a right twat, expecting you to come up with that sort of money out of the blue."

We pulled up next to Simon's car. Chloe ran around the car to help me get out. She acted like a crutch to help me get into the house; the back door was ajar. As we entered the kitchen, Simon appeared from the lounge, standing in the doorway as cocky as ever,

"Oh! Poppy, what's happened; why are you limping so bad."

Before I could utter a sound, Chloe burst into a tirade of abuse,

"Like you care, you two-timing good for nothing, arse hole. You screw around behind Poppy's back, you tell her to pay up or get out of her own home; what sort of a low-life are you, and where is that slag you ran off with? If she's here, she will have me to answer too."

I quickly butted in,

"Chloe, thank you! But I can handle it from here."

Then Simon piped up, still a little taken aback at the ferocity of Chloe's attack, but then, he gained his composure,

"It's none of your business, Chloe; please keep out of it."

"Well, that's where you're wrong. Poppy is my best friend; and if someone upsets her, they upset me; so yes, it is my business."

Chloe was getting louder and louder. She could certainly handle herself if I hadn't stopped her. I think she may have laid into Simon.

"Chloe, I think it might be best if you left us to talk. Sorry! Thanks for taking me to the hospital, love you loads."

Chloe gave me a hug, kissed me on the cheek and turned to go through the door.

"Poppy, just call me if you need me, see you soon."

Then, it was just me and Simon. It was dead silent and very awkward; then Simon spoke,

"Poppy! I still love you."

Before he could continue, my blood boiled, and I let rip,

"Love! Love! You don't know the meaning of love. Do you realise what you've done to my life, and you say 'You love me' going on? How you need the money from the house for your love nest in London, with that slapper."

"Poppy! She's not a slapper. You don't even know her; she's kind and clever, and…"

"Just stop right there, Simon! I don't want to hear about her. At the end of the day, she knew what she was up to, she knew you were in a relationship, and she continued screwing you all those years."

"Poppy, what are you talking about? I only left you here a few weeks ago, so why say years."

I looked at Simon and thought to myself, how could he lie to me and look me in the eye, like he was innocent and pretending to be hurt at not being trusted. I just couldn't help myself; and before I realised what I was saying, it just came blurting out of my mouth.

"Simon, I saw you with her, all those years ago, in London, at your office Christmas party and also at…"

I stopped abruptly, realising how stupid I had been, but it was too late. Oh my god! What had I done? I cupped my face with my hands. My mind was in a spin, trying to think of a way out of Simon's inevitable retort.

"You saw me in London with Lucy, years ago; and you never thought to mention it, have you gone around the twist; and anyway, how would you have seen me in London; were you following me."

"Simon, it doesn't matter, we are over, you've made your bed and you're welcome to lay in it."

I headed out of the kitchen door. My toe was still painful, but I had to get away from Simon. I walked over towards the pond and sat on the bench facing the pond, but Simon wasn't having any of it, and he came bounding over towards me.

"Poppy, I want to know what you meant. Were you following me, or have you made it up? Have you finally lost your mind, has it become too much, living here on your own for the past few weeks."

He was such an arrogant arsehole, Sam would have made ten of him. He obviously knew he was lying, but he still had to push me, thinking to himself that there was no way I could have seen him in London with Lucy, but, he didn't know I was a time traveller.

"Simon, we both know that I am right. You have been shagging Lucy the whole time we have been together. It doesn't matter how I know, I just know."

"Poppy, I want to know why you said you saw me in London. It's ludicrous. Why would you say such a thing if you hadn't seen me, or was it some vicious gossip from a so-called friend?"

It was obviously driving him mad, from what I said to him. He knew I was right, but for the life of him, he couldn't work out how I knew. Then as I stood up from the bench to get away from him, he grabbed me by the shoulders and started shaking me,

"Come on, Poppy, tell me who it was; who has it in for me."

He was shouting directly into my face. He was wild with rage. I felt spittle on my face from his abuse coming from his mouth,

"Simon, you're hurting me, let me go."

But he continued to shake me. He was so strong, his gripping hands squeezing my flesh. I put both hands on his chest and shoved as hard as I could. I couldn't believe what happened next. As he stumbled backwards, his feet caught a tree root running along the bank. There was a look of sheer bewilderment on his face, as the realisation of what was about to happen sank into his belligerent mind. It was like time froze as he went from standing on terror firmer, one second, to flying backwards into the pond the next. I watched as if in slow motion, he flung his arms in the air, frantically trying to get his balance, but to no avail. Just before he hit the water, like a large blue whale crashing into the sea, he shouted out with such anger,

"Poppy, you're dead."

His voice was silenced as his head entered the water. His whole body disappeared into the depths of the murky pond. The ducks scattered; they weren't too impressed with this intrusion into their space. I started to laugh, nervously I must add, but then I realised it was time to get out of there, but where could I go. Would I have time to find my van keys and get off the drive before he extricated himself from the water? He would be in a wild temper when he got out, I couldn't risk it. If he caught me, I'm sure he would have hurt me. As I ran towards the house, my foot throbbing with pain, I heard him surface from the water, shouting and swearing at the top of his voice. I briefly turned to see him pulling himself onto the bank of the pond; I was now scared. I entered the house and instinctively ran up the stairs towards my studio. I don't know why, the flimsy door wouldn't hold back Simon for long. I ran in, looking for something to block the door shut; then I noticed my easel. I grabbed it; the painting I was working on fell to the floor. I then attempted to wedge the easel leg into the carpet, and the top into the door; it was the best I could do.

I sat on the floor gasping for breath; then I heard a clambering on the stairs. Roscoe was barking; then I heard a yelp. Simon must have kicked the dog—the bastard—then I heard Simon shout out,

"Poppy, where are you; you just wait till I get my hands on you."

I began to cry; what was I going to do. Then I jumped out of my skin, as there was such a humongous force hitting the door; the easel held at the first attempt. Simon was determined to knock the door down, shouting so loud,

"Poppy, I know you're in there. When I get hold of you, I'm going to fucking kill you."

I now realised I was in serious danger, but then my prayers were answered. There was a resounding noise of the bolt on the 'Door' opening. I couldn't believe my look, or was the 'Door' looking out for me. I didn't really care at that moment. I ran to the 'Door', opened it and climbed inside. The 'Door' closed behind me, and I was safe.

Chapter 34
Sprecken Sie Deutsh

As soon as the 'Door' closed behind me, I knew I would be safe. There was no way Simon could open it. Besides, as far as he knew, the 'Door' didn't open anyway. He would certainly be scratching his head when he entered the room; he would be completely bamboozled as to where I had disappeared to. It brought a smile to my face, thinking how it would annoy the hell out of him. *Serves him right, the big bully,* I thought to myself. I made my way towards the light in the fog ahead. I had made this journey so many times now that it didn't faze me at all. In fact, I ran into the cold fog towards the light without a care in the world. I knew I would start falling any time soon, and I couldn't wait to see Sam. Strangely, I could hear the sounds of elephants trumpeting, and that low frequency rumble they make. Oh my god, I wasn't going back in time in to Africa, was I!

There was a bright flash of light, and I sort of fell onto a large round bale of hay, but it was wet and very cold. I was wearing jeans and a jumper but no coat. I scanned the scene all around me. I was surrounded by at least six elephants; they looked bewildered and were trumpeting so loud through their trunks, the noise was deafening. I was surely going to die. The elephant paying me the most attention had massive white tusks, obviously the dominant male, typical, out of the clutches of one crazy male and into the frenzy of a five tonne pissed-off male elephant. I definitely wasn't in Africa; it was absolutely freezing and everything was covered in snow. I must have arrived in a Safari Park. I looked around; and yes, there were high chain link fences all around me.

More to the point how the hell was I going to get away from these elephants. They weren't too impressed about me sitting on their lunch. Then came the sound of a high revving engine and the blare of a car horn. I turned around to see a Land Rover, painted like a zebra, speeding towards me; its lights flashing. There were two people inside, a driver and another person hanging out of the passenger window, gesticulating and shouting expletives at me, of which I couldn't make out, due to the noise of the elephants and the sound of the beeping horn. The Land Rover approached the elephants tentatively. Most of the elephants moved away backwards, but the bull elephant was standing his ground; his head and long trunk flailing around with loud trumpets of disdainful rebuke echoing out across the whole Safari Park. The elephant averted his attention from me and focussed on the vehicle, charging the Land Rover. I could see the fear on the two men sat in the vehicle. The driver must have put it into reverse and started speeding away backwards, with the elephant in pursuit. This allowed a gap to build between the chaser and the chased; and once a distance built up, the driver took his chance. The vehicle stopped, then started moving forwards, away from the elephant and towards me, with the annoyed bull elephant following up their rear. I could hear the engine being pushed to the limits; the vehicle bouncing in the air each time it traversed a bump in the ground. The vehicle pulled alongside the bale of hay I was stood on. The passenger was shouting out of the window,

"Jump onto the back and hold on tight to the roll bar."

The elephant was approaching fast and furious. I didn't have time to doubt if I could jump that far. I had no choice but to go for it. I leapt into the air, landing in the pick-up part of the Land Rover. With the force of the jump, I fell over, bashing my arm on some tools that were strewn over the floor. I looked up to see the passenger looking through the window, shouting,

"Hold on tight, for god's sake; it's going to be a hell of a ride."

Just as I grabbed the roll bar, the engine noise built to a crescendo. The driver let out the clutch, and we were off, hurtling towards the perimeter gates, with the elephant in chase. I was gobsmacked how fast a five tonne animal could run, thankfully not for too long. Finally, he stopped; his trunk in the air, with an ear-piercing trumpet of defiance; his annoyance at me sitting on his lunch abating.

I could see the passenger on his radio, obviously calling the gatehouse. As we approached, the tall steel gates started to slide sideways, allowing us to drive through to safety. After exiting the enclosure, the vehicle continued along the tarmac road towards a cluster of cabins. We went through another safety gate and pulled up outside an office. The driver got out of the vehicle, came around the back of the Land Rover and let rip.

"What the fucking hell were you doing in the elephant enclosure; not even in a vehicle, but you also sat on the elephants' breakfast."

What could I say; I couldn't tell him I was a time traveller. I had to think fast, "*Sprechen Sie Deutsch.*"

That's all I could think of saying. I just prayed he wasn't from the motherland and spoke fluent German.

"Well, you might be German, but you could have been a dead German if we hadn't turned up."

Stupidly, I almost responded in English by thanking him for saving my life, but stopped myself just in time.

"I'm sorry, young lady; and you probably don't understand what I'm saying, but you will have to stop in this office until the police arrive. It's a very serious and stupid thing you did this morning; not only did you risk your life but also ours."

The man grasped my arm. First of all to help me down from the back of the Land Rover, but then, without letting go, led me into the office. The office was quite sparse; an elderly lady was sat at a desk in front of a typewriter. The man told her to call the police, then proceeded to tell her where he found me; also that I was German and didn't understand a word of English. The lady was kind; you could see she was worried about me, offering me a drink, but I had to pretend I couldn't understand her. It then dawned on me, when the police turned up, and they got an interpreter, they would soon find out I wasn't German. I couldn't tell them who I really was. If they went to my address, and the original Poppy answered the door, that would be the end. I had to escape, but how on earth would I get out of the office. The two men who had saved me, suddenly left the office, saying they would come back when the police arrived. On their way out, the driver who was the more senior turned and said,

"Mabel, don't let her out of your sight; call us when the old bill get here."

Then they were gone, leaving me with the old lady; then a plan popped into my mind. If I could persuade her to let me go to the loo, I might be able to escape, but how would I ask where the toilets were; 'I didn't speak English'. I walked over to her desk; she looked alarmed. I grabbed a pen and a piece of paper and drew a toilet; she looked at it and laughed,

"You want the toilet, pet." She took my hand and led me out of the door into the reception area and pointed to the ladies,

"I will wait out here until you come out, pet."

I went into the toilet and locked the door. Luckily, above the loo was a window, just big enough for me to get through. I climbed onto the toilet and attempted to open the window. Shit! It was painted up, and it wouldn't budge. It was the only way out; the lady was waiting outside for me. I had no choice. I couldn't break the glass, she would definitely hear it. I had to use brute force. I grabbed the handle; and with all my might, I pushed it as hard as I could. I heard a crack; it was moving. I tried again; and this time, the window opened out. I scrambled up onto the window ledge and squeezed my body, head first, out of the small opening. I fell into a snow-covered bush, which was freezing. The sound of brittle frozen branches breaking alarmed me. I thought the lady would come running around the building to capture me, but all was quiet.

I picked myself up the floor, dusted myself down—the snow was quite powdery. Then I looked for my mode of escape. I peered through the bushes. I was adjacent to a car park; not far from me, stood a delivery vehicle. I watched the driver come out of the building, with a piece of paper in his hand. Just as he opened the cab door, I ran over and said,

"Morning! Are you going into the local town?"

"I am, young lady, why."

"Well, my car is in the garage, and I could do with a lift if you would be so kind."

He scratched his head and hesitated,

"Well, I'm not supposed to give lifts, Health and Safety, and all that, sorry!"

"Okay, it's not a problem," I replied.

As I began to walk away, he shouted, "Sod Health and Safety; come on, lass, jump in."

I was in the cab as fast as lightning, worried that the lady might come outside looking for me. Within minutes, we were leaving the Safari Park and heading for the local town. After approximately ten minutes, we reached the town. I knew it well; it was where Sam and I had bought our house. It seemed really strange that the 'Door' had delivered me to the local Safari Park and not to our home like previous times.

"You can drop me anywhere here if you don't mind. It's been a great help having a lift."

If only he knew what he had been party to, he had saved me from a lot of trouble. The delivery van slowed up and pulled to the side of the road. I opened the door and slid out on to the walkway,

"Thanks again! Have a good day, bye!"

The van pulled off, joining the busy traffic, and I headed home to see Polly. I guess Sam would be at work, because while in the van, I noticed the time on the driver's wristwatch; it was mid-morning. By the time I arrived at the end of our road, I was frozen solid. The jumper I was wearing was warm, but I could have done with a thick coat as well. It never ceased to amaze me, when I travelled back in time, what or who decided what I might be wearing when I arrived. As I turned into our *cul de sac,* my heart missed a beat. Sam's car was on the drive; I wondered why he wasn't at work. I ran to the front door, but instead of retrieving the hidden key, I thought I would surprise him; so I rung the door bell and waited. I was so excited, I had butterflies in my tummy; then, I heard the sound of the lock being turned.

The door opened, and Sam just stood there staring; then tears started rolling down his face, which in turn started me off, and I started crying. I pounced forward, wrapping my arms around the love of my life, squeezing the life out of him,

"Oh Poppy! I thought you were never coming back. I've missed you so much; my heart is broken."

He started to sob; his tears ran freely, wetting my face,

"But Sam, you know I always come back, and I love you so much. I know I've only been away a short while, but I've missed you so much."

"A short while, Poppy! I nearly gave up; I thought you had gone forever. I even thought about finding you in your time, never mind the consequences."

"Sam, what's the date," I said, dreading the answer.

"Poppy, you've been away almost two years; it's February 1993."

I stood there in shock. To me it had only been a couple of days; for poor old Sam, it had been two years, and still he waited for me. I sobbed at the thought of him waiting patiently for me, not knowing if he would ever see me again. I also sobbed, thinking of the hurt I had caused the man I loved. We must have stood on the doorstep for a good ten minutes holding each other, not wanting to be the first to let go,

"Well, are you going to make me a cuppa? I've had quite an experience, this morning."

"I'm sorry, Poppy, excuse my bad manners. Come in and make yourself at home again."

While we drank tea with some toast, I filled Sam in on the adventure I'd had with the elephants. He didn't say a word until I finished; then he just said,

"Oh my god, you could have been killed."

Then he went quiet for a minute, obviously thinking about what I had said; then, he spoke again,

"What on earth made you think to speak in German?"

I laughed; I just don't know. I guess I thought if I couldn't speak the lingo, they wouldn't ask me any stupid questions—questions I couldn't answer.

As we were talking, it suddenly occurred to me,

"Sam, where's Polly, is she alright?"

"Yes, she's fine. It's just that I've been working long hours; and with you not here, she was really lonely on her own, so she sometimes goes to stop with Sally. She has more time to spend with her."

"Oh okay, is she due back any time soon. I've missed her."

"Well, Sally was going to bring her back tomorrow. I can phone her and ask her to bring her today if you want."

"No, that's fine, we have a lot of catching up to do. I'm sure if I've been away for two years, you have a lot to tell me."

We spent all that day talking, and before we knew it, it was time to go to bed. We both had a shower and sat in bed, drinking a lovely cup of tea.

"Poppy, I'm so glad you're home; come here and give me a cuddle."

"Sam, I think you could do with more than a cuddle if I've been away that long."

Sam's face lit up. I disappeared under the covers and showed him how much I had missed him. After we had both been pleasured, I lay my head on Sam's chest and fell into a deep sleep.

Chapter 35
Tea Time

It was so fantastic to have Poppy back home. I had missed her so much; I loved her so much, it hurt. One thing for sure, I would definitely put that ring on her finger before she disappeared again. Over the next few weeks, we got back into our routine—Poppy painting in her studio and me off to work each day. Talking about work, I still had that hurdle to get across. While she had been away, I had thrown myself into work to help time pass by, and the big project I was working on was 'Beat fest' in Manchester. Poppy would be mad with me when I told her; she had warned me what was going to happen to me; but I figured if I knew the date of the accident, which I did, and I didn't go to work that day, then all would be okay, wouldn't it.

I got the feeling that something was troubling Sam. He seemed happy, but deep down I could see something was niggling him. I decided to have it out with him, so when he arrived home that night, I told him we were off to the pub for our tea. Sam was always pleased when I mentioned going to the pub; he really did like a pint. We both thought it would be nice to walk. The local was only about a 20-minute stroll away, and it would do us good. By the time we arrived, we were both gagging for a drink. I was quite thirsty, so I started with half a lager, and Sam had a pint. We settled into our seats, ordered our meals; then, I asked Sam what the problem was. He denied anything was wrong at first, but I persevered, and then he said,

"Well, Poppy, please don't go mad."

"Oh, Sam, what have you done?"

He took a gulp from his glass, paused for a while, then explained about the job at work. The job he promised he would never do, after how I told him about the awful accident that occurred.

"Sam, you can't be serious. You know what will happen if you work on that job; you just can't go, and that's all there is to say."

"Poppy, my boss insisted that I run that job. It's a massive prestigious contract that will bring a lot of money in for the company. I had no choice in the matter."

"Sam, didn't you believe me when I told you what happened to you."

"Of course, I do, but you told me the date it happens. I promise you I won't go to work that day, so everything will be fine."

Over the next hour or so, we discussed all the eventualities, and Sam promised me he wouldn't be on-site on the dreaded date of the accident. I have to say I was still concerned; maybe just being involved with the job might be the worst mistake of his life.

I can't remember eating my meal; my mind was all over the place. On the way home, Sam kept asking if I was okay. I said I was fine, but deep down I was worried sick. Anyway, Sam was adamant that he had to do the job, so all I could do was support him and hope for the best. We also didn't know if by changing what happened would change the future. I was certainly dreading the day of the accident. Everything might change; I might just disappear from Sam's life altogether.

The next day was fairly warm. It was Sunday, and I had just got back from a lovely walk in the woods with Polly. Sam had been tinkering in the garage when I left. I shouted to Sam to get the kettle on, but he shouted back,

"Poppy, can you come out to the back garden; I have something to show you."

I was intrigued, so I hung Polly's lead up and ran out to the back garden as requested. Sam was dressed in his best suit and stood under the oak tree just staring at me,

"Sam, what are you doing you nut; why are you in your best suit."

"Poppy, just come here, please. I have something to ask you."

The butterflies in my stomach were having flights of fancy. I was praying that my gut instinct was right. I approached Sam. He kissed me, then dropped onto one knee. He had a ring in his hand; my heart missed a beat.

"Poppy, my beautiful, beautiful love of my life… 'Will you marry me'?"

Oh my god, could life get any better.

"Samuel Devere, I love you with all my heart. Of course, I will marry you."

He slipped the ring on my third finger; it fitted perfectly. It was quite a rock; it was beautiful. We kissed, and I knew from that moment on, Sam and I would be together forever. It was a wonderful moment. We were both extremely happy; and naturally, we both went inside and up to our bedroom to celebrate.

We both stripped completely, then lay on the bed with our arms and legs entwined; we were both smiling like Cheshire cats. It's difficult to describe the feeling, but I will try. Although we had been together for years now, and we had always expressed our love for each other, now we were engaged, it felt official; and we wanted to shout it from the rooftops, but alas, we couldn't. Certainly we could tell Sally, Sam's sister, but until our time zones coincided, we would have to keep it low-key; so at least two years before we could get married.

"Sam, you do realise we will have to wait until 1995 before we can get married."

"Yes Poppy, I'd already thought about that, but it will soon pass, and we can start to plan. I'm just so happy that you said yes."

Sam kissed me so passionately that it sent a tingle down my spine. I lay on my back; Sam started kissing me, from my lips, then my neck. I had goose pimples all over. Then he licked my nipples; they responded by standing erect. I felt his fingers stroking the inside of my arms; he was being so gentle. His warm tongue then moved down to my tummy. I was so excited; I opened my legs wide.

He straddled me, in the 69 position; his hard wet cock dripping with love juice. My mouth engulfed his manhood; it tasted salty. Without warning, his wet tongue darted into my pussy, searching out my stiff clitoris; it was divine. He licked me, gently biting my lips, all the time thrusting his dick into my mouth. His fingers delved into my vagina; in and out with his finger, each time catching my clit, bringing me ever closer to an orgasm. I couldn't stand it any longer; he rubbed my clit so fast, my body went into spasm.

"Are you there, my beautiful fiancée," Sam asked, knowing full well that I was in the grip of a full-blown orgasm.

"Poppy, I'm also there, hhhmmmmm."

I felt Sam's body stiffen. I had been sucking his hard cock, wanking him with my mouth I squeezed his balls, as he shot his hot cum down my throat. We both came together; there is no better feeling than that union between two people becoming one. We both collapsed on the bed, both of us satisfied, with the feeling of peace and tranquillity you get after sex, flowing through our veins.

So it felt like we had consummated our engagement; we were going to get married in a couple of years, and we were both very happy. After a short sleep, we got up and went into the kitchen to make a cuppa. I noticed the calendar on the wall was two years out of date. I needed it to keep track of my comings and goings.

"Sam, remind me when we go out to buy a new calendar."

"Poppy, I did keep it up for about a year, but then I thought you weren't coming back, so I left it."

"Not to worry, Sam."

"Poppy, to celebrate our engagement, how do you feel like spending a few days by the sea. I have loads of holiday to take."

"That would be lovely, Sam, when can we go."

"How about in the morning, or is that too soon."

I was so excited. I loved the seaside, and the thought of spending time with Sam.

"I had better go and pack then, Sam. Oh! How about Polly."

"You had better pack Polly's bag as well; she will love the walks along the beach."

The next morning, we were up early. The bags were in the car, Polly was settled behind the dog guard; I was in-charge of the map, and Sam was our chauffeur.

"Well, Sam, where are we going, I can't wait to find out."

Sam seemed a bit hesitant to tell me for some reason,

"Poppy."

He hesitated again,

"Yes, Sam, spit it out."

"Well, Poppy, we're not going to a posh hotel. It's not the money, honest; it's just that my friend has a static caravan in West Wales, and it's such a beautiful spot."

"Fantastic, Sam, I love caravan holidays; well, come on then, Sam, let's go."

She just amazed me. Nothing ever fazed her, she was just perfect; whatever we did, she was happy; and if she was happy, I was happy. So off we went, off into the mountains along narrow roads with beautiful vistas, green grass everywhere and, of course, sheep; I've never seen so many sheep. Polly had her beady eyes on them; every now and then, she let out a staccato of excited barks, to let us know she had spotted them. I glanced to my left, Poppy was taking in the scenery, and I thought to myself, *How lucky are you, Devere.* I was certainly punching above my weight with this one; she was one in a million.

I didn't really need to read the map. Sam had travelled the country extensively through his work and basically knew his way to anywhere. As we drove along, I couldn't help but feel a little sad that my mum and dad could never meet Sam; and to see me so happy, he was just the nicest man you could ever hope to meet, better than that cad I had left in the future. Anyway back to the present, the sun was out. We were on the top of a mountain road, the scenery was breathtaking, and the tune on the radio was one I really loved—it was The Power of Love by Jennifer Rush. The song summed it up. There couldn't be a power stronger than love; it had the power to make you happy, sad, elated, put you off your food, make you strong, make you weak. It just depended on whether your love was equal. Luckily, we both felt the same way, and we sang at the top of our voices as we sped towards our destination.

We came to a spot on the road with a patch of neatly trimmed grass at the side of the road. The roaming sheep had nibbled it so short, it was like green carpet. We pulled over so that Polly could get out and stretch her legs and relieve herself. While Sam walked her around on her lead, just in case she took a liking to the sheep, I filled up her water bowel, which we kept in the boot of the car. The view was stunning; we could see the coastline and the long sandy beach. There were a few buildings visible; then Sam pointed out where our caravan was roughly situated,

"Do you see where the coast road swings inland?"

"Yes."

"Well, do you see the sand dunes to the left of it?"

"Yes."

"Well, can you see a few caravans dotted around?"

"Yes."

"Well, it's one of them. I can't tell you which one, but it's one of them."

"Sam, I can't wait to get down there; come on, let's go."

Sam made sure that Polly was settled down, then closed her back in the boot of the car; she wasn't amused. She must have thought her ordeal was over; never mind, it would only be about another 30 minutes. We sped off; the road wound left to right, dropping down steeply towards the sea; and it wasn't long before we were driving along the coast road towards the sand dunes. I pressed the button to wind my window down; Sam did the same. The smell of the salty sea air came flooding in. I could hear the waves crashing up onto the gently sloping beach. Wow, it was really beautiful.

"Sam, you were right; it is a gorgeous place and so quiet, there's hardly anyone around."

Sam smiled,

"I'm glad you like it, Poppy. The walks around here are amazing, and there's a lovely pub just around the corner from the caravan."

"Ha, Ha! I see, that's the reason you wanted to come here; a local little haunt of yours, is it!"

"No, Poppy, it's not just the beer. They do fantastic yummy food, and they sell Pino."

"Well, Sam, that's alright then. If they have my favourite tipple, they have my vote."

The car turned into a small opening, lined by gorse bushes, growing out of the fine white sand; they were covered in tiny yellow flowers. Protruding though the bushes stood a sign, 'Welcome to White Sands Caravan Park'. Sam wound his way along the twisty lane, and we arrived on a green grass field where a cluster of static caravans stood. They were all different; some were in a bad state of repair, some were new; painted in blues, creams, white and light green, all with a wicket-type fence marking the boundary around each van.

"Oh Sam, which one is ours; I can't wait to get inside."

"It's the cream one with the decking outside, next to the sand dune."

Poppy let out an excited squeal and opened the car door before I had even stopped; she got out and ran to the caravan door, trying to open it.

"Poppy, give me a minute to find the key."

My friend Nick, whose van it was, told me to look under a stone frog near the door, and I would find the key; and there it was. The key fob read, 'The resting Place'.

"There you go, Poppy; you do the honours."

I passed the key to Poppy, and she was in like a shot. I let her go ahead while I let Polly out of the boot; the car was a Rover SD 1, so the boot was large. But even so Polly was grateful to escape, she ran straight into the caravan to find Poppy. The caravan wasn't brand new, but it had all the mod cons, a TV, fridge, a bathroom with a shower, a galley kitchen with an oven, a separate bedroom with quite a large bed; that was going to see some action, that was for sure. The best part was the spacious lounge, with a large panoramic window over-looking the sea.

"Oh Sam, just look at the view; isn't it just wonderful."

Sam held me and kissed me saying,

"Poppy, everything is wonderful while you're in my life."

"Ditto,"

I replied. Even Polly seemed happy, running round from one room to the next, in a frenzy, yapping excitedly. Our bags only took a few minutes to unpack; then the first job was to visit the local shop to get provisions—the usual things like milk, tea bags, coffee, bread, cake, butter and, of course, beer and wine. The lady in the shop was quite a character, welcoming us to the area. She was about 40, a bit plump, with a rosy complexion, I suspect from a hard life and the sea breeze, or maybe from copious amounts of alcohol. Whatever it was, she liked you to know she was there.

"It looks like loves young dream, just married are we, holding hands and kissing."

She let out a cackle, laughing like a witch.

We both laughed, and then I spoke,

"We've just got engaged, and we hope to get married soon."

"I wouldn't bother lass; it never lasts. Just make the most of it while you can and save the money."

She laughed again, then went on with her business. We just looked at each other and smiled. We paid for our shopping, then set off back to the van, carrying two bags each. Sam had the heavy bags, the ones with the bottles and cans in.

"The first job when we get back, Poppy, is to get this alcohol in the fridge."

"Yes, Sam, the next job is to get the kettle on."

Sam laughed, then struggled on, spurred on by the thought of a nice hot cup of tea. We had left Polly in the garden. The wicket fence that surrounded the caravan was high enough to keep her safely inside. She saw us approaching and started barking. You could just see her nose breaching the top of the fence.

"Oh shit! You know what we forgot, Poppy."

"Don't worry, Sam. I packed a couple of tins of her favourite. It should do her until the morning. It takes a woman to organise things properly."

I sniggered as I said it,

"Yeah right! I suppose you want me to make the tea."

I put the shopping away and popped the kettle on. As I bent down to extract some cups from the cupboard, I glanced towards Poppy, who was stretched out on the sofa, under the window. She looked so sexy, she had a one-piece tight fitting short cotton dress on. It hugged her figure, showing off all of her curves. I thought to myself how lucky I was. I made the tea, then turned to ask if she wanted cake to go with it, oh my god! The sight that greeted me gave me an instant twinge in my groin. Poppy was leaning back on the sofa. She had pulled the top of her dress down, exposing her breasts; her legs were wide open. She had removed her white pants which were discarded on the floor, and she was rubbing her clit with her finger.

"Hi there, big boy, how do you fancy a bit of a tumble."

Well, I didn't need any persuading. My cock had reacted so fast that it was almost popping out the top of my trousers.

"Poppy, you really are a dirty girl; and if you carry on like this, you are going to get a good seeing too."

Poppy replied, in a deep sexy voice,

"Really! Do you know anyone with a cock big enough to give me this seeing too?"

She licked her lips as she spoke; she was such a naughty girl. I undid my buckle on my belt; my trousers dropped to the floor, followed by my boxers. The door to the caravan was wide open, but I didn't care. The only thing I was focussed on was the filthy bitch beckoning me to pay her some attention. My dick stood proud; the veins bulging from the pressure of blood rushing to the call for action. I ripped off my shirt; I was now completely naked and up for the challenge. I stood there with my erect cock in my hand and said,

"You keep teasing me, and you're going to get a piece of this."

As I spoke, I thrust my cock in the air with my hand,

"Well, I'm waiting, big boy if you're up for it."

That was it. Sometimes she was gentle when having sex—this wasn't one of those times—other times she was downright disgusting. Sex was like a drug to her, and when she wanted a fix, she was like a woman on a mission. I have to admit I loved the naughty Poppy; she was exciting, thrilling and so satisfying. It didn't matter what I did to her; she just lapped it up.

Sam was stood there, his massive stiff cock in his hand. I was so turned on; he stood there proud with his muscular legs and a fine torso. I almost came from the touch of my finger rubbing my clit. I so wanted him inside me, I noticed love juice dripping from the end of his penis. He approached me and knelt down between my legs; he placed each hand on the inside of my thighs and parted my legs further. His head went down; the next feeling was like all my birthdays had come together. He savaged my clitoris with his tongue, occasionally spitting on it, then licking it, like he couldn't get enough. I absolutely loved being muffed, but what I loved even more was a good hard fucking. I pulled Sam's head towards my face. He sucked hard on my nipples; then he snogged me. His kiss was so wet, I whispered in his ear,

"Darling, would you please fuck me now. I'm so close, I can't hold on much longer."

Sam smiled and reared backwards still on his knees. He grabbed his throbbing tool and smacked it against my pussy, several times before plunging it into my wet grateful slit. He rammed it up me so hard; my whole body moved up the sofa, each time I felt his balls smacking against my skin. I was lost, lost to the power of the orgasm; I had no control of my body. It felt like an explosion had ignited inside my tummy, and the shock waves were flowing right through me. My muscles stiffened, my eyes closed, and my back arched. Sam's cock was still inside me. I gripped him so hard I felt him wince; I just managed to say the words,

"Oh, Sam, I fucking love you."

Then I relaxed back into the sofa. My heart was beating like a drum, and my lungs still gasping for air. Could life get any better?

Poppy had come, and now it was my turn; just seeing her climax took me to the edge. I turned her over; her fantastic arse in front of me. I squeezed her cheeks with both hands, pulling her on to me. My dick slipped up her, she was so wet. She thrust herself backwards onto my shaft, trying to please me. As I slapped her arse, I shouted,

"Poppy, I love you, you dirty bitch."

She responded,

"Sam, shoot your cum all over me."

That was the last straw, hearing Poppy being so rude sent me over the edge. There was no return; no stopping the inevitable. I withdrew from her, just in time. I felt the rush of hot cum erupt out of me, like a kettle boiling, splattering all over the crack of her arse, leaving my balls empty and aching. I collapsed onto her, fighting for air, nuzzling into her hair, telling her how much I loved her. We were both quiet for a while, soaking up the calm feeling you get after sex. Then Poppy spoke,

"Shall we have that cuppa now?"

We both burst out laughing, Still hugging each other,

"Sam, that's it, our code for sex. If ever I say, 'Do you fancy a cuppa', that means I want sex. If you reply, 'With Cake', then it's a done deal."

"Also, Poppy, I think we should rename this caravan. It shouldn't be 'The Resting Place'."

Before I could say anything, Poppy piped up with,

"The Shag Shed, Passion Parlour, Cum Caravan, Orgasma Van."

Poppy was laughing so much, she had tears running down her face.

"No, Poppy, what I was about to say was, 'Poppy's Porn Pad'. It has a ring to it."

She screamed out again, holding her hand out, wiggling her fingers, "Yes, I have the ring."

Giggle. I don't think I had ever seen Poppy laugh so much. I don't think I would ever forget this moment; it was just the best.

Chapter 36
Déjà Vu

Over the next few days, we settled into the caravan life. Most of our time was spent walking Polly along the long stretch of beach near the van. Polly seemed to love the freedom, chasing into the incoming waves, barking her head off, then retrieving numerous sticks; some just too large for her to carry. I will never forget those walks with Sam, the sea breeze in our hair, holding hands, stopping every now and then for a cuddle; we were so much in love.

"Sam, do we have to go back home; this place is heaven."

"I'm afraid we do; bills to pay and all that. Besides, we have a wedding to plan, and they don't come cheap."

I obviously knew we had to go home, but I knew that when we got back, it wouldn't be long before Sam had to start the dreaded job up north—'Beat Fest'—and I really feared for our future. Just along the beach, about 20 minutes' walk from the van, stood a shack, where each day we would stop for a coffee and sometimes a slice of cake. Today was no different; it was about 11-ish, and we were both ready for a caffeine boost. There was a wooden deck in front of the cafe, with a lean to roof. We sat there, so Polly could sit with us. The owner even put a bowl of water out for people's pets to drink from. While enjoying our coffee and cake, we chatted about all sorts of things, but today Sam seemed intent on asking about my life in the future, which I didn't mind; but I was fretful that the more he knew, it might jeopardise the time line between now and 1995.

I didn't tell him where I lived; just about the house in the country, and where I found the 'Door'.

The 'Door' that allowed me to time travel, which if I hadn't, we wouldn't be together now. I told him about my paintings, and how I had found a small art shop in a local town, who displayed my work, I didn't tell him about my pseudonym 'Tony Le Meros'. So he knew roughly where I lived, that I still earned a living by painting, and that my partner was a cad. He also knew that time in the future did not move on at all when I travelled back in time, but while in the past, time moved towards the future. I told him about my best friends Chloe and Kim. He was dying to meet them, especially Chloe, who he thought might be a right handful; he wasn't far wrong there! Then, of course, last but not least, Roscoe the dog—the most important thing in my life in the future.

We must have been talking for ages; the coffee cups were cold, and Polly was getting impatient to chase more waves. We were just about to get up to go when Sam stopped. He grabbed my hand and sat down again; he looked at me, his face was serious; then, he spoke,

"Poppy, you said time stands still when you travel."

"Yes, each time I travel, when I get back, the clock in my studio hasn't moved at all; so each time I come back in time, the time moves towards the future. The future date being July 1995."

Sam's face froze, and then he sighed heavily,

"What's the matter, Sam, are you alright?"

"Poppy, you're in grave danger, and I don't know how to help you."

"What do you mean I'm in grave danger? How could I be; I'm with you."

"Poppy, you said when you travel back, no time elapses. Yes!"

"Yes, Sam, that's right, but what's the problem."

The dog started whining. She was desperate to go; she kept tugging on her lead.

"Poppy, think about what happened when you came back this time. You told me that Simon chased you up the stairs in a rage, and you blocked the door to your studio; then luckily, the 'Door' opened, and you escaped his wrath."

"Yes, that's right, Sam, but I don't see what your point is; what are you worried about."

Sam was getting frustrated with me. He held his head in his hands; then he looked me straight in the face and spoke,

"Poppy! If no time elapses, when you return back to the future, then Simon will still be there, trying to break down the door into your studio."

Then the reality of the impounding danger hit me, like a brick. Why I hadn't realised what Sam had just told me. I don't know.

"Sam! What am I going to do? The 'Door' could call me back any time, and there's nothing I can do about it. I will return to that danger that I thought I had escaped."

Sam gripped my hand, then spoke softly,

"Poppy, don't worry. We will think of something. The main thing to remember, if you are suddenly called back, you will be prepared for the chaos around you."

We set off back to the 'orgasma van'; our minds deep in thought. Polly was happy though. As soon as I let her off her lead, she was off, chasing the waves; her excited barking being drowned out by the incessant noise of water crashing onto the beach. That night, we lay in bed; I could hear Polly snoring on the sofa. Sam was in a deep sleep; we had walked miles during the day, and Sam was bushed. I couldn't sleep; my mind just kept going over what might happen when the 'Door' called me back. The only good thing was, at least I would be prepared when I suddenly appeared back in the future. I must have lay there for at least an hour; it was pitch black. Sam was lying on his back; his breathing was quite heavy but also soothing. Then came the patter of rain on the roof of the caravan. How I loved that sound, all tucked up, nice and warm, and that pitter-patter of rain drops hitting the thin covering between you and the outside world. It was mesmerising, and I soon drifted off into a deep sleep.

It was the last night of our holiday, and I would be sad to leave the tranquillity of this idyllic spot. We had got quite friendly with the staff in the pub, and I would certainly miss my favourite dish on the menu—beef and ale pie, with a flaky pastry topping, washed down with a cold glass of Pino. Sam rubbed his full tummy; he had just polished off a massive Cod and chips, followed by his fourth pint. For prosperity sake, we had a few photos taken with the couple who ran the pub—Gail and McKenzie. They were a lovely couple, telling us that we must visit again soon. Polly also loved the pub, because it was pet friendly. She was allowed to sit under our table, no doubt in wait for tasty morsels that were gobbled up in seconds. I think all three of us must have put on a few pounds this week. Sam kept teasing me, the cheeky so and so, calling me 'chunky', which I wasn't very happy about. As soon as we got home, it was definitely back to healthy food and more exercise, and that meant both of us.

The next morning we were up, bright and early. We soon packed our things; then after a quick simple breakfast of tea and toast, we had a cursory check around the caravan to make sure we hadn't left anything, and we were off. While I settled Polly in the back of the car, with some fresh water, Sam locked up and hid the key safely under the frog. We bid a fond farewell to the orgasma van, and we were off on our way home. The journey home was fairly uneventful. Our minds were on other things; and before we knew it, the two-hour drive was almost over.

Just before we arrived home, we started talking about Sam's work; it was the following week when Sam would have to start the job at the concert 'Beat Fest'. I was still worried sick that changing the events of time would change the future; and until we had passed the time when the accident originally happened, we wouldn't know if any changes would take place. Sam was quite *blasé* about it. He was convinced if he didn't turn up for work on the day, the accident couldn't happen, and that was the end of it. I had my doubts.

"Sam, what happens if, because you're not there, someone else gets injured, that would just be terrible; who will be doing what you should be doing on that day."

"Well! No one. The engineers will be rigging, but it's up to me to check everything off; so what's not checked that day will be done the next day. I suppose my second in command 'Mike' will be on site, so he might be checking."

"Sam, you will have to stop him. It might be him who gets injured."

"Poppy, I can't stop him going on site. The best I can do is to insist on all riggers to use safety harnesses, and I can arrange for an inflatable safety bag be erected under the rigging; so if anyone does fall, they will be fine."

I felt much better now. Sam was covering all eventualities, but still, if nothing happened, would the time continuum be intact? We wouldn't know until after the said date.

A week later, it was unfortunately time for Sam to travel up north to work on the 'Beat Fest' concert job. He didn't seem bothered, but I was a nervous wreck. We had a very quiet breakfast together; then Sam packed his case in the car and was ready for the off. He lent out of the car window, with a big smile on his face.

"Don't worry, Poppy, I will soon be home. All will be okay, see you in a few days."

We kissed passionately. I didn't want to let him go, but I had no choice. "Sam, promise me, you won't be on site on the dreaded day."

"I promise! Love you, Poppy, bye!"

His car pulled off the drive; the rumble of the powerful engine ebbing into the distance. Then I was on my own; I just stood on the drive, looking into thin air. I must have stood there for quite a while. What the neighbours must have thought if they had been watching, god only knows.

Because I was on my own, I had to get my car out of the garage. I would need some form of transport, now Sam was gone; also I thought it might be a good opportunity to put my plan into action. The plan that would shut Chloe and Kim up, once and for all, and prove that I was a time traveller. The plan was to visit the country house in the future and excrete a photo of Sam and me together in to a hiding place, so that when I travelled back to the future, I could retrieve the picture and show the girls; this would prove that I wasn't making everything up.

The next day, I was up bright and early. I walked Polly first. I decided not to take her with me, as she might bark and break my cover. Before I left, I looked through some recent photos of me and Sam together and chose a picture of us at the pub in Wales. Obviously, there was no reference to the date, so I decided to purchase today's newspaper on the way. Also I sorted out a plastic bag to wrap the items in. The house in the country was about 15 miles away. Crikey, I was so nervous; I knew I had to be so careful not to be seen. I took the same route that the removal lorry had taken when we had moved in, in June 1995. That was two years in the future, as it was only May 1993. I pulled up in the car, a few hundred yards away from the house. I had butterflies in my stomach. What the hell I was going to say if someone caught me; I didn't know. While I waited to pluck up the courage to attempt my undercover mission, I wrapped the two items carefully in the plastic bag. It was important because they would have to sit in the hiding place for at least two years, without getting wet.

Okay, so the newspaper and the photograph were wrapped; what was I waiting for... My heart was banging away like a drum; I had a stern word with myself,

Come on, Poppy, you can do it. Just get out of the car and start walking. I finally stepped from the car, locked the door and started walking towards the house. There was along hedge that ran along the road, which afforded me some cover. I planned to place the package into the stone wall at the gate entrance, where in the future I had noticed loose stones. I could hear ducks quacking on the pond, so I wasn't far from my target. I approached the gate; it was closed.

Oh my god, I could hear a car coming along the lane. If they stopped to ask me what I was doing, what would I say; I froze. I heard the car slowing. Oh! Shit, that was it then. I heard the car window being wound down.

"Excuse me, my dear, do you know where 'Banner Farm' is? We've been going around in circles for ages."

The relief was immense. It wasn't the owners of the house; just somebody lost who wanted directions. Luckily, I also knew where 'Banner Farm' was.

"Yes, you're not far away. Carry on up the lane, then take the next left turn. The road drops down quite steeply; then you will see the entrance on the right."

"Thank you so much."

The driver shouted out of the window as he pulled off at speed. I pulled myself together and looked for a spot in the stone wall where I could secrete the package. I stooped near the post box that was built into wall. There were several loose stones. I managed to extricate quite a large stone without loosening the rest of the frail wall. I pulled out the package from under my coat and placed it into the hole. I then expertly replaced the stone, forcing it tight into the gap. It was perfect; you couldn't see that a stone had been removed; no one would ever know until I removed it in two years' time.

I was feeling rather pleased with myself, as I rose up from my knees to make a speedy retreat. Then I had the shock of my life; staring right into my face was a man on the other side of the gate.

"Good morning, young lady, what are you doing down there."

I was in total shock; my throat went dry. I couldn't speak; I stuttered. I must have looked like a blithering idiot. The man spoke again,

"Are you alright, young lady; you look like you've just seen a ghost."

What he didn't know was that I had met him two years into the future. This was the man who we had bought the house off. It was George.

"I'm so sorry, sir. I seem to have lost my dog. I was just looking along the lane to see if she was hiding in the hedge."

It must have sounded ridiculous, because I was knelt down by the wall next to his gate. He thrust his hand forward, grabbing mine,

"Nice to meet you, young lady. I'm George, I live here with my wife Susan. Can I get you a cup of tea; you look a little upset."

"Oh! That's very kind of you! But I think I will get on with looking for my dog. Thank you anyway."

I started to walk away, desperate to get out of the situation,

"Shall I come with you; it will be quicker with two of us looking."

I shouted back; my steps getting faster,

"I'll be fine, thanks, have a good day."

My pace quickened and soon became a run, straight back to my car. I kept turning to make sure he wasn't following me, but he wasn't; he was just being kind, offering me help to find my dog. I sat in my car to get my breath back. My mind instantly surged forward to 1995. I remember now, when we looked at the house for the first time, I remember George saying to me,

"I've met you before, young lady." Of course, when we bought the house, I hadn't time travelled, so I hadn't met George, but he had met me back in 1993. I had no recollection of the meeting because I hadn't discovered the 'Door' at that time. My god, my head was spinning, trying to put all the facts together. One thing was for sure, I had now planted the evidence, to prove to the girls of my other life, in the past.

Chapter 37
Muddy Waters

Yesterday had been a bit stressful, bumping into George like I did. It still amazed me that from that short liaison, George could still remember me two years later, when I went along to buy his house. He may have been in his twilight years, but he was as sharp as a knife. I certainly wouldn't like to play poker with him. The best thing was, I had managed to place the items in the wall, and I couldn't wait to travel back to 1995. I would take the girls to the wall at the end of my drive, move the stone and retrieve the photo and the newspaper, dated 18 May 1993; that's if they hadn't been removed in those two years.

Now to more important things… Today was the day of the accident; well, let's hope there was no accident. I decided to phone Sam to make sure he wasn't at work.

"Hello Sam, how are you, still at the hotel I hope."

He seemed to hesitate, before he answered,

"Well Poppy, I've had to come in to work. There's been a major problem on site, and I'm the only one who can sort it out."

My blood ran cold through my veins. I couldn't believe Sam didn't heed my warnings,

"Oh Sam, you've really upset me now. I can't believe you would jeopardise our future."

I started to cry; the enormity of the situation just overwhelmed me.

"Sam, you need to leave the site right now. Please, Sam, just get off that site."

Poppy was screaming down the phone. I could tell she was extremely upset, but at the same time, I couldn't lie to her. I had to be honest with her. I had come to site because I had no choice. Mike, the other manager who reported to me, had called me in desperation. For some reason, the lighting rig wasn't talking to the receiving panel in the main control room, and so they called me.

"Poppy, I promise you I'm safe. I'm just about to leave the site now, so stop worrying yourself into an early grave; love you, my little poppet."

"Sam, I love you too! Please, please, leave the site now."

"Okay, Poppy, I promise you I'm leaving now."

The phone went dead. I was just about to leave the site when Mike shouted over,

"Sam, could you just look at the transmitter on the central section of lighting above the stage while I retune the receiver."

Now I was in a right dilemma. I couldn't tell him there would be an accident; he would think I was mad. So with great reticence, I shouted to the crew to move the inflatable safety bag directly under the area where I was about to climb. I then put on a safety harness. I climbed up the rigging to where Mike thought the problem might be; then I hooked my karabiner from my harness to the rig. My heart was going ten to the dozen, and I felt really bad that I had told Poppy I was leaving the site. I was just between a rock and a hard place.

I rummaged through yards of wires; then, I saw it. The connecting plug from the transmitter to the lighting rig had disconnected. I pushed the plug back in, and suddenly, a whole row of bright lights lit up. Then came the bellowing voice from below; Mike was shouting, "You've done it, you smart arse." I was so happy. I just wanted to get down from there. As I turned, I heard a high-pitched crack. Before I knew what was happening, I felt my whole body weight straining on the safety harness. I thought to myself, *thank god I had strapped onto the rig.* But then, without warning, the rig must have given way. The karabiner was still attached to the rig, but the spar I had attached to wasn't attached to the rig. For a split second, I stood still; then my whole life passed in front of my eyes, and I accelerated towards the ground. I hit the air bag with such a force; if it hadn't been there, my body would have crumpled on impact. Thank god, Poppy had warned me; otherwise I wouldn't have had the harness on or have ordered the air bag. I opened my eyes to see lots of faces staring into the dip in the air bag, where the weight of my body lay.

"Are you alright, Sam; grab my hand, let's get you out of there."

It was Mike, who extended his hand and pulled me up off the bag, then down onto the stage.

"My god, Sam, you're a lucky fucker. If you hadn't insisted on this safety bag, it would have been curtains for you."

If he had realised I had prior knowledge to the incident, and I had still gone up the rig, he would have thought I was bonkers. We then both looked at the harness, still intact, with the karabiner still attached to the spar; it had been a faulty spar that had been the cause of the accident. "Okay Mike, I think I'm okay, but I'm off to the hotel to have a stiff drink and a lie down. From now on, any ariel work has to be carried out with the bag. No exceptions!"

"Okay boss,"

Mike replied, with a playful salute to acknowledge the instruction; then I was off. How I was going to explain this one to Poppy, I had no idea!

About 20 minutes after coming off the phone with Sam, a strange thing happened. I was sat on the sofa with Polly, giving her some love, when the whole scene around me appeared to shimmer. I thought at first the 'Door' was calling me back, but the temperature stayed the same, and there was no flash of bright light. May be I was having a dizzy turn, I thought to myself, then just forgot about it. I went about my business, trying to forget that Sam was away until the weekend, so I concentrated on a new painting. It was in oil, and it was a woodland scene, with lots of silver birch trees. In the shade of the trees, you could just make out the image of a Roe deer, peering tentatively through the green ferns that grew around the base of the trees. After painting for a few hours, I fancied some fresh air; so I grabbed Polly's lead, and off we went to the woods. As soon as we were in the confines of the wood itself, I unclipped Polly's lead, and she was off like a rocket, no doubt after a rabbit or a squirrel. All I could see were the ferns moving as she bolted towards her goal. I was now on my own in the middle of the wood; it was very quiet apart from the occasional cooing of wood pigeons, and the distant sound of a woodpecker boring into the side of a tree. The smell of damp moss growing on the fallen trees entered my nostrils. I brushed my fingers through it; it felt like a wet sea sponge.

Then the shimmering started again, but this time much worse. First off all, the wood fell totally silent. As I looked at the trees, they all shimmered; the ground seemed to shake, I noticed my hand appeared translucent, as if part of me was disappearing. I was now quite frightened, I didn't know what would happen next. I slumped to the ground; and then in a nano second, everything returned to normal. I gathered my thoughts, *first of all, find Polly; then go straight home.* I shouted Polly; and within seconds, she came bounding towards me. I attached her lead, and we made our way back home. As soon as I got in to the house, I called Sam,

"Oh Sam, are you alright."

"Of course I am, Poppy. What's the matter with you; you sound upset, are you crying."

"Oh, Sam! Something is wrong. I'm not sure if the 'Door' is calling me, but weird things are happening. Can you come home, please; I'm scared."

"Poppy, calm down, sweetheart; are you in danger right now."

"No! But Sam, because we stopped the accident happening, I think it has upset the time continuum, parts of my body keeps disappearing."

She sounded delirious. Something must have really upset her; she was normally so level headed.

"Poppy! I'm on my way home. I should be with you in about one hour. I will phone Sally to come and be with you until I get home."

"I'm so sorry, Sam. I just feel really scared."

"Poppy, don't worry. I love you so much. I'm on my way right now."

I put down the phone and the guilt tore through me. Had I made things worse by going on site, after I told her I wouldn't; or just by preventing the accident, had we unleashed the wrath of time itself? I rang Sally and told her that Poppy was stressed. She offered to go straight to the house. I then threw my things in a bag, jumped into the car and sped down the motorway as fast as the traffic would allow me.

A few minutes after speaking to Sam, the doorbell rang. I opened it; it was Sally.

"Oh Sally, thanks for coming around. I really don't know what's happening."

"Poppy, just settle down; I'll put the kettle on while you bring me up to speed with what's going on."

Over the next hour or so, I told Sally about the 'Door', and how I had travelled back in time, met Sam, her brother, and consequently fallen in love.

Also how I discovered that Sam would have a serious life-changing accident if we didn't take action. I explained that the accident would have been today, but we avoided it by taking precautions; but in doing so, changed the time continuum, and it was this that probably caused the strange phenomenon that was occurring today. While I had been talking, Sally hadn't uttered a word. She seemed to be in deep thought, then she spoke,

"Poppy! First of all, don't worry! If you had changed the timeline for good, you probably would have disappeared altogether, to a different situation completely."

I couldn't believe she was so matter-of-fact; and also that she spoke with such confidence about the intricacies of time travel, I had to ask her, "Sally, how do you know these things."

"Poppy, put it like this. I've watched a lot of Star-trek movies, and, of course, it's quite logical if you think about it."

I was dumbstruck; she acted like it was an everyday occurrence to time travel and to say it was logical; well, I was blown away.

"What did you mean I would have gone to a completely different situation if we had changed the timeline."

She then tried to explain how the timeline might work; she paused, in deep thought, then spoke softly,

"When you travel back, you're going back in history. The events have already happened, and those events are the building blocks for future events."

She paused again to make sure I was with her, then continued,

"So if you travel back and change something big, like for instance, stop someone dying, that will have catastrophic changes on the future, and all the life connections with that person's timeline, it would be massive."

I nodded, like I was understanding what she was trying to get over.

"Now Poppy, what you did by stopping Sam getting injured has changed the timeline, but not as much as it could have; it will have consequences on the future, but my feeling is that there will be small changes, and what you are experiencing today is the timeline adjusting to the differences caused by Sam not being crippled."

"So Sally, do you think it will settle down, and these strange occurrences will stop."

"To be honest, Poppy, I don't know, but if you were going to be torn away into another timeline, I think it would have happened already."

I felt so much better having discussed my problems with Sally. God knows how she appeared to know the things she did.

Then Polly started barking; she had heard Sam's car pull on the drive. I ran out to greet him; I was so happy to see him. As soon as he was out of the car, I hugged him so hard, but he winced like I had really hurt him.

"Sam, are you alright; have you injured yourself."

"Let's get a cuppa, Poppy; and I will tell you all about it."

I was dreading telling Poppy about my fall. On the long drive home, my back had started aching. The impact, although on an inflatable bag, must have still bruised my muscles. Poppy was now fretting, begging me to tell her what had happened. Sally offered to make the tea, so once we all had a brew in front of us, I began. I felt really bad that I had let Poppy down, but it was best, all out in the open. Poppy told me what had happened to her, but I was relieved; we were past the accident, and so far, all seemed okay. Poppy forgave me. I think she was just happy that we could now move on,

"Sam, you poor thing, it must have been quite a shock falling like that. I will have to rub some soothing oil into you later."

She had that naughty grin on her face as she spoke, and I knew then that we were going to be alright.

In bed that night, after I had massaged Sam's back, we lay talking about all sorts.

"Sam, your sister is amazing; she was so calm today. After hearing everything, she wasn't fazed at all; are you sure she isn't a time traveller herself."

Sam burst out laughing, then replied,

"What, my sister, a time traveller; don't be so ridiculous. Don't you think she would have told me if she was."

"I suppose."

I said, but deep down I had my doubts. There was definitely something strange about her. Over the next few months, there were a couple of episodes of shimmering images around me, but I stayed calm and got on with my life, assuming that all was well. That summer we spent a lot of time in the garden. We built a fishpond and landscaped the rest of the garden. We even got a few chickens; it was great having fresh eggs. Sam built the hen house, and I have to say it was a fine job. I remember the day he finished it, he called me to look at it. It was roughly six feet long by five wide and about four feet high. He opened the door and said,

"Look in there."

As I bent down to see fresh hay covering the floor, he pushed me hard, and I ended up sprawled on the floor. I couldn't believe it; he locked the door, dropped his trousers, held his cock in the air and said,

"This cock is looking for a hen."

I have to admit sex in the chicken shed was a first for me, but I wasn't complaining.

I sometimes had to pinch myself when I thought about my life with Poppy; she was just the best. Life was a dream and sex was… well, interesting. I wasn't complaining, far from it. Poppy wasn't the sort of girl who had to have a bed to have sex on; she would do it anywhere. The best thing was in just over a year and a half, the two time zones we were living in would coincide, and we could get married at last. Deep down I prayed that the 'Door' wouldn't take her back again, but as we both knew, we had no control over the 'Door' at all.

It was a barmy September night. It had been sunny for days, and we were walking back home from our local. We had had a few drinks, we were laughing and joking and not far from home. The sky was filling up with really dark grey clouds, and you could tell a storm was brewing. Then there was an almighty clap of thunder; we both jumped out of our skin. The raindrops started falling, slowly at first, then the heavens opened. I had never seen rain like it. The raindrops were hitting the ground so hard, they were bouncing back up off the pavement; and within seconds, a river of water was flowing along the road. We were drenched to the skin, nothing we could do about it; we just carried on walking towards home.

When we arrived back, we went through the back door, into the kitchen. It had a tile floor, so the water from our wet clothes wouldn't hurt. As we stripped off, dropping our clothes to the floor, Poppy started laughing; she was up to something.

"Sam, are you a scared'y cat."

"What do you mean?"

"Well, Sam, are you a chicken…"

"Poppy, I have no idea what you're going on about."

"Sam, I dare you to run naked around the garden in the rain. In fact, I will race you to the top of the garden around the oak tree, and the first one back is the winner."

"Do you mean naked, naked as a j-bird, nothing on."

"Well, that's what naked means, isn't it."

"Just one proviso, Poppy. Can we wear wellies, in case we cut our feet."

"I suppose so. In fact, I think you might look quite fetching in a pair of green wellies, with nothing else on."

So we both stripped off. Poppy's body always gave me a twinge down below. I was hoping that I didn't get a full-blown erection; it might be embarrassing if the neighbours were watching. We both donned our wellies, and we were ready to go. I opened the kitchen door; the rain was coming down like stair rods.

I couldn't believe that Sam had a hard on; I couldn't stop laughing. I flicked his cock; he responded by slapping my wet arse.

"Right, Poppy, no cheating. The first one back wins. On your marks, get set, Go, Go, Go…"

Even with wellies on, it was still slippery. The lawn was so wet, it was tough going. Poppy was in front of me, her beautiful arse bouncing up and down, and she was screaming with excitement; the first part of the garden was sloped upwards. She reached the archway at the top of the slope and turned; it was surreal seeing her naked in the garden. Her hair was flat to her face; the pounding rain was running off her breasts, and her pubes glistened. She shouted,

"Come on, slow coach, catch me if you can."

Then she was off again, towards the chicken house. It was really muddy there. I put on a spurt, I got close enough to grab her around the waist; she squealed. The mud was splashing everywhere; then she stumbled, ending up face down in the mud. I was hysterical; I landed on top of her. My cock slipped between the cheeks of her slippery arse,

"Poppy! I bet you did that on purpose, you dirty girl."

"No, I didn't, I'm still trying to win this race," she replied. She was so determined; she hated losing. She rolled over; I went sideways, landing in the mud on my back, and she was up again and off like a shot. I just managed to catch her welly, which brought her down again, giving me a chance to get back on my feet. She accelerated towards the oak tree, with me in hot pursuit. My heart was pounding—god, she was fit. As she rounded the tree, she grabbed the trunk, catapulting her towards the house, but she spun so fast, she lost her balance, landing on her back, sliding down the grassy slope. I was moving at such a pace, I couldn't avoid her. I also faltered and landed on top of her. We were both absolutely knackered. I could feel Poppy's heart pounding in her chest. We must have looked like mud monsters. We both fought for the next breath, laughing and then gasping,

"Poppy,"

I took another breath,

"I love you so much."

I wrapped my arms around him, opening my legs. I could feel his hard cock searching for me. He smiled as he penetrated me.

"Sam! I guess it's a draw."

"Oh no! Poppy, I'm the winner. I get the spoils. I get to shag you in the rain."

As he vented all of his passion into me, the mud flew in every direction, making a squelchy sound each time our bodies came together. It was such a turn on having sex in the mud, I soon reached a climatic orgasm, with Sam not far behind. His eyes bulging as he shot his hot cum inside me. But then, without having the time to enjoy the moment, it happened. Instead of feeling all warm and relaxed, like you normally do after sex, the temperature dropped dramatically,

"Sam! Sam! Help me! The 'Door', it's taking me."

I just heard Sam shout,

"Poppy! Be prepared, he will be waiting for you."

Then the image around me shimmered, followed by a flash of bright light, and I was gone.

Poppy just disappeared from under me. I crashed face first into the muddy grass. I took a big breath in, then started choking on the water I had breathed in. I pushed myself upwards, out of the muddy water, and regained my composure. I sat there for a minute, contemplating what Poppy's fate might be. What I must have looked like, god only knew. I scraped away the mud from my eyes, with both hands; then as my vision cleared, I saw her. Oh my god! I froze, not knowing what to do next; should I pretend I hadn't noticed her, or should I wave. The lady next door was in her bedroom window, looking straight at me. *Bollocks*, I thought to myself. It was the only part of the garden overlooked by neighbours, and I had to be sat stark naked in the mud in full view of what looked like a very shocked but bemused middle-aged lady.

Chapter 38
You're Nicked

In a flash, I was lay in the chair in my studio. I instantly remembered what Sam had shouted to me before the 'Door' had torn me away from the man I loved and unceremoniously delivered me into the dangerous path of a man I definitely didn't love. The noise of the studio door being rammed was frightening. I jumped up, and without thinking, grabbed a vase from the side, then stood behind the door. Then came the almighty sound of cracking wood, as the easel I had wedged against the door disintegrated, splintering all over the place. The studio door flung open with such force, I was lucky it didn't knock me out. Simon's body then came crashing into the room, ending up on his hands and knees just in front of me. Before he could regain any sense of what was going on, I smashed the vase across the back of his head; the flowers and the water cascaded all over the carpet. Simon let out a growl, like a wild animal, but thankfully, dropped to the floor, incapacitated by the force of the blow.

I didn't waste any time. I stepped over Simon's limp body and ran down the stairs, as fast as I could; my foot was still painful. I met Roscoe on the way. I ran into the kitchen, grabbed my phone, which was on the kitchen table, but I couldn't see the van keys. They weren't on the hook where I would normally have left them. Roscoe was running around the kitchen, whining; he must have sensed the panic I was in. Then I heard a rumble on the stairs. Simon must have regained consciousness. I heard him shout, but couldn't quite make out what he said. I was now in serious danger. Simon would want revenge for my incredulous attack on him. I decided to run, but then as I went to leave, I noticed my coat by the back door. I checked the pockets, and bingo… I found the van keys. I ran out of the back door, followed by the dog and headed for my van.

The van was quite old, so didn't have remote locking. I had to fiddle with the key to undo the door, and in my panic, I dropped the key on the floor. I heard Simon shouting; this time I did hear what he said,

"Poppy, you're going to regret hitting me, you bitch."

I managed to open the door. The dog jumped in first; I scrambled in and locked the door. As I turned the ignition key, I noticed Simon coming through the kitchen door; he was holding his head. He seemed a bit disoriented; then he heard the engine start on the van. He immediately ran in front of the van to block my escape. He threw himself onto the bonnet, shouting to me to stop. Roscoe was jumping at the screen, barking violently, trying to get at Simon. If I didn't get away, I knew it wouldn't end well, so I revved the engine, dropped the clutch and fled forwards, towards the pond, with Simon still hanging on to the windscreen wipers. I then braked really hard. The van came to a sudden stop, but unfortunately, Simon didn't. He went rolling off the bonnet, down the slight slope, and into the pond. If I hadn't been so scared, I probably would have wet myself with laughter. Instead I drove off the drive as fast as the engine would allow me to.

I sped down the lane, constantly looking in my wing mirrors to see if Simon's car was in pursuit, but nothing. May be he had cooled down after going in the pond. Yet again, a smile came to my face. Just when I thought my escape was succeeding, the engine started coughing and spluttering. "Oh no!" I shouted at the top of my voice, "not now." I looked at the dashboard, an orange light was flashing. The fuel gauge read empty; then I remembered I had meant to put some fuel in from a backup jerry can I kept at home. I thought if I could just make it to the local town, I could phone Chloe; she would come and help me. But it was not to be; the engine gave out its last splutter, backfired, then died. I was now coasting in neutral, looking for a safe place to pull over. Just ahead was a small lay-by, so I pulled in to get off the road. I glanced at my wing mirror and went cold with fear. In the distance, I could see a vehicle heading towards me at great speed; it was Simon. I started shaking. If I got out now and made a run for it, he would surely catch me. I decided to call the police. I retrieved my phone from my bag and dialled 999. The operator calmly asked, "What emergency service do you require." I was not so calm, screaming down the phone that I needed the police asap. I looked into the mirror; Simon was just pulling in behind me. I started to cry,

"Please, help me; a man is attacking me."

The operator calmly asked where I was. I told her; she replied,

"Sit tight! An officer is on his way. Can you describe the man who is attacking you?"

I couldn't believe the questions she was asking; then Simon's face appeared at my driver's side window. I screamed so loud, even the dog yelped. I could hear the operator asking,

"Are you alright?"

Then in my panic, I dropped the phone. Simon started banging on the window; he looked demented. He was so angry, he was shouting at the top of his voice.

"Open the fucking door, you bitch. I'll kill you when I get my hands on you."

I looked around the cab to see if there was anything I could use to defend myself, but there was nothing. I had never been so frightened in all my life; and from looking at Simon's face, he looked like he'd lost the plot. He continued to bang the window with such a force, I wasn't surprised when the window exploded inwards, showering me with bits of glass. Simon's hand reached in, grabbing me around the neck. He was so strong, I couldn't push him off. I tried to scream, but he was crushing my windpipe. Then Roscoe flew at him, biting deep into his hand. The blood squirted everywhere; Simon pulled back, shouting again, "You little bastard, get your fucking mutt off me."

I scrambled over to the passenger seat while Simon was trying to deal with the dog; then Roscoe yelped in pain. Simon had yanked him out of the cab and discarded him on to the road. Then in the distance, I heard a faint siren. Hopefully it was the police, and they were on their way to save me. I don't think Simon heard; he was just intent on getting to me. He had now got his whole body through the window, frantically grasping at me. I lashed out, landing a few blows to his head, but it didn't seem to have any effect. He was like a devil possessed; he was bleeding profusely, but all he could focus on was me. The siren got louder and louder. Then there was the noise of a vehicle breaking hard on the road— they had arrived. Simon glanced back, then turned to me and said,

"You fucking bitch! You called the police."

He lurched forwards, grabbing my hair; he pulled my head close to his. The blood was gushing out of his wound. His eyes stared straight into mine, bulging with anger; the last thing he said was,

"I'll have you!"

Then suddenly, he seemed to retreat backwards. The two officers, who had come to my rescue, had grabbed his legs; and with great force, ripped him from the cab. They then manhandled him to the ground, pushing his face into the gravel. Then while one officer knelt on his back, the other one bent his arms behind his back and cuffed him. The older of the two officers spoke first, "Not so big now, are you, picking on a lady half your size. I've seen bullies like you many times before; well, you're nicked."

The other officer read him his rights, while Simon just scowled, not saying a word. A couple of minutes later, another police vehicle arrived; it was a van with compartments in the back. The driver got out to speak to the arresting officer, "I suppose you didn't want the blood in the back of your car, hey Sarg!"

"No, I didn't, put him in the paddy wagon. I'll take the young lady to the station in our car."

The officer then turned to me and, in a soft reassuring voice, said,

"Are you injured? There seems to be a lot of blood spattered all around the vehicle."

"No! It's not mine. My dog was trying to defend me and bit him; is the dog alright?"

The officer hesitated before he answered,

"Well, the dog is still laying in the verge. I'm not sure. First things first, let's make sure you're okay; then we can get the vet to look at the dog."

I wasn't bothered about me. I was just a bit shaken up, so I climbed out of the passenger side door, and there was Roscoe, lying prostrate on the ground. I knelt down; he was still breathing. I rubbed his neck and kissed him. He was so groggy, I think the force that he hit the ground with must have knocked him out. He did look sorry for himself.

"Officer, I want Simon charged for this. He could have killed him."

The officer replied,

"I think that's the least of his problems after what he's done to you. Anyway, I think we should get down to the station now. You best lock up this vehicle; and after you've given us your statement, we will drop you back here to collect it."

I quickly retrieved my phone from the van floor, then locked the van. Not a lot of point though, the driver side window was missing. Before we left, the officer checked Simon's car. In his hurry to get at me, he had left the keys in the ignition. So they locked it, and we all left for the police station.

I sat in the back of the squad car, with Roscoe on my lap. If only I could talk to Sam, I really needed him right now. I just couldn't believe how Simon had turned so nasty. I really thought he wanted to kill me. With my mind wandering, it only seemed like minutes, and the car turned into the secure parking of the impressive police station. The van containing Simon went into a different entrance—I assumed the custody suite. We parked up, and the rather sweet PC escorted me to the waiting room; there was a strange smell lingering in the corridor. I then called Chloe to let her know what had happened. She insisted on coming to the station immediately, and I didn't complain; I needed someone to comfort me. Before I even went into the interview room, Chloe arrived, which was great. It meant she could look after Roscoe while I was talking to the police. Because I expected the statement to take a long time, I asked Chloe to take Roscoe home. He seemed fine now, but I thought he would prefer to be at home. Besides, he needed feeding.

"Poppy, give me your keys to the van as well. I will get Tom to get it back home for you, and I will ask Kim's Colin to change the locks on the house. That bastard had better keep away if he wants to keep his balls."

The police officer, who was stood right next to me, gave Chloe a very stern look, then spoke,

"I hope you're not threatening to harm Miss Day's partner; are you, young lady."

Chloe looked up, a little indignant at being cautioned by the young officer,

"Well, you just make sure that the low-life gets what's coming to him. If you don't, I will."

Then she made a hasty retreat out of the station, with Roscoe in tow. The officer looked at me and said,

"She's a feisty one. I wouldn't want to get on the wrong side of her."

"No! She stands her ground, that one, but I love her to bits."

I was in the interview room for at least three hours before the questioning finally came to an end. I was exhausted and couldn't wait to get home to have a drink. Before I left the room, I asked the sergeant, "What will happen to my ex?"

"Well, Miss Day, he will be up in front of the magistrates, first thing in the morning—the first charge of assault and the second of criminal damage."

I was sad that things had gotten so bad, and now, Simon would end up with a criminal record. I sighed; then the officer spoke again,

"Look miss, if he had lashed out and hit you while in a rage, that would be bad enough; but to jump in his car and chase you down the road to attack you, well, that's premeditated. He wanted to hurt you; you're better off without him."

I already knew that, but I didn't want to see him in prison. As promised, the arresting officer arranged a lift home for me; and as we neared the house, we passed the lay-by where it all happened. My van had gone, but Simon's car was still there. The police officer could see I was concerned, "Yes, he will have to come and retrieve his motor, but don't worry, he now has a restraining order against him; so if he comes within a hundred yards of you, he will be arrested and put behind bars."

I didn't feel very reassured if I was honest, but what could I do. A couple of minutes later, we pulled on to the drive. Chloe's car and also Kim's were parked at the top of the drive that made me feel better straight away. I thanked the officer for the lift, then waved him goodbye; then the girls came running out of the house and hugged me.

As soon as we got in the house, I could smell something cooking. Chloe had put a large pizza in the oven, and the wine glasses were already primed.

"Right Poppy, have something to eat and drink; there's nothing to worry about. Roscoe is fine, Colin has changed the locks, Tom refuelled the van and brought it back, and Kim cleaned the blood from the cab. We still need to replace the window though, so all we have to do now is get pissed."

We all burst out laughing; then Kim proposed a toast,

"Here's to Roscoe for biting the bastard. May his teeth be forever sharp."

We all raised our glasses and repeated,

"Here's to Roscoe for biting the bastard. May his teeth be forever sharp.'

Chapter 39
End of the Line

My one eye opened. I could see a bare foot; the toenails were pink, so I assumed they were female. Then I remembered, the girls stayed over last night. I was in the middle of the bed, my head at the headboard end, and the two girls were lay either side of me, the opposite way around, with their heads at the foot of the bed. My head was thumping; god knows how much wine we had put away last night. I decided then, I would never drink a drop again. Kim was the first to stir, "I'm going to put the kettle on. Anyone fancy a cup of tea."

Chloe responded, before I even had the chance to speak,

"Do bears shit in the woods, does Dolly Parton sleep on her back! Of course we want a cup of tea."

She was holding her head, cursing the booze,

"Polly, why did you make us drink so much; it's your fault."

She laughed out loud while blaming me for her banging headache. In fact, it was her who kept filling the glasses up. Kim had been a bit more sensible. She had gone on to water about midnight; now she was reaping the rewards. Kim jumped out of the bed. She was stark naked; she had a fine body, very slim and toned; her bottom was a lot smaller than mine, and so were her boobs.

"Polly, is it okay if I wear this robe hanging on the back of the door."

"Of course Kim, it's one that Simon left behind. I don't think he will be wanting it."

Then Chloe piped up!

"Yes, the only thing he needs is a damn good slap; and when I see him, he will be getting it."

Kim just smiled. She knew Chloe was the fiery one, out of all of us, and she also knew that Simon would get a slap when Chloe saw him. Kim then disappeared down the stairs to fetch the tea.

Chloe then spun around and lay next to me,

"Poppy, my dear, how are you feeling today, apart from the hangover."

"What hangover, I haven't got a hangover."

I lied through my teeth,

"Oh Poppy! You're such a terrible liar. You drank at least as much as I did last night. I just know you're suffering the headache from hell."

I couldn't pretend any longer. My head was throbbing, and I felt like throwing up,

"Chloe, I'm never going to drink with you again. I'm just not in the same league as you. You were drinking at least two glasses to my one; and look at you, you look as bright as a button."

She started laughing; then she threw the covers back, exposing her large firm breasts,

"Just look at these babies. Aren't they just the best boobs you've ever seen."

She held them in her hands, shoving them upwards, not that they needed lifting; the expensive boob job she had had made sure of that they seemed to defy gravity.

The bedroom door flew open. First of all, Roscoe came bounding in, followed by Kim, who was carrying a large tray. She placed it down on the dresser, next to the window,

"Right then, ladies, who's for tea and toast."

I shouted out, "I bagsy the crust if there is one."

Kim very kindly brought my tea and toast over to me. Then both girls helped themselves and joined me on the bed with Roscoe. It went a bit quiet while we gulped our tea, all of us anxious to rehydrate our suffering bodies—it was heaven. Even Roscoe managed to bag a crust or two. We must have looked a sight—Kim in a man's gown, Chloe naked and me just in knickers. The main thing being, I had the best friends ever trying to support me in my hour of need.

"Girls, I just want to thank you for being here for me. I don't know what I would have done without you. I know Sam would appreciate what fantastic friends I have."

Then, Kim spoke,

"Talking about Sam the man, you promised you would bring some proof back with you, to show us what a hunk this Sam really was."

I smiled to myself, because I knew that at last I could show them that yes, I was a time traveller.

"Well, girls! The good news is, I do have proof; and as soon as we all get dressed, I will show you my hunk, as you call him."

The girls were so excited, insisting that they see the evidence straight away, I explained that we had to go outside to retrieve the proof and they just had to wait a little bit longer.

By the time we all got dressed, the morning was nearly over. It was 11:30 a.m., and the heavens had opened; the rain was coming down hard. Chloe wanted to know why we had to get soaked to retrieve the evidence.

"The thing is, Chloe, I need you to see where the proof is hidden, so you will understand how I managed to get the picture from 1993 to now, 1995."

I then explained to both of the girls how I had hidden the package in the wall, near the gate, back in 1993. Then how I had been almost caught by the owner of the house, just so they would believe that I was a time traveller. We then donned our coats, grabbed a couple of brollies which were hung by the back door and made our way down the drive to the stone wall by the gate.

The rain was bouncing off the surface of the pond. The ducks seemed oblivious to the tirade of water falling from the sky. We on the other hand were soaked, even with the brollies fending off most of the rain. We arrived at the gate. Kim pulled back the bolt, securing the gate to the post and swung it open. We walked through the opening to the left, where the post box sat; then we stopped, "Well Poppy, where is the package."

"It's just there behind that stone, with the moss growing on it, I think."

Kim spoke, "You think! There's a lot of stones in this wall. If we have to try all of them, we will be here all day."

"Well! It was two years ago when I hid the package, and I'm still a bit bleary eyed after last night."

Kim then knelt down, to remove the stone, while Chloe and me held the brollies over all of us to fend off some of the rain. Kim pushed her fingers into the crack between the stones. Using both hands, she pulled, but with no success,

"It's stuck solid, Poppy, are you sure it was this one."

I stood back a little; my mind whizzing back two years, trying to remember where I was stood when the man from the house appeared over the gate. I was positive that was the correct stone,

"Kim, give it another go! I'm sure it was that one."

Kim moaned. She was kneeling in a puddle, and the rain was pouring off the two brollies and soaking her. Chloe started laughing, which started me off. Kim wasn't amused, "You two can shut the fuck up as well. It's me knelt in the mud, and I'm bloody soaked."

This just set us off again. Chloe was crying with laughter. I had tears running down my face, but you couldn't see them due to the water everywhere; then Chloe spoke,

"Kim, come on! Think of the stone as Simon's head, and you want to pull it off."

That did the trick. Kim had been so intent on pulling Simon's head off, she shot backwards so quickly, she almost knocked us over. She landed on her back in the mud, still holding the stone in her hands. A cheer went up from me and Chloe,

"Well done, Kim; you've done it."

She threw the stone to one side, and we all peered into the hole in the wall, "Is it there, Kim?"

I asked, nervously.

Kim reached into the hole, searching from right to left; she glanced up at us, "Absolutely nothing, there's nothing here."

My heart sank. I was sure that was the rock; someone must have removed it in the past two years. Then Kim's face changed, and she smiled, "Only joking." She pulled a plastic bag from the hole and held it up towards us,

"Is this what we're looking for?"

I squealed with excitement, so did Chloe. I grabbed the bag from Kim, unceremoniously, desperate to make sure it was the one.

"Yes, that's the bag. You'll see now that I'm not making it all up."

I tucked the evidence under my coat, and we all ran up the drive towards the house, not bothering with the brollies; we were soaked to the skin anyway. We piled into the kitchen; I tossed the bag onto the kitchen table; then as if in unison, we all gathered around the AGA to get some comforting warmth. We ended up all stood there in our pants, our clothes sprawled over the AGA steaming, the water being driven out by the incessant heat which the AGA gave out. If anyone had come to the back door and looked through the window, they would have had a pleasant shock. Three almost naked ladies huddled together in anticipation, waiting to see if the evidence in the bag would prove once and for all that Poppy Day was a time traveller. We all wrapped up in towels, which were stored in a cupboard next to the kitchen. We then sat around the table, each with a hot cup of tea and a chocolate digestive. The package covered in cobwebs, lay in the middle of the table, awaiting for one of us to open it,

"Well, Poppy, are you going to open it, or do you want one of us to?"

"I can't bear to look. I think one of you should open it."

I was dreading that a mouse or some sort of animal had got into the bag, to make a nest or something, eating up the evidence.

Kim tentatively reached forward, picking up the package; she unfolded the plastic bag carefully and peered inside. She instantly closed the bag and stared towards us; she was being so dramatic, she should have been an actor.

"What's in there?" asked Chloe. Kim replied, in a slow eerie voice,

"It looks like a newspaper and a photograph."

Kim was being so silly. Chloe couldn't wait any longer, so she took the bag and retrieved the objects, placing them on the table in front of us. The girls' faces dropped towards the photograph, so they could focus on the image,

"Oh my God, Poppy, it's you and the hunk, my word, he is a dish," exclaimed Chloe.

Then Kim joined in,

"I see why you want to travel back in time now; he is rather dishy."

Then Chloe picked up the newspaper,

"So why did you include the newspaper, Poppy."

"Well, the photo only shows us together, but the newspaper which I bought on the same day as I planted the package shows the date, which proves that I must have travelled back in time."

They then both scrutinised the date at the top of the page, and both of them recited the date at the same time,

"The 18th of May 1993."

They both looked at me, as if in a trance; then Kim spoke,

"So you really are a time traveller. Our friend, Poppy Day, is a bona fide time lord; from now on, I'm going to call you Doctor Who."

The girls both started to laugh. I didn't think it was really that funny, but deep down, I was happy that they now both believed me.

The day was getting on. The girls would have to go soon, but before they could leave the house, we all had to do something about our hair. We took turns in the shower, then congregated in my bedroom. Chloe had first dibs with the hair dryer while me and Kim attempted to look something like with a bit of make-up. Even with the noise from the hair dryer and the constant chat from the girls, I could vaguely hear a tapping sound in the background,

"Shush, shush! Can you hear that tapping sound?"

Chloe turned the hair dryer off, and we all went silent.

"I can't hear a thing,"

Kim exclaimed.

"No wait! Did you hear that?" replied Chloe.

"I think it might be a woodpecker," I said. They often visited the tall trees by the pond. Then Kim, who was stood by the window, held up her hand, as if to beckon us to listen,

"I think you better come and see this, Poppy."

We all rushed to the window and peered out. At the end of the drive was a small white van, and next to the gate was a man stood with a white post in his one hand and a large hammer in his other hand. The noise we could hear was the sound he made each time he banged the top of the post into the ground. Then it hit me; in big red letters, the sign read, 'For Sale'.

We all looked at each other in dismay. Then Chloe spoke,

"Poppy, did you put the house on the market?"

"No, I bloody didn't. I'll bloody kill him; this is Simon's doing."

I ran out of the house, followed by the girls; what we must have looked like, god knows. Chloe had grabbed a coat from the hook on the way out, and Kim and I were in our dressing gowns.

As we proceeded down the drive, the man heard us coming. He looked up, bewildered; but before he could open his mouth, I shouted out,

"What the hell do you think you're doing, you stupid man. I haven't put the house up for sale, you imbecile; now take that down before I do."

The man looked a little shaken up. I guess the sight of us three girls, approaching with menace in our eyes, must have worried him.

"Well, my dear, the owner of the house has instructed the estate agents to sell the property as soon as possible, and I'm just doing my job. So I'm sorry, but you will have to speak to them."

He then turned, put his tools in the back of the van and drove off, leaving us just stood there, staring at the sign. I looked at the sign again in disbelief. It read, For Sale; underneath that, the name of the estate agent, Herbert Banks; then in black writing, four-bed country residence with land, then the phone number of the agent. I was absolutely fuming; how could he do this to me. I ran back to the house and phoned the agent. The call was answered almost immediately.

"Good morning, Herbert Banks Estate Agency, how may I help you?"

"Hello, can I talk to the agent dealing with 'Ducklands Farm House' sale please."

"One moment please."

There was a click on the line; then music started playing. I knew the piece—Pachelbel Canon in D major—I loved this piece of music, I was just getting into it when it was interrupted by a female voice.

"Good morning, this is Judith Smyth-Banks speaking."

"And this is Poppy Bloody Day speaking. Who gave you permission to put my house on the market; who do you think you are. My name is on the ownership papers of this property, and you have no right to attempt to sell it without my authority."

There was a silence at the other end of the phone. In fact, I thought they had put the receiver down on me. Then the posh voice unshaken by my outrage spoke again,

"Miss Day, if you can just calm down a little and let me speak, I will explain our actions."

I had been rather rude. I didn't even know this woman, so I did calm down, but first I apologised,

"I'm very sorry Miss Banks, but I'm so upset and was shocked to see your man putting up a for sale sign."

She then went on in a very calm voice and explained how Simon Bridges had been into the office and instructed them to place the house on the market. Apparently, he had explained how our relationship had broken down, and because of the restraining order, he wasn't allowed to come near me. Because the house had recently been on the market with the same estate agent, they were told to use the same photos and details they held on file, which is why no one had visited to measure up the place; also, the house was to be sold on a sealed-bid basis. I then spoke, "But Miss Banks, I don't want to sell the property. I am trying to raise the capital to buy my ex-partner out."

"I understand that Miss Day, but from what Mr Bridges said to us was that he is stopping the mortgage payments from the end of this month; and if you don't make those payments, it's a slippery slope to repossession."

She then went quiet, and so did I; just the word 'repossession' sounded alarm bells in my head. My heart sank; deep down I knew I was in trouble. Then she spoke again,

"Miss Day, I realise this has come as a shock, but it does give you options."

"What do you mean options?"

"Well, you say that you want to raise the money to buy Mr Bridges' share of the property. Well, this way you can continue to pursue that avenue; but if all else fails, we will strive to find a buyer."

I thought for a moment. Then I realised she made sense; I just hated admitting it. Then with a heavy heart, I agreed with her,

"Okay Miss Banks, I guess it's the only option. You have my permission to market the property. I just don't want any contact with the prospective buyers, I just couldn't bear to. Meanwhile, I will try to raise the funds to buy my ex out."

"That's agreed then, Miss Day, we will actively promote the property; and if you made yourself scarce during the viewings, we will show them around the property. If you could let us have a key, that would be marvellous."

She then bid me farewell, and the phone went dead. I stood there feeling numb; it seemed like it was all over.

"Well, Poppy, what's happening, you look upset."

I explained to the girls what had transpired on the phone. They both went quiet, not really knowing what to say; then Kim spoke,

"At least you now have options. Come on, Poppy, keep positive; you just don't know what might happen."

Deep down I knew it was going to be impossible to raise the funds, and I knew there and then that keeping this beautiful house in the country was looking more and more precarious by the day.

Chapter 40
On the Trail

It had been months since Poppy had left me in the mud in our back garden. I was constantly worried about her and what might have happened on her return, with her ex waiting for her. There wasn't a lot I could do but be patient and await her return; we were in the hands of the all-powerful 'Door', and time itself. I got some comfort from Sally my sister. At least I could talk to her about Poppy and how much I missed her. She after all seemed to understand the intricacies and the frustrations of time travel; god only knows why! Work continued to be busy, which helped occupy my confused mind. I had all sorts of conflicting thoughts, should I try and find her, even though the time lines weren't aligned. Or should I try and forget her; she might never come back. I knew one thing for certain, I was sick of this time travel malarkey; why couldn't I have fallen in love with a normal girl.

Over the next few months, I got more and more angry, coming home to an empty house; even the dog was depressed without Poppy in our lives. I decided to sell the house; I'm not sure why. Besides, it was too big for me to live here on my own; also it kept reminding me of Poppy and the fantastic times we shared together. Sally offered to put me up if I sold the house, until I could work out which way my life was heading; I was so confused. After a year of waiting and still no sign of Poppy, I was really down. I had lost my spark. I was drinking far too much, drowning in my sorrows; I was so sad. On several occasions, I was even late for work, going into work with a hangover—how shameful is that. Then I had an offer on the house; and after careful consideration and a long talk with Sally, I decided it was the best solution; so I accepted the offer and spent the next couple of weeks packing up all of our stuff.

I even found grateful homes for the chickens, at least their lives would continue happily. The hardest thing ever was packing Poppy's things. I remember the day I packed her clothes into a cardboard box. Each and every item I pulled out of the wardrobe brought back memories. One item in particular, which I retrieved from the hanging rail, overwhelmed me. It was the dress we had bought in London, for my work's Christmas party. I sat on the bed and buried my head into the fabric. The smell of Poppy was overpowering; just as if she was in the room, images of us together flashed into my mind. Then the greatest feeling of loss you could imagine. My eyes welled up. I once again buried my head into the dress and sobbed my heart out.

I had never been as sad as I was right now. It must have taken me 20 minutes to regain my composure; the dress was soaked in my tears. I don't know why, but I decided to write a note, which I tucked into the folds of the dress. It read,

Poppy Day,
I love you now as much as I ever did,
I miss you so much, it hurts,
I hope one day, to be together,
Our hearts as one.
Love Sam x

All of the boxes were then sealed up and ready for the storage container. All of my stuff included, I just kept back a few clothes and photos of Poppy. That's all I would need if I was living with Sally.

Three weeks later, the dreaded day was upon me. The furniture van arrived; all the stuff for storage was loaded and taken away. I put my two cases of belongings into the car and was about to leave for Sally's, but then realised Polly wasn't anywhere to be seen. I checked all of the rooms to no avail. I was stood in our empty bedroom when I happened to gaze through the window. Polly was sat under the oak tree; her head down between her legs, looking so sad. The only reasonable explanation was that was the spot where Poppy reappeared so many times when she travelled back. Polly was so desperate to see Poppy again that she thought she would wait for her, in a place she knew Poppy might reappear. The sight pulled on my heartstrings; how I was going to console the dog, I had no idea.

I had been with Sally now for several weeks. Polly the dog had settled in; although you would often find her looking forlorn out in the garden. We were both living a life, with a large piece of it missing, Poppy, she was constantly on my mind. It was worse than losing someone who had died. At least when you buried someone, it was final, and you knew you could never see them again. But in this instance, I knew Poppy was out there somewhere, but we weren't together. Then one night, I was in my bedroom lay on the bed with a beer in my hand, and Polly the dog stretched across me, when an image of Poppy burst into my mind. It was the image of her face; the image I got the first time I ever spoke to her when I wound the car window down at the side of the road to ask her out for a drink. I remember how nervous I had been, seeing her at the side of the road, slowing the car down; my stomach churning with anticipation. Then hearing her voice for the first time and trying to appear as calm as a cucumber. Although she hadn't accepted my offer of a drink together, at least we had made contact; and I knew as I drove away, it was the start of a very long friendship.

Over the next few days, I came up with a plan, enough of the self-pity and more of the Samuel Devere that Poppy had met all those years ago. Poppy had always mentioned about the past catching up with the future; the time now and the time she lived in 1995 when we could live as a normal couple. Well, it was now May 1995, I wasn't sure what the date was in Poppy's time line, but I had

had enough. I knew roughly where she lived, and I was going to go and find her and sod the consequences.

I started by listing all the things that I knew about Poppy's life. I remember her mentioning a place called Toddminster a local town and also a village called Leyton-Somer. She had a dog called Roscoe, and an ex called Simon who worked for my sister company. Hhmmm, I might be able to get a lead from HR, but it could get a bit tricky. I decided to only use that as a last resort. Poppy mentioned two girlfriends a lot, Chloe and Kim, but I didn't know their surnames, so that was going to be a long shot. I know she lived in a country house, it was quite old, and it sat on a decent-sized piece of land, with a large pond in the garden. Also the house had an attic where she painted. This is where the infernal 'Door' was situated. Not that this fact would be of any help to me, because no one knew about the 'Door'. I remember her saying about a five bar gate at the entrance to the drive and also an arched top window in the attic, which she used to like looking out over the pond in her garden. Poppy told me that she sold her paintings through an art shop in the local town, but she didn't mention which town it was.

At least now I had a plan. I felt better that I was on the case. I couldn't just give Poppy up without a fight; she was the best thing that had ever happened to me. The next day, I didn't go into work; I phoned in sick. This was more important than pleasing my boss. Then a thought occurred to me, *Samuel Devere, how stupid could you get. If Poppy were to reappear, she would probably materialise under the oak tree in the garden of the house which I had sold.* The first job of the day was to call back at the house to try and minimise any stress, should Poppy appear in the garden looking for me. I drove straight to the house in the hope that the people who bought it were amiable. I pulled onto the drive; then rang the bell. Within seconds, the door was opened by a gorky young lady, "Hello, can I help you, Oh! You're not selling stuff, are you."

"Uummm no, I'm not selling anything. I used to live here, and I just wondered if you could do me a favour."

"If you want favours, you better ask my dad."

She turned quickly and shouted at the top of her voice,

"Dad! Dad! There's a man at the door who wants a favour. Come and talk to him, will you; I've left my curling tongs on."

Then she was gone, leaving me stood at the door, waiting for her dad to come and speak to me. A minute later, a gentleman in his late 40s arrived at the door,

"Can I help you, what is it you want."

I then explained how I used to live in the house, and a female friend might come looking for me, and could he possibly pass on the address where she might find me. He kindly took my details; then just before he closed the door, he winked, then said,

"A bit on the side, is she; don't worry, your secrets safe with me."

Then the door closed. I was flabbergasted. Why would he think she was a bit on the side; anyway, at least now if Poppy turned up, she would know how to get in touch with me.

The next step in my plan was to find Toddminster. I had never been there before, but I had heard it was quite a posh place to live. I drove towards the town a little anxious. I had no idea where to start looking, so I entered the town and looked for a car park. I soon found a spot to park. I put several hours on my ticket, then went in search of a coffee shop. I was sure that a shot of strong caffeine would focus my mind on the job in hand. I drank my coffee, thinking about Poppy and wondering if she was nearby. Maybe she was doing her shopping. Then the reality hit me. There were hundreds of people milling around the streets. The chances of bumping into her were minimal.

I asked the cafe owner if there were any art shops in the town. He told me about two that he knew about. I wrote the details in a notebook which I kept in my pocket. The first one apparently was on the same road as the cafe, just a few hundred yards away, next door to a furniture shop. I set off excited that I was actually doing something positive in my search for the love of my life. I reached the shop and looked through the window. It was quite expensive-looking, very well lit; paintings adorned the white walls. I opened the door and went in. The door opening triggered a bell to ring; and as quick as lightening, a middle-aged lady appeared in front of me.

"Good morning, sir, my name is Jillian, how may I help you."

I hadn't rehearsed what my spiel was going to be, so I probably came over as a bit of a div,

"Well, I'm looking for an artist."

"Well, you've come to the right place, sir. We have copious amounts of artists supplying work for us to sell."

I started looking around at the art on the walls. None of them had the same look that Poppy's paintings had.

"What is the name of the artist you're looking for, sir, are they male or female, what genre do they paint in."

I thought very carefully before I answered,

"Well, the artists name is Poppy Day, and she paints wildlife and country scenes but also fantasy erotic art."

The lady stopped in her tracks. Her hand moved to her mouth, as if in disgust,

"I'm afraid I've never heard of an artist called Poppy Day, and we certainly do not sell erotic paintings."

She just turned around and went back to her desk in the middle of the shop, leaving me stood there. I decided to leave; this place wasn't the sort of establishment that Poppy would patronise anyway.

I have to admit I was a little disappointed, not the best of starts, but c'est la vie upwards and onwards. I asked a passer-by where the next shop was. It was about a ten-minute walk from where I currently was, which I didn't mind. It would give me time to practise my intro. The shop I was looking for was called 'Smart Art', and it was my last hope. The shop was hidden away down a narrow cobbled alley. There were small shops on both sides, and I noticed a sign sticking out from above the door, with the name, 'Smart Art'. I peered through the window. This was more like it; no fancy lighting and paintings all over the place.

I felt more confident this time as I entered the cluttered shop. I looked around; there were landscape paintings, modern art and on the back wall I noticed some paintings of nudes. I heard someone shout out from behind a screen,

"I won't be a minute, have a browse."

I continued looking through the hordes of paintings. Some were stuffed into cardboard boxes, some just leant against the wall, but none of them had Poppy's signature on, and not one resembled her type of painting. Then the lady appeared from behind the screen; she was about 30 years old, short black hair, quite slim, a lovely figure and a smile to melt anyone's heart.

"Oh hello! My name is Samuel, pleased to meet you."

"You too! My name is Jane, but everyone calls me J. What is it you're looking for: watercolour, oil, prints… I have them all."

"Yes, I can see you have a lot of stock, but I was looking for a particular artist."

"Okay! Who is it you're after?"

"The artist's name is Poppy Day."

Her face went blank; then she scratched her head,

"I'm sorry, Samuel, I've never heard of her. What sort of paintings does she do?"

"Well J, I know she does country scenes, but she's rather good at erotic art, but I don't see any of that sort here."

"Well, it's funny you should mention that, Samuel. My friend who also runs an art shop is doing rather well in that field. I even thought about stocking that genre myself."

I now got quite excited,

"Where is your friend's shop if you don't mind me asking?"

"Not at all if it's of any help. Catherine's shop is about ten miles from here, in a village called Leyton-Somer."

I remembered that name. I was sure that Poppy had mentioned it when she told me about her paintings.

"That's really helpful of you, J. You don't happen to know the name of the shop, do you."

"Yes, I do! It's called 'Art in your Heart'."

I thanked J for her help and ran back to the car. It only took me 20 minutes to find the shop in Leyton-Somer; and being a village, I managed to park right outside. As I glanced out of the car, my heart missed a beat. In the window of the shop was a painting, it was exactly like Poppy's style.

I stood looking into the shop. The painting was erotic; it was of a couple. The man was naked apart from a black leather jacket; the women topless, with black leather tight-fitting trousers. They were in an embrace across the bonnet of a red sports car; the atmosphere was electric. You could see they were very much in love. The painting was beautiful; I just knew it was one of Poppy's. I entered the shop; this one was a lot more organised than the last one. Then a lady approached; she spoke eloquently. She was blonde, slim and dressed immaculately,

"Hello, I'm Catherine. May I be of assistance, sir?"

"Hi! I'm Samuel. I would love to look closer at the painting in the window if I may."

I pointed at the picture.

"Do you mean the erotic scene?" she asked politely,

"Yes, that's the one, isn't it just so powerful; I love it."

She removed the painting from the window and placed it on an easel, so I could view it at ease; she then spoke again,

"The name of the painting is, *Black Leather Together*; and yes, you're right, it does portray a powerful feeling of dominance, love and, if you don't mind me saying, lust."

I then looked down to the right hand corner of the picture. My heart sank; this couldn't be right. The painting was signed, 'Tony Le Meros'.

I was convinced that this was Poppy's work, but why hadn't she signed it,

"Are you sure this wasn't painted by a young lady called Poppy Day, Catherine."

"Sir, we sell all of the paintings in goodwill for the suppliers of the work, that's as far as we get involved."

"Catherine, I know this painting has something to do with Poppy Day, so I will take it. Could you wrap it for me, please?"

"Of course I can, sir!"

She took the painting out the back of the shop; and a few minutes later, reappeared with it wrapped in plain brown paper.

I felt bad having to lie to the lovely young gentleman, but I had promised Poppy never to divulge her real name to anyone, so that was that; nothing I could do. While he was writing out the cheque for his purchase, I looked him up and down. He had wavy blonde hair, blue eyes, and you could see he took pride in the way he dressed; all in all, a very nice young man indeed.

Just before I left the shop, I passed a note to the shop keeper with my name and contact details written on,

"Catherine, I understand you have a criteria to work to, but I would greatly appreciate it if you could pass my details to whoever the artist of this painting is."

She took the note from my hand, read it, then said,

"Okay, Mr Devere, I will."

I then left the shop with the painting under my arm, jumped into my car and drove home feeling frustrated and annoyed that I still hadn't found my Poppy.

Chapter 41
Out of Kilter

The next day I woke up to the sound of pounding rain, which further depressed me. Yesterday, the girls had been a marvellous support, but they had their own lives to lead, so I was on my own once again. I was desperate to see Sam; I missed him terribly. If he was here with me, I just knew things would turn out okay. The trouble was, even if I travelled back, I still had the massive problem of raising the finances to buy Simon out when I returned. If it was just the house I was going to lose, it wouldn't be so bad, but it was the 'Door'—the gateway to Sam—that was the biggest hurdle. The last time I travelled back, the date was roughly about a year and a half short of the future, which I was in now, so I couldn't just go and find Sam now in 1995. The time zones had to be equal.

To try and put things out of my mind, I decided to have a good tidy up. After all, the estate agent would be showing people around the house very soon. I started in the attic; the smashed up easel was still scattered across the floor after the incident with Simon. I also picked up the vase, which miraculously didn't break when I had hit Simon over the head with it. The water had dried, leaving a faint stain on the carpet. I glued the easel back together, then wrapped tape to support it while the glue hardened. I couldn't afford to buy another one. After straightening up the attic room, I worked my way through the whole house—cleaning, dusting, hoovering—and I also removed all of the personal pictures that were dotted around the rooms. I didn't want total strangers looking at my photos or any of my fantasy art. They might link me with the name 'Tony Le Meros', and I wanted to remain anonymous.

The weather outside was getting worse. The sky was black, and I could hear the rumble of thunder. I think a storm was heading my way. I had almost finished hoovering in the lounge when I dropped my duster. As I knelt down to retrieve it, my eye caught sight of an envelope under the sideboard. I stretched my arm underneath; it was right at the back against the wall. I could only assume that because the top was so shiny it had slid and dropped down the back of the sideboard. As soon as I looked at it, I knew who it was from. I recognised the logo at the top left of the envelope; it was a painter's palette. It was a letter from the art shop who displayed my paintings. I was excited; they must have sold another painting. I ran my finger along the flap ripping the letter open. I took out the folded piece of paper and read it,

'Art in your Heart'
12 Crawley Lane
Leyton-Somer
14/07/95

Dear Poppy,

I thought I should let you know that the young man, Samuel Devere, who came into the shop two weeks ago and bought your painting, *Black Leather Together,* came into the shop again today. He seems desperate to contact you, even though I told him that I didn't know who Poppy Day was. I realise that it's none of my business and don't want to pry, but he seems like such a nice guy. So please forgive me for including his contact details again at the end of this letter,

Yours sincerely, Catherine x
Samuel Devere Tel. 0779 602 7268

I sat on the sofa, staring at the letter, trying to make sense of it. I looked again at the date. It was dated July 14th 1995, that was just two weeks ago! I was confused, how could this be. When I saw Sam the last time I had travelled, it was late in the year of 1993. I knew I would have to go back straight away to see Sam; something was wrong. I ran up the stairs to the attic and sat in my reclining chair. I just prayed that the 'Door' would cooperate and open, so that I could go back in time to see Sam. Then there was an incredible flash of lightening, followed by the loudest clap of thunder I had ever heard; it shook the whole house. The storm was getting worse. I thought I had better go downstairs and comfort Roscoe; he would be fretting. As I turned to leave the room, the resounding clonk of the lock on the door releasing rang out. I was torn between Roscoe or Sam, who should I go to; then it occurred to me, if I went through the door, no time would elapse anyway; so I might as well go to Sam first.

I ran to the 'Door' pulled the handle down and went inside. The 'Door' closed behind me; the cold fog swirled around me as normal. I headed for the distant white light. But then something weird happened. The white fog turned blue, waves of electric energy seemed to short out all around me, like a mini lightning storm within the time machine. I panicked and turned towards the 'Door', but like each time before the handle was solid, the only way out was forward, towards Sam. As I moved nervously forward through the plasma like fog, there was an almighty bang, like a bomb going off. I think the house had taken a direct hit from a lightning bolt. The time machine reacted; the blue plasma all around me exploded into millions of electric bursts of energy. My body felt like it was on fire. I ran towards the distant light. I had to get out of here as fast as I could. Then, my body was falling; thank god I would soon be with Sam, safe and sound.

I could hear a dog barking. It must have been Polly waiting for me by the oak tree; but then, a bright flash of light filled my vision, and I fell into long grass next to a fence. I gained my senses, but I was really confused. As I looked around, there was no oak tree. I felt really strange. I noticed my shoes; they were red patent, with a tee bar and a buckle. I had white ankle socks on, and a red and white pinafore dress. I realised I was also very small; although my mind was from 1995, my body, well my body was, oh my god! I was just a little girl. What the hell had happened to the time machine, instead of transporting me back to Sam in 1993, I had travelled back much further. I remember wearing clothes like this when I was about eight or nine years old. Oh my god! What was I going to do now; the thunderstorm must have interfered with the fine balance of time control that the 'Door' had reliably used up to now.

Was I now lost in time forever, would the time machine ever recover back to normal after being hit with such catastrophic force. Would I ever be delivered back to 1995, to lead a normal life with the man I loved—how about Roscoe. I just hoped that Chloe remembered our plan, should I not return. I began to cry; yes, I cried like a young nine-year-old girl, scared and wanting her mummy. The tears rolled down my face, dripping off my chin onto my dress, creating quite a wet patch. I lifted the hem of my dress and wiped my eyes dry. When my eyes opened and focussed on the view in front of me, I was in total shock. I looked through the chain link fence, and what I saw shook me to my core.

I was looking into a garden; more to the point, it was my garden when I was a child. My fingers grabbed the wire; my head pressed firmly against the mesh. The scene that my eyes relayed to my brain amazed me. The other side of the fence sat my father in his deck chair. He was reading his paper, like he always did. He loved doing the crossword and to help him concentrate, he puffed on his pipe, plumes of smoke rose sporadically into the air. I still to this day remember the smell of the tobacco he used. I think it was called 'Golden Virginia'. My Mother was also there; my heart fluttered with joy. I missed her so much. She was wearing a floral dress and flat dolly shoes and curly blonde hair. I heard her saying to my father,

"Darling, would you like another cup of tea."

My father rarely refused a cup of strong tea; and as always, my mother dutifully delivered and placed a fresh cup at his side. The most shocking thing about this scene was me. When I say me, I mean the other me, an exact copy of me, dressed in the same clothes as me. I was playing with the dog, a beautiful shaggy haired dog, a Dulux dog called Carol. I remember pretending she was a pony; I would put rains on her and run behind her, imagining I was riding her.

I was completely engulfed watching us as a family, all those years ago, but then without warning, I noticed the dog stop in her tracks. Her ears raised into the air, her nose twitched, then her head turned; she stared straight at me. I froze; they couldn't see me. God knows what might happen if anyone of them saw another me; it would blow their minds. The dog bounded towards me; the other me shouted out, "Carol, Carol, come back here."

Has the dog approached at speed, her beautiful coat floated from side to side, as if in slow motion. Then she abruptly stopped just the other side of the mesh; her face was so close I could smell her rancid breath. Her tongue was hanging out of her mouth, wet with slobber; it dripped incessantly onto the floor. She just stared into my eyes. Her brain trying to compute why there was another me outside the fence; she started to whine. I could see that the other me started running towards us, obviously wondering why the dog was at the fence. I had to leave and leave quickly. I moved away from the fence, gaining cover in the long grass. I ran away as fast as my short legs would carry me, and then without warning, I ran into a cold fog. The image around me shimmered, and I was on my way, hopefully to my Sam.

Chapter 42
Giddy Heights

It had been at least a week since I had visited the art shop in Leyton-Somer, and I was still convinced that the painting I had bought was painted by Poppy. I had hung the picture on my bedroom wall; looking at it made me feel closer to Poppy. My life now without her was meaningless. I just had to find her and find her I would. I decided I would visit the shop again to see if 'Catherine' had any more news. If that failed, I had a back-up plan. I could stake out the shop in case Poppy visited with more pieces of art; and if that failed, I knew what type of house she lived in; so I would drive all around the region looking for her. I realised the plan was a little weak, but what else could I do. I was desperate and lonely.

The following day, I had a word with my boss and arranged a few days off work. That way, I could concentrate on the job in hand. The next morning, I jumped out of bed with such enthusiasm that I startled Polly, who was fast asleep at the bottom of the bed. I made a flask of tea and loads of sandwiches. I put some dry food and water for Polly in the car; then I found the most recent photo of Poppy that I had and placed it in my wallet. I was all set for my stake out; how difficult could it be. After all, I remembered watching a film called *The Stake Out*. I think it was a 1987 film, where the two detectives were watching a house opposite, and the one detective fell for the lady in the target house. Well, I had already fallen in love with my target, so all I had to do was find her.

Being a small village where the shop was situated proved to be a hindrance. My car stuck out like a sore thumb. Then I sat there for hours, with a bored dog in the passenger seat, just staring at the art shop. I bought a newspaper, which I raised up to cover my face, pretending to read it each time a passer-by took an interest in me. Then there were several walks with Polly to satisfy her calls of nature and also mine.

Unknown to Samuel, if Poppy had visited the shop, she would have entered through the back door, so he wouldn't have seen her anyway.

Then after spending all day watching the shop, eating all of the sandwiches, drinking all of the tea and being gassed by the constant silent farts from the dog, I gave up.

I decided to call in the shop and have another word with the owner Catherine. I walked through the door, Catherine was serving a customer. She glanced over, and I'm sure she recognised me. She said,

"I won't be long, have a browse while you're waiting."

Which I did. I looked to see if there were any more of Poppy's paintings in the shop. On the back wall, slightly shielded by a false screen, I spotted a picture that got my attention. It was a small painting, approximately 15"x12". It was in oil and painted in bold colours. It was of a couple having sex on a washing machine. It instantly took me back to the time when Poppy and me had first met, and we had made love with the help of the spin cycle in my kitchen at the flat. Although you couldn't recognise Poppy's face from the painting, it was absolutely without a doubt the two of us depicted in the picture. I again looked at the signature on the painting, and yes, there again was the name 'Tony Le Meros'. This had to be Poppy's work, I was convinced. Then I heard the doorbell chime as the customer left the shop. Catherine came over to speak to me,

"Hello again, how can I help you."

"Well, Catherine, I've just been admiring another painting by Tony Le Meros."

"Oh! Yes! Which one."

"The one on the back wall called *In a Spin.*"

"Oh that one! I've had quite a lot of interest in that painting."

"Catherine, we both know who painted it. I could even tell you who featured in the painting. I realise you have an etiquette to adhere to, but it's really important that I contact Poppy Day, so please, will you get in touch with Tony Le Meros and let him, her know I'm trying to make contact."

Catherine sighed, then rubbed her chin, like she was struggling with something,

"I will do my best, Mr Devere, but you will have to leave it with me."

I then pulled the photo from my pocket and showed it to Catherine. She glanced at it, but she was still non-committal,

"You see, we are together in the photo. I'm not a stalker; I'm her friend."

I then thanked her and left the shop; I believed her. I went away confident that she would contact Poppy to tell her I was trying to get in touch. I returned back to the car and gave Polly some food and water. While she was busy, I sat and thought about my next step in search for Poppy. I then reluctantly drove home disappointed again.

That night, I lay in bed in deep thought, thinking about all the things that Poppy might have said to me regarding her life in the future. I racked my brains, going back to the first time we had met, trying to glean any information I could that would give me a clue as to where to look for her. Then a conversation we had had, popped into my consciousness. I remember her saying how steep the hill was on the way to her house, and how beautiful the view was from the top. Now I know this wasn't a lot to go on, but if I searched a ten-mile radius around the art shop on an ordinance survey map, the map would show contours on the land. If I then drove to all the raised pieces of land and looked for a house with a pond, an arched window in the roof, a five bar gate etc., I might just find my Poppy's house. I felt pleased with myself that I now had another source of hope, and I couldn't wait for the morning to arrive, so I could get started.

Chapter 43
The Power of Love

I was so lucky to get away without being seen, although it was a joy to see my mother and father again. Now the 'Door' had called me back. I was just hoping that I would be delivered to my precious Sam. But instead of appearing in my reclining chair, I landed with a bump in complete darkness. I was engulfed in dust, which caused me to sneeze. I stood up, attempting to feel my way to a faint glow of light, a few feet away from me. But I tripped on something under foot and fell heavily to the floor. I lay there for a minute; my eyes were slowly adjusting to the darkness, gradually the scene around me unfolded. I was so confused. I recognised the arch-topped window; the moonlight was beaming through the glass and shining onto the very dusty wooden floor. I was in my attic room at the country house, but it was derelict—no carpet, no reclining chair, thick with dust; then the reality hit home. The 'Door' had brought me home, but to the wrong time. It had delivered me back to the house before we had bought it. I was just mulling over in my mind what to do next when I heard a man calling out,

"Who's there?"

He shouted. I could hear him climbing the wooden stairs, getting ever closer to catching me in his attic. There was no escape, other than climbing through the window, but we were two stories up so that wasn't an option. Then I heard the clonk of the lock on the 'Door' being released. I sprang to life, and in a jiffy, I was entering the time machine. The cold fog like air spilled into the room, then just before the 'Door' closed behind me, the attic light came on. The 'Door' as ever closed automatically with a resounding bang. At least I was safe, and I wouldn't have to try and explain why I was in his attic. The swirling fog inside the time machine was still tainted in a blue colour, but did not have the electric plasma effect like the last time. Maybe things were slowly returning to normal, and I was now going to be reunited with my Sam in 1993. I ran towards the distant defused light in the fog. I began falling. I was in free fall, but without fear, I had complete trust in the 'Door' to deliver me safely. It was almost surreal; I was falling at quite a pace. I was completely at ease, and my ears were filled with the sound of classical music—the beautiful sound of Ave Maria by Schubert. I fell on to a very soft golden yellow sofa. The music was all around me; the room was sort of familiar. There were paintings on the wall, set in gold filigree frames; one was of a nautical scene. On the highly polished sideboard stood a crystal decanter filled with a bronze liquid, probably brandy. As I scanned the room further, my eyes focussed on a picture frame; now I knew why the room looked familiar. The picture was of my mum and dad, and I was sat in the middle of them. I must have been about ten years old in the photo. I then panicked; I had reappeared in my family home, but what if the original Poppy was also here. Before I could react, my mum came in from the garden, through the open patio doors,

"My word, Poppy, you gave me a fright. I didn't hear you come through the front door, but then I wouldn't, would I, with the music playing so loud."

She went over to the gramophone and turned off the music; then, she spoke again,

"I wasn't expecting you home from uni, Poppy; is everything alright?"

"Yes Mummy, everything is absolutely fine. I just thought that I would come and spend some time with you and Daddy before I go off on holiday."

"Oh, Poppy, that's nice of you. Where are you off to, somewhere hot I hope."

"Yes, we are off to Malta for two weeks, so I thought it might be nice to come home for a couple of days."

She then went through to the kitchen, saying that we couldn't have a proper catch up without a cuppa. My mind was going ten to the dozen, trying desperately to get things straight in my head. Then, with great sadness, I remembered this visit home to see my parents. My eyes filled with tears; this visit home stuck in my mind for all the wrong reasons. I now remembered the tragic events at the end of my fast approaching holiday. This would be the last time I saw my mum alive. I burst into tears. I cried uncontrollably; then Mum came running into the room. "Poppy, what on earth's upset you, you're literally shaking."

I had to think on my feet and think fast. What the hell I was going to say to her; then I just blurted it out,

"Mummy, I just miss you so much, living away from home. Not being able to see you when I want to and you're so far away."

She wrapped her arms around me; just her smell comforted me. I missed her so much; then she whispered in my ear,

"My darling, Poppy, you don't have to worry. I'm always here for you. As soon as you finish your degree, you can come back home to live if that's what you want."

If only she knew what the near future held in store for her, and I couldn't do a damn thing about it. I did wonder if the 'Door' was helping me to relive that short time I had with my mum to make it more special. Over the next couple of days, I spent as much time as possible with my mum and, of course, with my dad. I couldn't really understand why the original Poppy wasn't on the scene. Was it because the 'Time Machine' was in melt down due to the lightning strike, or were there more mysterious powers at work.

That night, I lay in my own bed, in my own room. It felt safe and homely; the thought of my mum and dad tucked up in the room next door filled me with warmth. I began thinking about my life, how I had wasted all those years with Simon, and how stupid I had been not realising what was going on. Then, of course, Sam—I missed him so much. I wondered if I would ever see him again.

Was I trapped in time, the wrong time, or would the 'Door' regain its equilibrium and eventually deliver me back to 1995. The last two time travel events were completely weird. First of all, I travelled back to my childhood, then 25 years forward to the country house. My memory then went back to the time when Simon and I went to view the house for the first time when George told us about the time when he had heard someone in his attic. Of course, it was me; I knew that now. It just seemed like the 'Door' had everything mapped out. Deep down, I just knew that the 'Door' was looking after me; it had its reasons for these out of schedule visits. Ever since I had visited the house in the country, I had felt its pull, its attraction; it was almost like I was destined to become a time traveller, almost like I had been recruited, but recruited for what.

The next day was really sunny, so daddy took the day off work, and we went to a local beauty spot for a picnic. We spread our chequered burgundy and cream-coloured blanket on the grass, next to the river. Daddy retrieved his fold out chair from the boot of the car, then sat in it, lit up his pipe and started another crossword. Mummy and I made our selves comfortable on the blanket. Because Daddy was driving, he had tea; I drank ginger beer, and Mummy, of course, had wine. She did like a drink. I think that's where my love of wine must have come from. In the wicker basket that Mum had packed were loads of goodies—ham, cheese and tuna sarnies, crisps and, of course, cake. My mum made the best Victoria sponge ever; and although I had stuffed myself with sandwiches, I still made room for a slice of cake. The time that day spent with my parents was magical, especially talking about all sorts of stuff with my mum. Deep down I was so sad, but at least the 'Door' had given me this chance to spend precious time with my mum before her untimely departure from this world.

That night in bed, I was in a dilemma. I so wanted to stay with my mum much longer than the couple of days, I had originally told her. But the problem was, I was scared stiff that the other Poppy might turn up; and also, I didn't want to be sat talking to my mum when the 'Door' decided to take me away again. Me just disappearing in front of her eyes would be too much for her to take in; she would panic and probably call the police. Then they would think she had lost her marbles. So the next morning after breakfast, I told Mum I had to leave. It was one of the hardest things I have ever done, knowing that I would never see her again. Mum was obviously oblivious to what the future held, so after a prolonged hug, I said farewell. She seemed bemused when I started crying,

"Oh Poppy, why are you so upset again. I will see you when you get back from your holiday, silly; now come on, cheer up."

I hugged her once again, burying my face into her neck. I breathed her smell into my lungs, as if committing it to my memory. Tears streamed from my eyes, wetting her skin,

"I love you so much, Mummy."

"I love you too, my dear, dear Poppy."

I pulled away; my heart broken. Daddy looked up from his paper, pulled his pipe from his mouth and said,

"See you when you get back, safe journey."

Then it was time for me to leave. I glanced back towards my mum for the last time and closed the door behind me.

Chapter 44
Shattered Dreams

It was a beautiful sunny day, and I have to say I was feeling confident. I was armed with a flask, food, an ordnance survey map and, of course, my main weapon in the field of search and rescue, Polly the dog. If she got the faintest whiff of my lovely Poppy, she would soon let me know. The night before, I had studied the map and found several areas where the land around Leyton-Somer was raised quite a bit above sea level. To save more time, I had ringed the areas of interest in red pen, so it was easier to see them while I was driving. I had five target areas, ranging from 800 feet to 2,000 feet above sea level. The plan wasn't guaranteed to find my Poppy, but it was the best idea I had.

I arrived at the small village of Leyton-Somer and pulled up opposite the art shop. I thought it might be a good place to start. Besides, you never know your luck. I might just bump into her by chance. While I studied the map, working out my best route, I poured a cuppa from my trusty flask. I couldn't resist dunking a chocolate digestive into the cup; then Polly's nose started twitching, so she had to have one as well. She woofed it down in seconds, then looked at me with those big brown eyes, hoping for another,

"That's enough, Polly; you know you shouldn't eat chocolate."

I rubbed her head, then cupped her face between my hands,

"Right then, Polly, let's go and find the love of our lives."

The nearest hill on the map was just a quarter of a mile away, so I started the engine, put it in gear, and we were off. About five minutes later, the road started to climb, twisting and turning; and eventually, the road levelled out. The land surrounding the road was mainly agricultural, and from the car window, you could just see over the hawthorn hedges. I drove fairly slowly, getting excited each time I saw a five bar gate. The problem was, most of the country properties had a five bar steel gate at the entrance to their properties. The key was to find the gate, a pond and an arched top window in the roof all at the same house. An hour later, after seeing approximately 30 houses, I had had enough. I was getting nowhere, so I thought a nice cup of tea might refresh my enthusiasm. I pulled over into a lay-by right next to a wooden gate; I got out to stretch my legs. The view was amazing. I was looking over a deep valley; sheep were grazing everywhere. I then noticed on the opposite side of the valley, a road winding up the side of a very steep hill, and at the top were several properties. I wish I had brought my binoculars. I could have saved so much time if I could only see them up close. While I drank my tea, I looked at the map to see which hill; opposite I was looking at. It turned out to be the 2,000 feet above sea level hill, which I had marked on the map. I now had a very excited feeling. There was something about that hill that was talking to me. I set off; the car radio was playing My Girl by The Temptations. It must have been a sign; Poppy was my girl, and I was coming for her.

I descended from the hill I was on and headed for the other side of the valley. It was farther than it looked, and it took me 40 minutes before I started snaking upwards. The hill was a lot steeper than the previous one. As I levelled off at the top of the hill, my ears actually popped. I then remembered Poppy saying how it had happened to her when she first visited her country house. Surely, I was now on the right track. On my left, there was a run-down farm. Its barn was adjacent to the road. Almost opposite stood a five-bar gate; I pulled in and looked up the drive, but, unfortunately, stood at the end of the drive was a bungalow. I wasn't too disappointed though. I had a renewed vigour, and I was positive I would find the house. I drove on up the lane. Polly was sat next to me, with her paws on the dashboard, tail wagging and her tongue out.

I came to a rather straight part in the road. The grass verge was well tendered, and the hedge was trimmed. I slowed down; there was a property set back off the road. Very tall popular trees rose into the air. Then I noticed something red and white in the hedgerow, further up the lane. As I got nearer, I realised what it was. It was a For Sale sign. Then it couldn't be Poppy's place; she would never sell her beloved house in the country. Polly started barking; she was excited about something. Then I noticed the entrance to the property. At the end of the curved drive, there stood a five-bar steel gate. It was closed, so I pulled over onto the verge. Across the top of the gate was a wooden sign, and in handwritten paint, it read 'Ducklands House'. I stood at the gate a little nervous, at first. Deep down, I had a feeling I had found her. Polly was going mental in the car. She seemed to sense something, but at this stage, I thought it better to leave her in the car.

I peered over the gate, and to my left was a rather large pond. Ducks were chasing each other around smacking their wings into the water. I looked up to the house. From the look of the windows and front entrance, it appeared to be Georgian. It boasted quite tall chimneys, at either end of the building—one looked damaged and scorched. Then my eyes caught sight of something that confirmed that this was indeed Poppy's house. Standing proud from the dark grey slate roof was an arched top window, overlooking the garden and pond. Poppy always talked about the attic window; how she used to sit in her chair and admire the view. This last piece in the jigsaw confirmed to me that Poppy was probably in this house, and I couldn't wait to see her.

I let Polly out of the car. She was so excited, she wet herself. I held her collar while I opened the gate, then let her go. She was off like a shot, running at a fair old lick towards the house. There were two cars and a van parked at the top of the drive, so someone was probably in. I heard the dog squealing with excitement; she must have found Poppy. I closed the gate and ran towards the sound. As I approached the vehicles, I noticed the back door. Then without warning, the dog flap shot open with such force, it startled me. Polly came bounding out, followed by a smaller dog—a terrier I think. The two dogs chased each other around the garden, yelping with such excitement; it was as if they knew each other. But that was impossible, wasn't it. As the dogs played like life-long pals, I noticed movement through the window next to the back door. I shouted out,

"Poppy! I've found you at last."

The back door opened. I fully expected Poppy to rush out and smother me in kisses, but it wasn't Poppy. Two young women appeared in the entrance of the doorway; both about the same height. The one was quite busty, and the other very slim, but both of them were very attractive.

"Oh hello, I'm sorry to bother you, my name is…"

I was cut off by the busty young lady,

"Your name is Samuel, Samuel Devere."

I was gobsmacked. I had never seen this person in my life before, but she knew my name. Then the other lady spoke,

"You're looking for Poppy, aren't you?"

"Well, yes I am, but how do you know who I am. I've never seen either of you before, but you know my name."

The busty one reached out with her hand,

"I'm Chloe, and this is Kim; we are Poppy's best friends and, we know who you are, because Poppy showed us a photo of you two together, the last time we saw her."

I was aware of Poppy's friends, but still confused, why Poppy wasn't here with her friends.

"When you say the last time you saw her, do you mean she's not here."

They both looked at each other. They also seemed confused; then Kim spoke,

"Do you mean that Poppy is not been in touch with you either."

"No, she's not. I haven't seen her for months; that's why I've been driving everywhere looking for this house."

The two girls looked at each other. They both seemed concerned; then Chloe spoke again,

"Samuel, I think you had better come in, we need to talk."

Chapter 45
Deliverance

I entered the kitchen, following the two girls. It was so hot in there and completely stifling. Chloe asked me to sit at the table; then she offered me a drink,

"Sam, would you like tea, coffee, beer or a glass of Pino."

Just the word Pino reminded me of Poppy. It was her favourite tipple.

"A beer would be fine if you don't mind. Thank you, Chloe; and if you don't mind, can we open the window. It's sweltering in here."

Kim immediately lent over the sink to reach the catch on the kitchen window and opened it as wide as the stay would allow. I heard the fridge door open. Chloe retrieved the beer, removed the top and placed it in front of me. She then topped up the two wine glasses on the table; then they both sat at the table opposite me.

It seemed surreal being in Poppy's house. I don't know why, but I felt at peace amongst her belongings. There was a painted sign above the AGA; it read, 'There's Always Time for a Glass of Wine'—typical Poppy. I also felt torn because I hadn't got a clue where she was. The two girls took sips of their wine, then looked me in the eye expectantly, obviously hoping I was about to enlighten them about Poppy's whereabouts. There was an awkward silence as we all waited for someone to speak. It was Chloe who spoke first,

"Well, Sam, it's really nice to meet you. We've heard so much about you from Poppy, and, of course, she showed us a picture of you and her together; that's how we recognised you."

I wondered to myself how Poppy had managed to show them a photo of us together, and then what Poppy had actually told them about me. It couldn't have been too bad though, as they seemed quite friendly.

"Ditto, Poppy never stopped talking about you two and the dog, of course. I can't believe how Polly and Roscoe get on together. It seems like they know each other."

Then it was Kim's turn. She was more reserved than Chloe but still quite confident.

"Sam, we haven't seen Poppy for a few days now. I know that doesn't seem like a long time, but when she used to travel, she was never away for longer than a few minutes. She always told us that when she travelled back to you and then returned, no time had elapsed at this end. Now if she isn't with you in the past, and she's not here with us, where the hell could she be."

We all pondered for a couple of minutes; then Chloe put forward an idea.

"Sam, Poppy's been travelling back in time to see you right, and she told us that your time and our time were going to coincide soon, and then we could meet you."

"Yes, Chloe, that was the ultimate goal. When the two time zones matched, then we could live a normal life together, and the two timelines have now converged; it is 1995, isn't it."

"Yes Sam, it is 1995, and now you've arrived, but Poppy's disappeared. Do you think the time machine has gone haywire or do you think that Poppy has gone forward in time, in to the future maybe."

We all took another drink as if it would help us to think; then a thought came to me,

"Girls, I know this may sound strange, but do you think I might look at the 'Door'. Poppy used to talk about it all of the time, but obviously, I've never seen it. You never know it might give me inspiration on what may have happened to Poppy."

Both of the girls stood up immediately, with their glasses in hand,

"Come on then, Sam, follow us."

They left the kitchen with me in toe. We went through a rather nice lounge area, which had a massive fireplace. Sat in the fireplace was a rather grand firedog, with a back plate featuring a knight on a horse back. Next to the grate stood a wicker basket, full of split logs, ready for the outbreak of a cold spell. Either side of the fireplace stood built-in cupboards, which stretched right up to the very tall ceiling, which must have been at least ten feet tall. The room was quite elegant. Pictures adorned the ochre walls; above the fireplace hung an oil painting of three oriental women, playing some obscure instruments, which I didn't recognise. There were two large three-seater green leather sofas, sitting on what looked like a designer carpet. I imagined Poppy sitting there, with a glass of Pino; then feeling really sad that she wasn't here.

The two girls went through another door, leaving me stood there pondering about Poppy.

"Come on, Samuel, keep up," shouted Chloe. I went through the next door into the hallway. The front door was at least three feet wide, with an arched top-glass facade above it. It was exactly like the entrance at No 10 Downing Street in London. The girls were already at the top of the wooden staircase. I grabbed the dark, wooden, highly polished handrail and whisked up the flight of stairs. The girls looked at me; then Kim spoke,

"Come on, slow coach, we have another flight to climb yet."

Then both of the girls giggled, then led the way up a rather rickety dogleg creaky staircase. Chloe led the way, pushing open a ledge and braced old wooden door, which led into the attic room.

I entered and had an immediate feeling of peace. I sensed a warm emotion of closeness with Poppy; then I spotted the 'Door'. The 'Door' that had brought us together, which I would be eternally grateful for, but also the same 'Door' was now keeping us apart.

"Well, Sam, there it is; the formidable stubborn 'Door' that only opens when Poppy is here on her own."

I looked at her inquisitively; she realised I wanted more,

"Well, Sam, I sat here with Poppy for hours, one night, waiting for the unpredictable stupid 'Door' to open, but no chance; we gave up in the end. Poppy said that it would only open for her and her alone. It seems you have to be a time traveller for it to open."

It was so frustrating to think that my Poppy, who travelled from this room to my time to see me for all those years, was probably the other side of the 'Door' to me. Now I was this side without her, and I was worried sick what might have happened to her. Kim slumped into the reclining chair. Chloe sat on the floor, still holding their glasses of wine. I then noticed that the easel had been repaired and taped up.

"What happened here then, Chloe; the easel has been broken and taped up."

"Aaarrggh, yes, you probably haven't seen her since the incident with her ex."

"What incident, is she alright, what happened?"

"Apparently, she confronted him about his long-standing affair with some trollop called Lucy. She had proof that he had been seeing her for years."

"Yes, I was with her when she saw Simon with her some years ago."

Chloe looked surprised, but then carried on,

"Anyway, he wasn't too happy about being challenged. He's an arrogant bastard, so he attempted to beat her up, because she refused to say how she knew."

"I told her to be prepared when she travelled back. I said he would be waiting."

Chloe interjected,

"You mean you knew he would be waiting, and you still let her put herself in danger."

"Chloe, just stop right there, that's not fair. You must know I love Poppy, and I would never knowingly put her in danger. I'm not sure if you know the intricacies of Poppy's time travel, but she had no control over when the 'Door' would call her back. So the only thing I could do was to warn her to be vigilant when she travelled back."

"I'm sorry, Sam. I wasn't thinking straight. I know you love her, and you would do anything for her. I'm just worried about her. She must be stuck somewhere, because she would never allow us to worry, like we are."

"So Chloe, is she alright after the attack? Was she injured badly... My god, I will swing for him when I see him."

Kim answered, turning from her chair,

"Yes, Sam, she was shaken up. Most of the blood in the cab was from Simon. Apparently Roscoe the dog didn't take too kindly to Simon hurting Poppy, so he bit Simon on the hand, and then the police turned up and arrested the twat. We haven't seen him since, due to the restraining order. She was absolutely fine the last time we saw her before she travelled through that damn 'Door'."

I walked over to the arched top window. Poppy was right. There was a lovely view over the garden and pond from up here. I looked towards the end of the drive and noticed the 'For Sale' sign.

"So why was Poppy selling the house; she loved this house."

Chloe piped up, aggressively,

"That was down to the twat; he wants his money to buy a slapper pad in London for him and the bitch."

She certainly didn't mince her words, did Chloe. You wouldn't want to get on the wrong side of her; that was for certain.

As I turned to come away from the window, I noticed the sky had turned black. Strange, because the forecast had been quite positive towards a sunny day. Then came the sound of barking; both of the dogs were at the edge of the pond, barking at something in the pond; they appeared stressed.

"I think we had better go and see what's bothering the dogs. It's probably just the ducks, but we had better check."

The girls jumped up and lead the way downstairs. Chloe asked,

"So Sam, did you get any inspiration from seeing the 'Door'. Have you got any ideas where Poppy might be."

Unfortunately, even after seeing the place that Poppy would have travelled from, so many times, I still had no idea where she might have disappeared to.

"I'm sorry girls, it's still a mystery to me where Poppy might be. We just have to pray that she is well and will come back to us asap."

We arrived in the boiling hot kitchen. I took a swig from my warm beer before going outside to see what was spooking the dogs. The girls followed me; we approached the edge of the pond where the two dogs were barking incessantly. Kim tried to calm them by stroking them but without success; something was definitely upsetting them. The sky continued to darken, and angry clouds gathered; yet in the distance, you could see bright blue sky. *Weird*, I thought to myself. I looked around; the tall popular trees were being whipped around by the powerful wind. I looked at the house and again noticed the damaged scorched chimney above Poppy's studio in the attic. I asked the girls,

"What happened to the chimney; it appears to be damaged and burnt."

The girls both looked up to witness what appeared to be damage from a lightning strike. Maybe it was this that interfered with Poppy's time travel; we might never find out.

Then to our amazement, there fell total silence. The dogs stopped barking, the ducks stayed silent, and the wind died completely—you could have heard a pin drop. The girls just stared at me as if, for some sort of explanation, but I was just as surprised by the anomaly as they were. The clouds above the pond converged, almost biblical in nature, rolling upwards, focussing your eyes northwards. A hole appeared in the thick grey tumultuous swirling mass of cloud, then came the piercing bright white light shooting from the hole and down into the pond. Where the light struck the water, the water seemed to boil; then what happened next took us all by surprise.

From the epicentre of the light, emanating from the clearing in the cloud, came the screams of what appeared to be a woman. Then within seconds, a body of a woman came shooting through the hole, accelerating towards the surface of the pond. Her arms and legs were flailing in the air, trying to gain some semblance of control, but to no avail. Chloe shouted out,

"It's Poppy! It's Poppy!"

Just as I realised what was happening and the image of Poppy registered in my confused brain, she hit the water at great speed.

The force of the impact sent a tidal wave of water in all directions, away from the impact point. Poppy disappeared into the depths of the murky pond. Within seconds came the first wall of angry water crashing up the bank of the pond and completely engulfing us in smelly pond water. It came with such force that Chloe and Kim were knocked off their feet, and the two dogs were washed away towards the house. I managed to keep my balance, trying to focus on the impact point, hoping to see Poppy resurface from the bottom of the pond. I knew deep down that to survive such an impact would be almost impossible.

But then I saw a hand emerge from the water. Kim screamed out,

"Look, it's Poppy, she's come back up."

Then her head appeared above the swirling water. We heard her shout,

"Help me, please help me, I can't breathe."

Then the massive wave of water that had been ejected from the impact point had reached its peak and started to return. I had to reach Poppy before it did. I dived into the pond and swam as fast as I could. I shouted out at the top of my voice,

"Poppy, hang on, I'm coming. I love you!"

But the returning water had quite a pace. It overtook me and headed towards Poppy with such menace, and before I could get to her, it swamped her once again. She was submerged for the second time. I reached the place I last saw her and dived down. The pond water was so murky, I couldn't see a thing, but then my searching hand caught hold of her hand. I pulled her towards the surface. My heart was pounding like a drum. I found it difficult to breathe myself; god knows how Poppy was managing. Her face emerged from the water. Her eyes were closed. I shouted at her to breath, but she was unresponsive.

I struck out for the edge of the pond; my hand around Poppy's chin. I could hear Kim and Chloe screaming from the bank. As soon as I neared the bank, the girls were in the water, helping me to drag Poppy on to dry land. Both of the dogs were going mad with excitement; they hadn't got a clue of the gravity of the situation. We lay Poppy on her back. She wasn't conscious; I couldn't detect a pulse. Kim was crying. Chloe started chest compressions, and I gave the kiss of life.

"Come on, Poppy, we all love you. Come on, breathe, please, breathe."

It was a desperate situation. Poppy's skin was white; she was cold and then came an eruption of dirty water gushing out of her mouth. We all shouted encouragement at her. She started to cough which was a good sign. Then she opened her eyes. We all burst into tears. I spoke first, "Oh Poppy, you're back with us. I love you so much, don't you ever leave me again."

Both of the girls were crying uncontrollably. They were so happy that she was back with us. Poppy looked up at me and said,

"Sam, I love you with all my heart."

Before I could respond, her eyes closed, and her head fell to one side, and I instinctively knew she was gone.

Chapter 46
Last Hope

Chloe and Kim just stared at me in disbelief; tears were streaming down their faces. Kim was holding Poppy's hand. I think they were both in shock because they just sat there talking to Poppy, like she was just asleep. They were begging her to wake up; I had to take control,

"Girls, Poppy's gone! There's nothing else we can do!"

They both flipped. They were hysterical, telling me to do something. Chloe started heart compression again, in a desperate attempt to bring Poppy back to life. I was sobbing; they were crying. Then Kim shouted,

"Call an ambulance, they might be able to save her. Sam, please just call 999."

I knew deep down that no one could save my beautiful Poppy now. It was too late; she was gone forever. I think Chloe realised that we had done all we could because she started comforting Kim. I lay my head on Poppy's chest and sobbed my heart out. I couldn't believe I had lost her. I started ranting; I was so angry with the 'Door'.

"That god forsaken 'Door', why did it have to take my Poppy. Sodding time travel; ten years of travelling and for what, just to drown her in a dirty pond."

Kim ran towards the house shouting,

"I'm going to get my phone. I'm going to call the ambulance."

I looked at Chloe and said,

"We will have to call them sooner or later and the police. They will want to know what's been going on. How we will explain this one, god only knows."

Then as I turned to get up, I looked at the scorched chimney and thought to myself, *I bet that had something to do with Poppy's demise.* It must have interfered with the time machine, and somehow instead of bringing her back to the attic, like it always had, it had dumped her unceremoniously into the pond. Then a spark of hope lit up in my broken heart,

"Chloe, I have an idea. Stop Kim calling the police."

"But Sam, why, what are you thinking; what can we possibly do."

I then explained to Chloe my idea. How if we could get Poppy into the time machine, she could travel back in time, and maybe she would be returned at a different time and place and consequently not be drowned in the pond.

"Oh Sam, that's a fantastic idea. I will go and stop Kim calling the police."

She ran off to the house. I just hoped that she was in time to stop Kim making that call. Then it hit me like a ton of bricks, what Chloe had said earlier up in the

said the 'Door' would only open for a time traveller, so if we were in
[...] with Poppy, the 'Door' wouldn't open. So how would Poppy get into
[...] machine; she was dead. I had to think away around the problem, but it
[...]ed impossible, then I had a flash back. I remembered Poppy saying how
[...]markable my sister Sally was, and how she thought she might be a time
[...]raveller. She was my last hope. I remembered I took my coat off in the
sweltering kitchen; my phone was in the pocket. I raced towards the kitchen to
retrieve it. Chloe and Kim were arguing; Kim was insisting on making that call.
I had to calm them down and get them both on side, because without them, I was
going to struggle getting Poppy up to the attic room.

"Girls please! This is the only option to give Poppy another chance of life.
We have to get her upstairs as soon as we can; now please, help me."

I then phoned Sally. It was a bit of a weird phone call to say the least,

"Sally, it's Sam. I need your help and I need it now. I know you will think
I'm mad, but are you a time traveller."

"Sam, have you been drinking; what sort of a question is that to ask your
sister."

"Sally, Poppy is dead! If we don't get her back in the time machine, I will
have lost her forever. Now please, can you help me?"

The line went very quiet. I thought she had put the receiver down on me;
then came the response,

"Where are you, Sam. I'm on my way."

I gave her the address, and then the line went dead. My heart lifted; at least
she didn't deny she was a time traveller. At least, we now stood another chance
to bring my Poppy back to me.

"Girls! Girls! We have to get Poppy up to the attic room immediately. It's
the only chance we have; now please, come and help."

They both looked at me. They looked a mess. They both had eye make-up
running down their faces; then Kim spoke,

"Sam, do you really think we can save her. Honestly, do you."

"Yes, I do. If we can get her into the machine, I honestly believe that we
stand a chance of getting Poppy back alive."

It was a grim task picking Poppy up from the ground. She was completely
limp, which made it even more difficult to carry her. In the end, I found it easier
to throw her over my shoulders, as in a fireman's lift and struggle up the stairs
on my own. Kim was ahead, so she opened the attic door for me. I had to stoop
to get through the opening, being careful not to bash Poppy on the door frame. I
then lay Poppy onto the reclining chair and tried to catch my breath. Then Chloe
spoke,

"Sam, it's not going to work. The 'Door' won't open while we're in the
room; and if we leave, and the 'Door' does open, how will Poppy get into the
time machine."

"I've already thought about that. It will be fine, I promise you."

She responded quickly,

"Sam, you don't understand. If we wait outside for the 'Door' to unlock and then rush in, it will lock again before we can even move the handle. It just won't work."

I then heard a car come shooting up the drive. I ran to the arched top window to see Sally arrive. I opened the window and shouted down to her,

"Sally, we're up here in the attic, please hurry."

Then Kim asked,

"Sam, how can your sister help? It's another time traveller we need, not another pair of hands."

Chloe ran down the stairs to meet Sally. She didn't know how Sally could help, but she welcomed any help we could get. The girls came charging into the room,

"Kim, Chloe, this is my sister Sally. She's come to try and help Poppy."

Sally said hello to the girls, then immediately knelt down by Poppy's body. She held her hand, then looked at me,

"Sam, it's imperative that we send her back in time as soon as possible. It might already be too late."

I then explained to Sally what Chloe had said about the 'Door'. The 'Door' would not open while we were still in the room, so she would have to struggle on her own to get Poppy into the time machine. Then Kim suggested that we should move Poppy nearer to the 'Door', so that when the handle did release, Sally wouldn't have too far to move poor old Poppy.

After I lifted Poppy up and placed her on the carpet near the 'Door', I squeezed her hand and then kissed her forehead. I whispered in her ear,

"Poppy, my dearest friend, I love you with all my heart. Please, come back to me soon."

Tears rolled down my face. My heart was pounding. Then the girls joined me; they said their goodbyes; they were in pieces. Our tears were running off our faces and onto Poppy. Sally grabbed my arm,

"Sam, we should really move on. Time is of the essence. The sooner she travels back, the more chance of success."

We all stood up, preparing to leave the attic. I hugged Sally and thanked her for what she was doing. She said,

"Sam, you do realise that what we are about to do might not work. The 'Door' might not even open."

I replied, confidently,

"Sally, of course, it will work. As soon as you hear the 'Door' releasing the bolt, open the 'Door', place Poppy inside, then close the 'Door' behind you; then we just have to wait for poppy to return."

I then kissed Sally on the cheek, gave her a loving squeeze, looked once more at Poppy and then left the attic, with the girls.

I pulled the creaky attic door shut, made sure the latch was on. Then all three of us sat on the stairs and waited. I don't know why because we didn't know how long it would be before the 'Door' would open, but what else could we do, just wait. Chloe and Kim were true friends to Poppy. You could see how upset they were, but they still found the strength to comfort me, even though they had only met me a couple of hours ago. It was Chloe who spoke first,

"So Sam, how long have you known your sister was a time traveller."

"Well, to be honest, I didn't know. It was something Poppy said to me a while ago. At the time I didn't give it much thought, but then today, it just flashed into my mind. When I spoke to Sally on the phone and asked her, she denied it. Then as soon as I said Poppy had died, she offered to help."

"Well, Sam, let's hope she can work her magic; it's our only hope."

We then all sat in silence, awaiting the sound of the 'Door' releasing its lock. It might be a long wait.

After Sam and the girls left the room, I settled down on the reclining chair. I couldn't bear to look at poor Poppy's body, which lay lifeless on the carpet near the 'Door'. It had come as a shock, having to let Sam, my brother, know that I too was a time traveller, but these were desperate times, and desperate times called for desperate measures. I had endeavoured throughout my life to keep it secret, and not telling Sam had been difficult to say the least. But now he and two others knew my secret; I just prayed that it would go no further. I assumed that Sam and the others were waiting outside and would reappear as soon as I placed Poppy in the machine and closed the 'Door' behind me. All I could do was be patient and wait for the sound; the sound that might save Poppy's life.

About an hour later, I got up to stretch my legs. I was looking out of the window when I heard a solid 'clonk'. It sounded like metal on metal; it had to be the lock opening. I ran to the 'Door' and pressed down on the handle; it moved—the 'Door' released. There was the sound of air being released. I pulled the 'Door' until it was wide open. The room was filled with a cold fog. I had been through a few time tunnels in my life, but none like this one. The temperature in the room must have dropped by at least 20 degrees, but the clock was ticking. I had to get Poppy inside and quick. I bent down towards her limp body and wrapped my arms around her. I grasped my hands together; then pulled her backwards to the opening in the wall. Although Poppy was quite slim, I still struggled to move her inside the time machine. My heart was thumping from the exertion, and even though cold fog surrounded me, I could still feel sweat on my brow. The plan was to place her inside, then to leave and close the 'Door' behind me. I could see a light at the end of the tunnel, shining through the fog. I thought it might be best to place Poppy as close to the light as possible. As I lay Poppy down on to the floor, fog was swirling around my ankles. I squeezed her hand; then turned to leave.

Bang! The door closed behind me, trapping me inside with Poppy.

We had been sat on the stairs for such a long time. Kim had fallen asleep, and Chloe was sprawled out on the landing. All I could think about was my poor Poppy; would Sally be able to save her, would the 'Door' even open. Then after at least an hour of waiting patiently, I heard movement in the room. We all heard a resounding 'clonk'; then the sound of air being released under pressure. Chloe looked at me, then Kim; we all focussed on the attic door. We heard the sound of the 'Door' being opened. We were all transfixed on the wooden door in front of us, praying that Sally would succeed in her mission. Then without warning, came the sound of metal hitting metal; an almighty bang rang out and then silence.

We all stared at each other; then I spoke,

"Do you think we should go in? It's awfully quiet in there. Sally might need our help."

And with that, we entered the room. The room was full of cold swirling fog. We just stood and stared at each in shock. Sally and Poppy were both gone.

The End